"Stayed in from recess to read it . . . **CAN'T WAIT FOR NEXT ONE!**"
—Zac A., age 9, Hood River, Ore.

"*Hilo* was **SO GREAT** I couldn't stop reading until I'd finished it. I want to read the next one **NOW**!"
—Jack A., age 10, Brooklyn

"**GINA WAS MY FAVORITE** character because she's into science and soccer like me! I also liked D.J.'s family because it looks like mine!"
—Kiran M., age 7, Carlsbad, Calif.

"*Hilo* is **REALLY, REALLY FUNNY.** It has a **LOT OF LAUGHS.** The raccoon is the funniest."
—Theo M., age 7, Miami, Fla.

"My big brother and I fight over this book. **I CAN'T WAIT** for the second one so we can both read a Hilo book at the same time."
—Nory V., age 8, Montclair, N.J.

"**FANTASTIC. EVERY SINGLE THING ABOUT THIS . . . IS TERRIFIC.**"
—Boingboing.net

"**BETTER THAN THE BEST!**"
—Matteo H-G., age 9, Oakland

"**HIGH ENERGY** and **HILARIOUS!**" —Gene Luen Yang, National Ambassador for Young People's Literature

"**ACTION-PACKED** and **AMAZING FUN.**"
—Brad Meltzer, THE FIFTH ASSASSIN

"*Hilo* is loads of **SLAPSTICK FUN!**"
—Dan Santat, winner of the Caldecott Medal

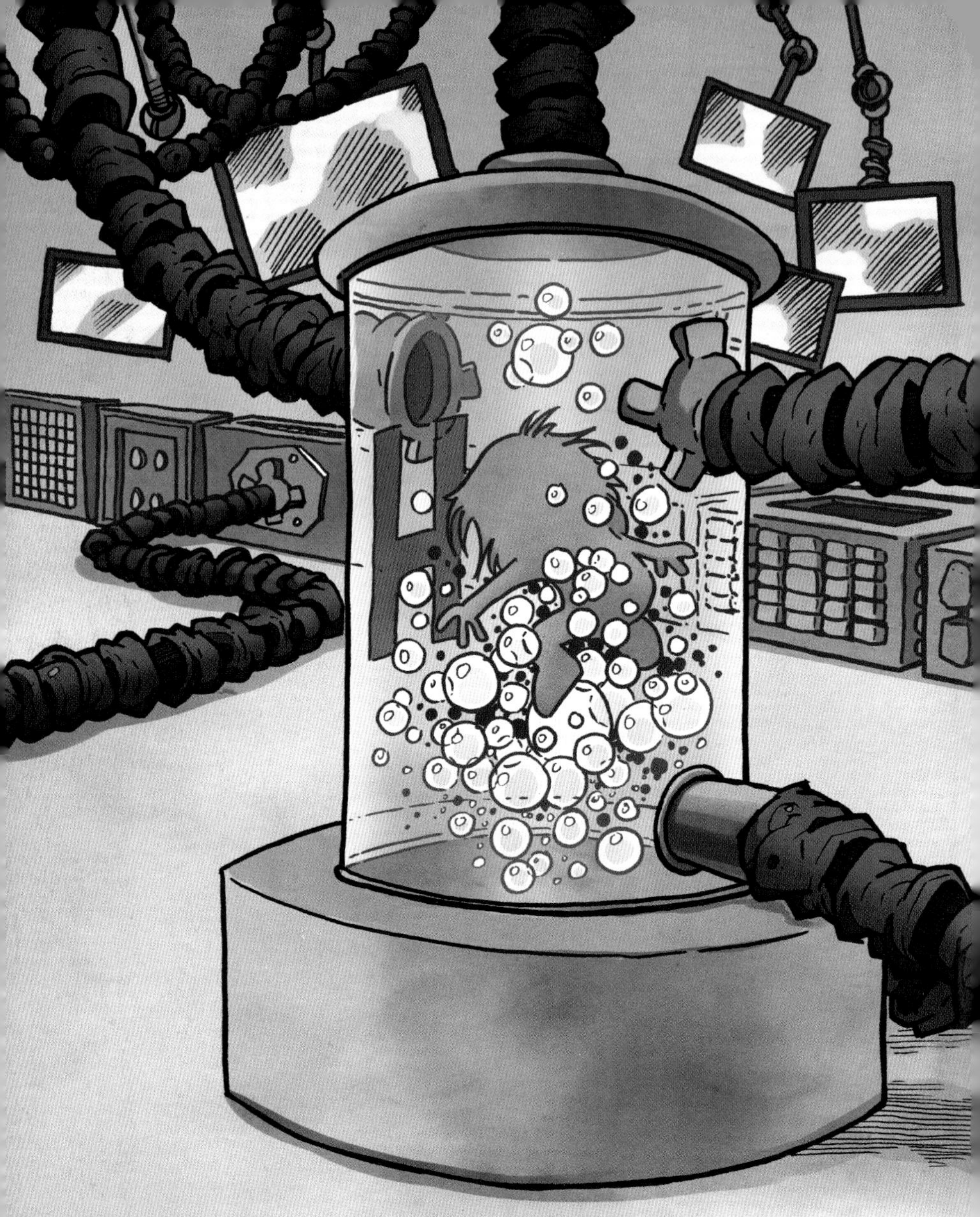

## READ ALL THE HILO BOOKS!

**HILO #1** THE BOY WHO CRASHED TO EARTH
**HILO #2** SAVING THE WHOLE WIDE WORLD
**HILO #3** THE GREAT BIG BOOM
**HILO #4** WAKING THE MONSTERS
**HILO #5** THEN EVERYTHING WENT WRONG

BOOK 3

# HiLO

## THE GREAT BIG BOOM

# BY JUDD WINICK

### COLOR BY
### STEVE HAMAKER

RANDOM HOUSE 🏠 NEW YORK

Copyright © 2017 by Judd Winick
All rights reserved. Published in the United States by Random House Children's Books,
a division of Penguin Random House LLC, New York.
Random House and the colophon are registered trademarks of Penguin Random House LLC.
Visit us on the Web! randomhousekids.com
Educators and librarians, for a variety of teaching tools, visit us at RHTeachersLibrarians.com
Library of Congress Cataloging-in-Publication Data
Names: Winick, Judd, author, illustrator.
Title: Hilo : the great big boom / by Judd Winick.
Description: First edition. | New York : Random House, [2017] | Series: Hilo ; book 3 | Audience: Ages 8–12. |
Summary: Hilo and DJ, with the help of Polly, the magical warrior cat, travel through a mysterious portal
and battle bad guys, face disgusting food, an angry mom, and powerful magic to save their friend Gina.
Identifiers: LCCN 2016005216 | ISBN 978-0-385-38620-3 (hardcover) |
ISBN 978-0-385-38621-0 (hardcover library binding) | ISBN 978-0-385-38622-7 (ebook)
Subjects: LCSH: Graphic novels. | CYAC: Graphic novels. | Robots—Fiction. |
Extraterrestrial beings—Fiction. | Friendship—Fiction. | Science fiction. |
BISAC: JUVENILE FICTION / Comics & Graphic Novels / Manga. | JUVENILE FICTION /
Action & Adventure / General. | JUVENILE FICTION / Social Issues / Friendship.
Classification: LCC PZ7.7.W57 Hin 2017 | DDC 741.5/973—dc23
MANUFACTURED IN CHINA
10 9 8 7 6 5
Book design by John Sazaklis
First Edition
Random House Children's Books supports the First Amendment and celebrates the right to read.

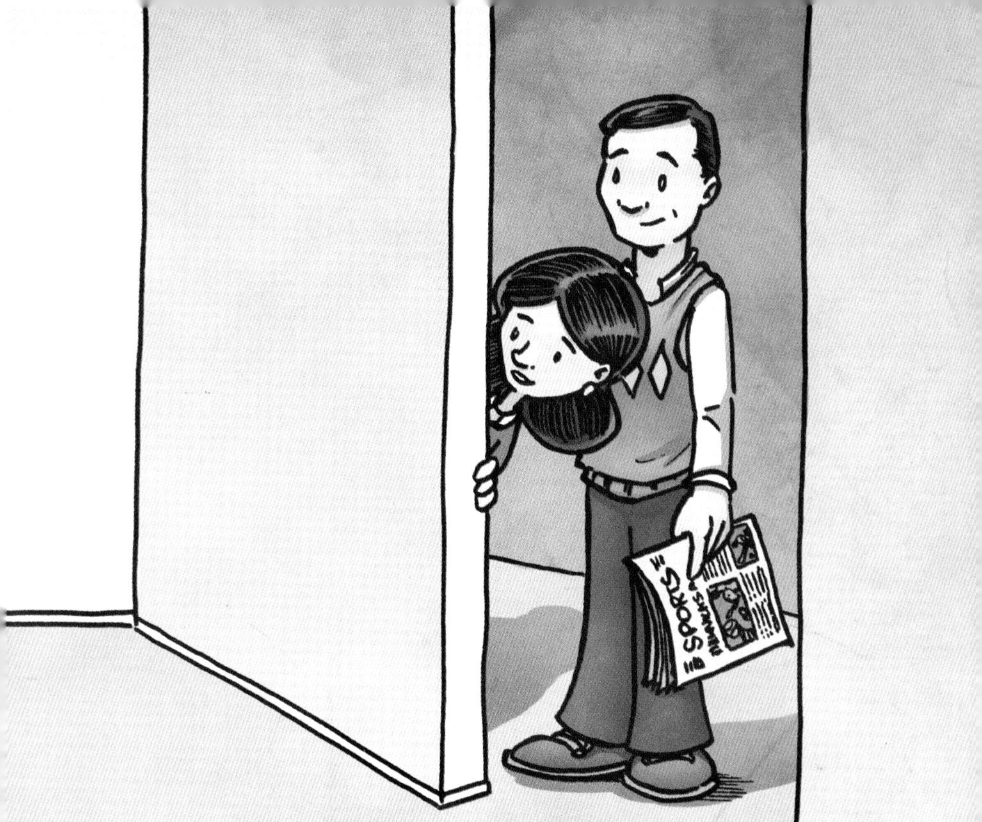
SPORTS

FOR
MOM
AND
DAD

# CHAPTER

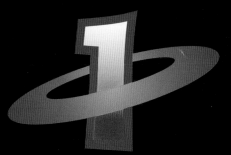

## SECRETS

MY NAME IS **DANIEL JACKSON LIM.** BUT EVERYONE CALLS ME **D.J.**

I HAVE TWO BEST FRIENDS.

**GINA.**

AND **HILO.**

**HANG ON!**

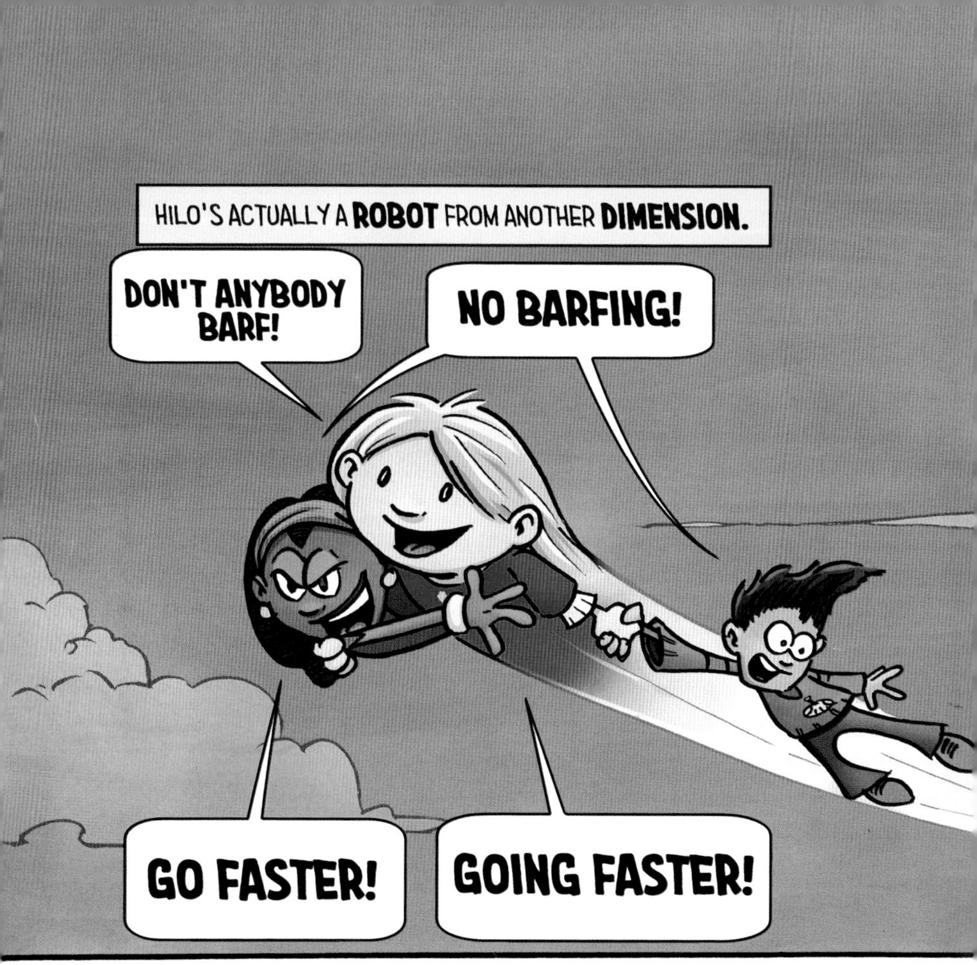
HILO'S ACTUALLY A ROBOT FROM ANOTHER DIMENSION.
DON'T ANYBODY BARF!
NO BARFING!
GO FASTER!
GOING FASTER!

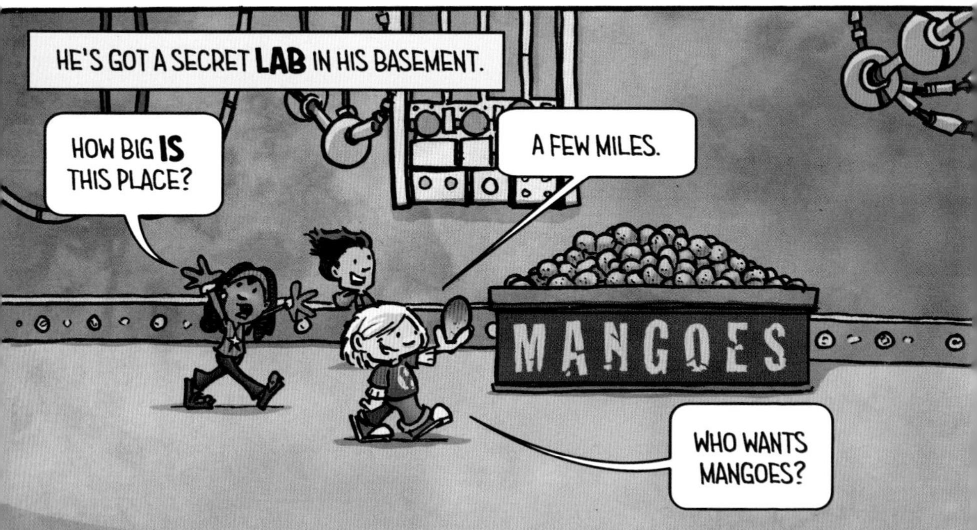
HE'S GOT A SECRET LAB IN HIS BASEMENT.
HOW BIG IS THIS PLACE?
A FEW MILES.
MANGOES
WHO WANTS MANGOES?

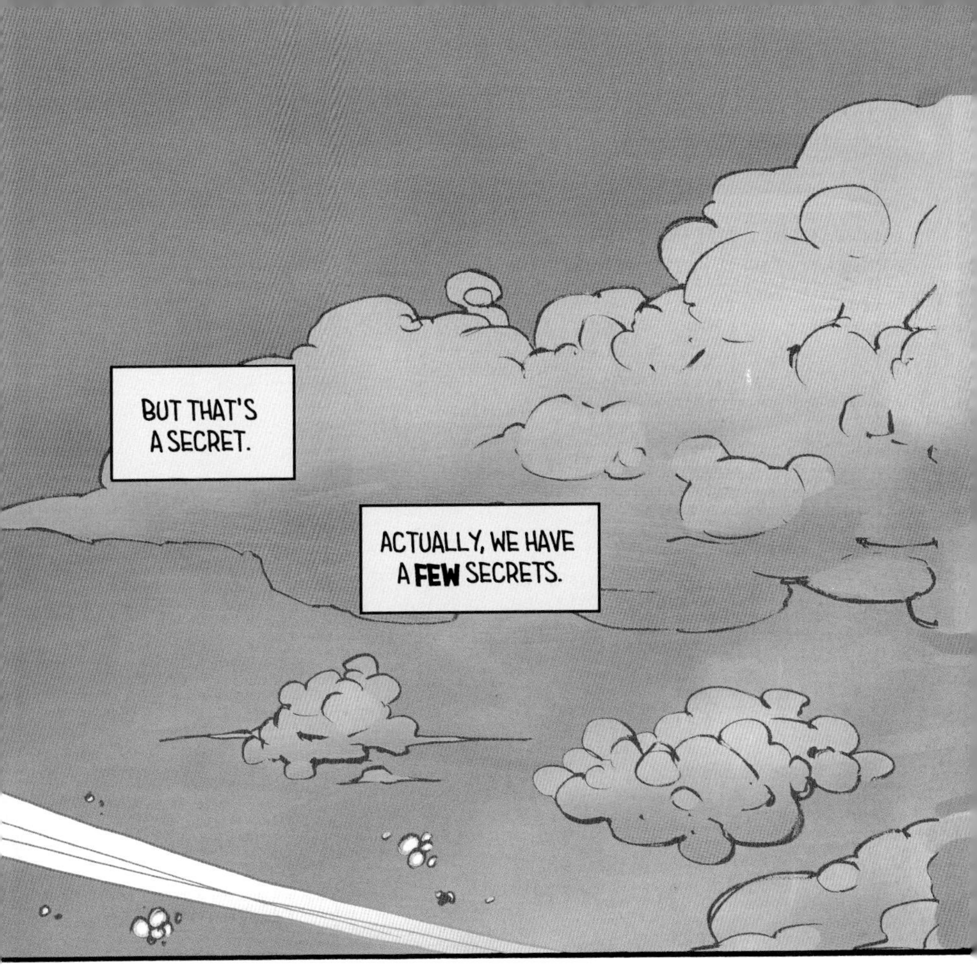
BUT THAT'S A SECRET.
ACTUALLY, WE HAVE A **FEW** SECRETS.

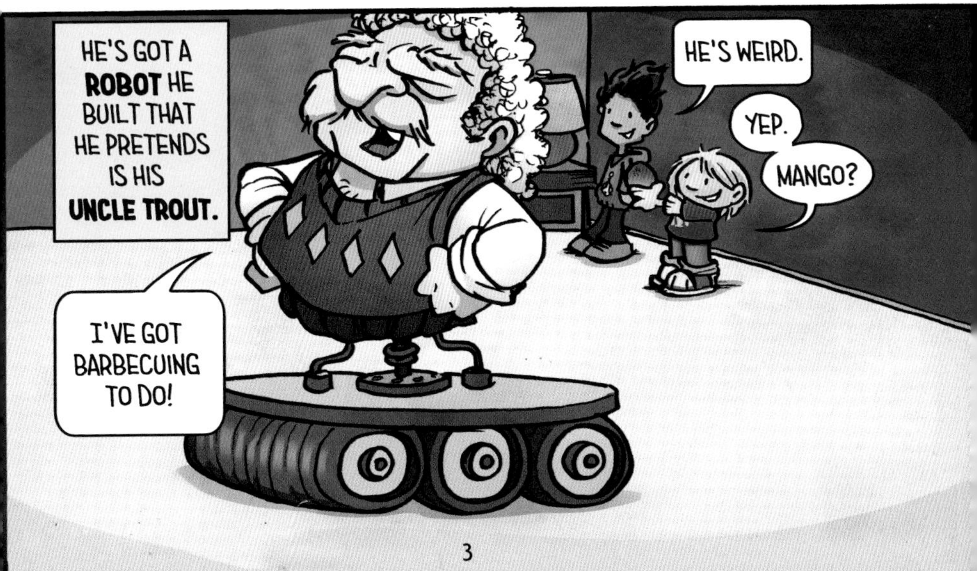
HE'S GOT A **ROBOT** HE BUILT THAT HE PRETENDS IS HIS **UNCLE TROUT.**
HE'S WEIRD.
YEP.
MANGO?
I'VE GOT BARBECUING TO DO!

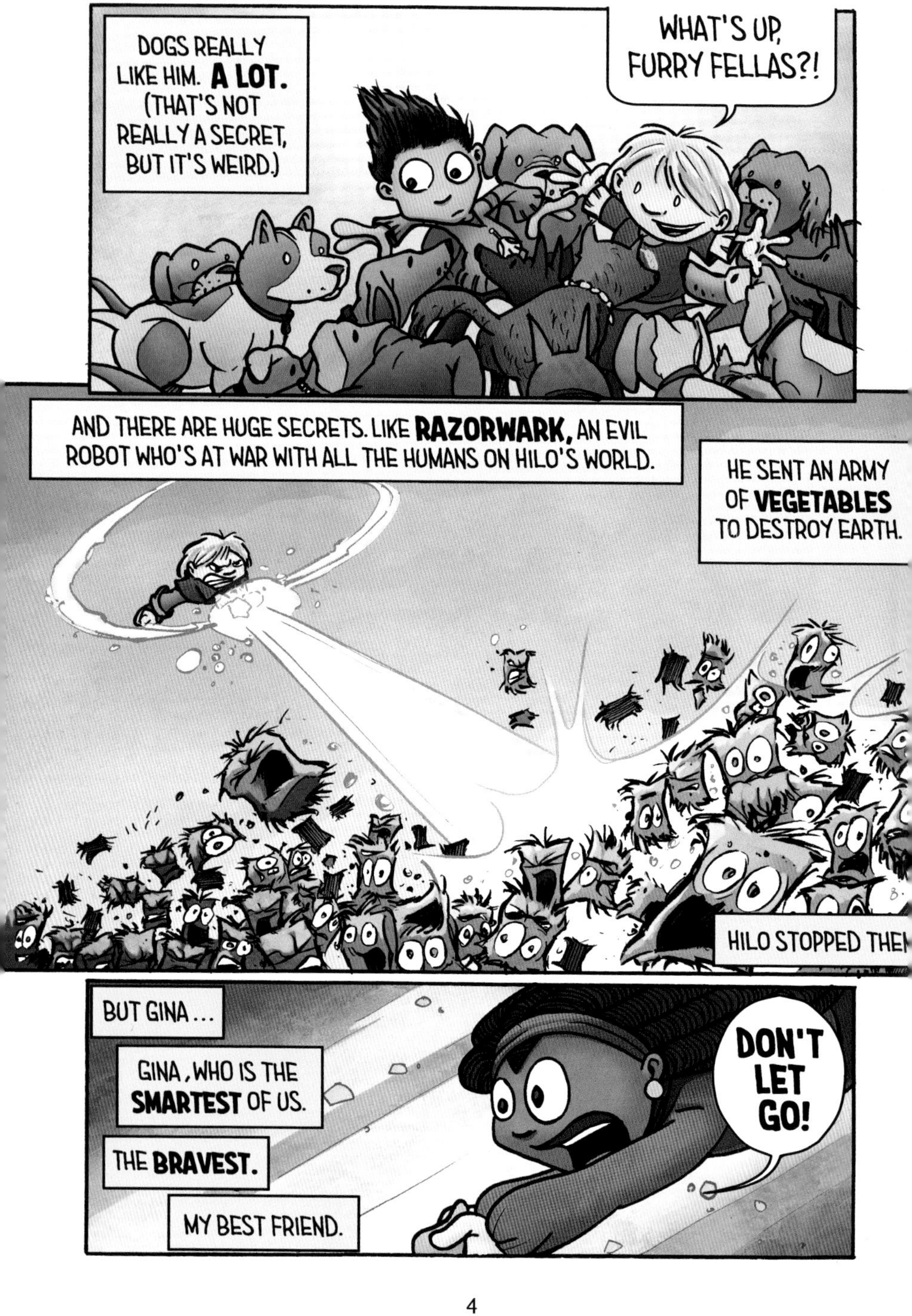

DOGS REALLY LIKE HIM. A LOT. (THAT'S NOT REALLY A SECRET, BUT IT'S WEIRD.)
WHAT'S UP, FURRY FELLAS?!
AND THERE ARE HUGE SECRETS. LIKE RAZORWARK, AN EVIL ROBOT WHO'S AT WAR WITH ALL THE HUMANS ON HILO'S WORLD.
HE SENT AN ARMY OF VEGETABLES TO DESTROY EARTH.
HILO STOPPED THE
BUT GINA . . .
GINA, WHO IS THE SMARTEST OF US.
THE BRAVEST.
MY BEST FRIEND.
DON'T LET GO!

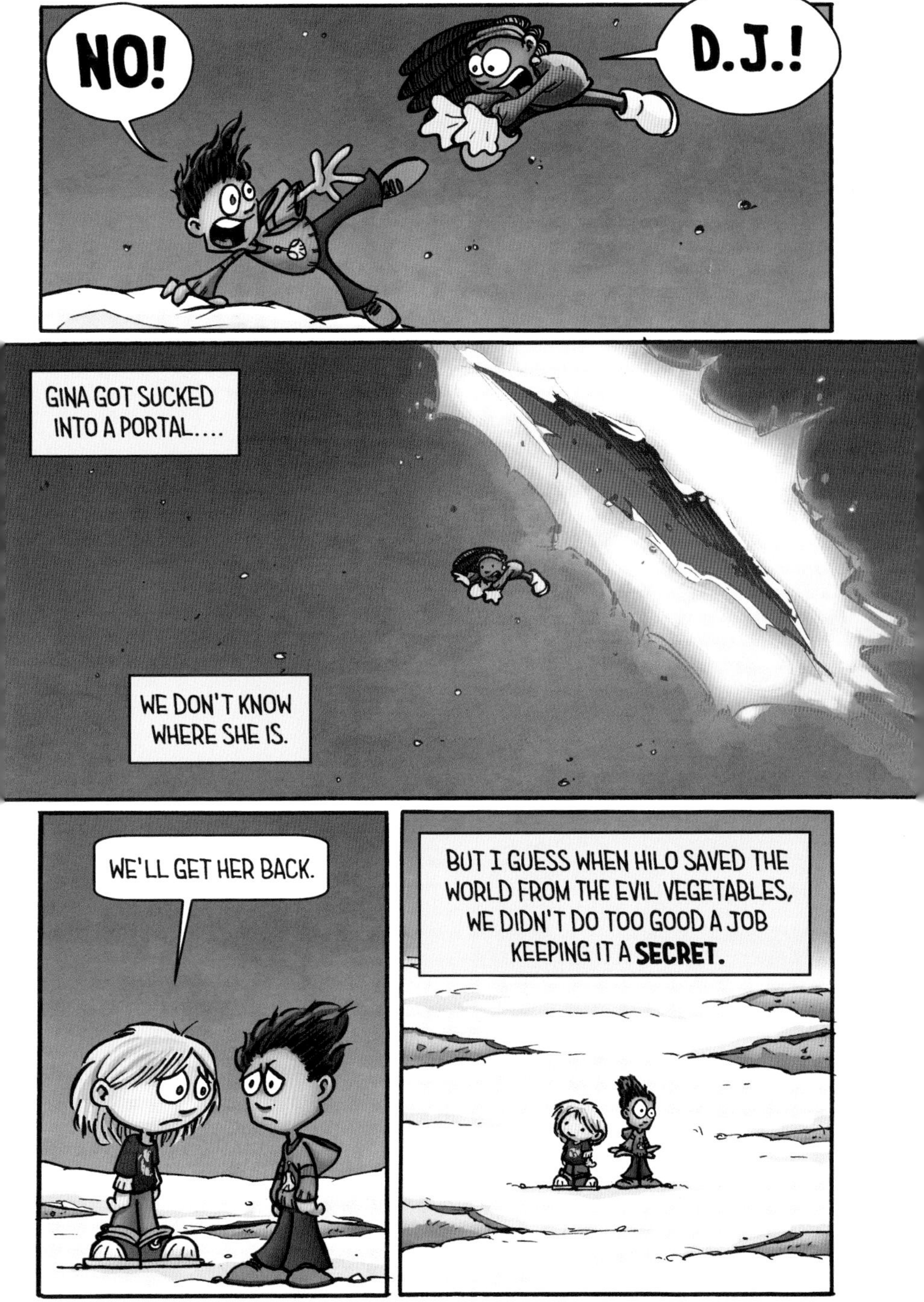
NO!
D.J.!
GINA GOT SUCKED INTO A PORTAL....
WE DON'T KNOW WHERE SHE IS.
WE'LL GET HER BACK.
BUT I GUESS WHEN HILO SAVED THE WORLD FROM THE EVIL VEGETABLES, WE DIDN'T DO TOO GOOD A JOB KEEPING IT A SECRET.

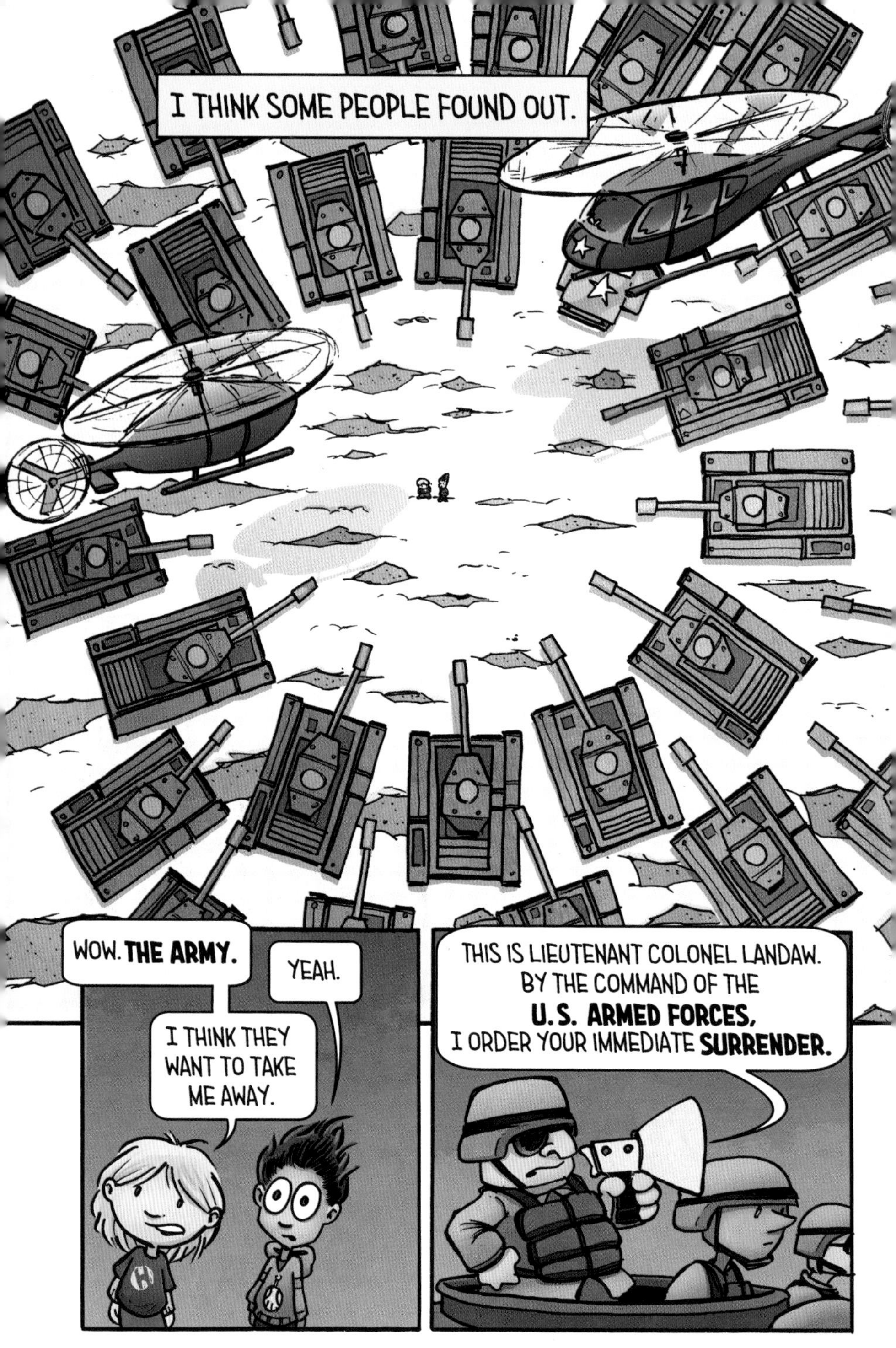
I THINK SOME PEOPLE FOUND OUT.
WOW. **THE ARMY.**
I THINK THEY WANT TO TAKE ME AWAY.
YEAH.
THIS IS LIEUTENANT COLONEL LANDAW. BY THE COMMAND OF THE **U.S. ARMED FORCES,** I ORDER YOUR IMMEDIATE **SURRENDER.**

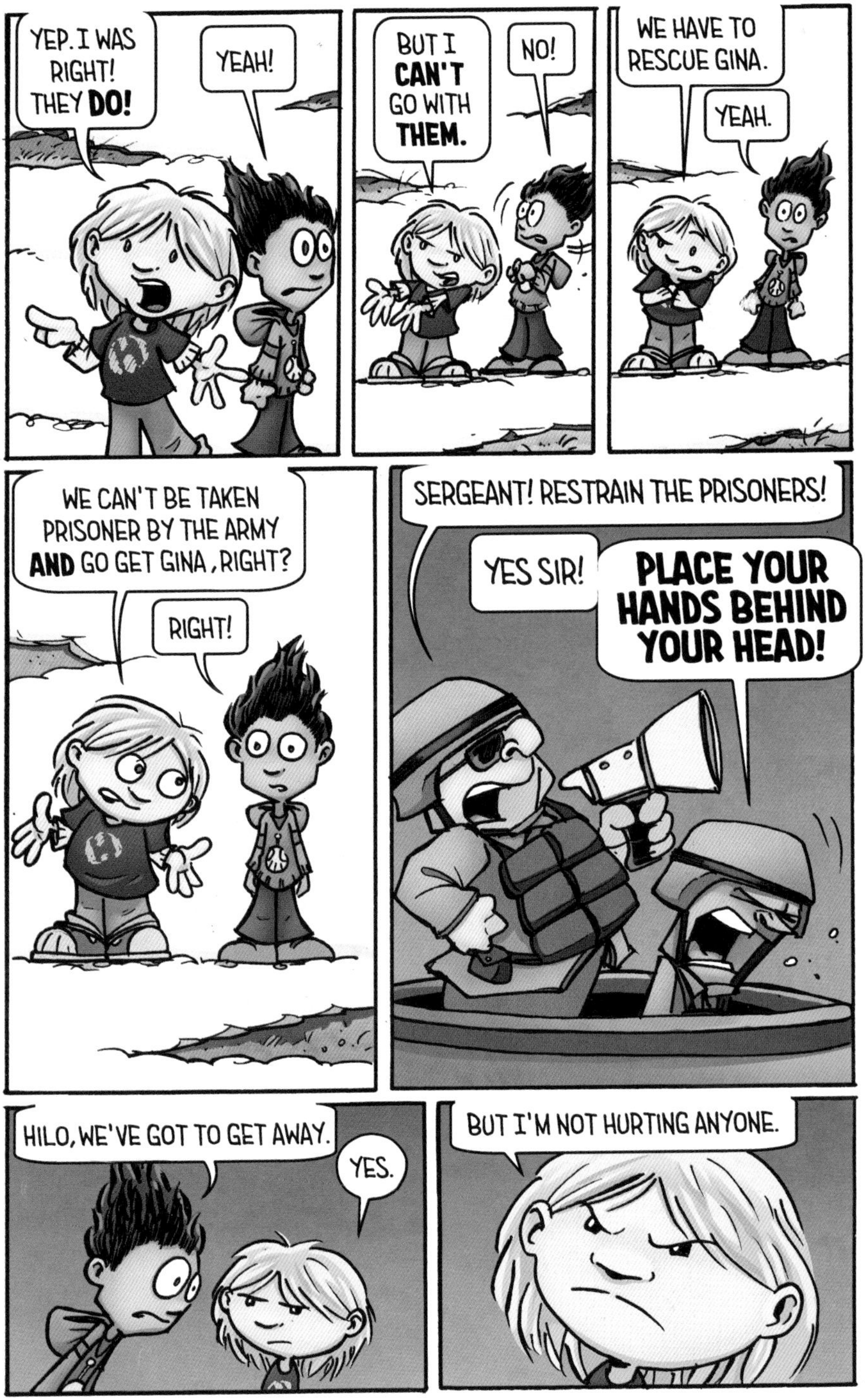
YEP. I WAS RIGHT! THEY **DO!**
YEAH!
BUT I **CAN'T** GO WITH **THEM.**
NO!
WE HAVE TO RESCUE GINA.
YEAH.
WE CAN'T BE TAKEN PRISONER BY THE ARMY **AND** GO GET GINA, RIGHT?
RIGHT!
SERGEANT! RESTRAIN THE PRISONERS!
YES SIR!
**PLACE YOUR HANDS BEHIND YOUR HEAD!**
HILO, WE'VE GOT TO GET AWAY.
YES.
BUT I'M NOT HURTING ANYONE.

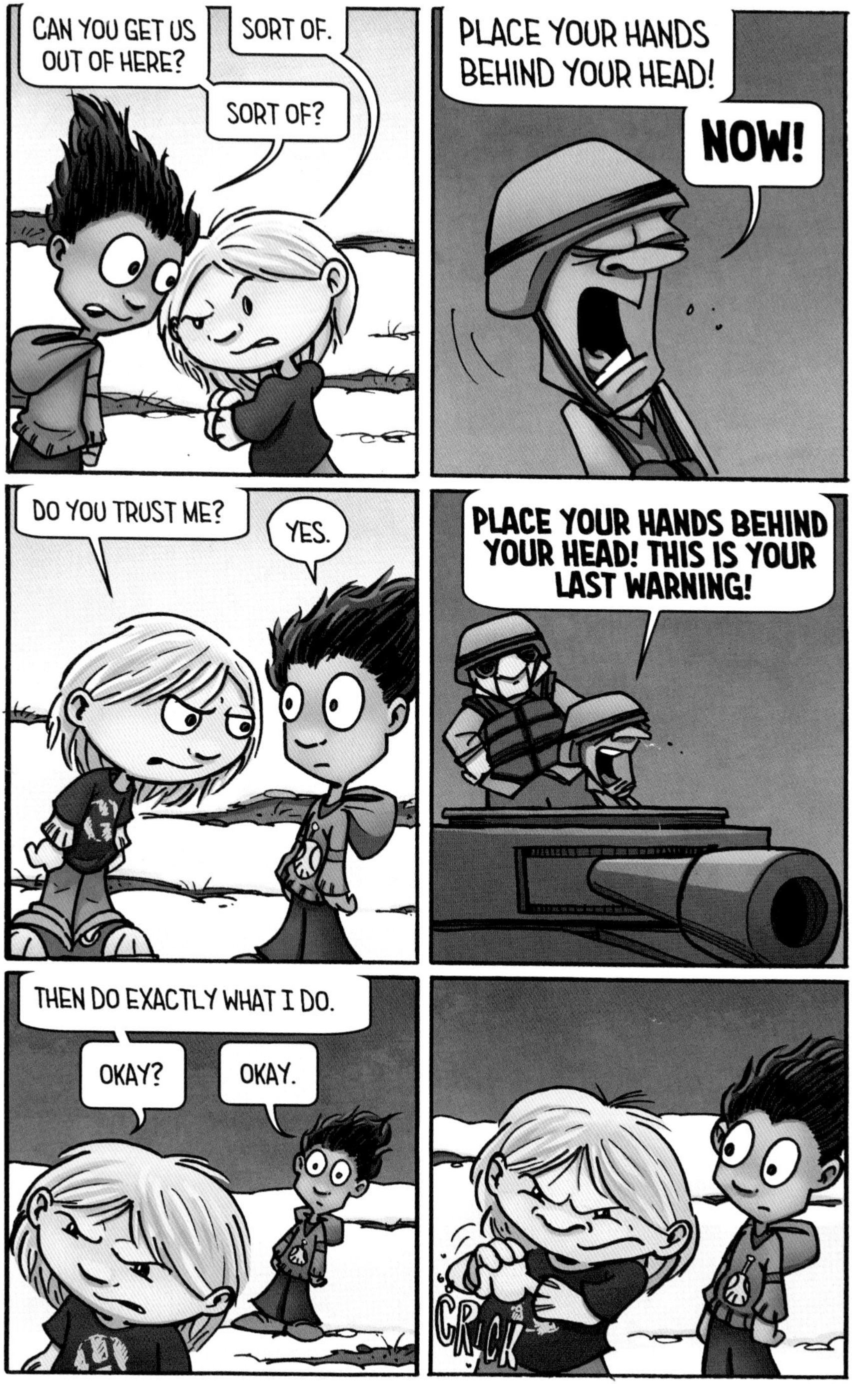
CAN YOU GET US OUT OF HERE?
SORT OF.
SORT OF?
PLACE YOUR HANDS BEHIND YOUR HEAD!
NOW!
DO YOU TRUST ME?
YES.
PLACE YOUR HANDS BEHIND YOUR HEAD! THIS IS YOUR LAST WARNING!
THEN DO EXACTLY WHAT I DO.
OKAY?
OKAY.
CRICK

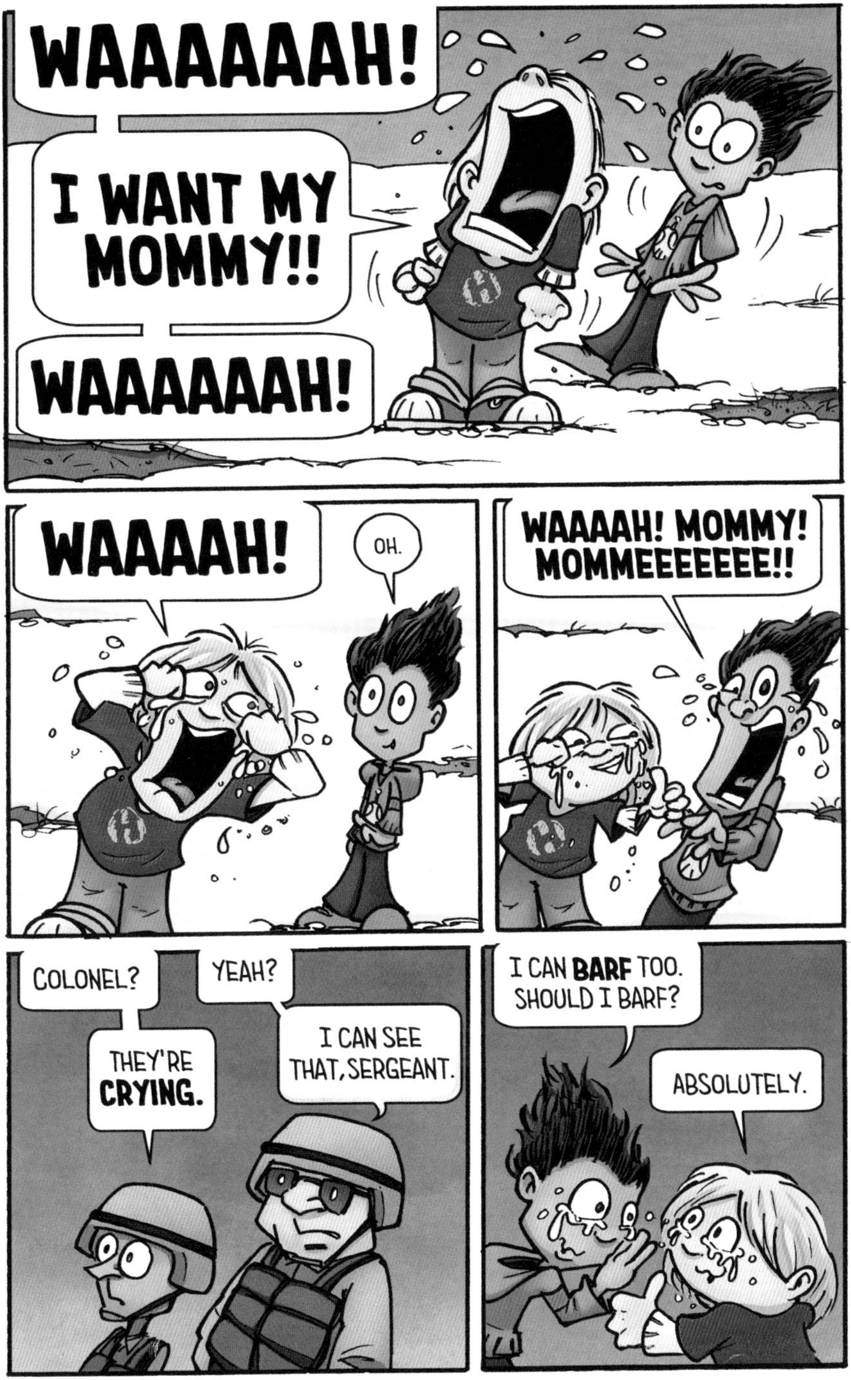
WAAAAAAH!
I WANT MY MOMMY!!
WAAAAAAH!
WAAAAH!
OH.
WAAAAH! MOMMY! MOMMEEEEEEE!!
COLONEL?
YEAH?
THEY'RE CRYING.
I CAN SEE THAT, SERGEANT.
I CAN BARF TOO. SHOULD I BARF?
ABSOLUTELY.

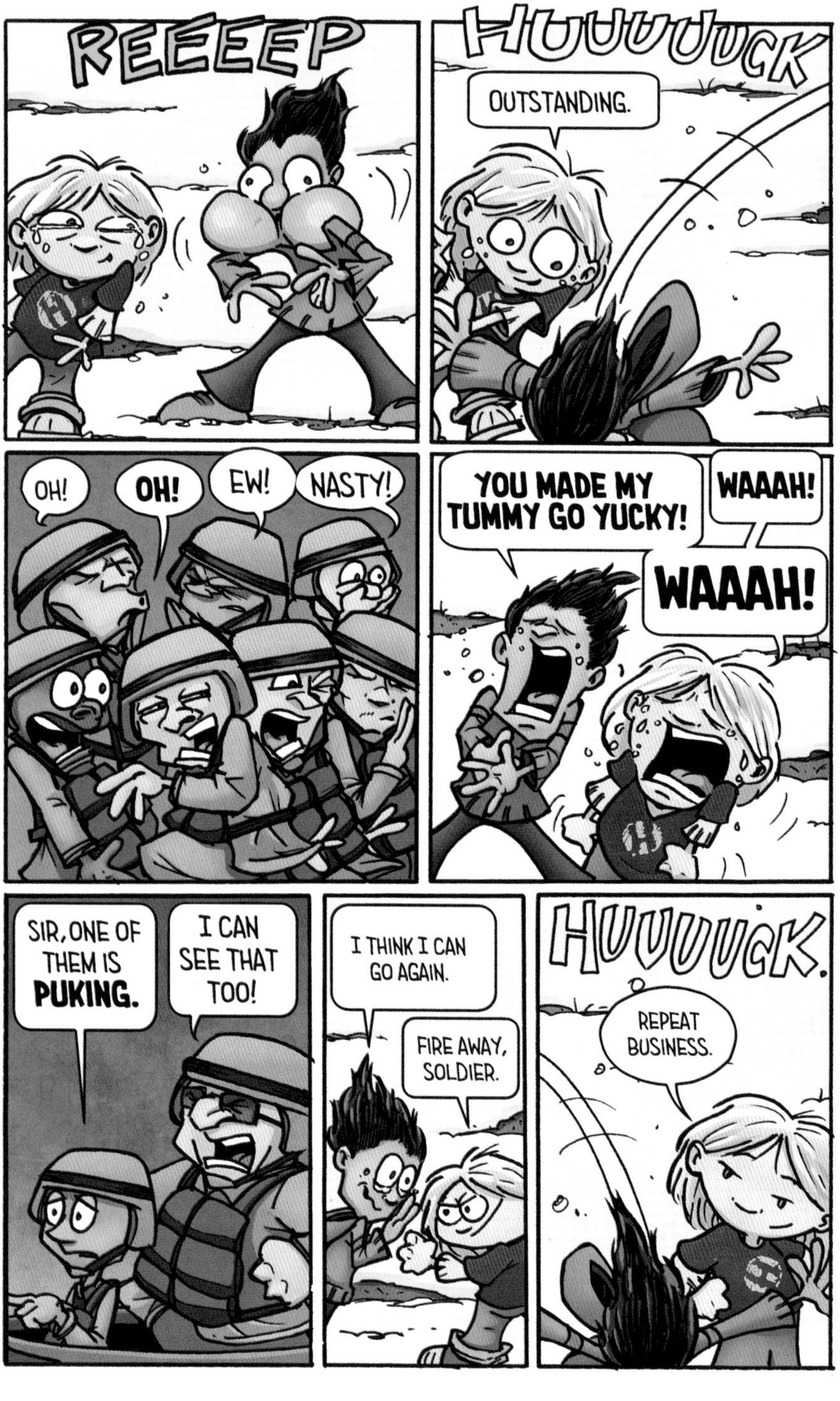
REEEEEP
HUUUUUCK
OUTSTANDING.
OH!
OH!
EW!
NASTY!
YOU MADE MY TUMMY GO YUCKY!
WAAAH!
WAAAH!
SIR, ONE OF THEM IS PUKING.
I CAN SEE THAT TOO!
I THINK I CAN GO AGAIN.
FIRE AWAY, SOLDIER.
HUUUUCK.
REPEAT BUSINESS.

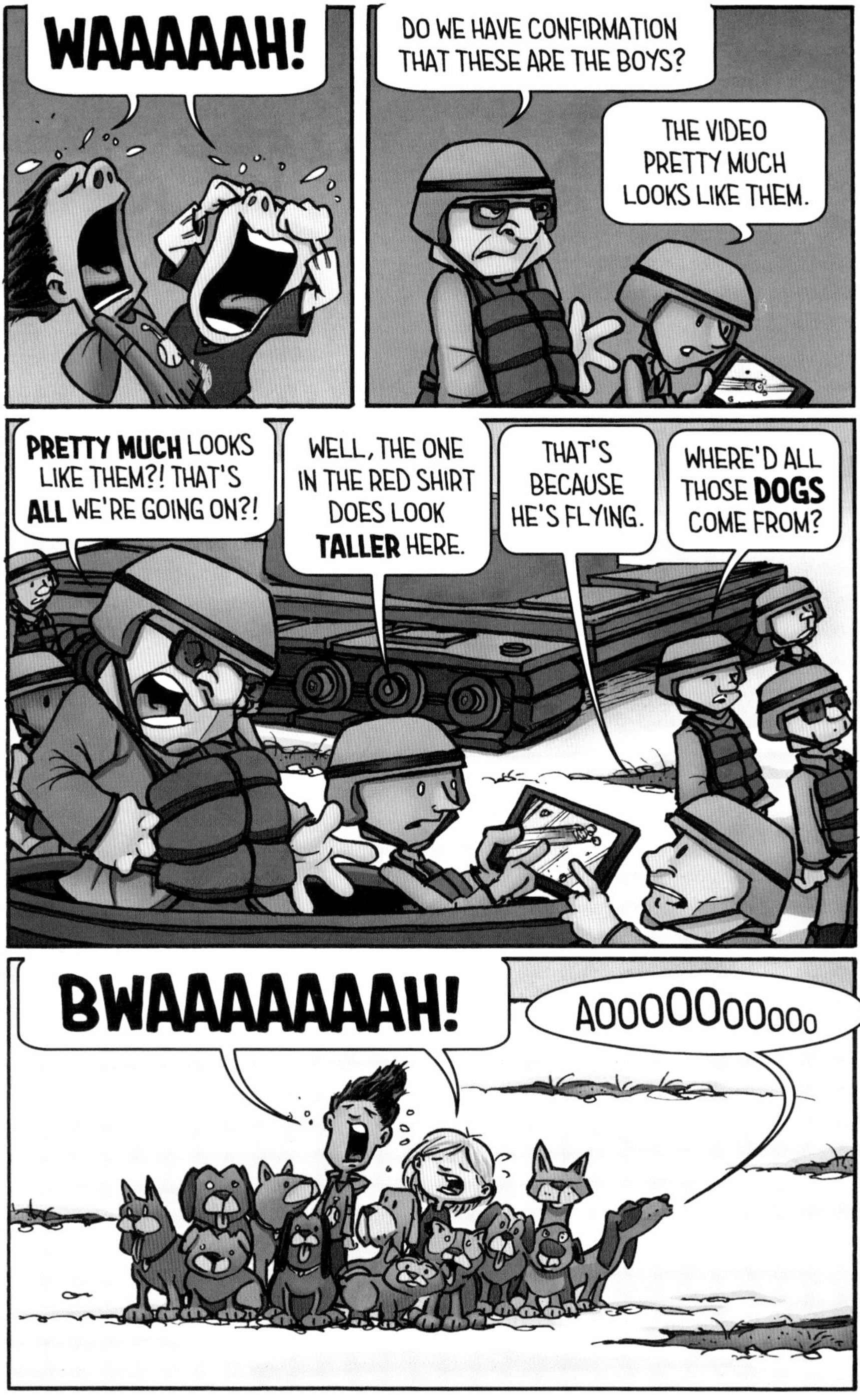
WAAAAAH!
DO WE HAVE CONFIRMATION THAT THESE ARE THE BOYS?
THE VIDEO PRETTY MUCH LOOKS LIKE THEM.
PRETTY MUCH LOOKS LIKE THEM?! THAT'S ALL WE'RE GOING ON?!
WELL, THE ONE IN THE RED SHIRT DOES LOOK TALLER HERE.
THAT'S BECAUSE HE'S FLYING.
WHERE'D ALL THOSE DOGS COME FROM?
BWAAAAAAAAH!
AOOOOOooooo

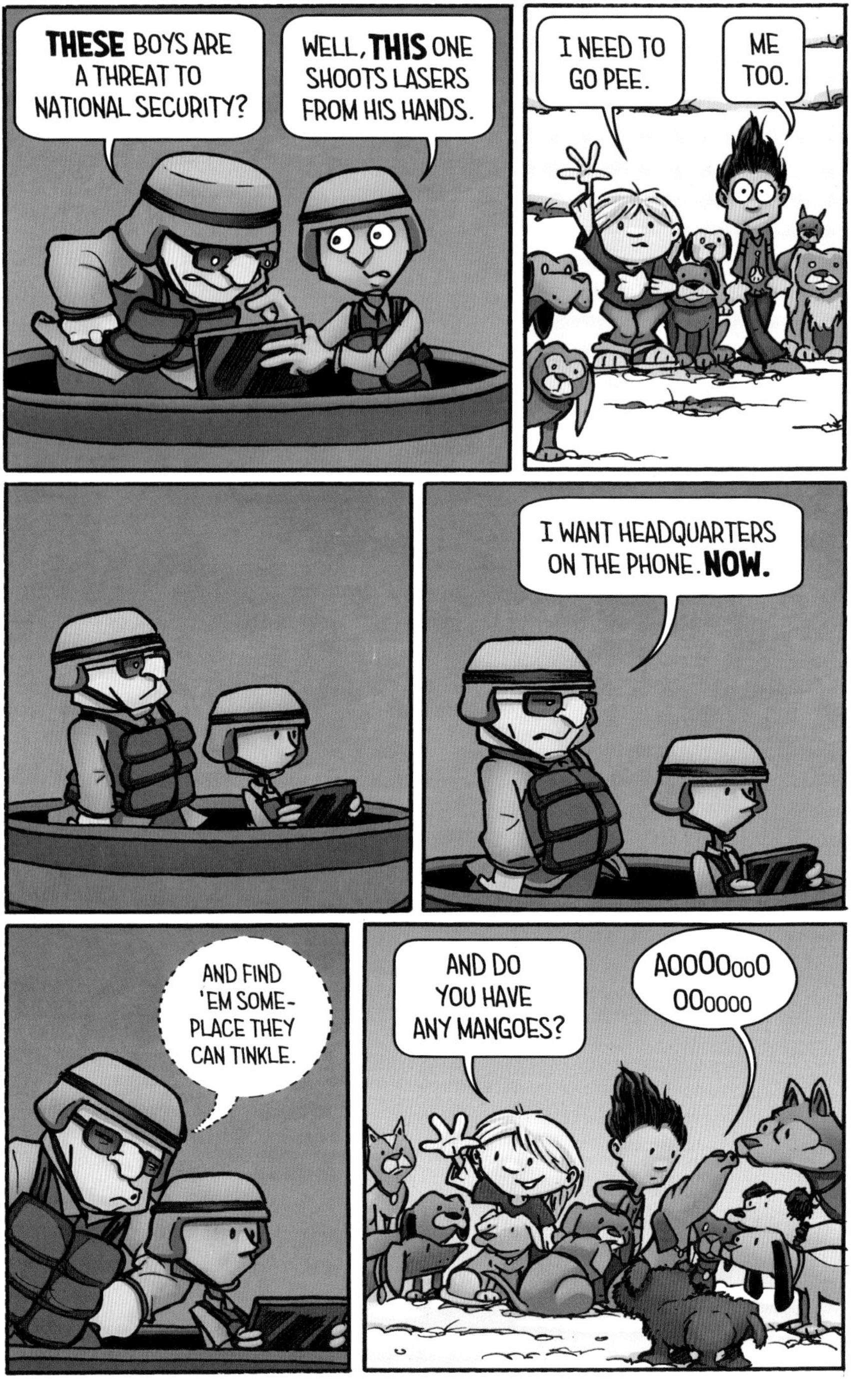
THESE BOYS ARE A THREAT TO NATIONAL SECURITY?
WELL, THIS ONE SHOOTS LASERS FROM HIS HANDS.
I NEED TO GO PEE.
ME TOO.
I WANT HEADQUARTERS ON THE PHONE. NOW.
AND FIND 'EM SOME-PLACE THEY CAN TINKLE.
AND DO YOU HAVE ANY MANGOES?
AOOOOooO OOoooo

# CHAPTER 2

## HELP

FORT RISPLER ARMY BASE.
I GOTTA SAY... THIS PLACE IS **IMPRESSIVE.**

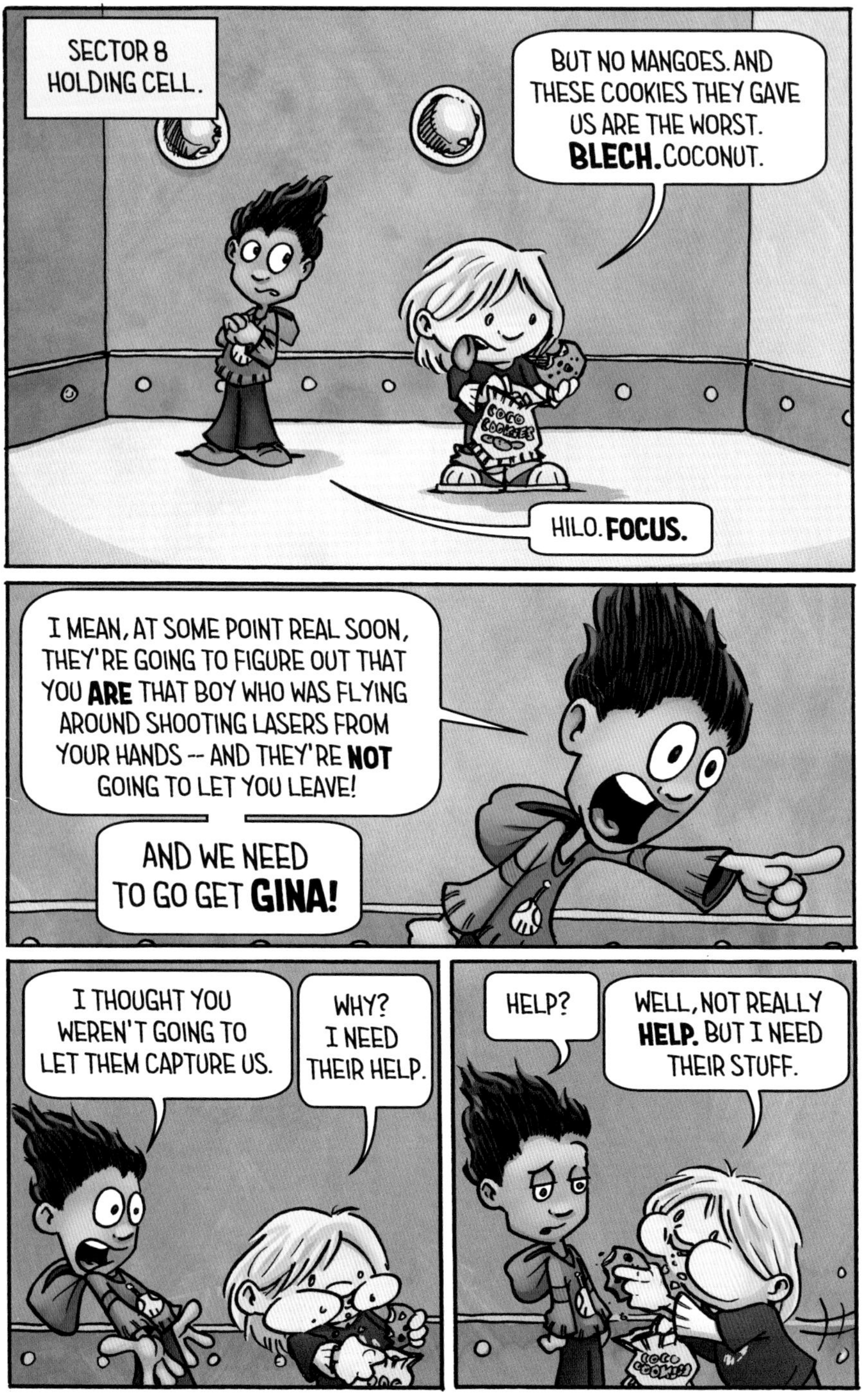
SECTOR 8 HOLDING CELL.
BUT NO MANGOES. AND THESE COOKIES THEY GAVE US ARE THE WORST. BLECH. COCONUT.
COCO COOKIES
HILO. FOCUS.
I MEAN, AT SOME POINT REAL SOON, THEY'RE GOING TO FIGURE OUT THAT YOU ARE THAT BOY WHO WAS FLYING AROUND SHOOTING LASERS FROM YOUR HANDS -- AND THEY'RE NOT GOING TO LET YOU LEAVE!
AND WE NEED TO GO GET GINA!
I THOUGHT YOU WEREN'T GOING TO LET THEM CAPTURE US.
WHY? I NEED THEIR HELP.
HELP?
WELL, NOT REALLY HELP. BUT I NEED THEIR STUFF.

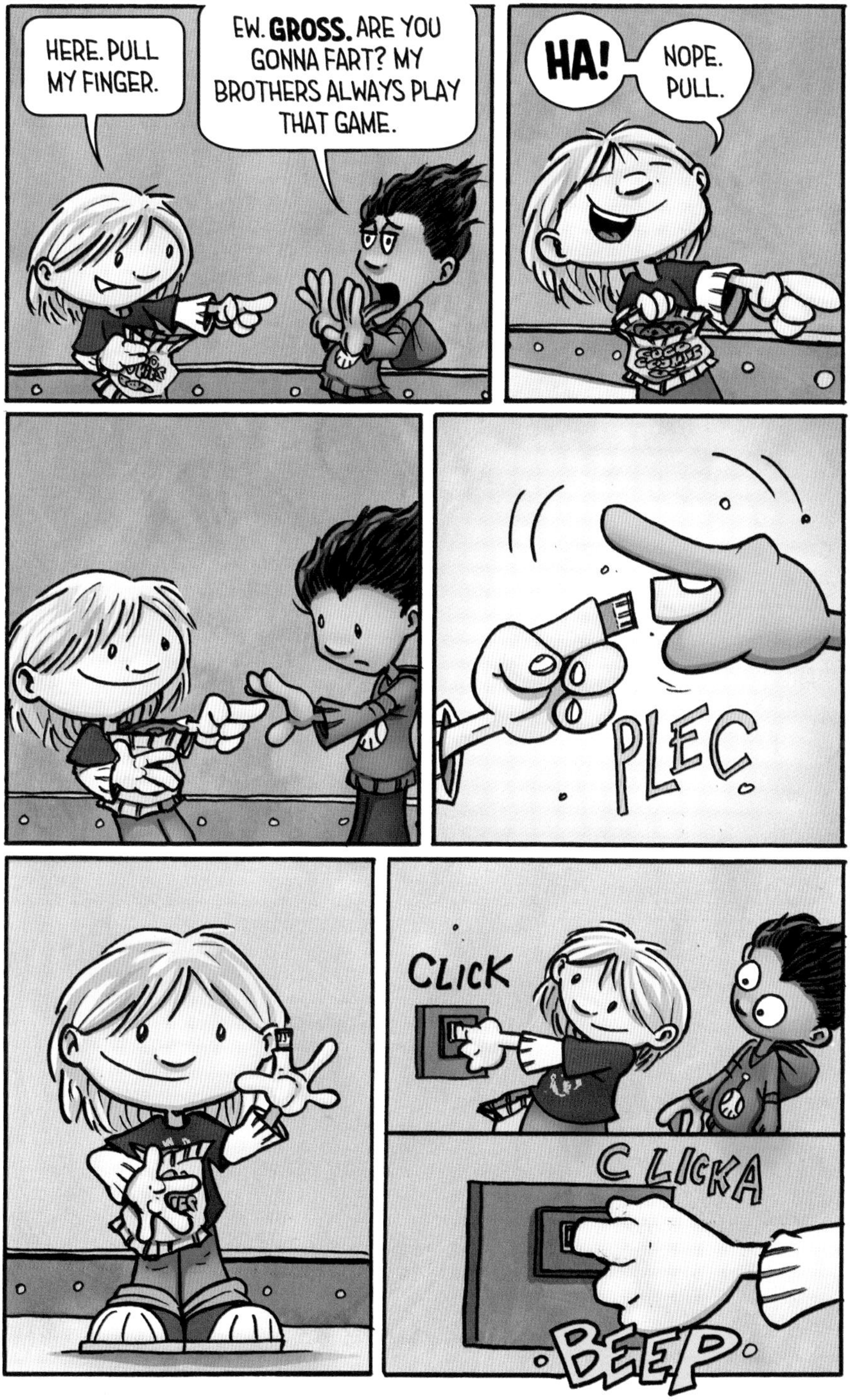
HERE. PULL MY FINGER.
EW. GROSS. ARE YOU GONNA FART? MY BROTHERS ALWAYS PLAY THAT GAME.
HA!
NOPE. PULL.
PLEC
CLICK
CLICKA
BEEP

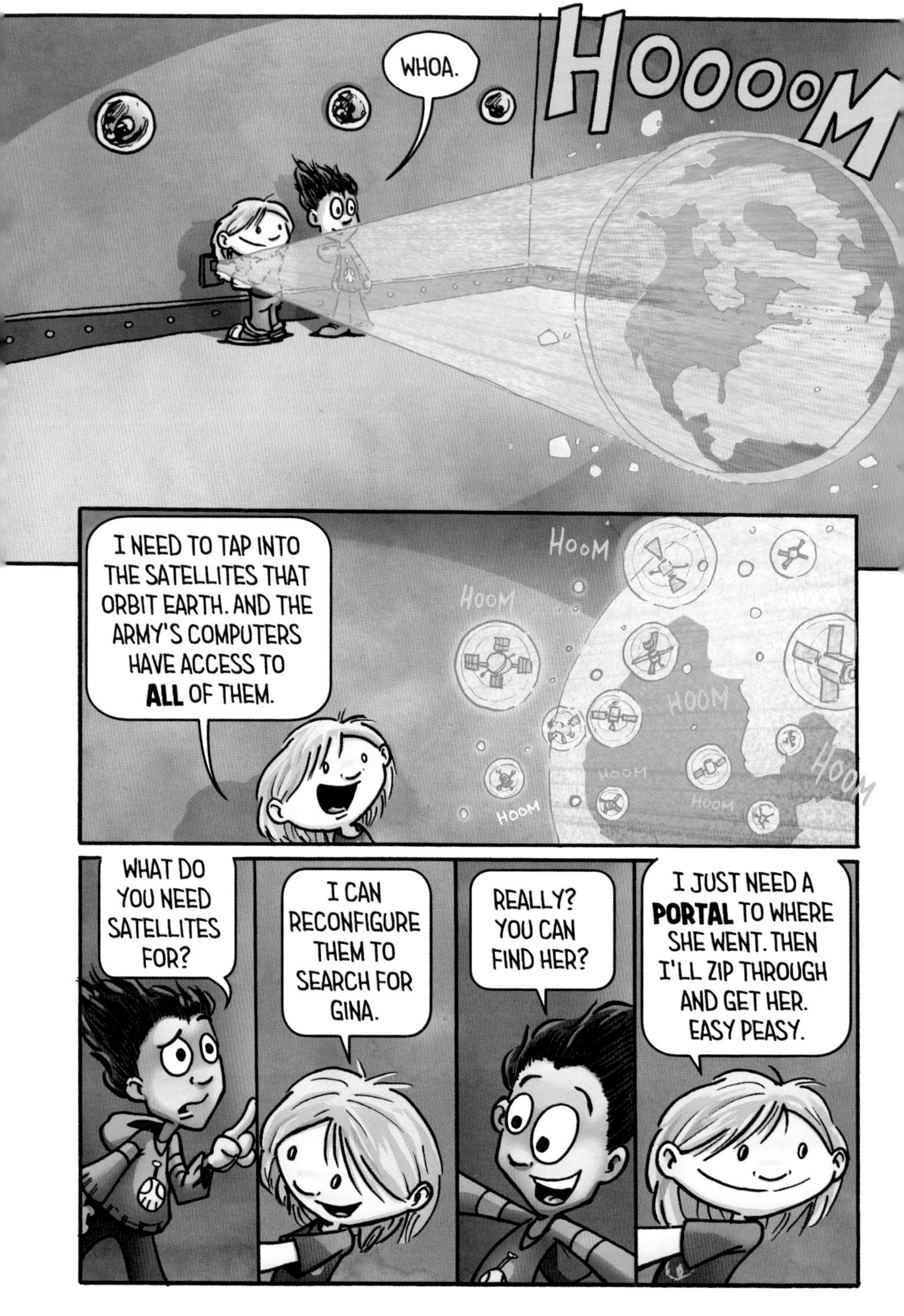
WHOA.
HOOOOM
I NEED TO TAP INTO THE SATELLITES THAT ORBIT EARTH. AND THE ARMY'S COMPUTERS HAVE ACCESS TO **ALL** OF THEM.
HOOM
HOOM
HOOM
HOOM
HOOM
HOOM
HOOM
WHAT DO YOU NEED SATELLITES FOR?
I CAN RECONFIGURE THEM TO SEARCH FOR GINA.
REALLY? YOU CAN FIND HER?
I JUST NEED A **PORTAL** TO WHERE SHE WENT. THEN I'LL ZIP THROUGH AND GET HER. EASY PEASY.

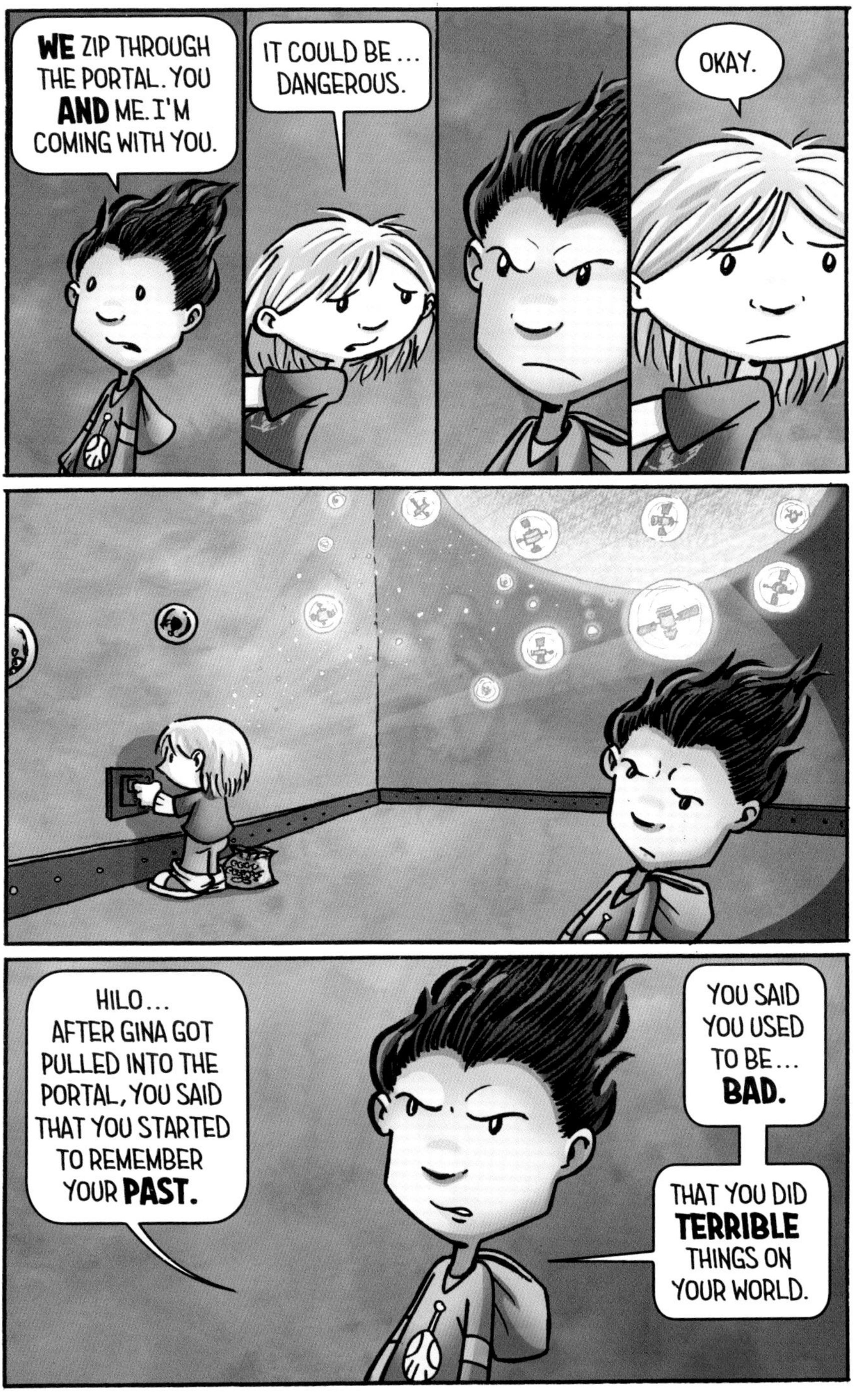
WE ZIP THROUGH THE PORTAL. YOU AND ME. I'M COMING WITH YOU.
IT COULD BE... DANGEROUS.
OKAY.
HILO... AFTER GINA GOT PULLED INTO THE PORTAL, YOU SAID THAT YOU STARTED TO REMEMBER YOUR PAST.
YOU SAID YOU USED TO BE... BAD.
THAT YOU DID TERRIBLE THINGS ON YOUR WORLD.

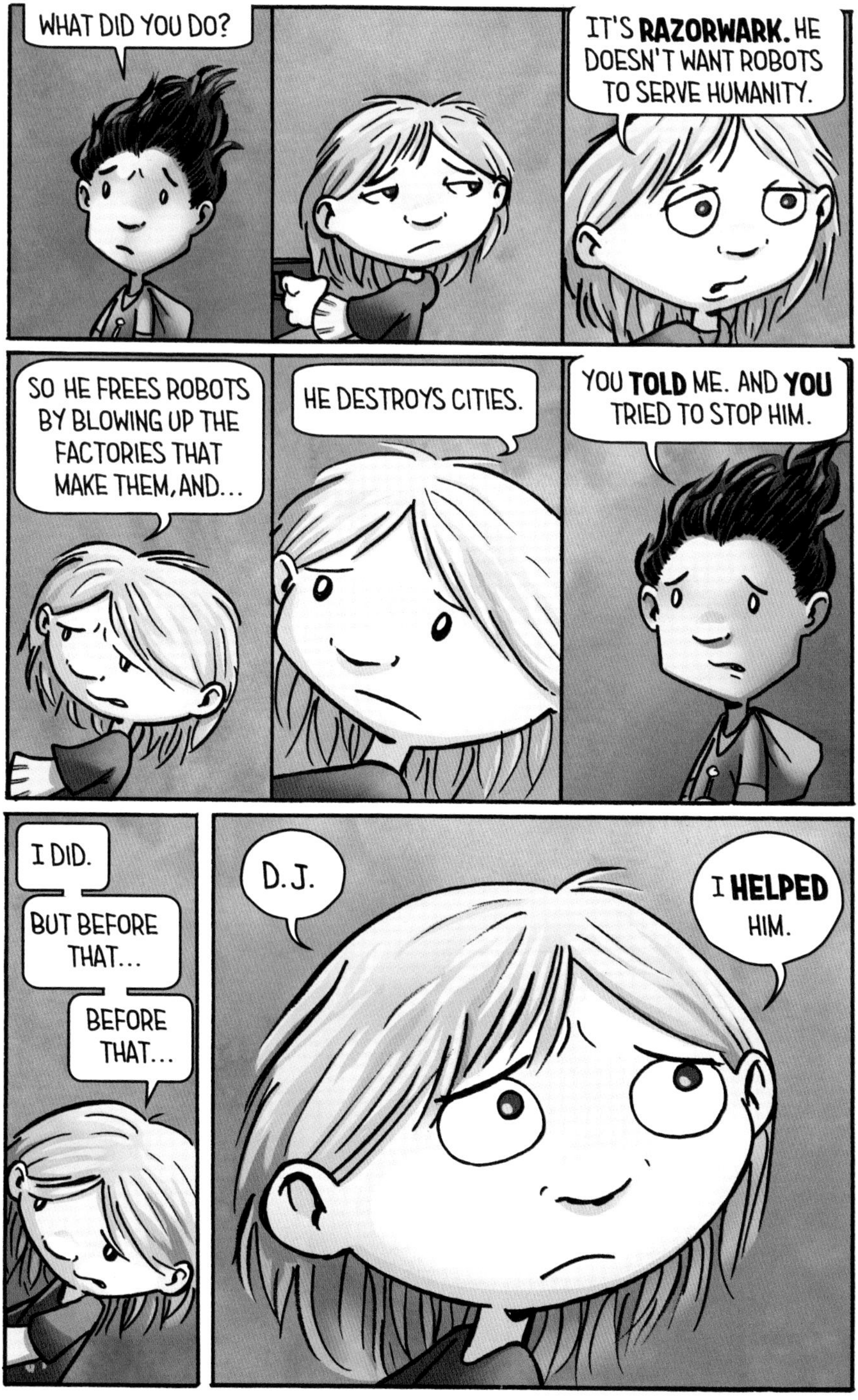
WHAT DID YOU DO?
IT'S **RAZORWARK.** HE DOESN'T WANT ROBOTS TO SERVE HUMANITY.
SO HE FREES ROBOTS BY BLOWING UP THE FACTORIES THAT MAKE THEM, AND...
HE DESTROYS CITIES.
YOU **TOLD** ME. AND **YOU** TRIED TO STOP HIM.
I DID.
BUT BEFORE THAT...
BEFORE THAT...
D.J.
I **HELPED** HIM.

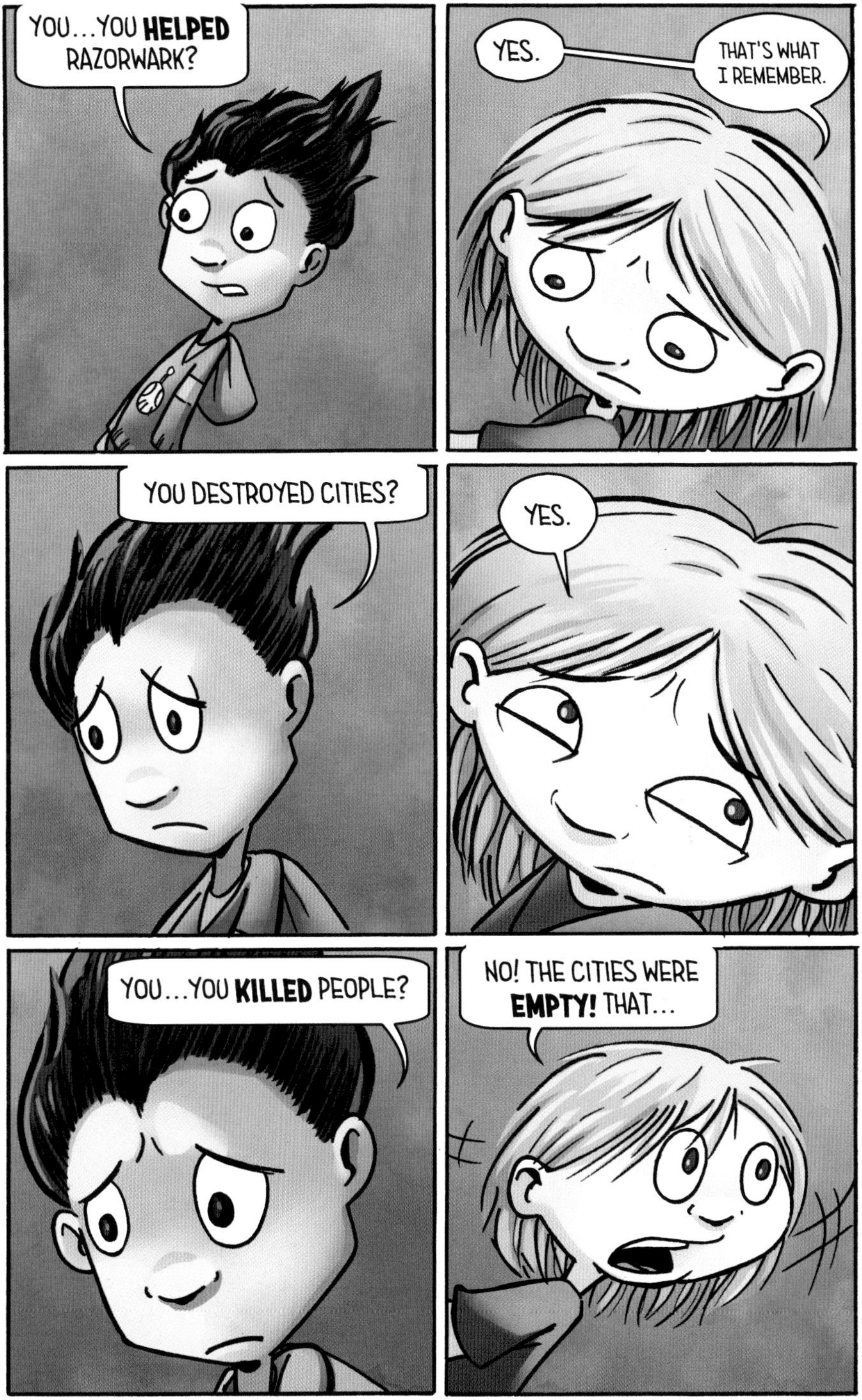
YOU...YOU **HELPED** RAZORWARK?
YES.
THAT'S WHAT I REMEMBER.
YOU DESTROYED CITIES?
YES.
YOU...YOU **KILLED** PEOPLE?
NO! THE CITIES WERE **EMPTY!** THAT...

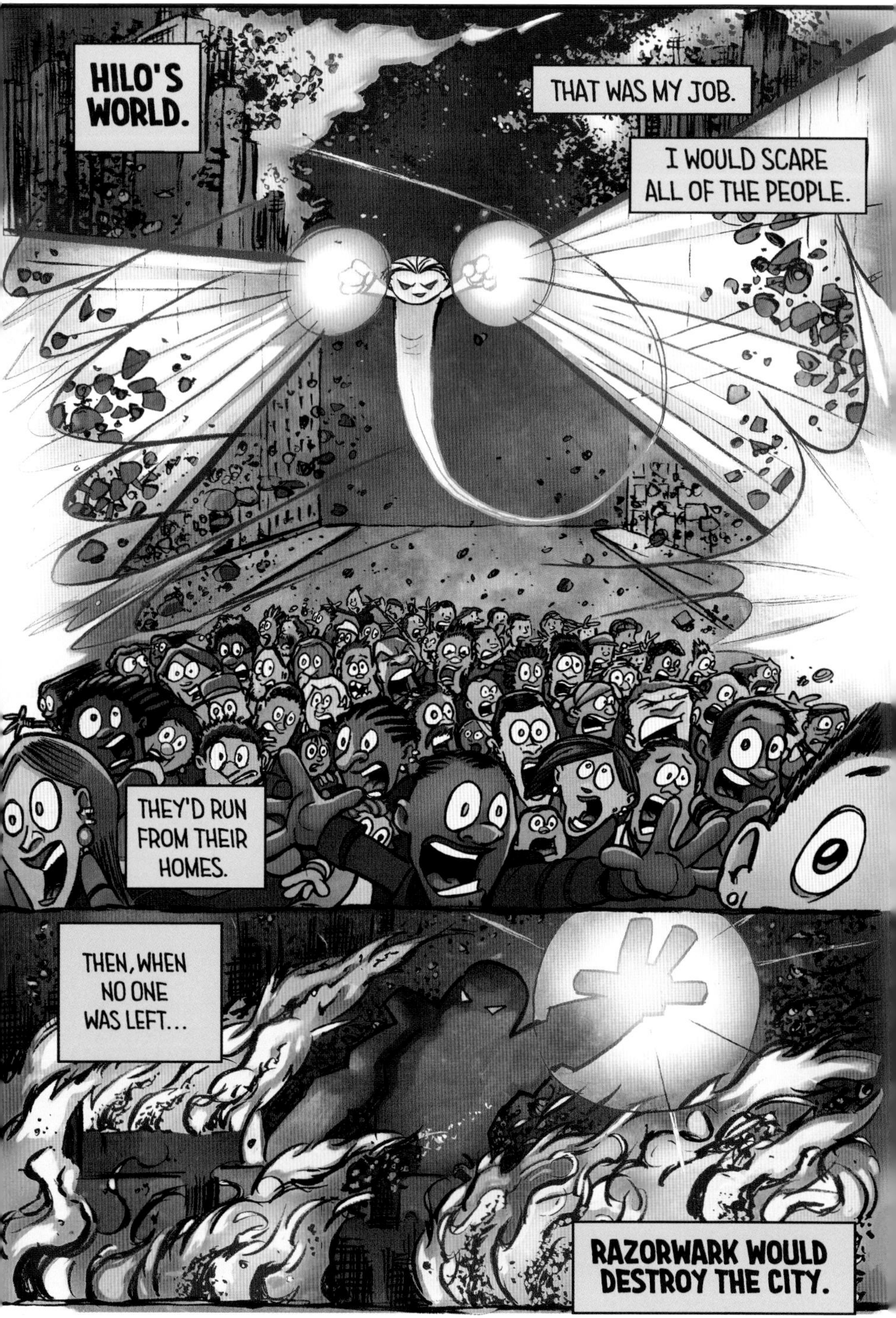
HILO'S WORLD.
THAT WAS MY JOB.
I WOULD SCARE ALL OF THE PEOPLE.
THEY'D RUN FROM THEIR HOMES.
THEN, WHEN NO ONE WAS LEFT...
RAZORWARK WOULD DESTROY THE CITY.

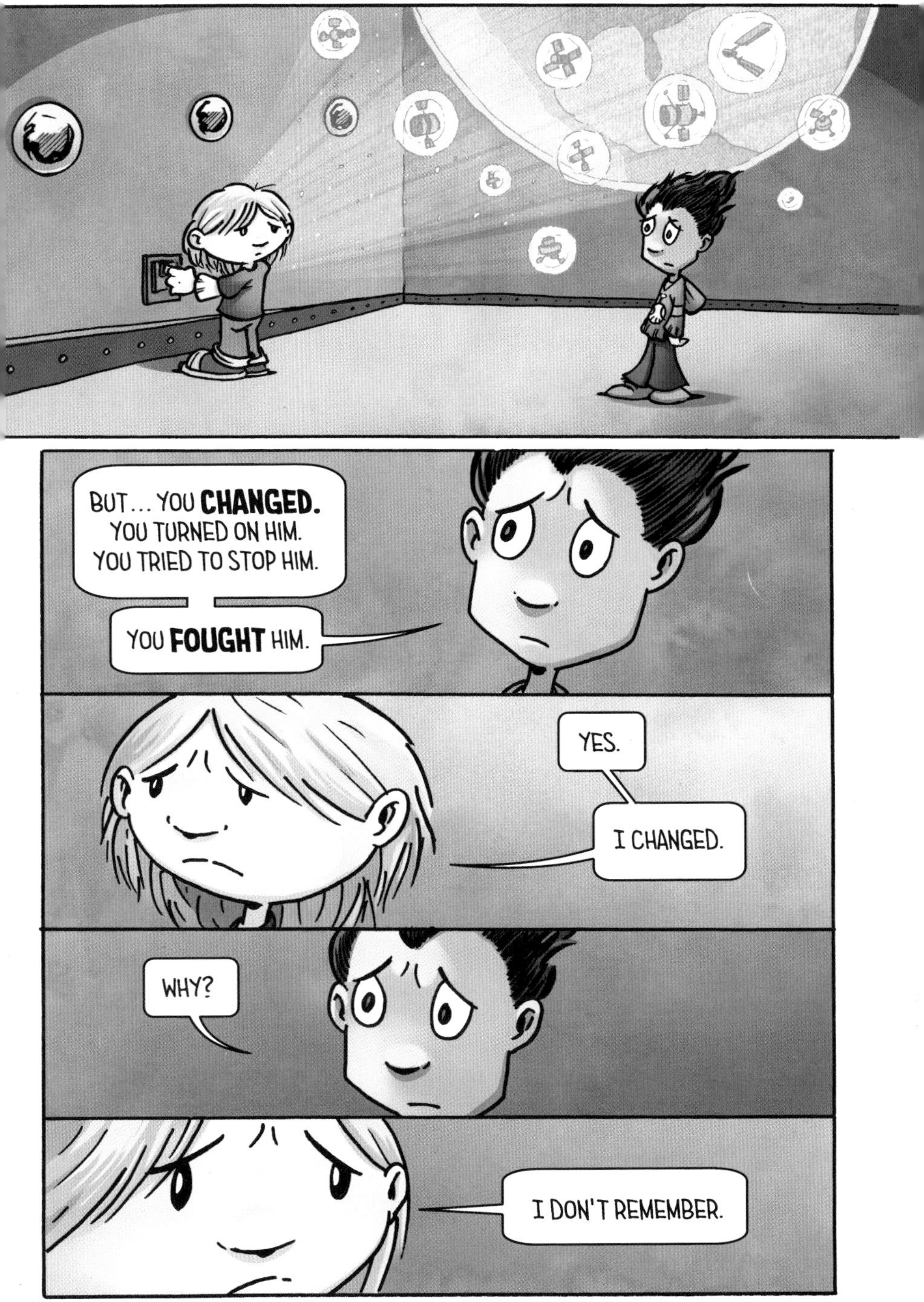
BUT... YOU **CHANGED.** YOU TURNED ON HIM. YOU TRIED TO STOP HIM.
YOU **FOUGHT** HIM.
YES.
I CHANGED.
WHY?
I DON'T REMEMBER.

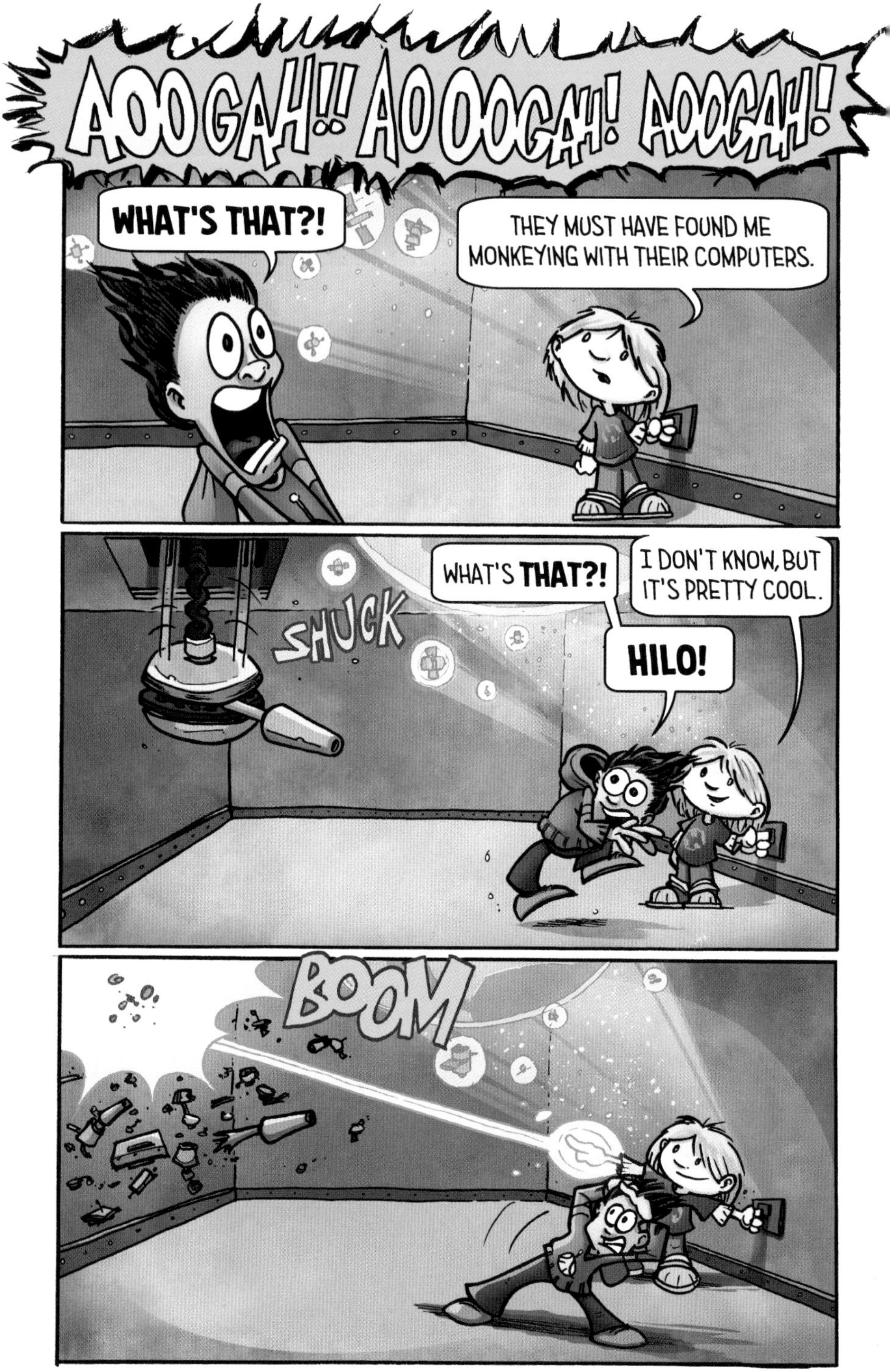
AOOGAH!! AOOOGAH! AOOGAH!
WHAT'S THAT?!
THEY MUST HAVE FOUND ME MONKEYING WITH THEIR COMPUTERS.
SHUCK
WHAT'S THAT?!
I DON'T KNOW, BUT IT'S PRETTY COOL.
HILO!
BOOM

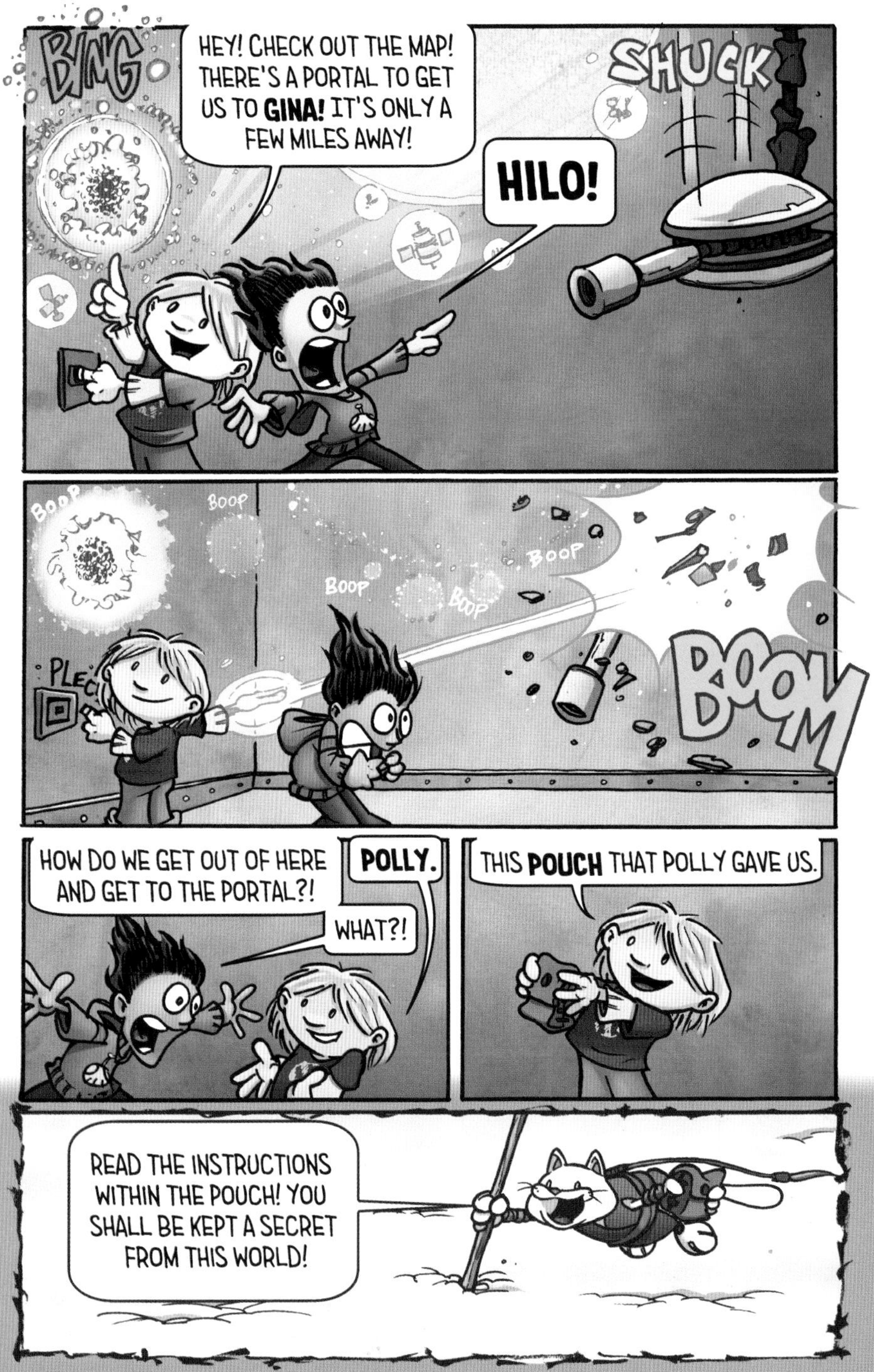
BING
HEY! CHECK OUT THE MAP! THERE'S A PORTAL TO GET US TO **GINA!** IT'S ONLY A FEW MILES AWAY!
SHUCK
HILO!
BOOP
BOOP
BOOP
BOOP
BOOP
PLECK
BOOM
HOW DO WE GET OUT OF HERE AND GET TO THE PORTAL?!
POLLY.
WHAT?!
THIS **POUCH** THAT POLLY GAVE US.
READ THE INSTRUCTIONS WITHIN THE POUCH! YOU SHALL BE KEPT A SECRET FROM THIS WORLD!

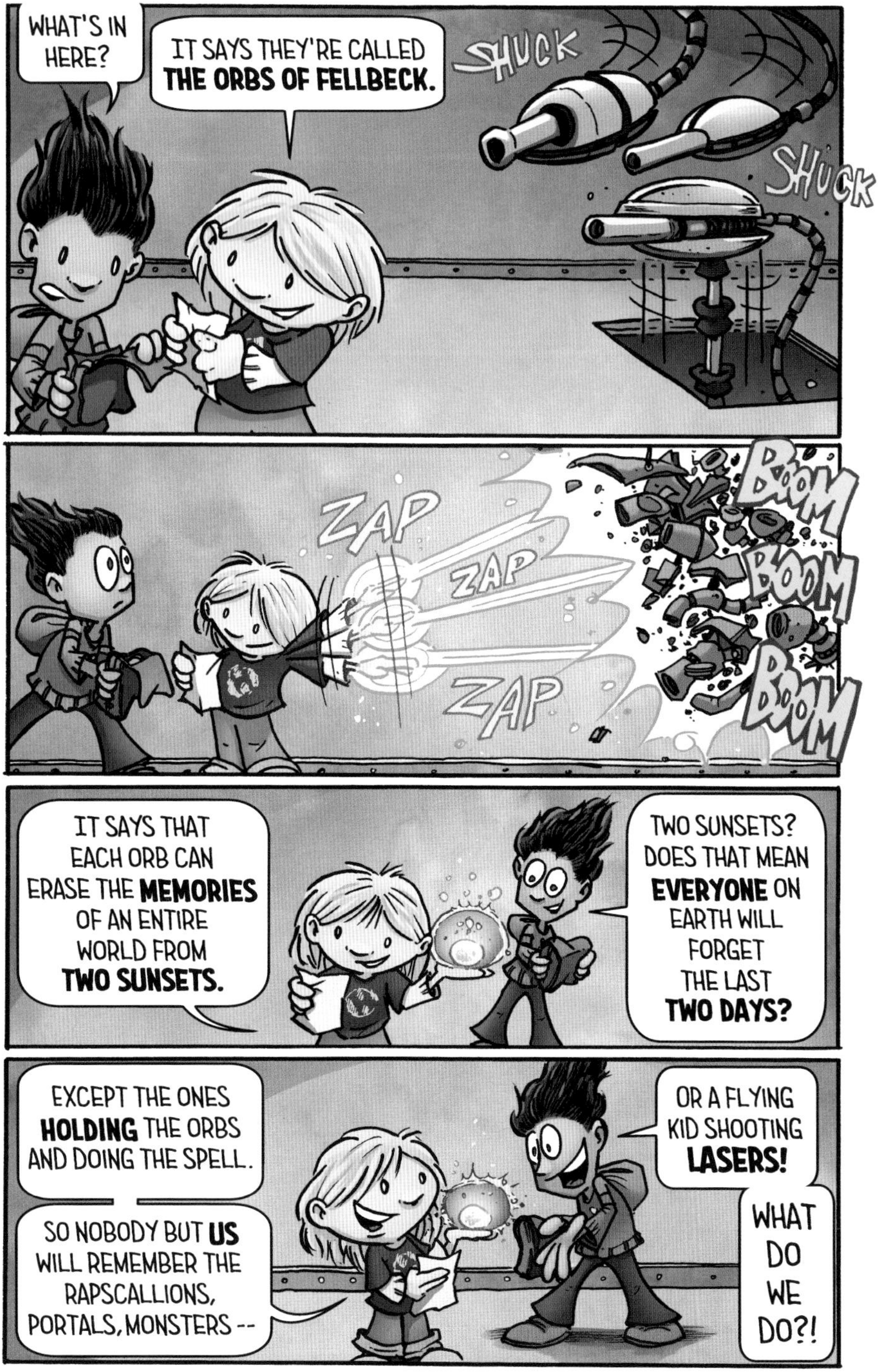

WHAT'S IN HERE?
IT SAYS THEY'RE CALLED **THE ORBS OF FELLBECK.**
SHUCK
SHUCK
ZAP
ZAP
ZAP
BOOM
BOOM
BOOM
IT SAYS THAT EACH ORB CAN ERASE THE **MEMORIES** OF AN ENTIRE WORLD FROM **TWO SUNSETS.**
TWO SUNSETS? DOES THAT MEAN **EVERYONE** ON EARTH WILL FORGET THE LAST **TWO DAYS?**
EXCEPT THE ONES **HOLDING** THE ORBS AND DOING THE SPELL.
SO NOBODY BUT **US** WILL REMEMBER THE RAPSCALLIONS, PORTALS, MONSTERS --
OR A FLYING KID SHOOTING **LASERS!**
WHAT DO WE DO?!

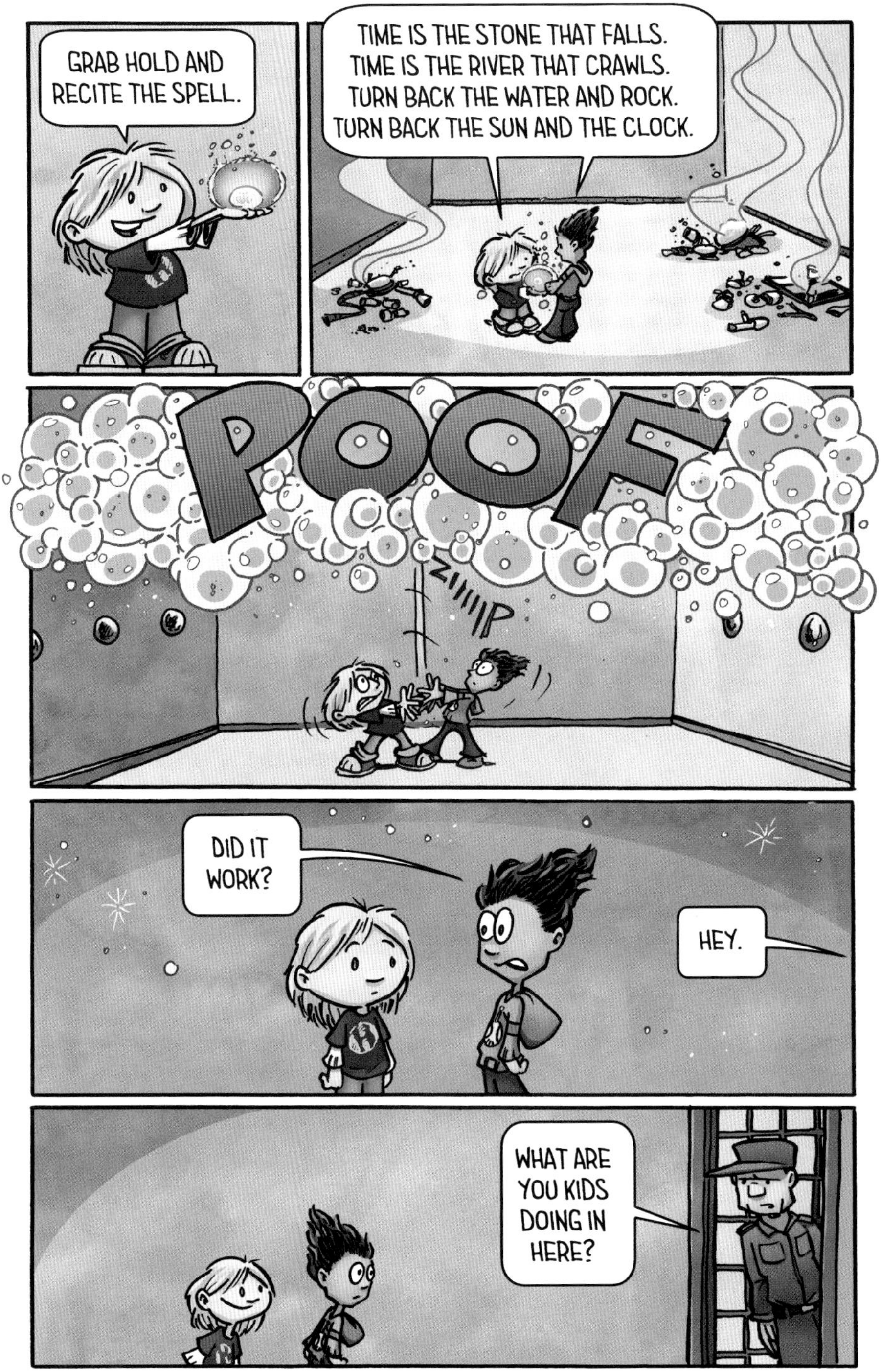
GRAB HOLD AND RECITE THE SPELL.
TIME IS THE STONE THAT FALLS. TIME IS THE RIVER THAT CRAWLS. TURN BACK THE WATER AND ROCK. TURN BACK THE SUN AND THE CLOCK.
POOF
ZIIIIP
DID IT WORK?
HEY.
WHAT ARE YOU KIDS DOING IN HERE?

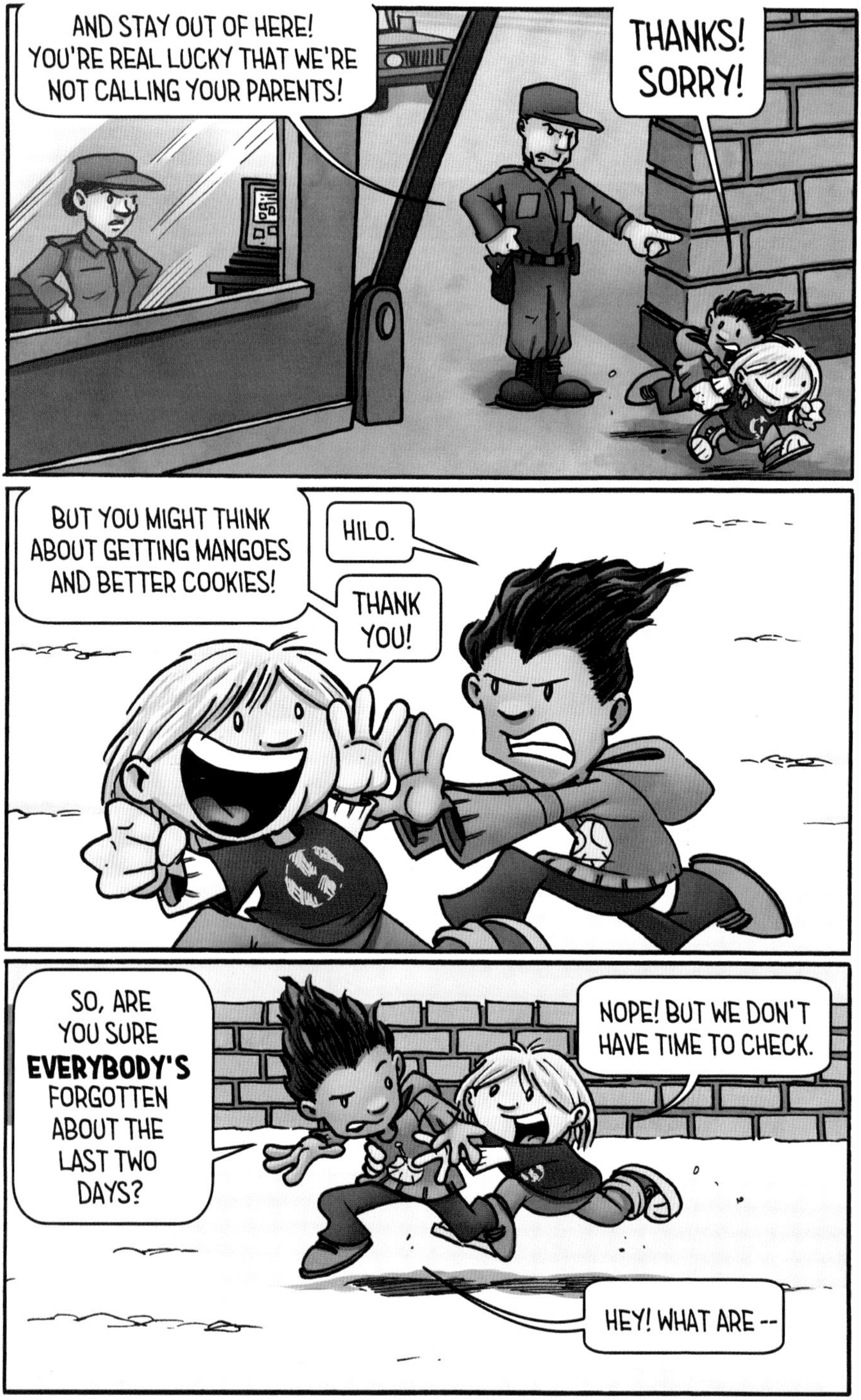
AND STAY OUT OF HERE! YOU'RE REAL LUCKY THAT WE'RE NOT CALLING YOUR PARENTS!
THANKS! SORRY!
BUT YOU MIGHT THINK ABOUT GETTING MANGOES AND BETTER COOKIES!
HILO.
THANK YOU!
SO, ARE YOU SURE **EVERYBODY'S** FORGOTTEN ABOUT THE LAST TWO DAYS?
NOPE! BUT WE DON'T HAVE TIME TO CHECK.
HEY! WHAT ARE --

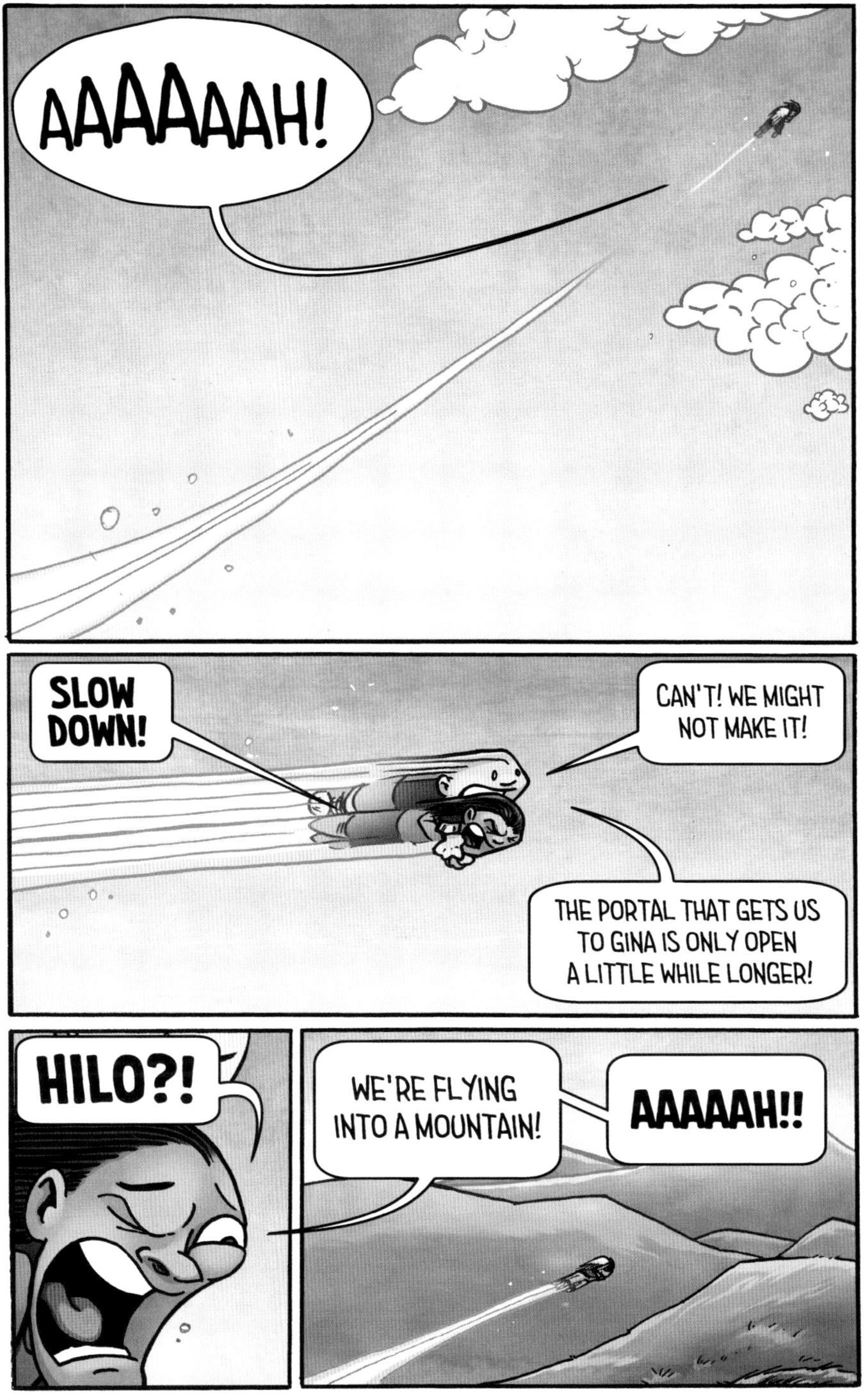
AAAAAAH!
SLOW DOWN!
CAN'T! WE MIGHT NOT MAKE IT!
THE PORTAL THAT GETS US TO GINA IS ONLY OPEN A LITTLE WHILE LONGER!
HILO?!
WE'RE FLYING INTO A MOUNTAIN!
AAAAAH!!

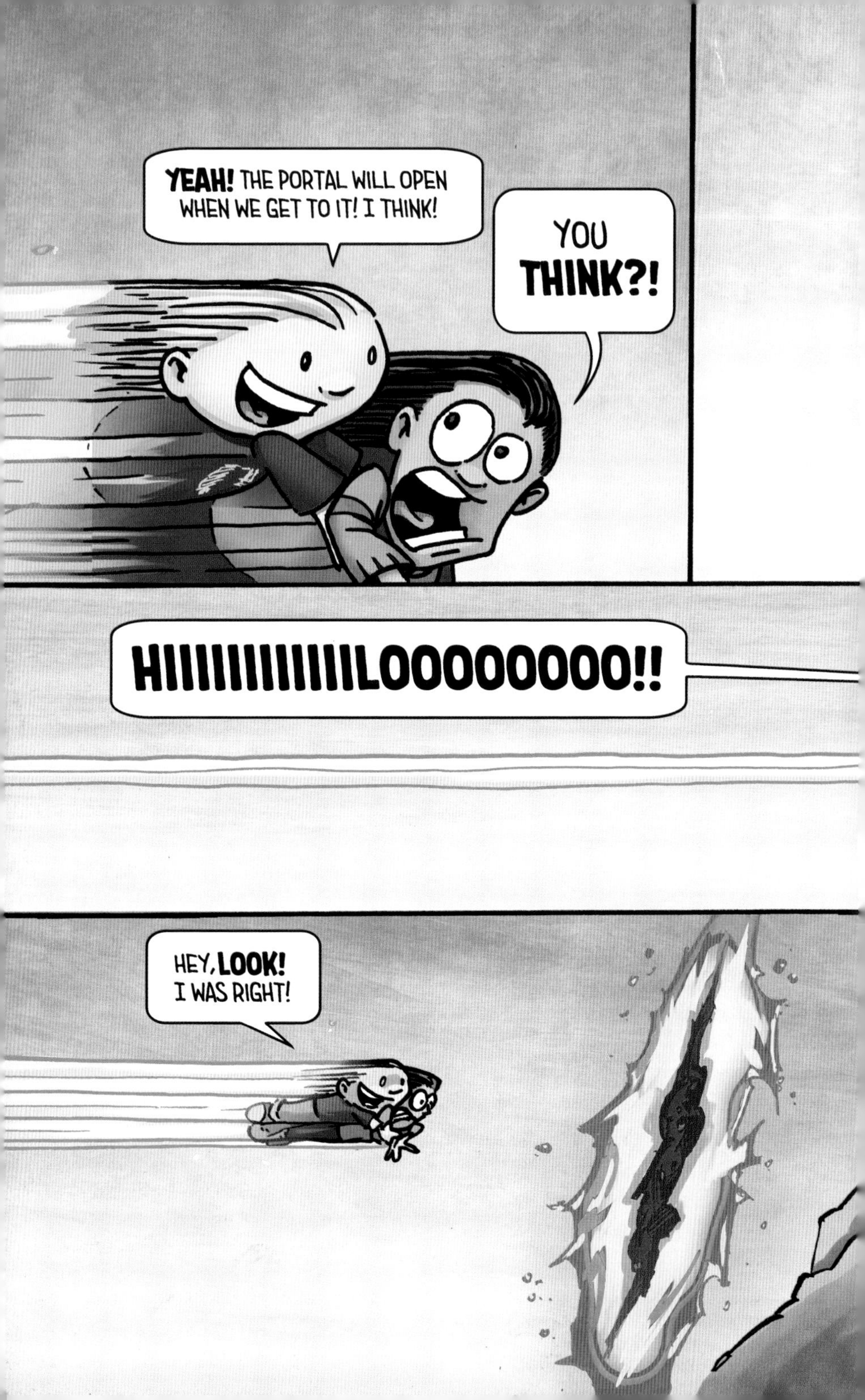
YEAH! THE PORTAL WILL OPEN WHEN WE GET TO IT! I THINK!
YOU THINK?!
HIIIIIIIIIIIILOOOOOOOO!!
HEY, LOOK! I WAS RIGHT!

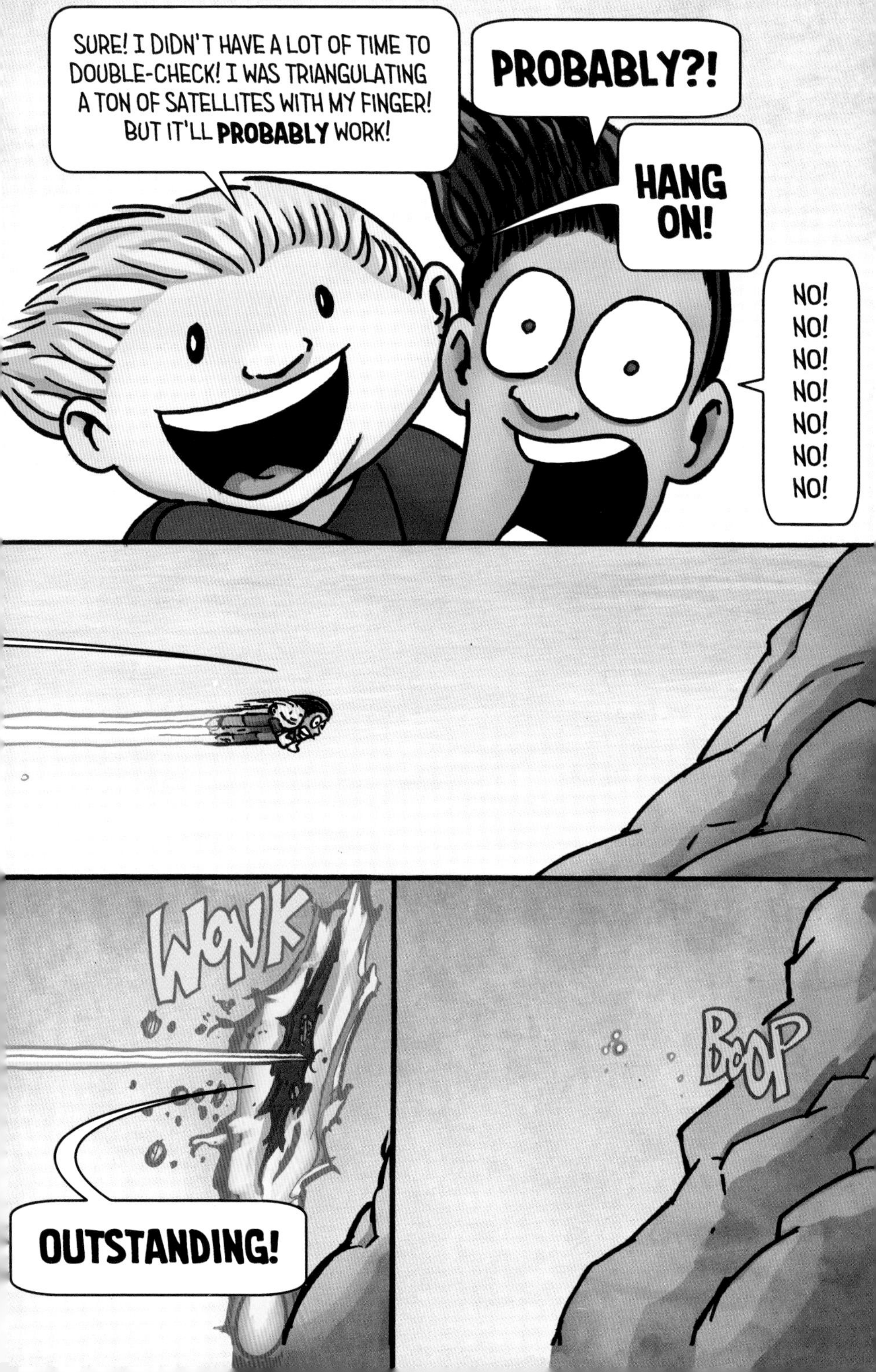
SURE! I DIDN'T HAVE A LOT OF TIME TO DOUBLE-CHECK! I WAS TRIANGULATING A TON OF SATELLITES WITH MY FINGER! BUT IT'LL **PROBABLY** WORK!
PROBABLY?!
HANG ON!
NO! NO! NO! NO! NO! NO! NO!
WONK
OUTSTANDING!
BOOP

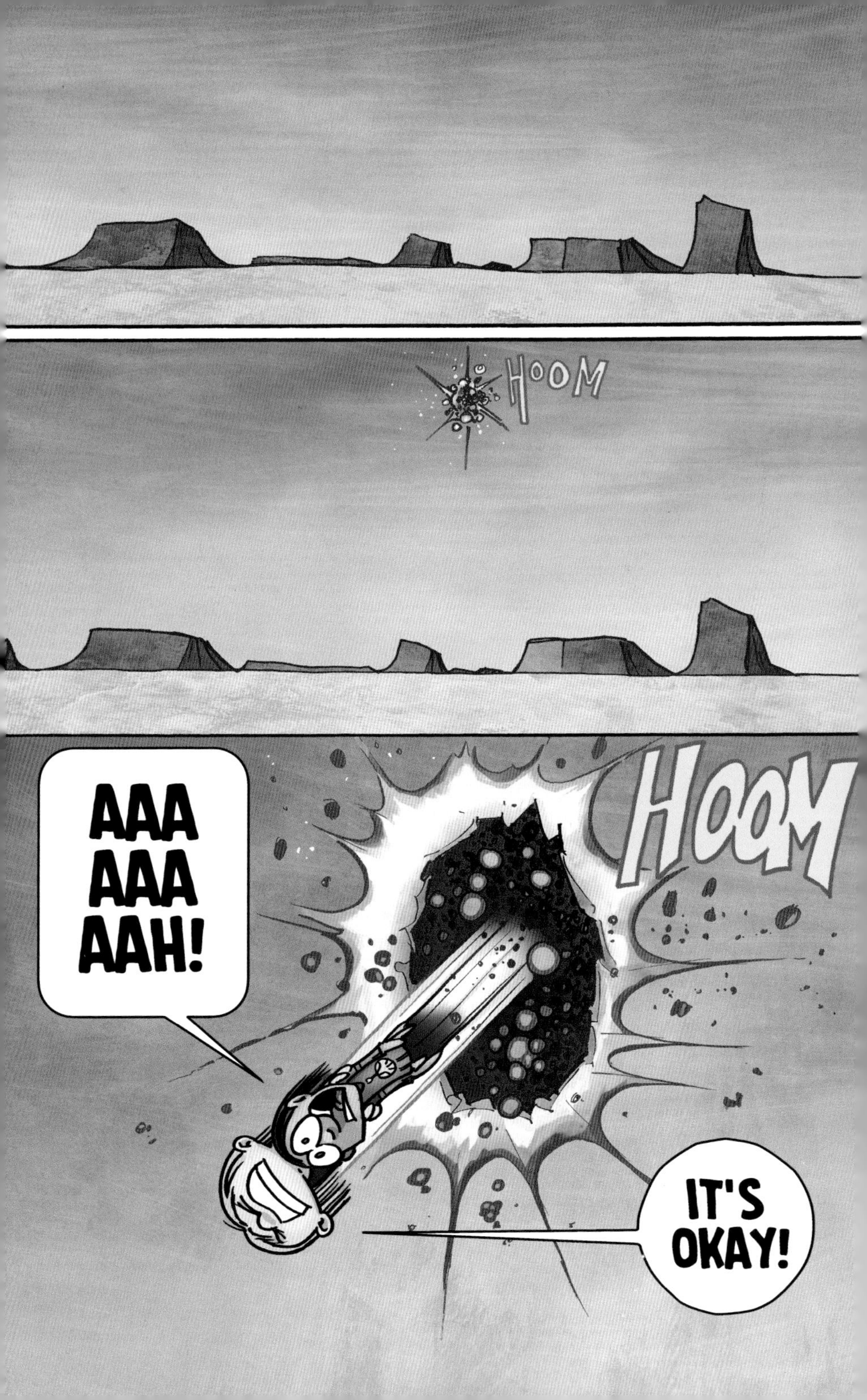
HOOM
HOOM
AAA AAA AAH!
IT'S OKAY!

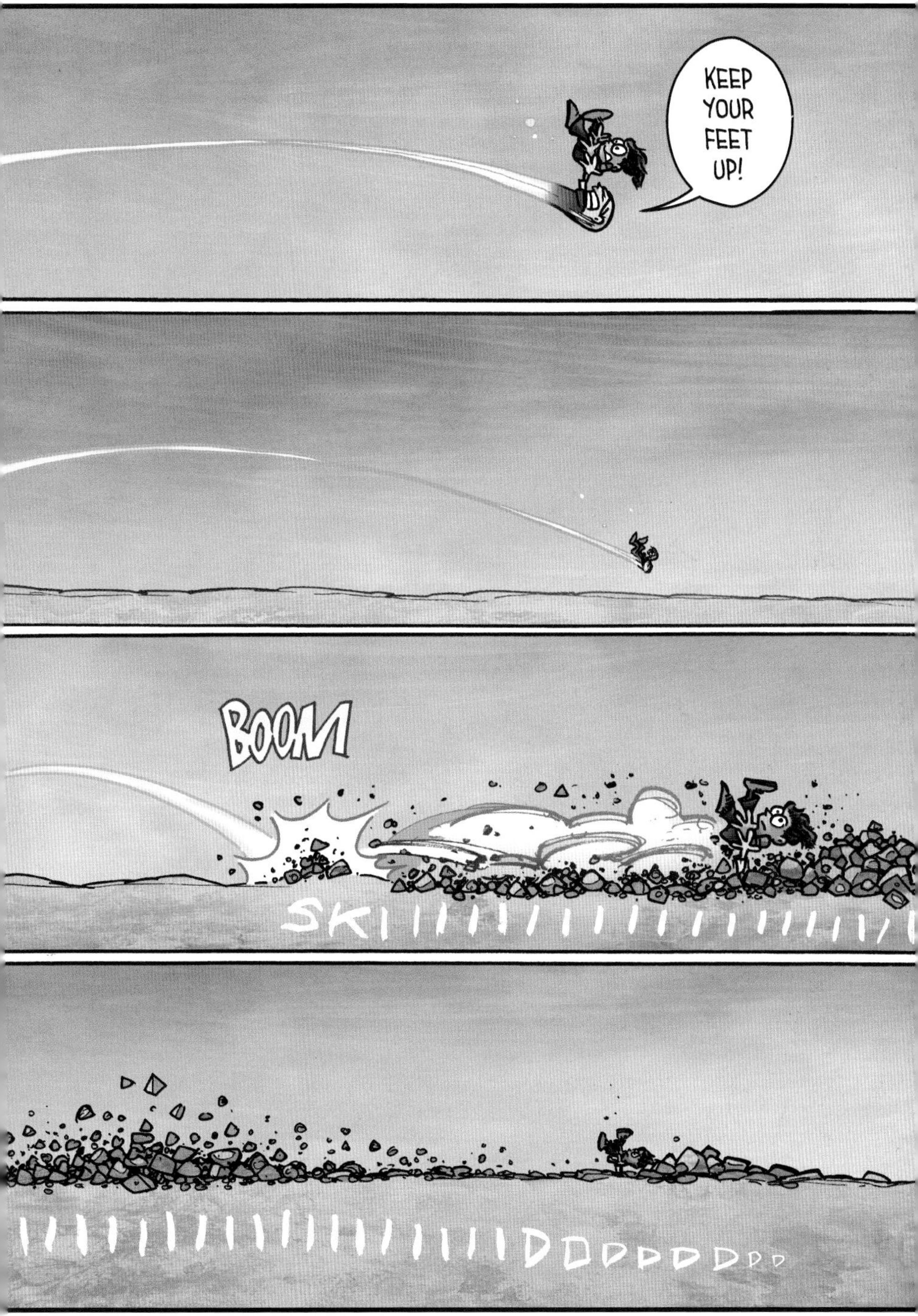
KEEP YOUR FEET UP!
BOOM
SKIIIIIIIIIIIIIIIIIIII
IIIIIIIIIIIIIIIIIIDDDDDDDDD

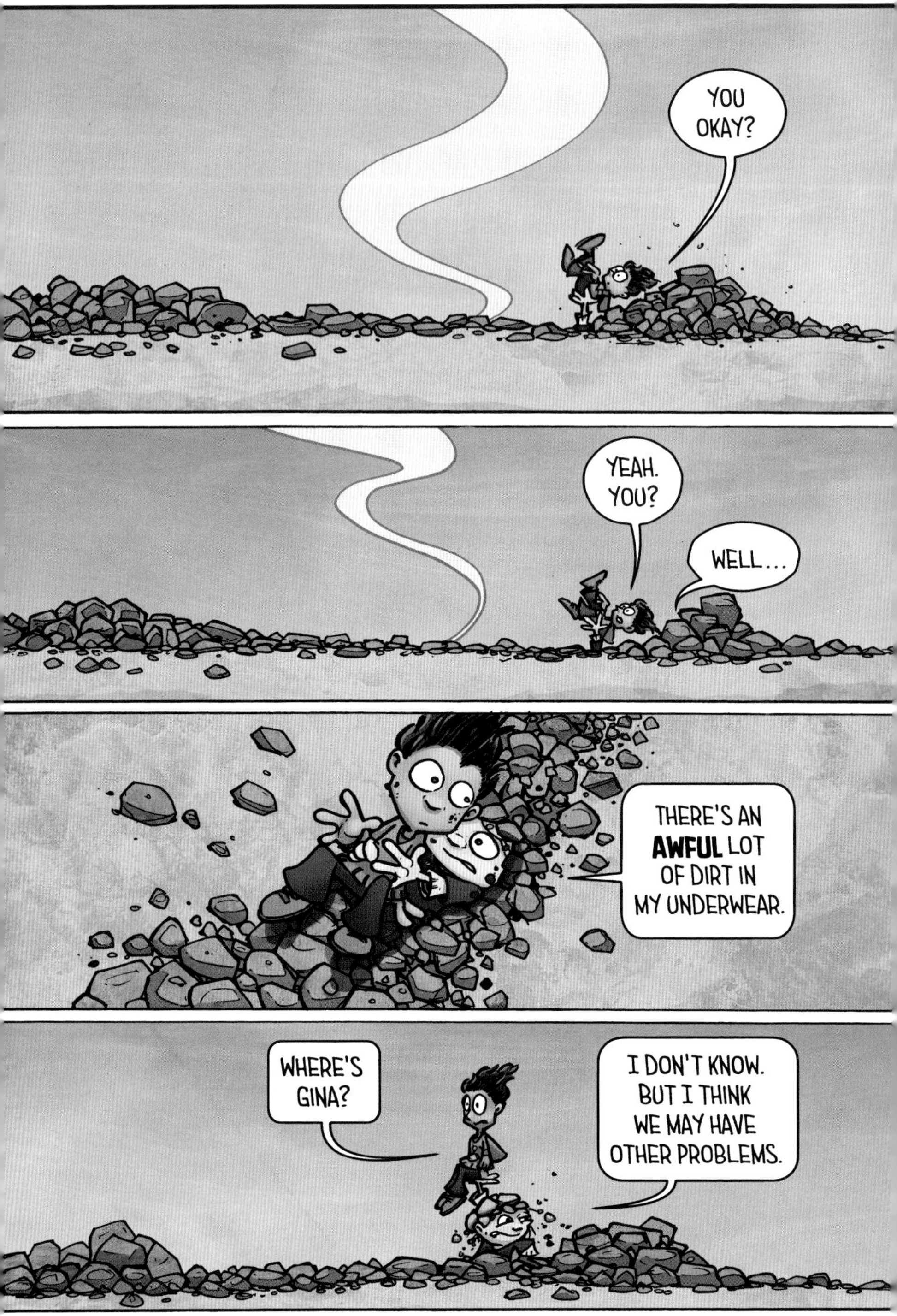
YOU OKAY?
YEAH. YOU?
WELL...
THERE'S AN **AWFUL** LOT OF DIRT IN MY UNDERWEAR.
WHERE'S GINA?
I DON'T KNOW. BUT I THINK WE MAY HAVE OTHER PROBLEMS.

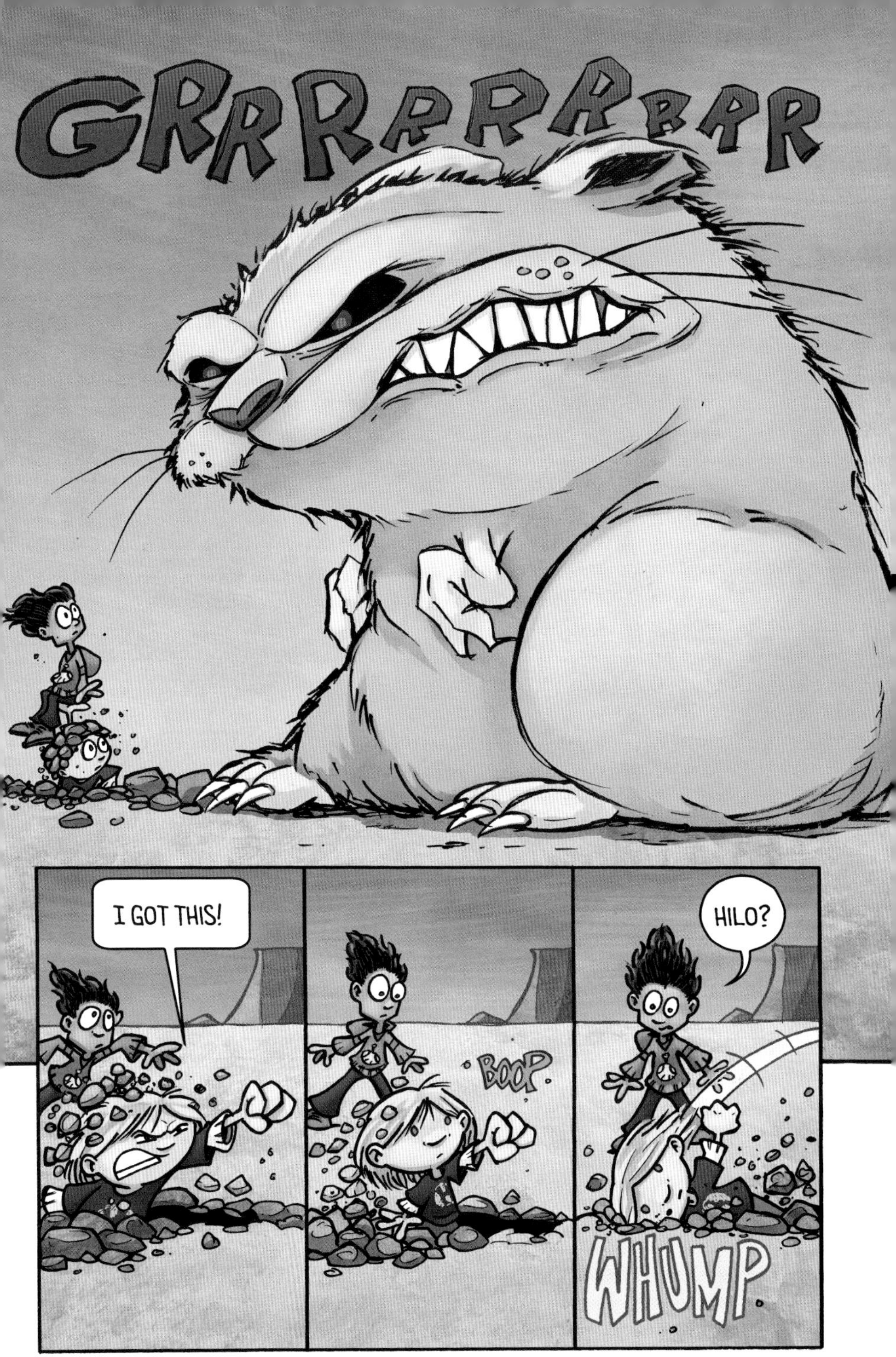
GRRRRRRRRR
I GOT THIS!
BOOP
HILO?
WHUMP

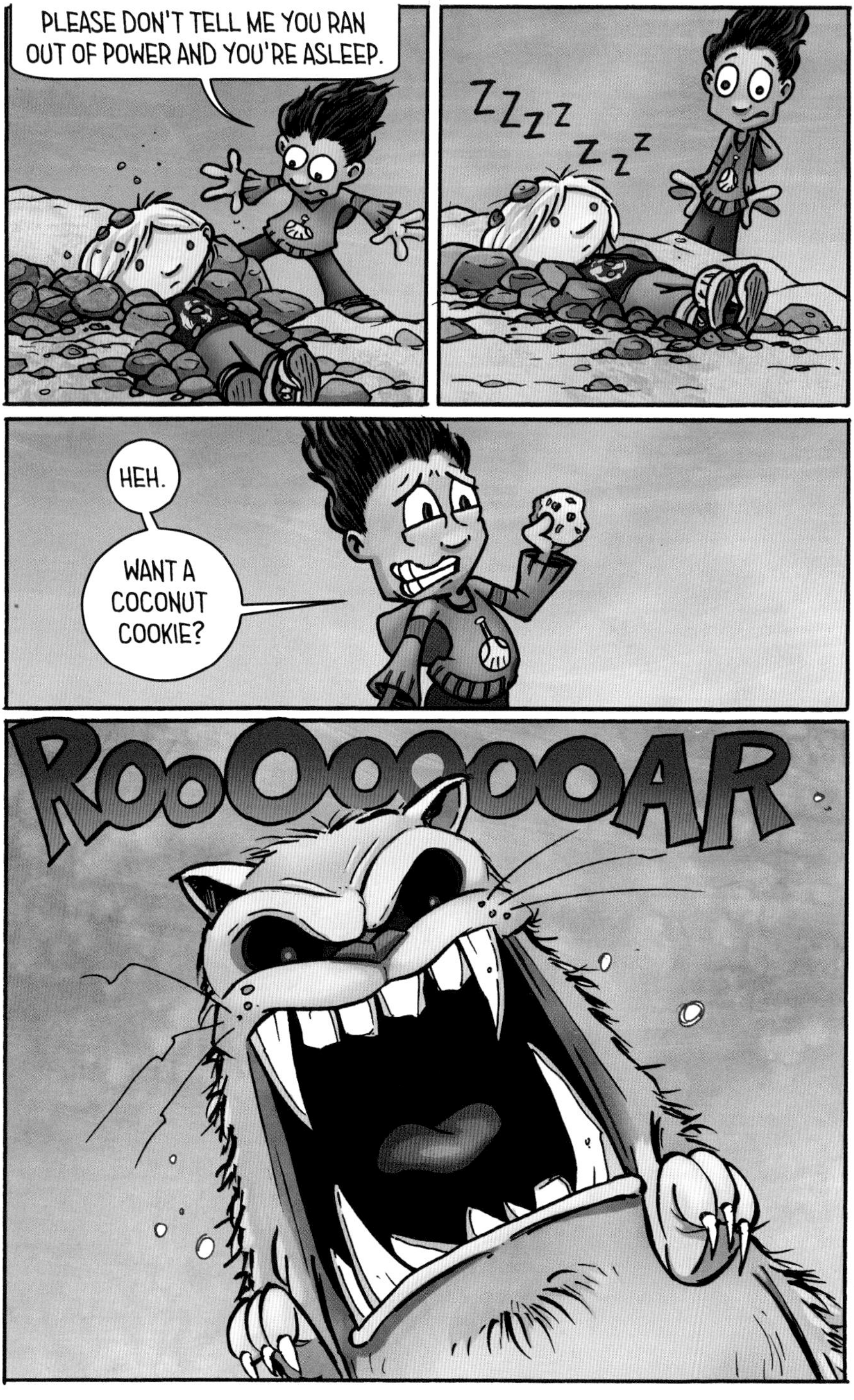
PLEASE DON'T TELL ME YOU RAN OUT OF POWER AND YOU'RE ASLEEP.
ZZZZ ZZZ
HEH.
WANT A COCONUT COOKIE?
ROOOOOOOAR

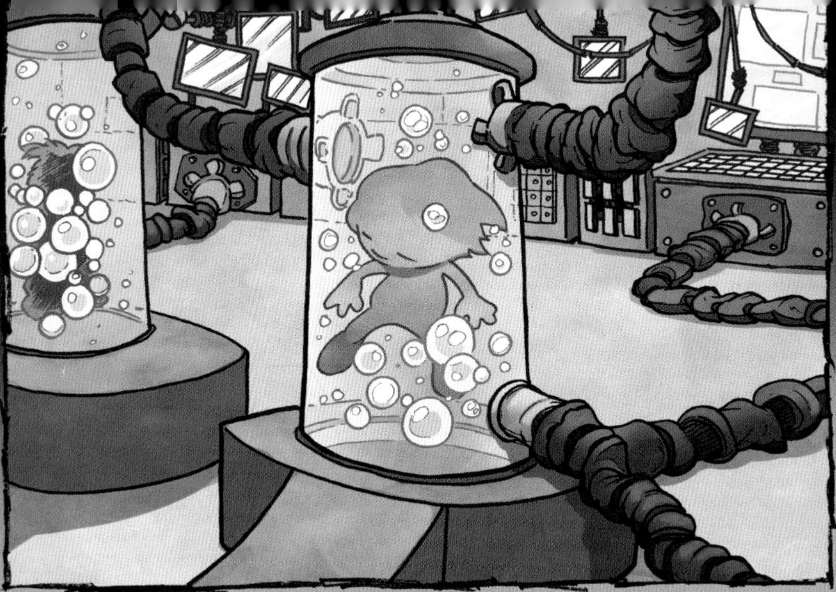

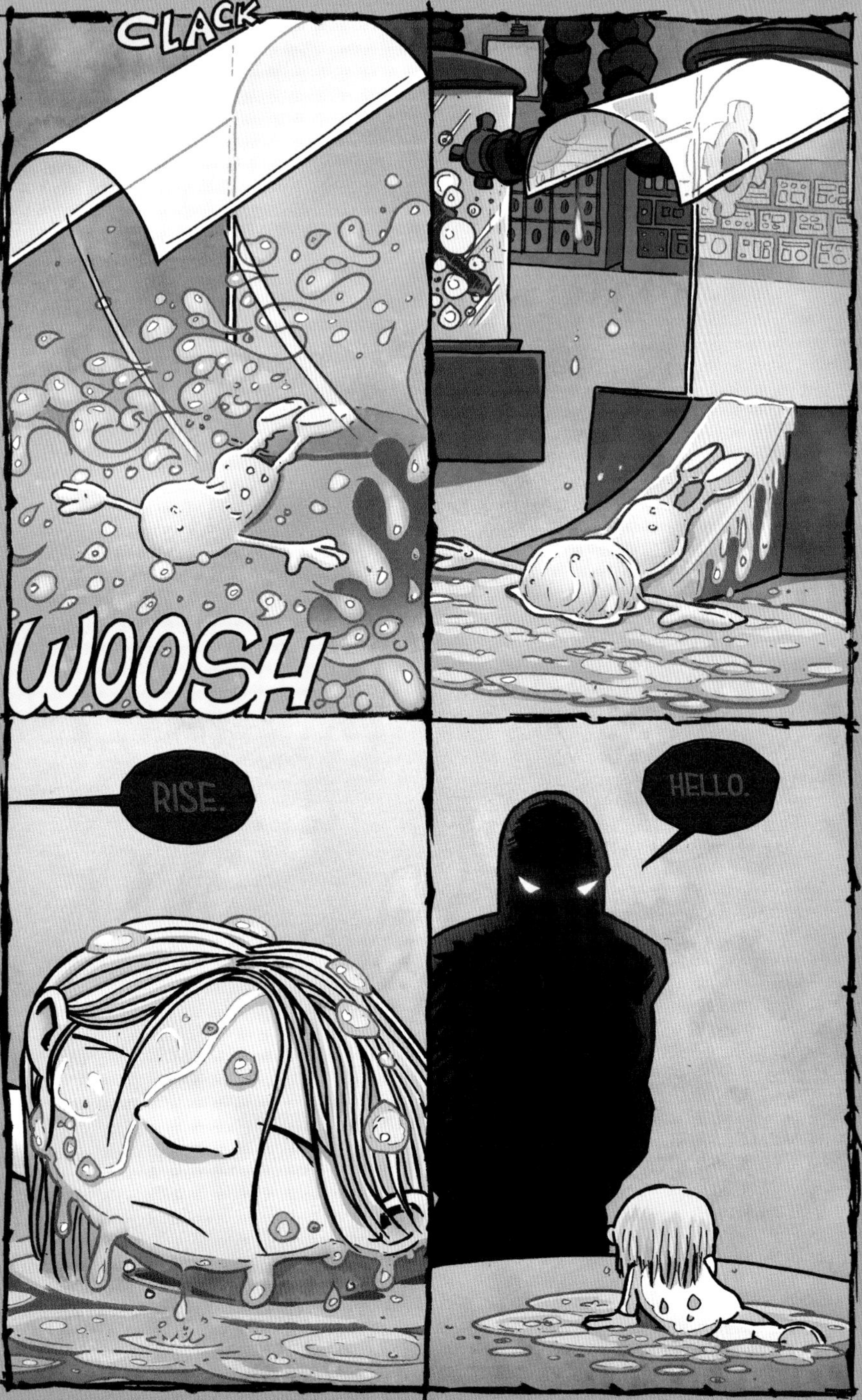
CLACK
WOOSH
RISE.
HELLO.

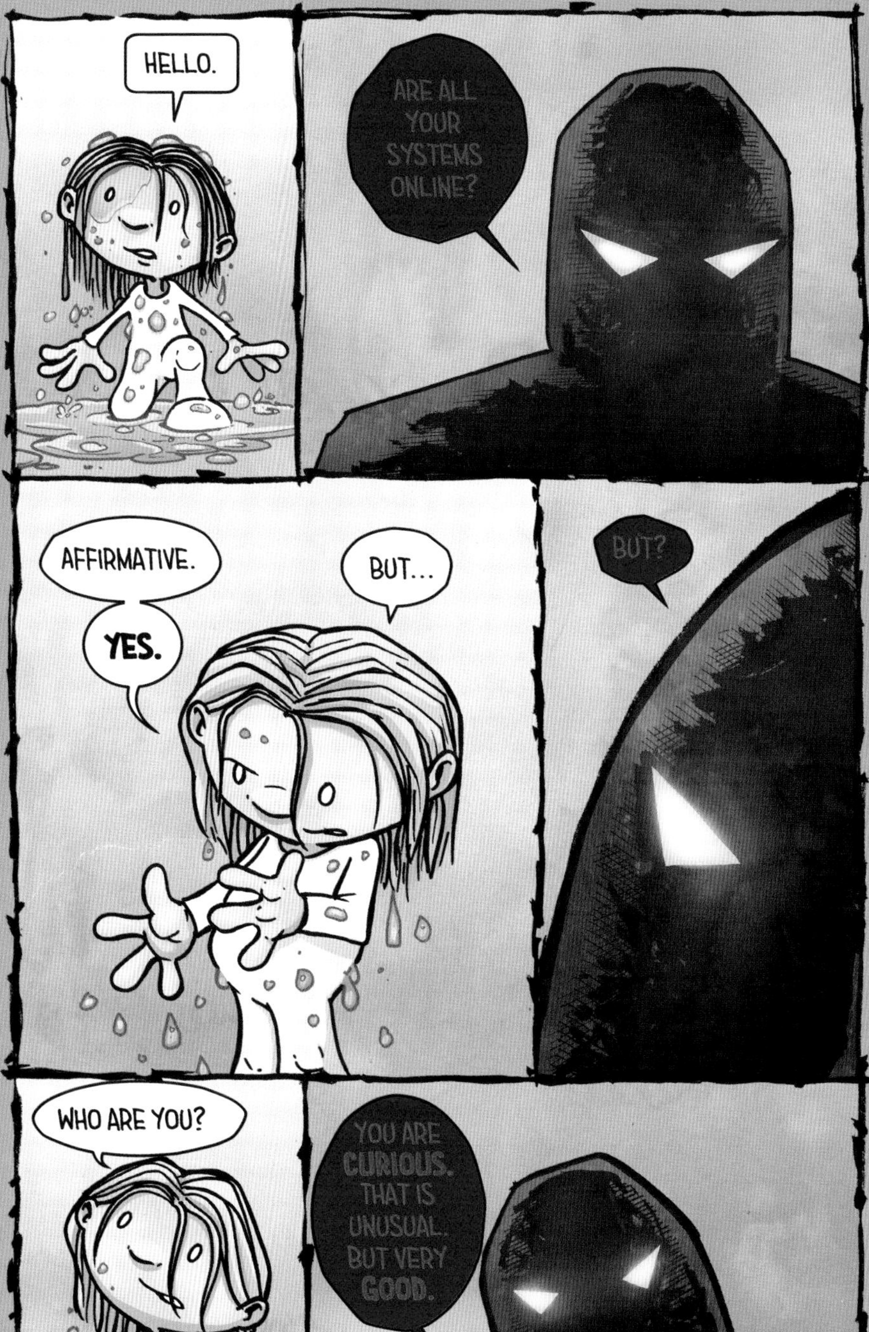
HELLO.
ARE ALL YOUR SYSTEMS ONLINE?
AFFIRMATIVE.
YES.
BUT...
BUT?
WHO ARE YOU?
YOU ARE CURIOUS. THAT IS UNUSUAL. BUT VERY GOOD.

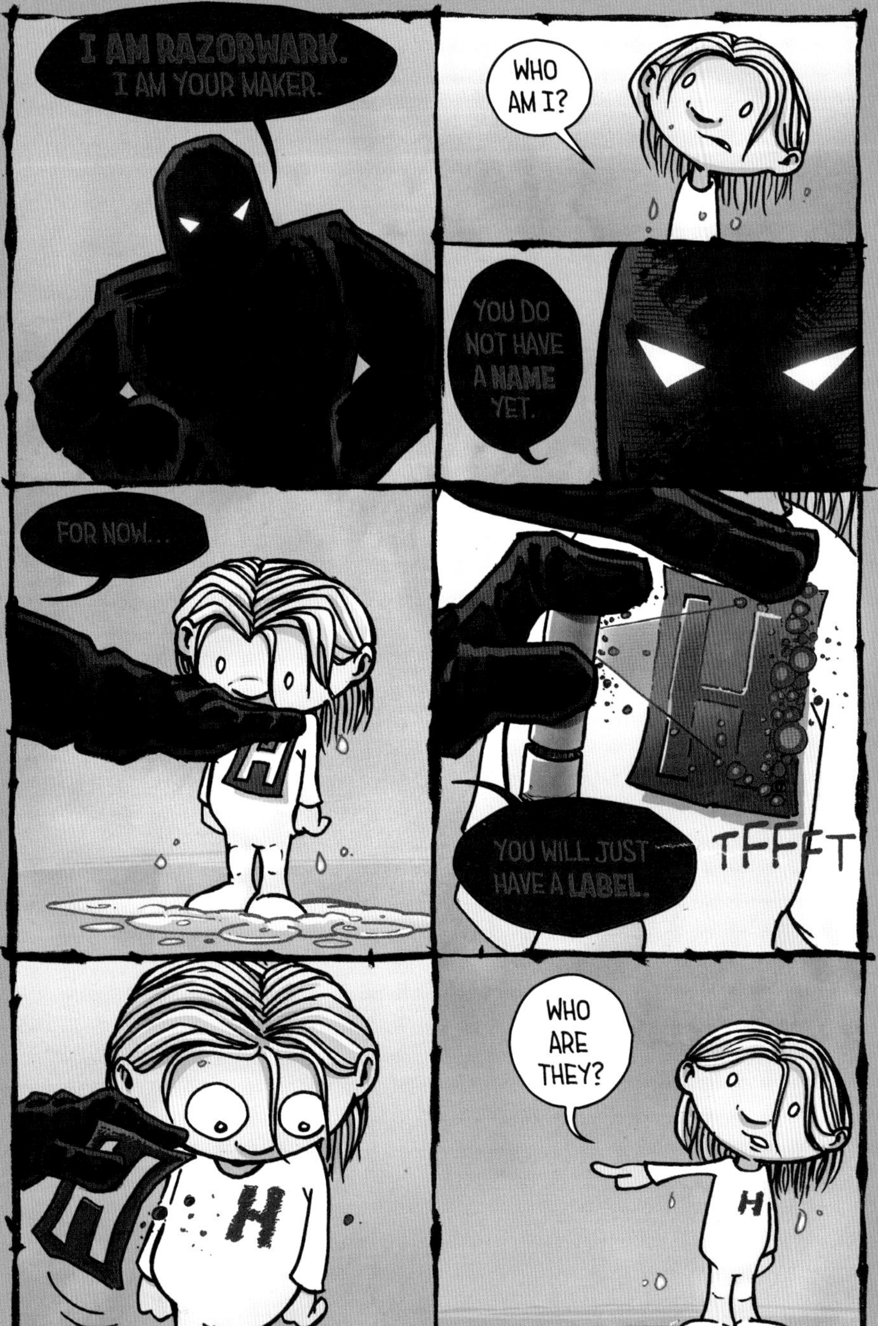
I AM RAZORWARK.
I AM YOUR MAKER.
WHO AM I?
YOU DO NOT HAVE A NAME YET.
FOR NOW...
YOU WILL JUST HAVE A LABEL.
TFFFT
WHO ARE THEY?

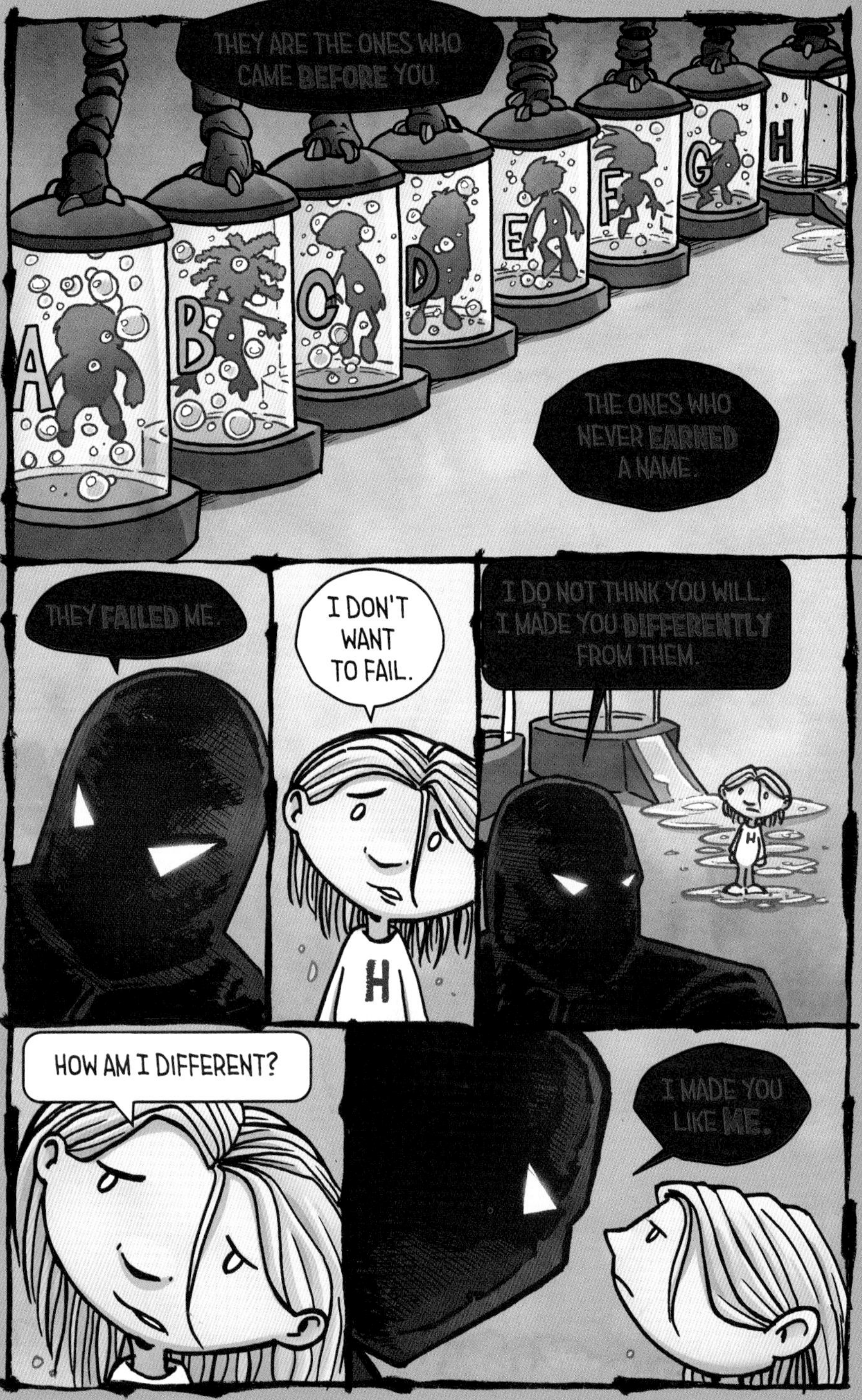
THEY ARE THE ONES WHO CAME BEFORE YOU.
A
B
C
D
E
F
G
H
THE ONES WHO NEVER EARNED A NAME.
THEY FAILED ME.
I DON'T WANT TO FAIL.
I DO NOT THINK YOU WILL. I MADE YOU DIFFERENTLY FROM THEM.
HOW AM I DIFFERENT?
I MADE YOU LIKE ME.

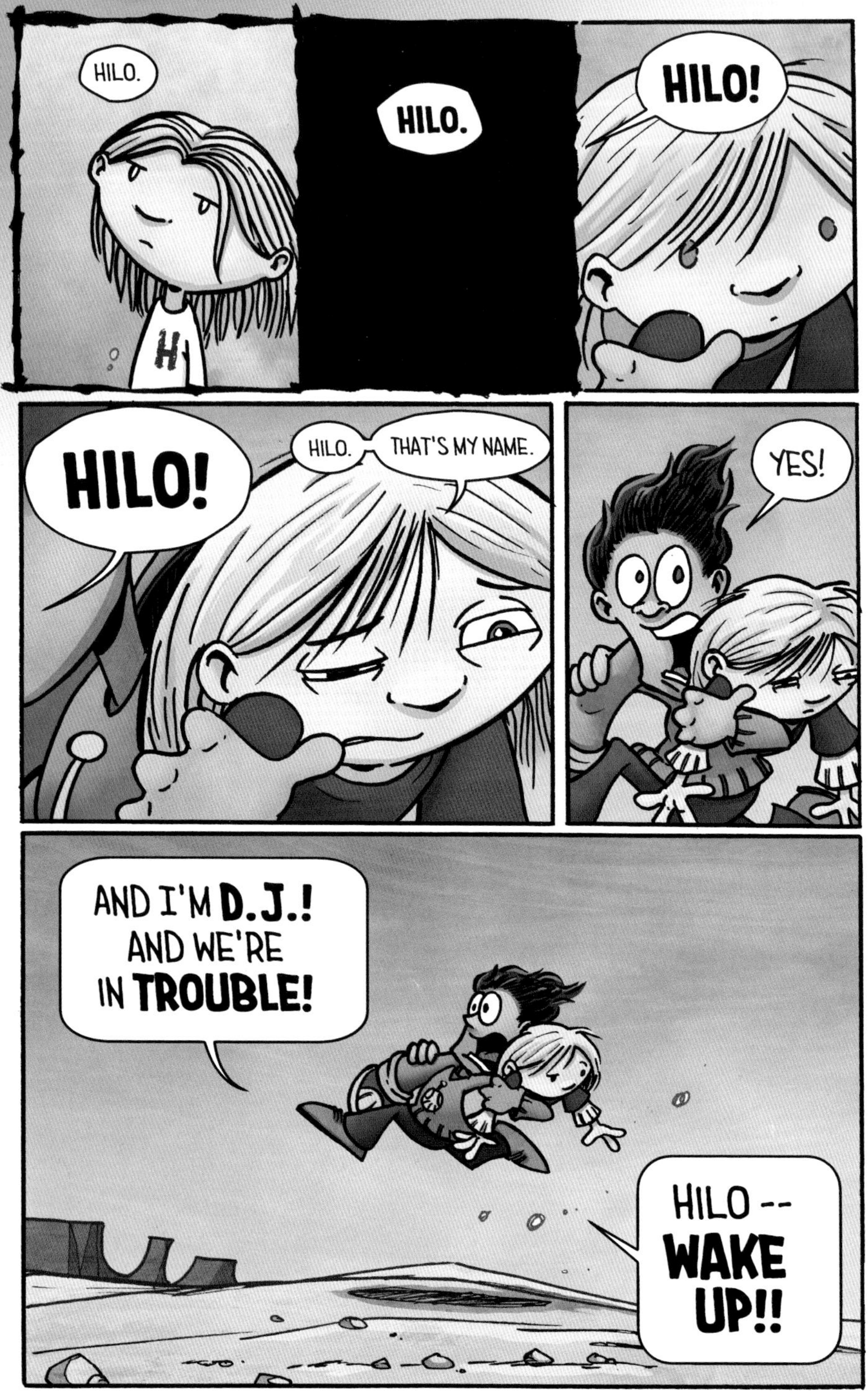
HILO.
HILO.
HILO!
HILO!
HILO.
THAT'S MY NAME.
YES!
AND I'M D.J.! AND WE'RE IN TROUBLE!
HILO -- WAKE UP!!

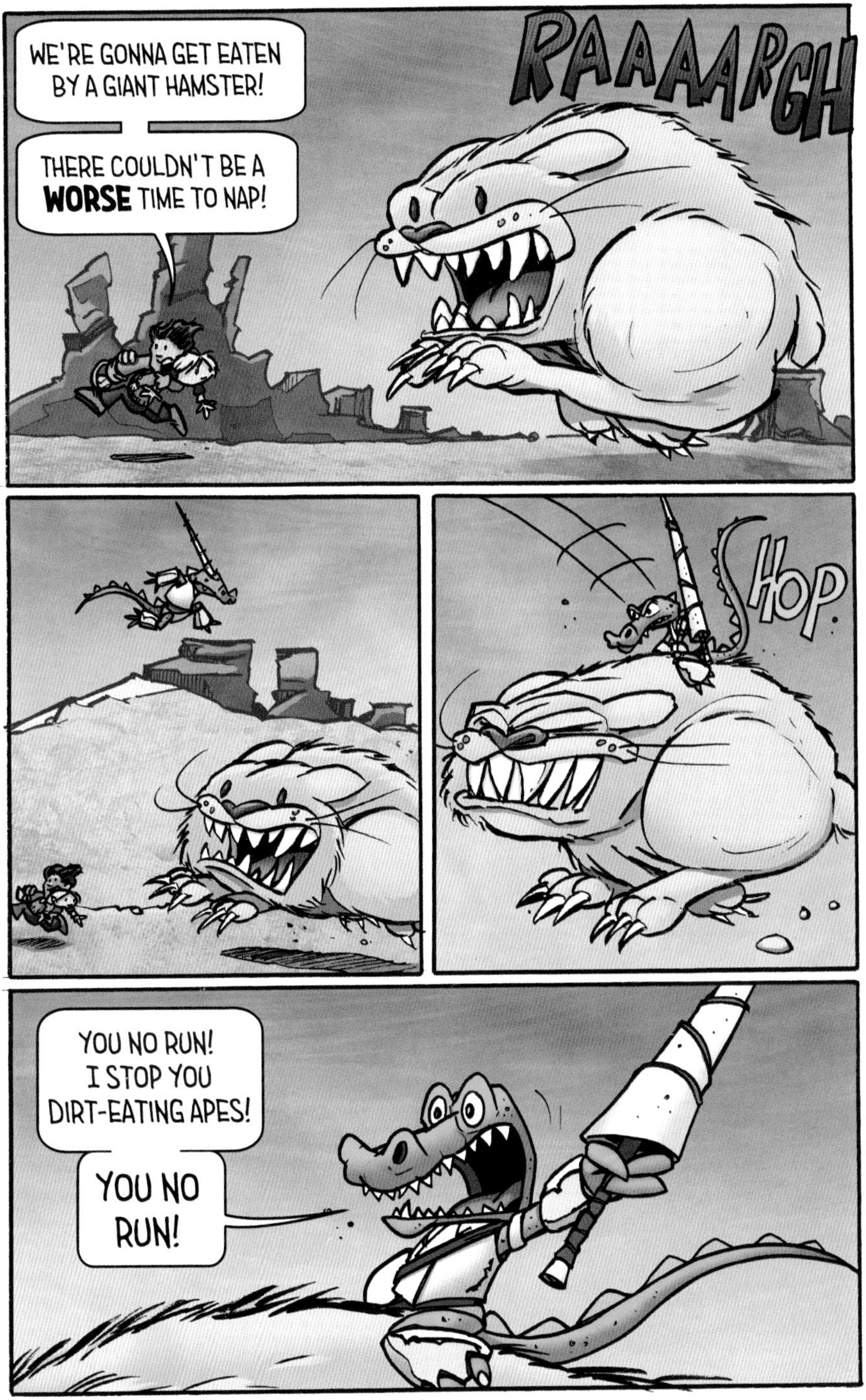
WE'RE GONNA GET EATEN BY A GIANT HAMSTER!
THERE COULDN'T BE A **WORSE** TIME TO NAP!
RAAAARGH
HOP
YOU NO RUN! I STOP YOU DIRT-EATING APES!
YOU NO RUN!

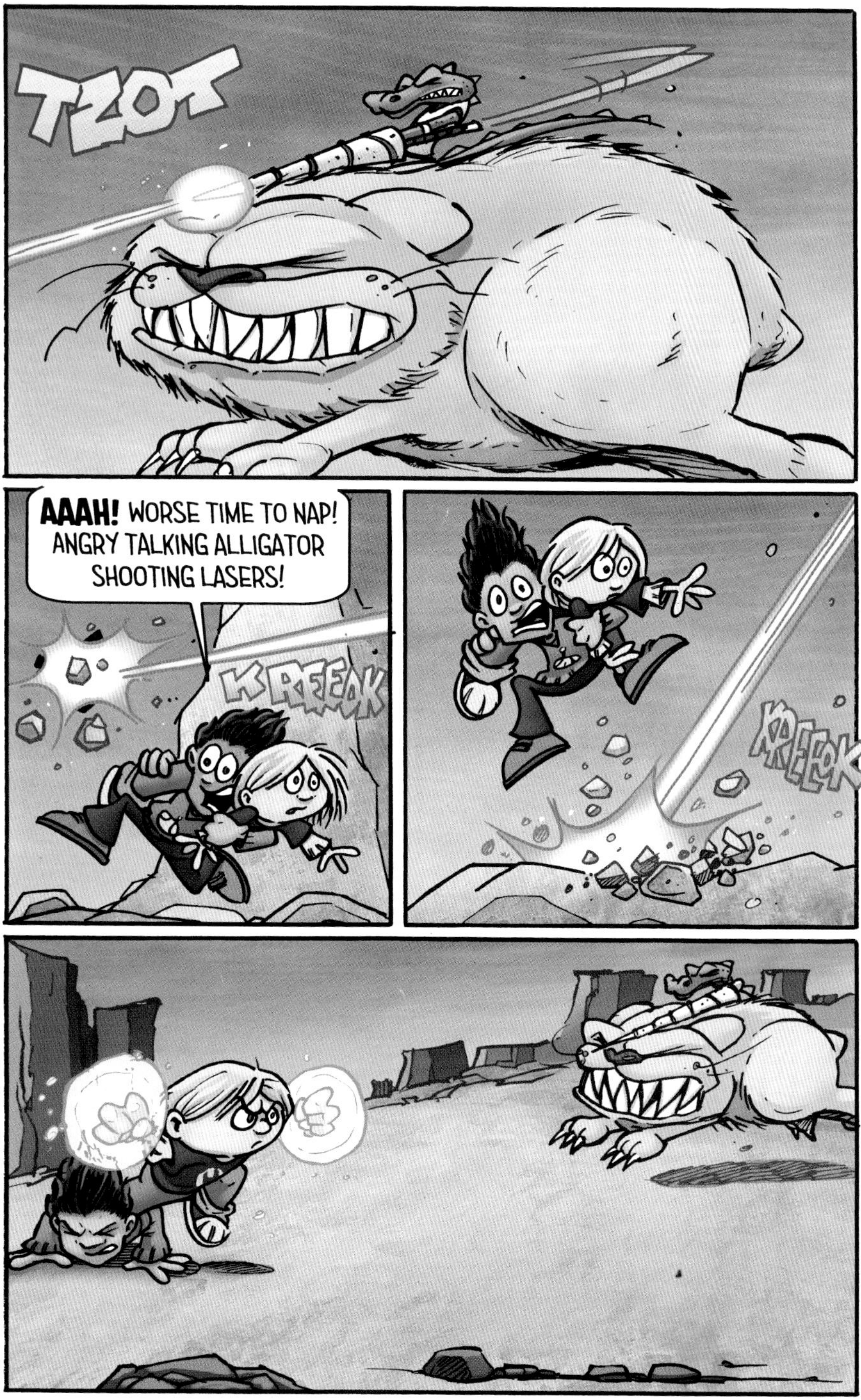
TZOT
AAAH! WORSE TIME TO NAP! ANGRY TALKING ALLIGATOR SHOOTING LASERS!
KREEAK
KREEOK

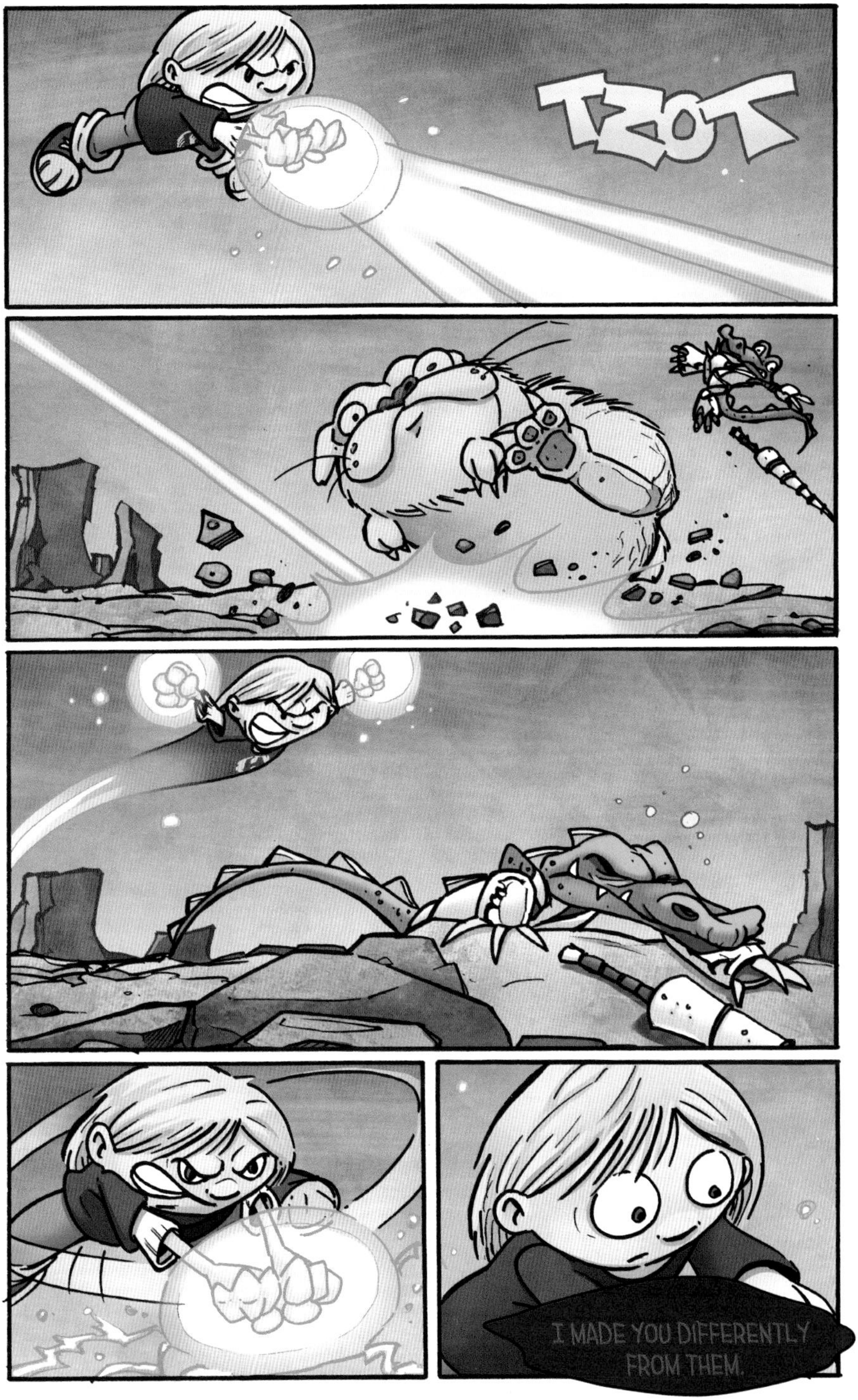
TZOT
I MADE YOU DIFFERENTLY FROM THEM.

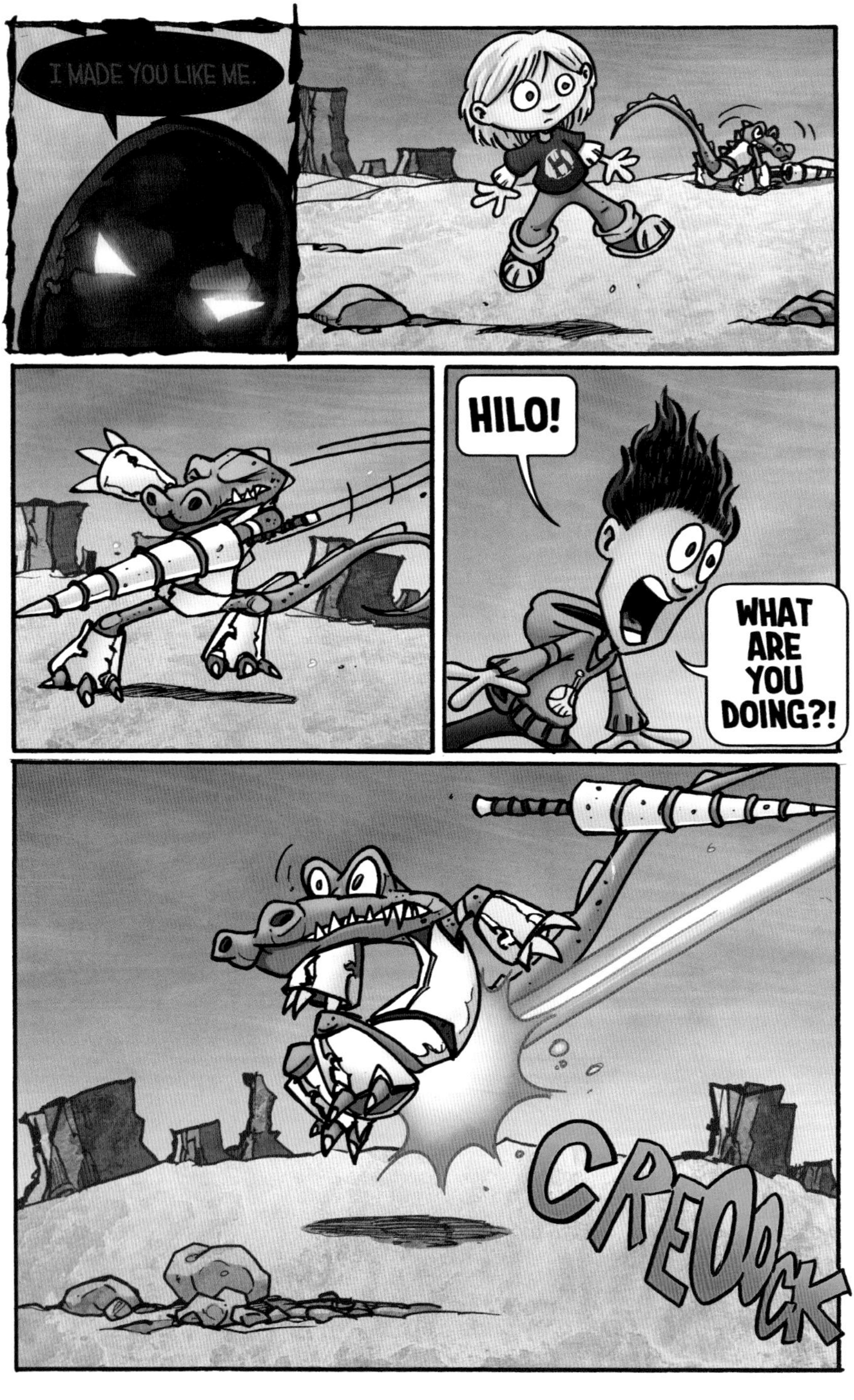
I MADE YOU LIKE ME.
HILO!
WHAT ARE YOU DOING?!
CREOOCK

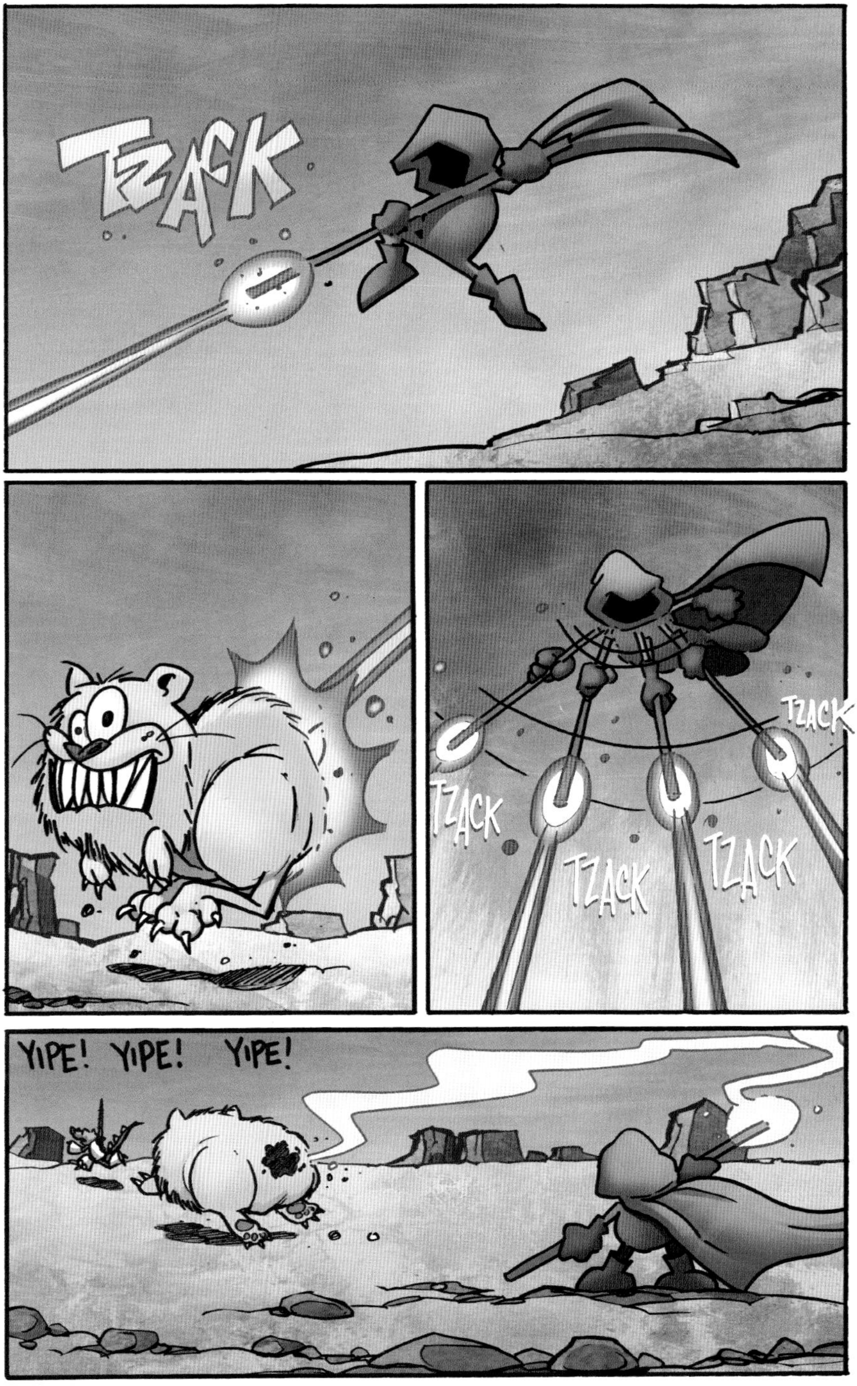
TZACK
TZACK
TZACK
TZACK
TZACK
YIPE! YIPE! YIPE!

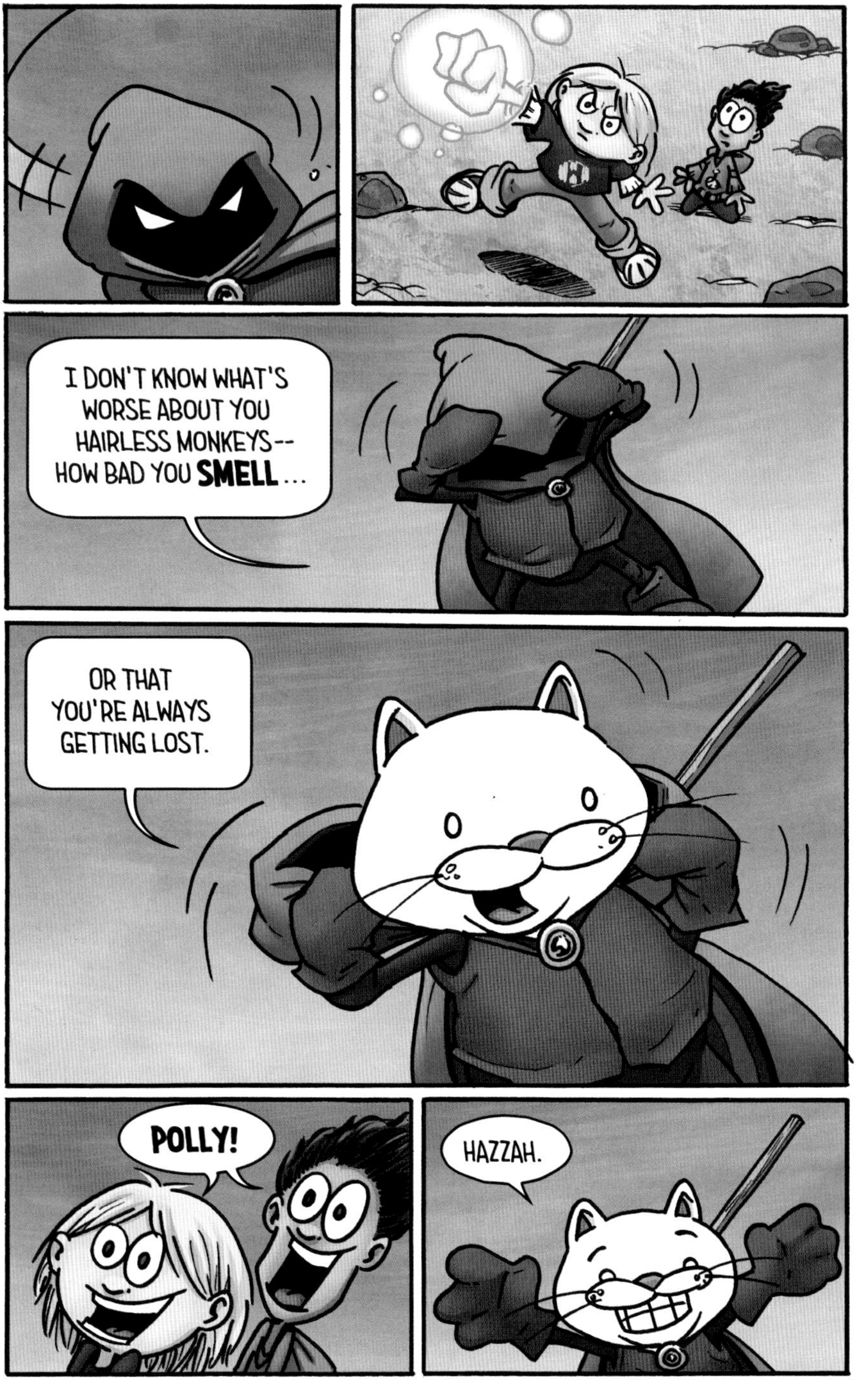
I DON'T KNOW WHAT'S WORSE ABOUT YOU HAIRLESS MONKEYS-- HOW BAD YOU **SMELL**...
OR THAT YOU'RE ALWAYS GETTING LOST.
POLLY!
HAZZAH.

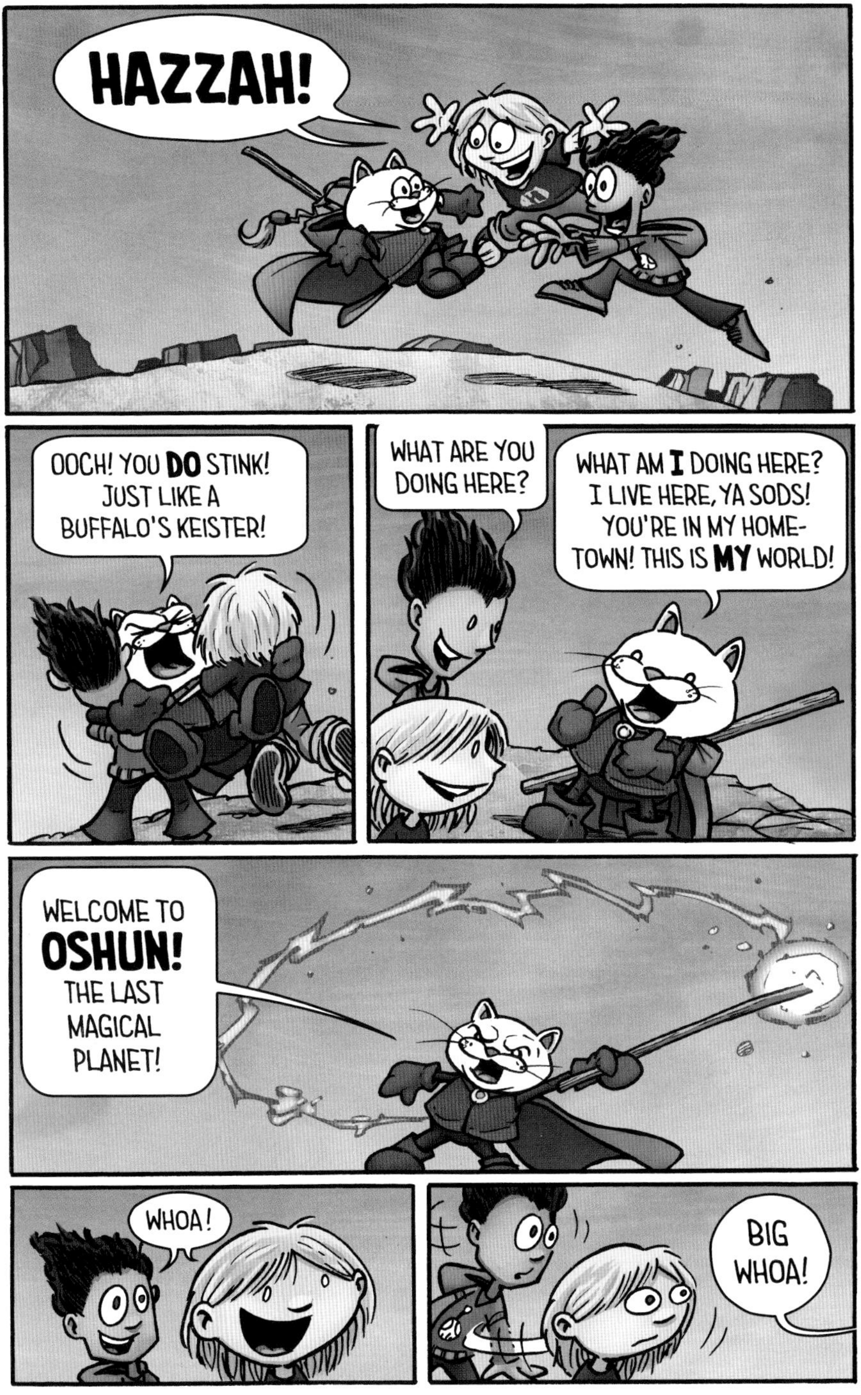
HAZZAH!
OOCH! YOU DO STINK! JUST LIKE A BUFFALO'S KEISTER!
WHAT ARE YOU DOING HERE?
WHAT AM I DOING HERE? I LIVE HERE, YA SODS! YOU'RE IN MY HOME-TOWN! THIS IS MY WORLD!
WELCOME TO OSHUN! THE LAST MAGICAL PLANET!
WHOA!
BIG WHOA!

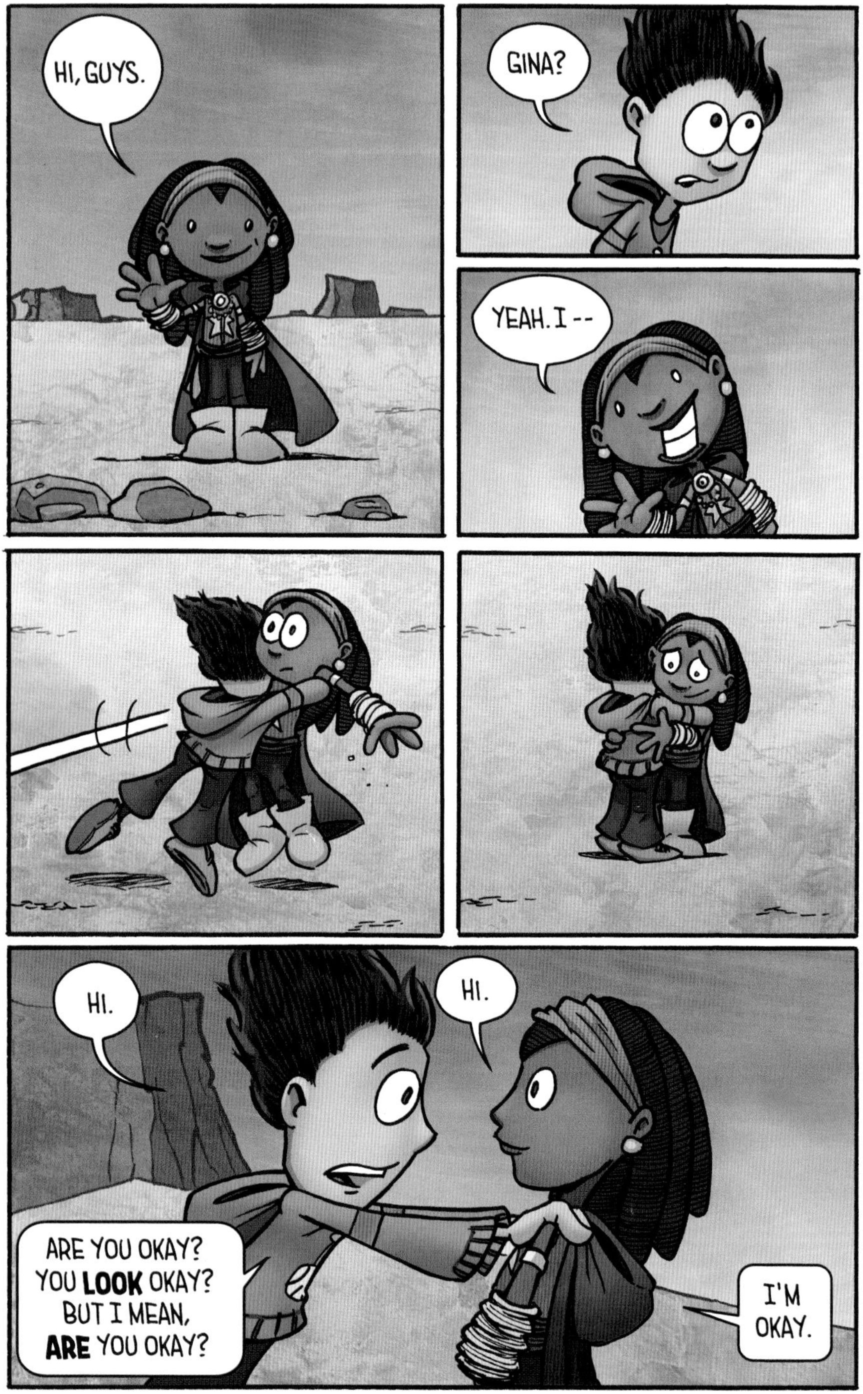
HI, GUYS.
GINA?
YEAH. I --
HI.
HI.
ARE YOU OKAY? YOU **LOOK** OKAY? BUT I MEAN, **ARE** YOU OKAY?
I'M OKAY.

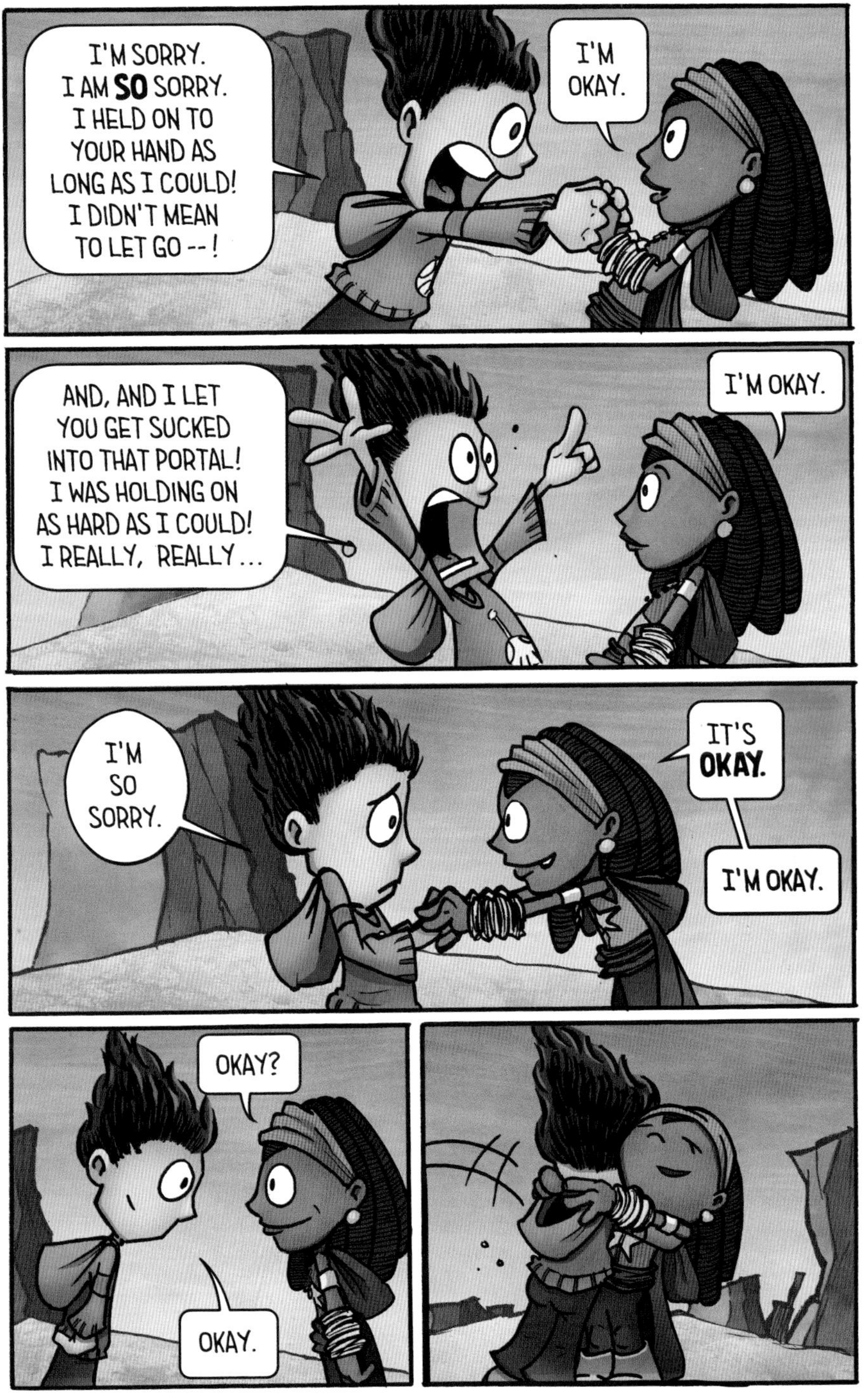
I'M SORRY. I AM **SO** SORRY. I HELD ON TO YOUR HAND AS LONG AS I COULD! I DIDN'T MEAN TO LET GO --!
I'M OKAY.
AND, AND I LET YOU GET SUCKED INTO THAT PORTAL! I WAS HOLDING ON AS HARD AS I COULD! I REALLY, REALLY...
I'M OKAY.
I'M SO SORRY.
IT'S **OKAY.**
I'M OKAY.
OKAY?
OKAY.

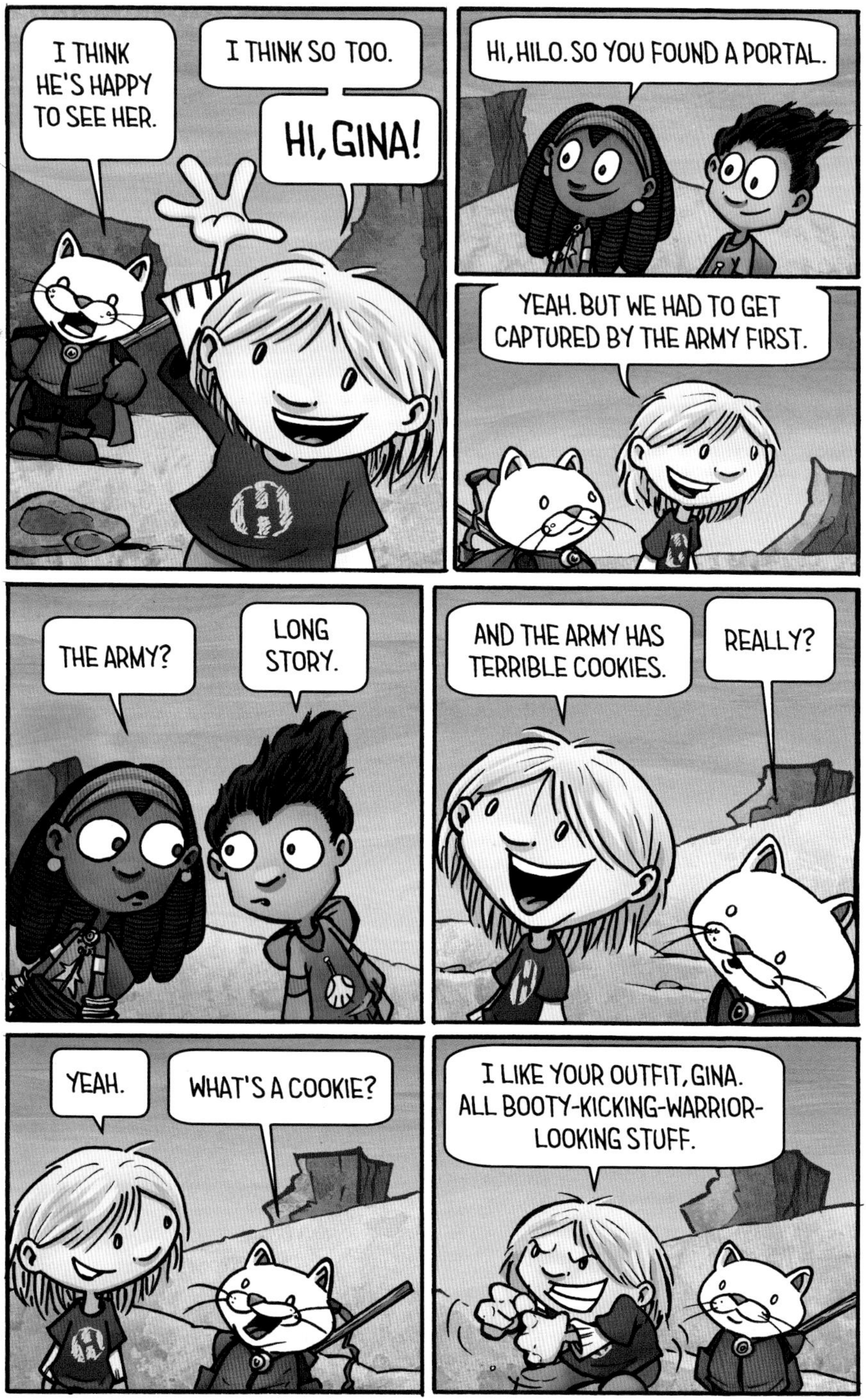
I THINK HE'S HAPPY TO SEE HER.
I THINK SO TOO.
HI, GINA!
HI, HILO. SO YOU FOUND A PORTAL.
YEAH. BUT WE HAD TO GET CAPTURED BY THE ARMY FIRST.
THE ARMY?
LONG STORY.
AND THE ARMY HAS TERRIBLE COOKIES.
REALLY?
YEAH.
WHAT'S A COOKIE?
I LIKE YOUR OUTFIT, GINA. ALL BOOTY-KICKING-WARRIOR-LOOKING STUFF.

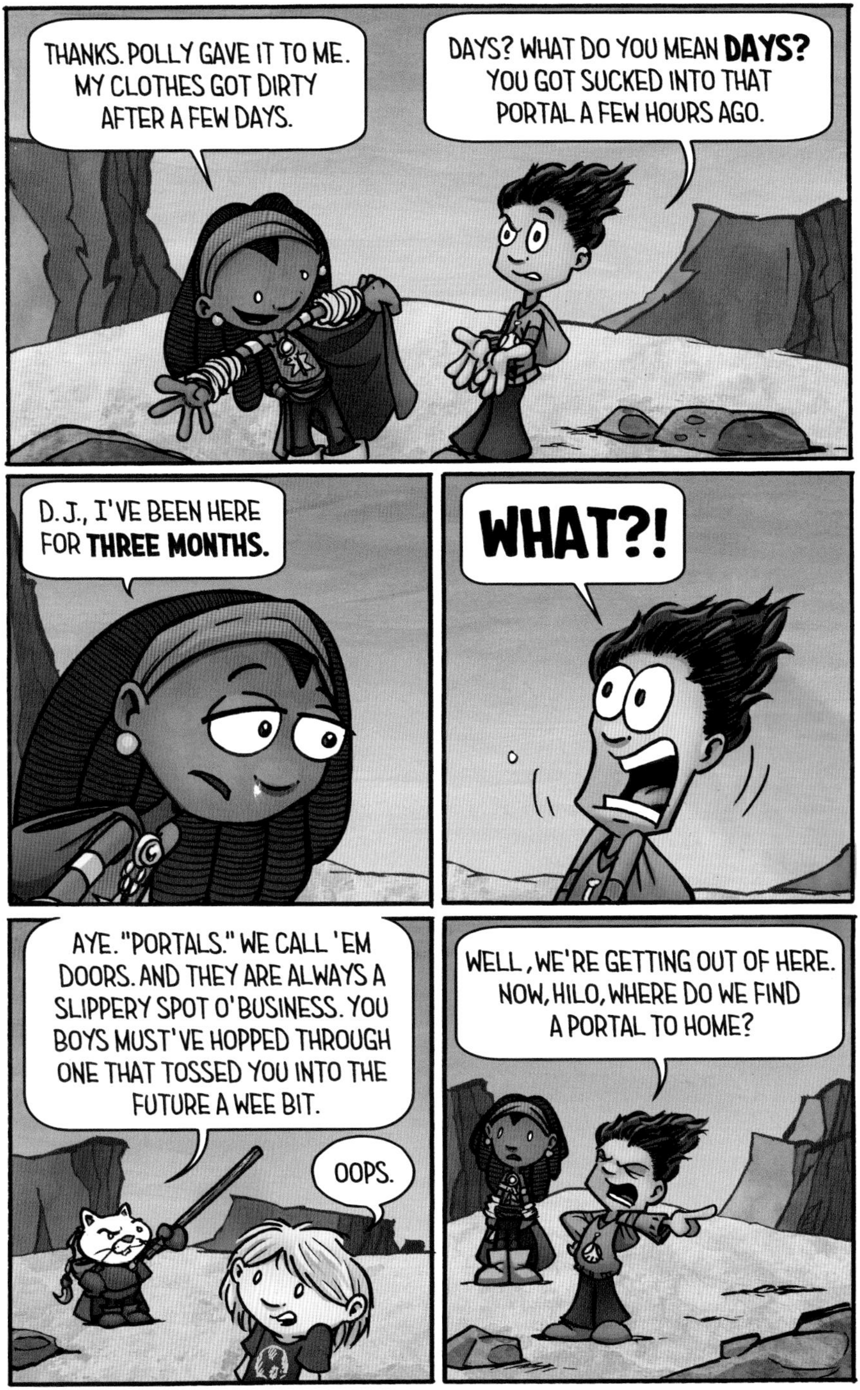
THANKS. POLLY GAVE IT TO ME. MY CLOTHES GOT DIRTY AFTER A FEW DAYS.
DAYS? WHAT DO YOU MEAN **DAYS?** YOU GOT SUCKED INTO THAT PORTAL A FEW HOURS AGO.
D. J., I'VE BEEN HERE FOR **THREE MONTHS.**
**WHAT?!**
AYE. "PORTALS." WE CALL 'EM DOORS. AND THEY ARE ALWAYS A SLIPPERY SPOT O'BUSINESS. YOU BOYS MUST'VE HOPPED THROUGH ONE THAT TOSSED YOU INTO THE FUTURE A WEE BIT.
OOPS.
WELL, WE'RE GETTING OUT OF HERE. NOW, HILO, WHERE DO WE FIND A PORTAL TO HOME?

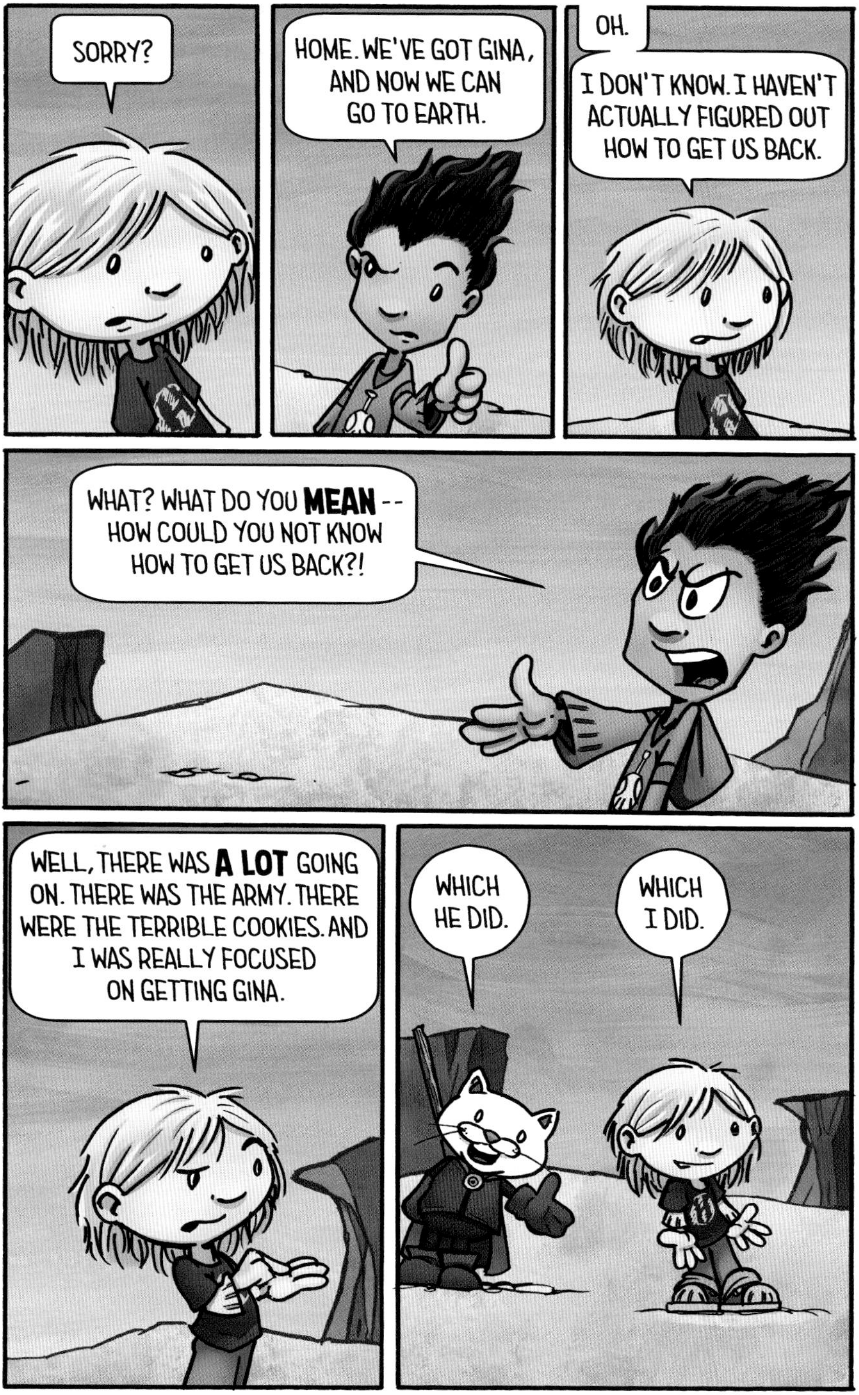
SORRY?
HOME. WE'VE GOT GINA, AND NOW WE CAN GO TO EARTH.
OH.
I DON'T KNOW. I HAVEN'T ACTUALLY FIGURED OUT HOW TO GET US BACK.
WHAT? WHAT DO YOU **MEAN** -- HOW COULD YOU NOT KNOW HOW TO GET US BACK?!
WELL, THERE WAS **A LOT** GOING ON. THERE WAS THE ARMY. THERE WERE THE TERRIBLE COOKIES. AND I WAS REALLY FOCUSED ON GETTING GINA.
WHICH HE DID.
WHICH I DID.

YEAH! THREE MONTHS INTO THE FUTURE WITH NO WAY HOME?!

TRUE. I KIND OF BLEW IT THERE.

KIND OF?!

OKAY, D. J. IS HAVING A WEE BIT OF A **NUTTY.** AND I LIKE A GOOD NUTTY, BUT WE NEED TO BE ON OUR WAY BEFORE WE'RE UP TO OUR ARMPITS IN LIZARDS.

WHAT?

KIND OF?!

AYE, WE NEED TO BE OFF. THAT PUTRID, SLIME-CAKED SALAMANDER RIDING THE GIANT BALL OF HAIR IS PART OF THE **SCALE TAIL CLAN.**

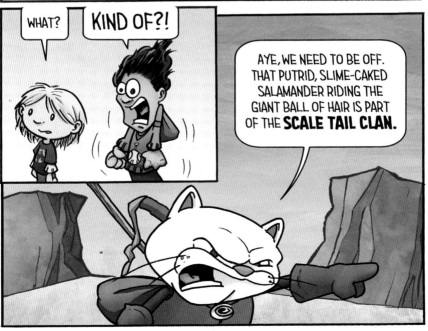

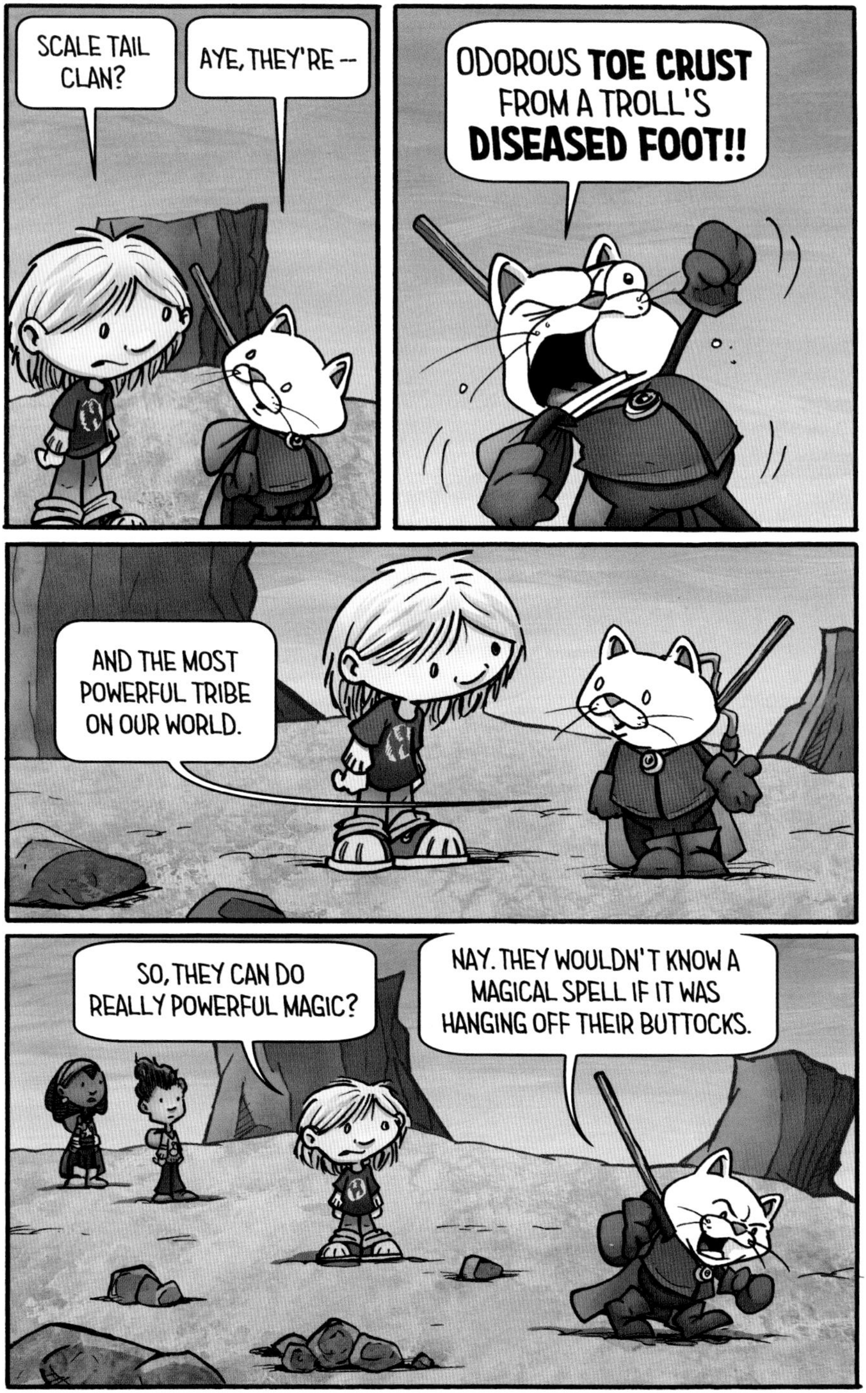
SCALE TAIL CLAN?
AYE, THEY'RE --
ODOROUS **TOE CRUST** FROM A TROLL'S **DISEASED FOOT!!**
AND THE MOST POWERFUL TRIBE ON OUR WORLD.
SO, THEY CAN DO REALLY POWERFUL MAGIC?
NAY. THEY WOULDN'T KNOW A MAGICAL SPELL IF IT WAS HANGING OFF THEIR BUTTOCKS.

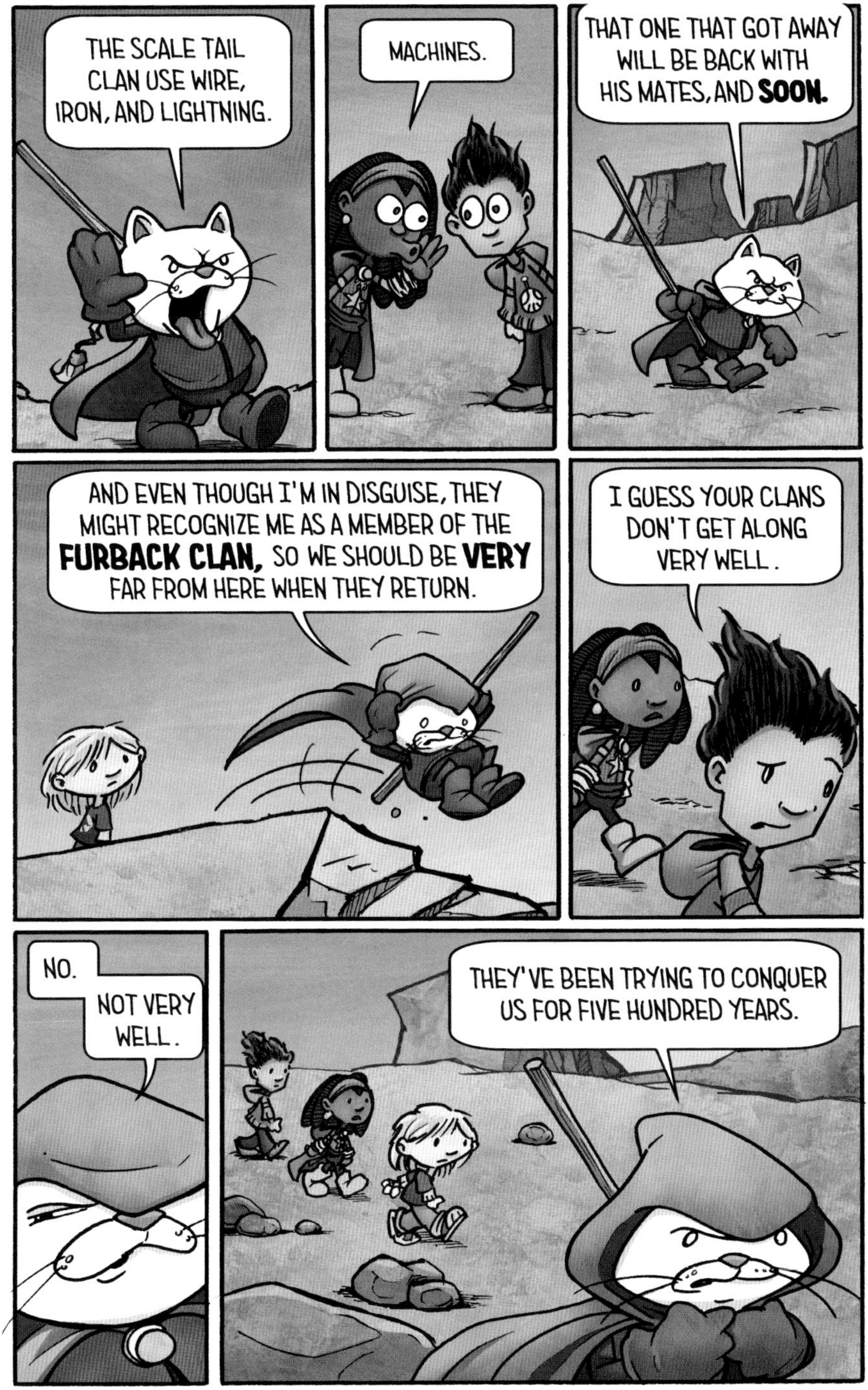
THE SCALE TAIL CLAN USE WIRE, IRON, AND LIGHTNING.
MACHINES.
THAT ONE THAT GOT AWAY WILL BE BACK WITH HIS MATES, AND **SOON.**
AND EVEN THOUGH I'M IN DISGUISE, THEY MIGHT RECOGNIZE ME AS A MEMBER OF THE **FURBACK CLAN,** SO WE SHOULD BE **VERY** FAR FROM HERE WHEN THEY RETURN.
I GUESS YOUR CLANS DON'T GET ALONG VERY WELL.
NO.
NOT VERY WELL.
THEY'VE BEEN TRYING TO CONQUER US FOR FIVE HUNDRED YEARS.

# CHAPTER

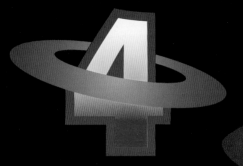

## 4

## FUR
## AND SCALE

THE VILLAGE OF THE **SCALE TAIL CLAN.**

BUT, **GREAT BOOMBA,** THE SMALL HOODED ONE WAS POWERFUL.

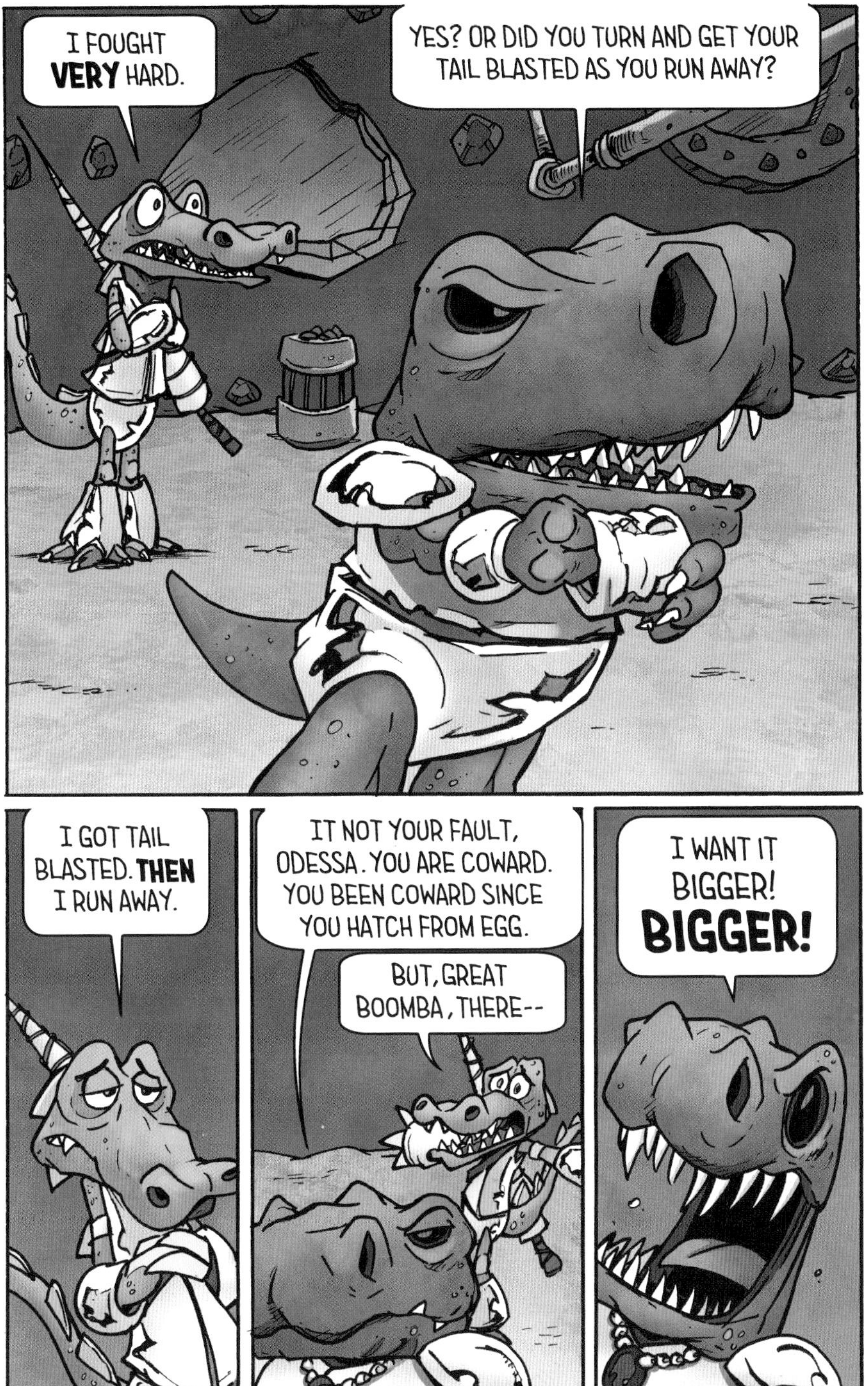
I FOUGHT **VERY** HARD.
YES? OR DID YOU TURN AND GET YOUR TAIL BLASTED AS YOU RUN AWAY?
I GOT TAIL BLASTED. **THEN** I RUN AWAY.
IT NOT YOUR FAULT, ODESSA. YOU ARE COWARD. YOU BEEN COWARD SINCE YOU HATCH FROM EGG.
BUT, GREAT BOOMBA, THERE--
I WANT IT BIGGER! **BIGGER!**

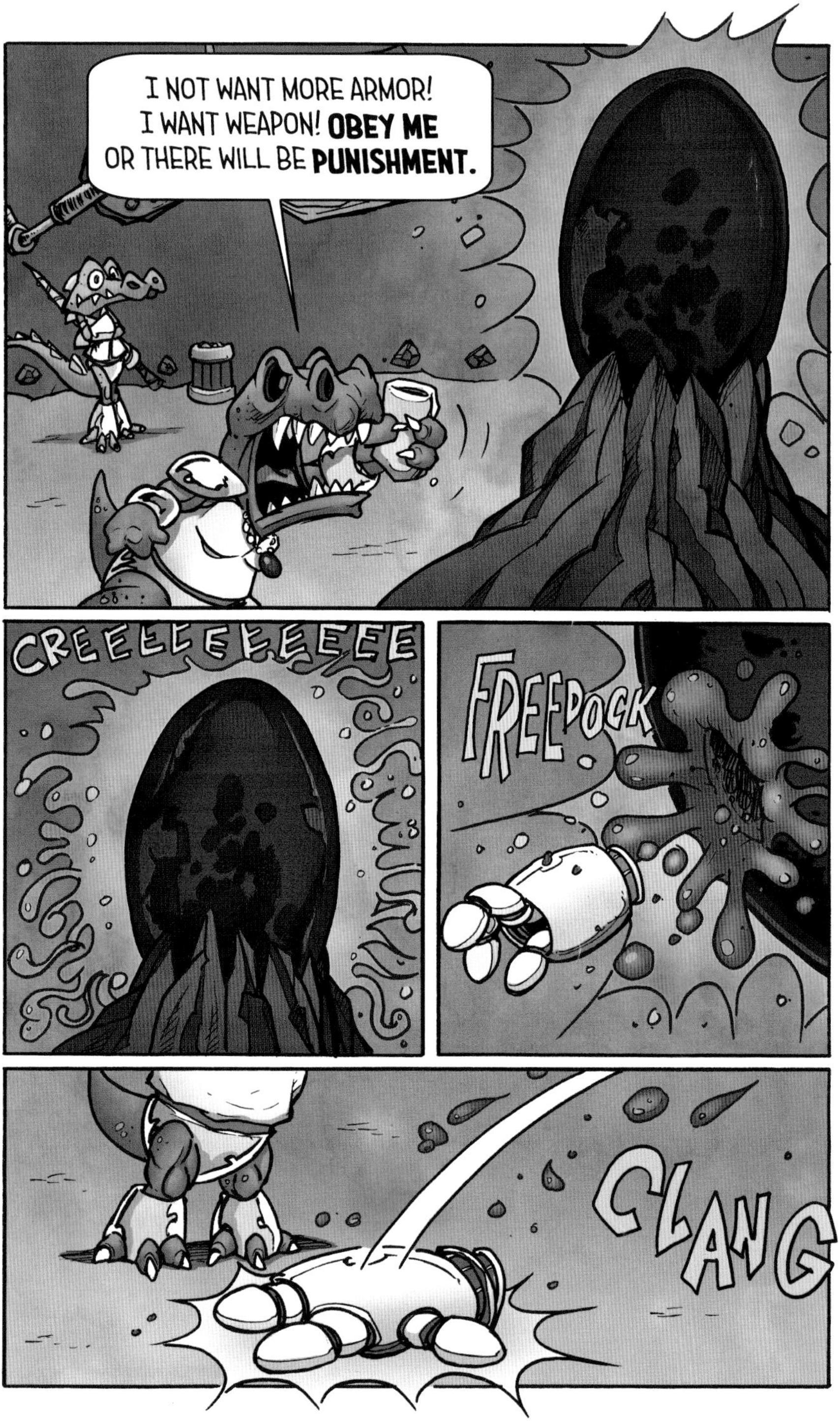
I NOT WANT MORE ARMOR! I WANT WEAPON! **OBEY ME** OR THERE WILL BE **PUNISHMENT.**
CREEEEEEEEEEE
FREEDOCK
CLANG

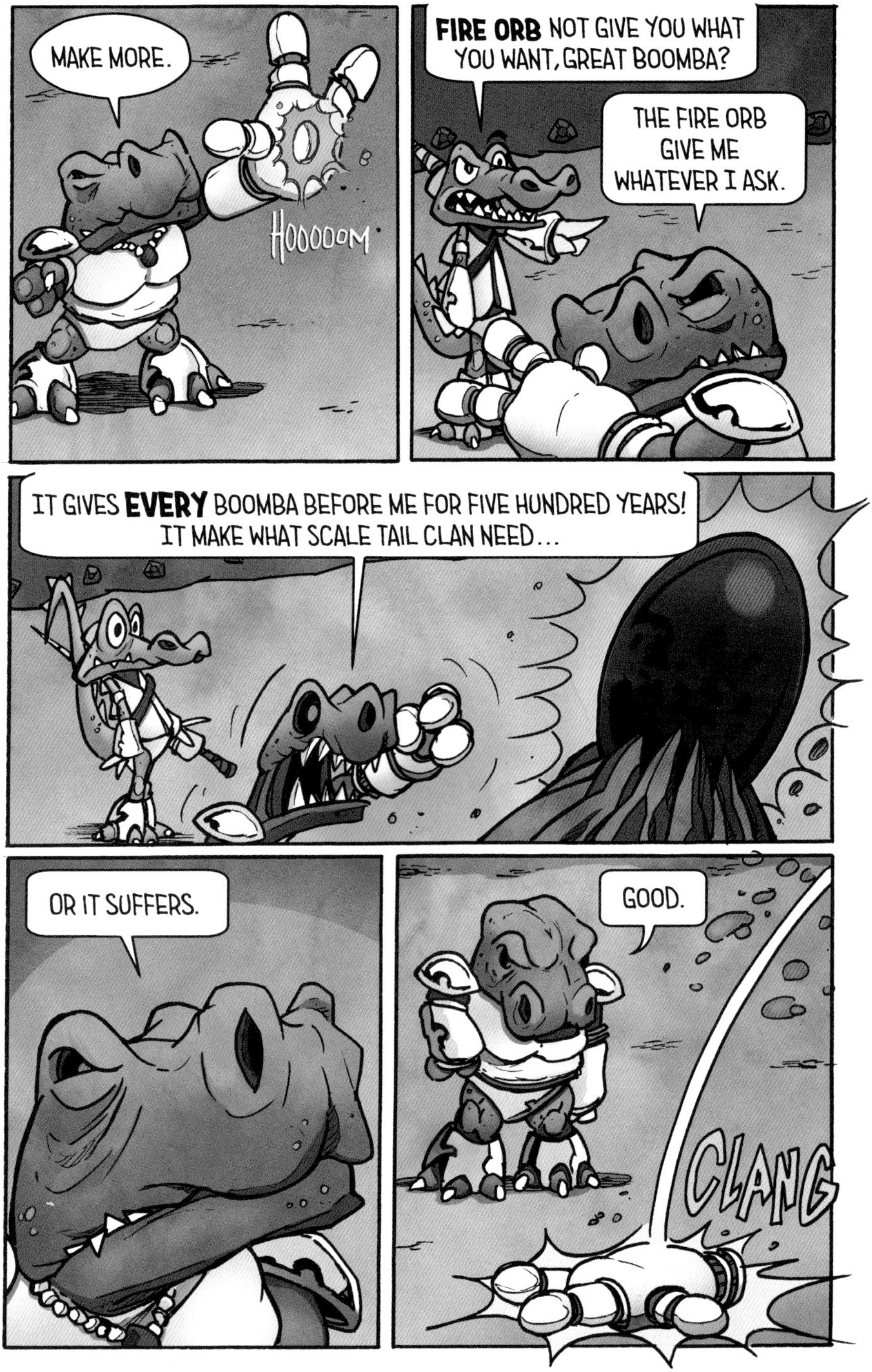
MAKE MORE.
HOOOOOM
**FIRE ORB** NOT GIVE YOU WHAT YOU WANT, GREAT BOOMBA?
THE FIRE ORB GIVE ME WHATEVER I ASK.
IT GIVES **EVERY** BOOMBA BEFORE ME FOR FIVE HUNDRED YEARS! IT MAKE WHAT SCALE TAIL CLAN NEED...
OR IT SUFFERS.
GOOD.
CLANG

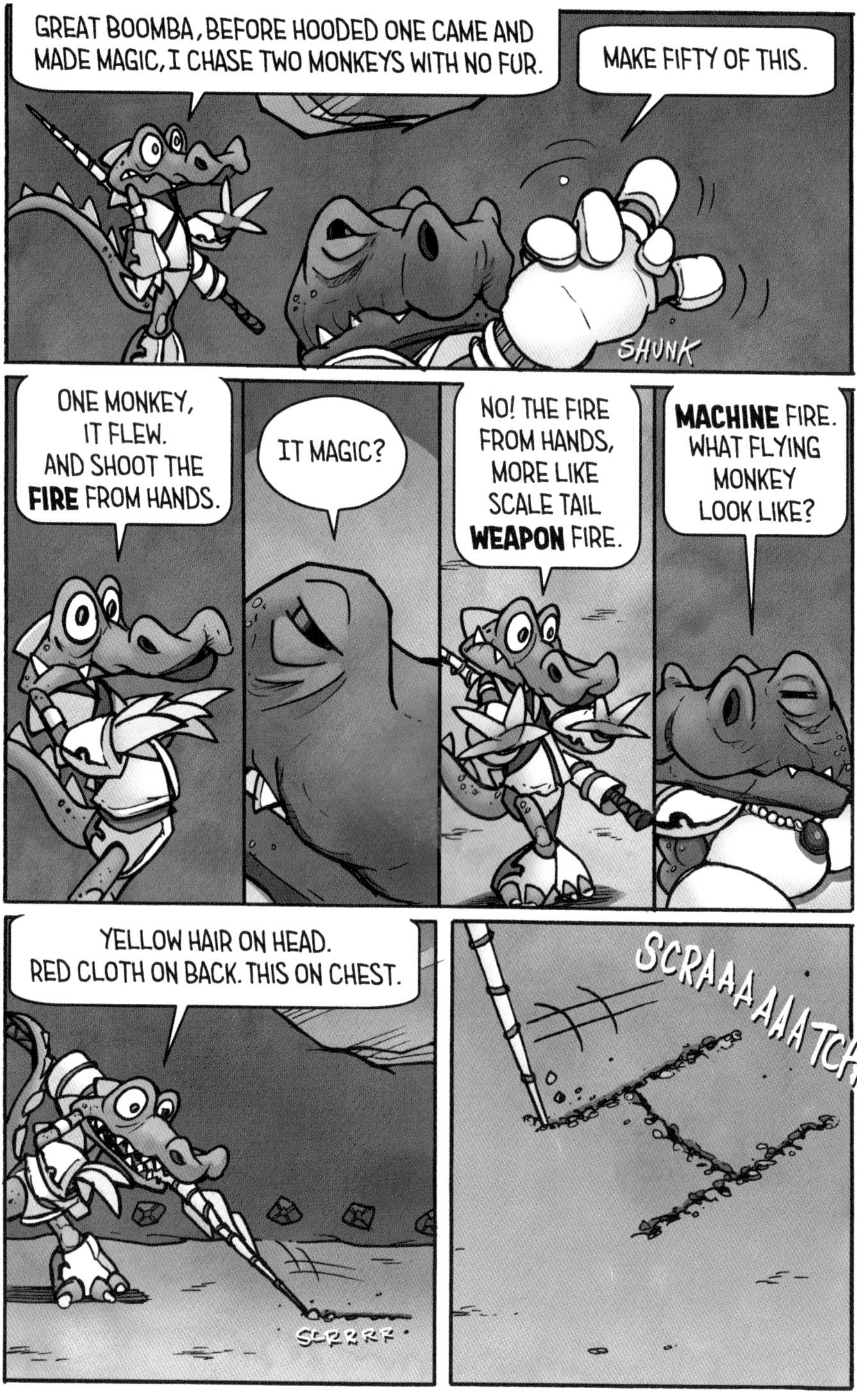
GREAT BOOMBA, BEFORE HOODED ONE CAME AND MADE MAGIC, I CHASE TWO MONKEYS WITH NO FUR.
MAKE FIFTY OF THIS.
SHUNK
ONE MONKEY, IT FLEW. AND SHOOT THE **FIRE** FROM HANDS.
IT MAGIC?
NO! THE FIRE FROM HANDS, MORE LIKE SCALE TAIL **WEAPON** FIRE.
**MACHINE** FIRE. WHAT FLYING MONKEY LOOK LIKE?
YELLOW HAIR ON HEAD. RED CLOTH ON BACK. THIS ON CHEST.
SCRRRR
SCRAAAAAATCH

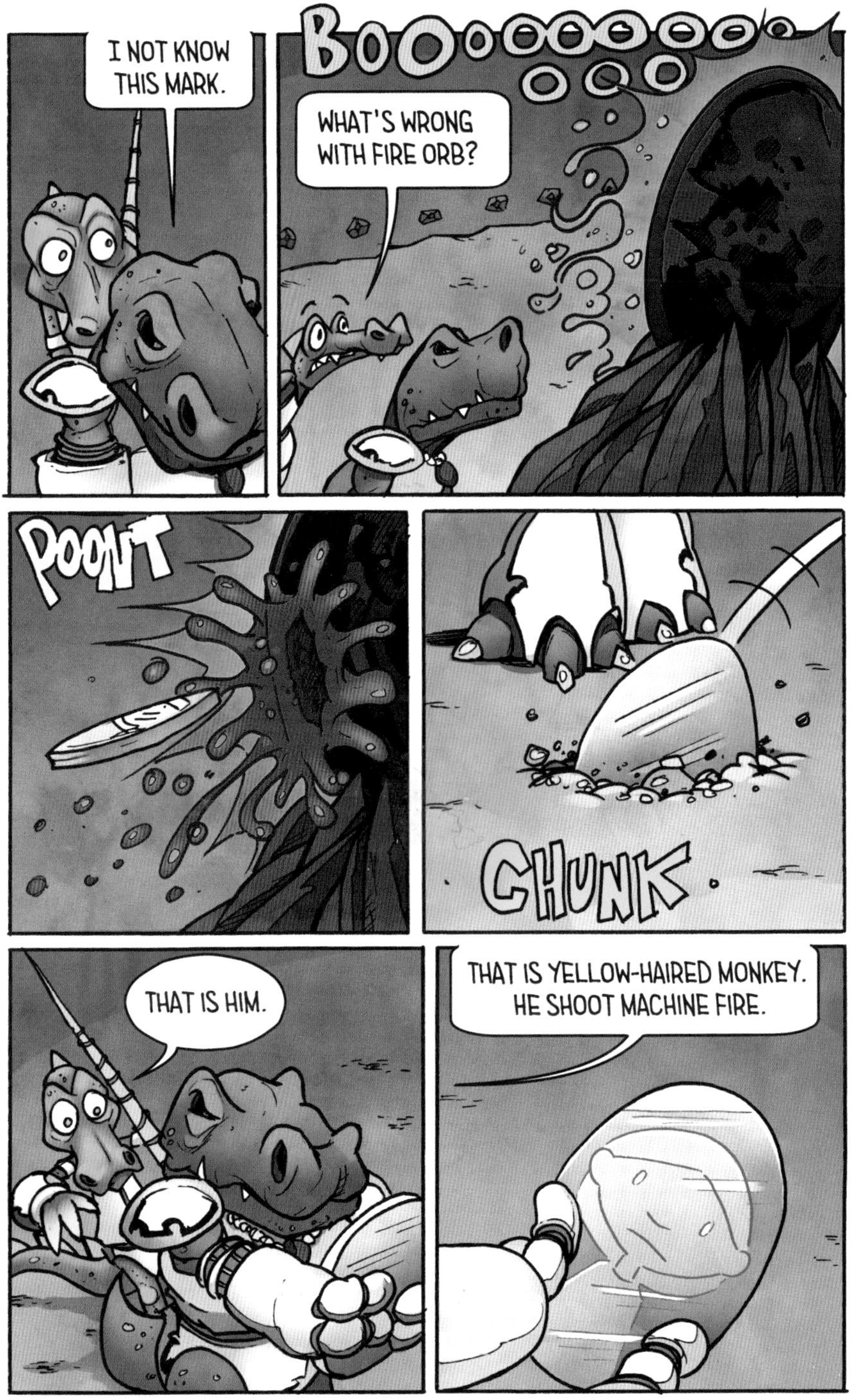
I NOT KNOW THIS MARK.
BOOOOOOOOOOOOO
WHAT'S WRONG WITH FIRE ORB?
POONT
CHUNK
THAT IS HIM.
THAT IS YELLOW-HAIRED MONKEY. HE SHOOT MACHINE FIRE.

HOW FIRE ORB KNOW THAT?

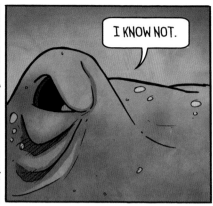

I KNOW NOT.

ODESSA, GET LARGE FIGHTER SQUAD TOGETHER. SEARCH FOR THIS YELLOW-HAIRED ONE.

SEARCH WHERE?

EVERYWHERE.

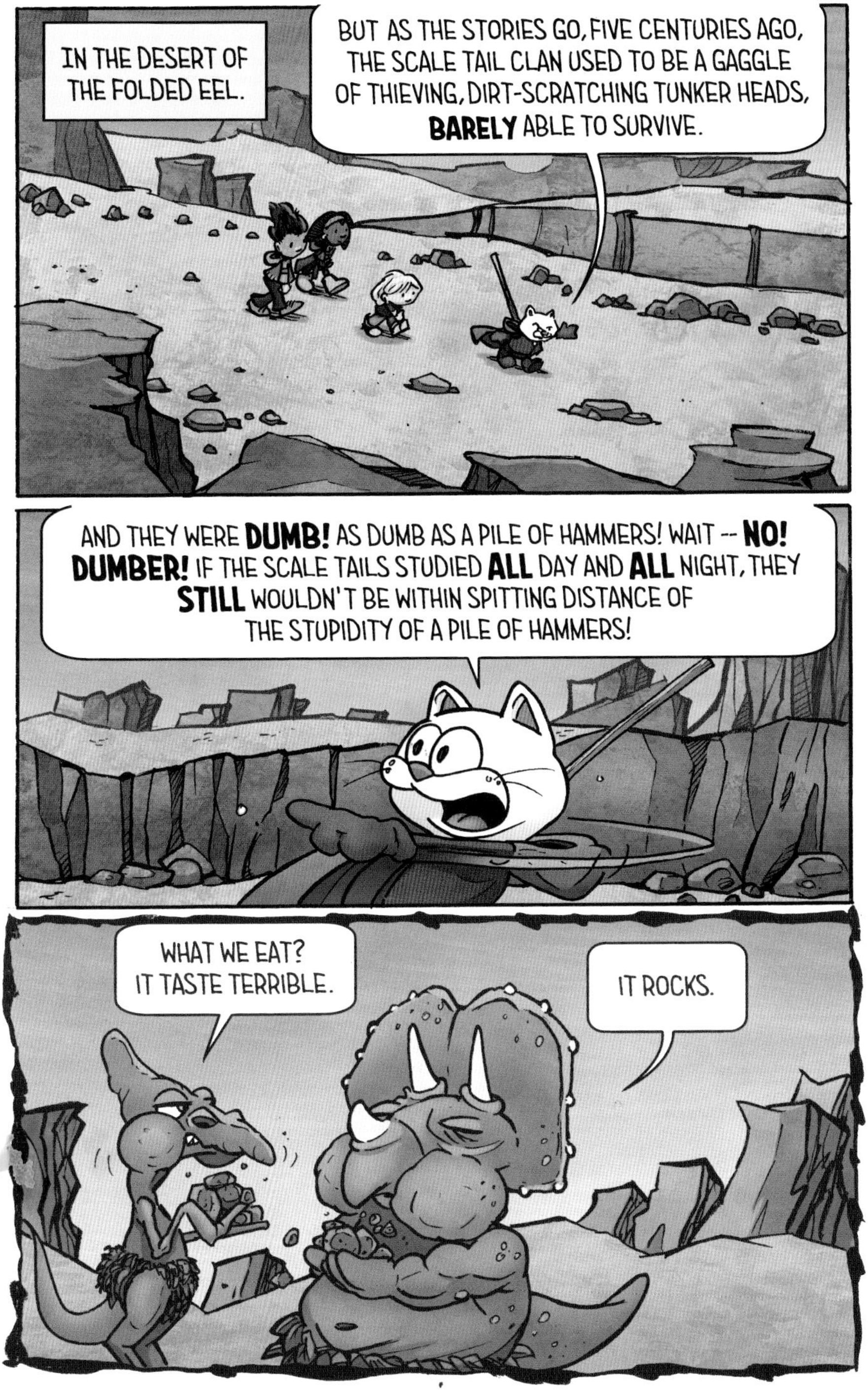
IN THE DESERT OF THE FOLDED EEL.
BUT AS THE STORIES GO, FIVE CENTURIES AGO, THE SCALE TAIL CLAN USED TO BE A GAGGLE OF THIEVING, DIRT-SCRATCHING TUNKER HEADS, **BARELY** ABLE TO SURVIVE.
AND THEY WERE **DUMB!** AS DUMB AS A PILE OF HAMMERS! WAIT -- **NO! DUMBER!** IF THE SCALE TAILS STUDIED **ALL** DAY AND **ALL** NIGHT, THEY **STILL** WOULDN'T BE WITHIN SPITTING DISTANCE OF THE STUPIDITY OF A PILE OF HAMMERS!
WHAT WE EAT? IT TASTE TERRIBLE.
IT ROCKS.

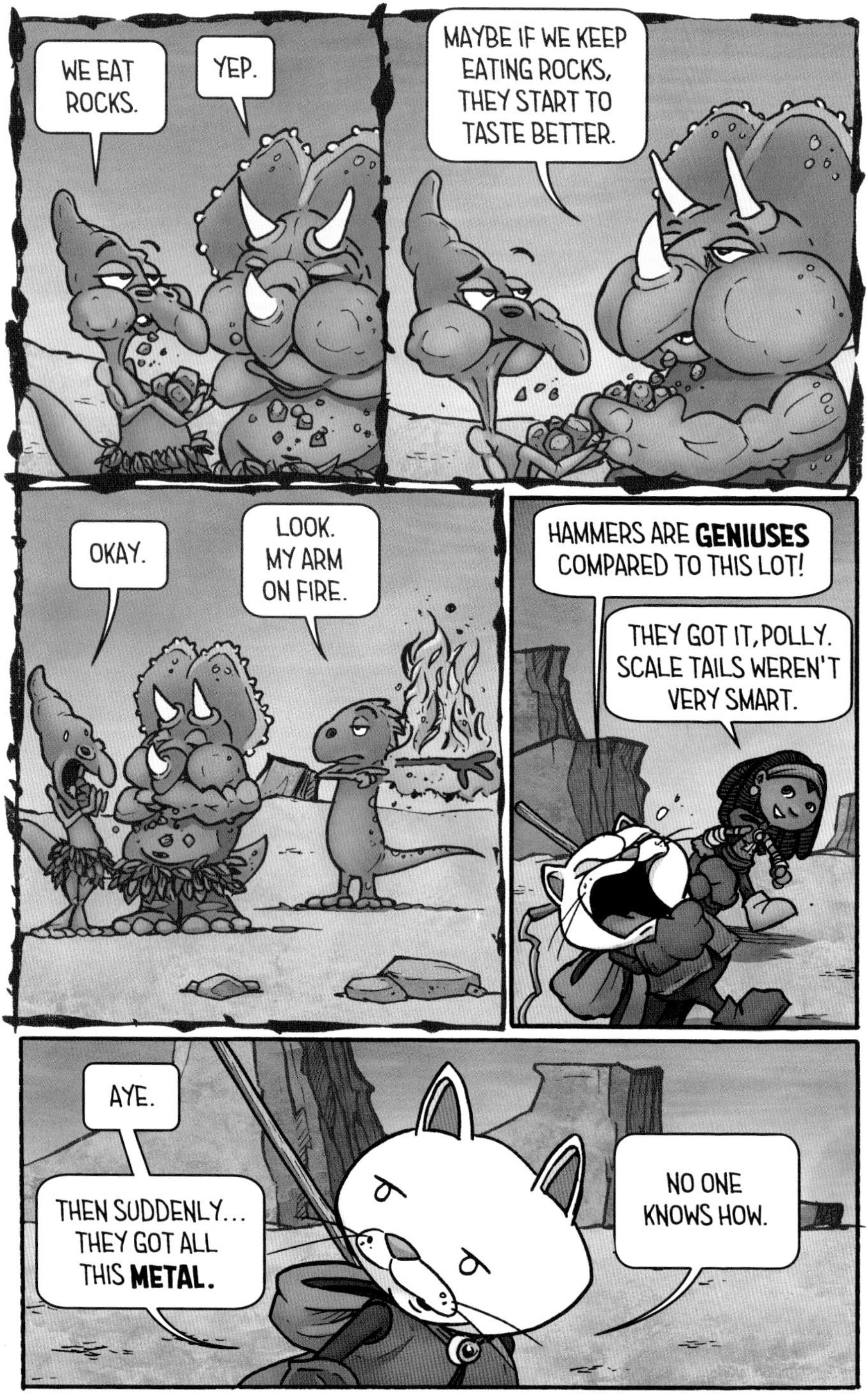

WE EAT ROCKS.
YEP.
MAYBE IF WE KEEP EATING ROCKS, THEY START TO TASTE BETTER.
OKAY.
LOOK. MY ARM ON FIRE.
HAMMERS ARE **GENIUSES** COMPARED TO THIS LOT!
THEY GOT IT, POLLY. SCALE TAILS WEREN'T VERY SMART.
AYE.
THEN SUDDENLY... THEY GOT ALL THIS **METAL.**
NO ONE KNOWS HOW.

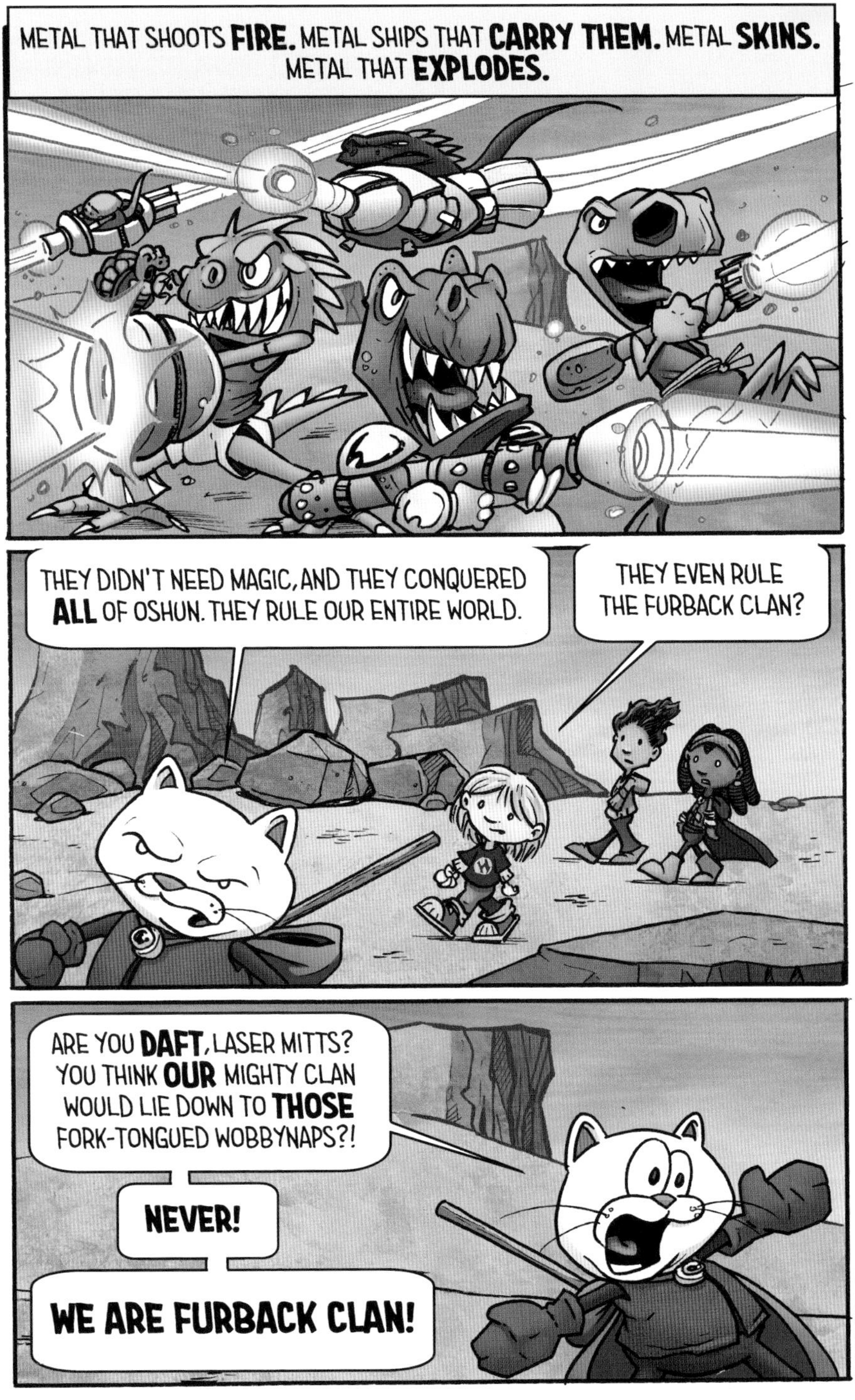
METAL THAT SHOOTS FIRE. METAL SHIPS THAT CARRY THEM. METAL SKINS. METAL THAT EXPLODES.
THEY DIDN'T NEED MAGIC, AND THEY CONQUERED ALL OF OSHUN. THEY RULE OUR ENTIRE WORLD.
THEY EVEN RULE THE FURBACK CLAN?
ARE YOU DAFT, LASER MITTS? YOU THINK OUR MIGHTY CLAN WOULD LIE DOWN TO THOSE FORK-TONGUED WOBBYNAPS?!
NEVER!
WE ARE FURBACK CLAN!

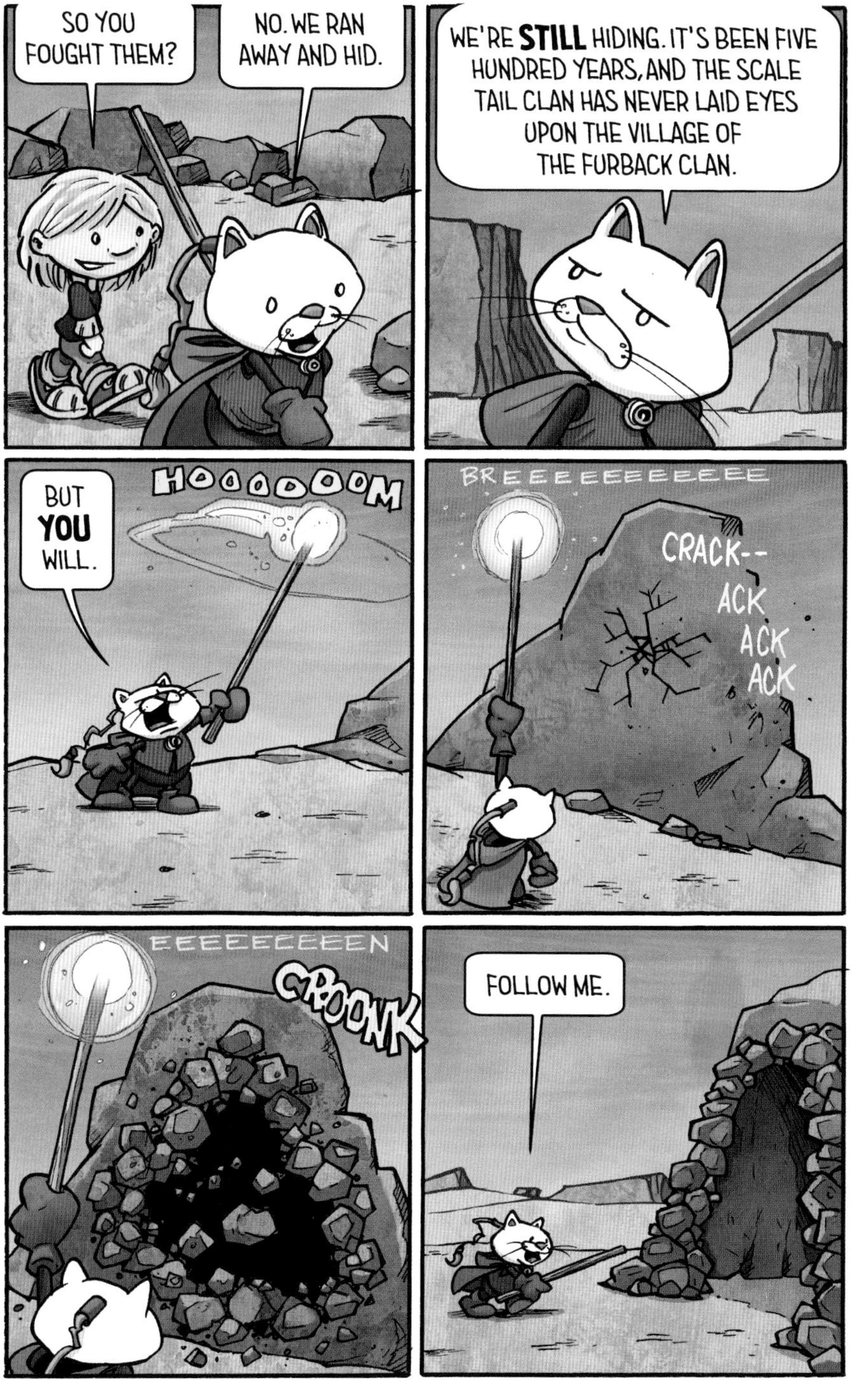
SO YOU FOUGHT THEM?
NO. WE RAN AWAY AND HID.
WE'RE **STILL** HIDING. IT'S BEEN FIVE HUNDRED YEARS, AND THE SCALE TAIL CLAN HAS NEVER LAID EYES UPON THE VILLAGE OF THE FURBACK CLAN.
BUT **YOU** WILL.
HOOOOOOM
BREEEEEEEEEEEE
CRACK--
ACK
ACK
ACK
EEEEEEEEEEN
CROONK
FOLLOW ME.

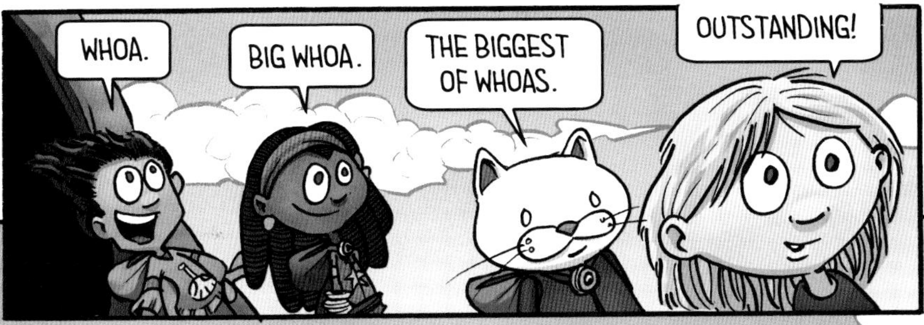
WHOA.
BIG WHOA.
THE BIGGEST OF WHOAS.
OUTSTANDING!

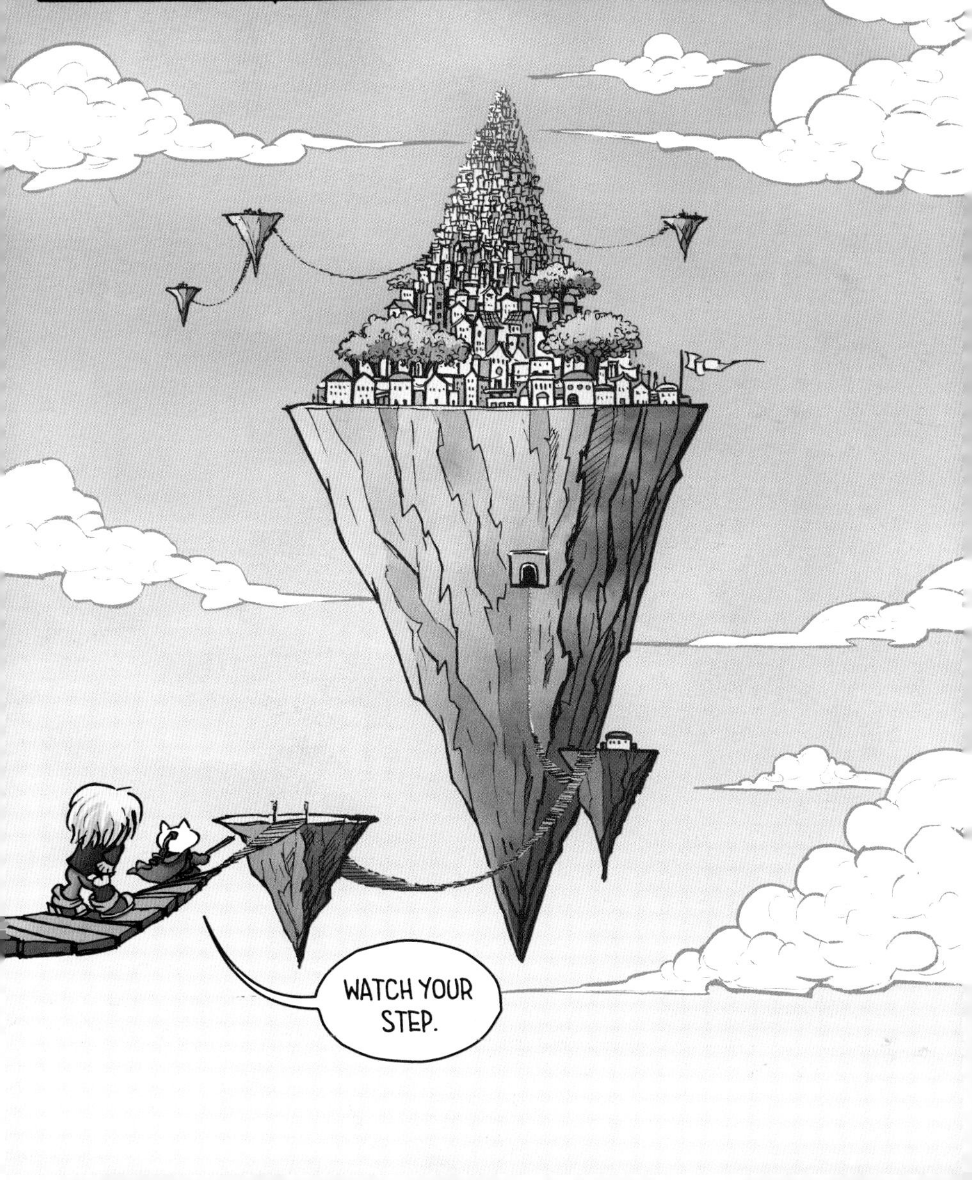
WATCH YOUR STEP.

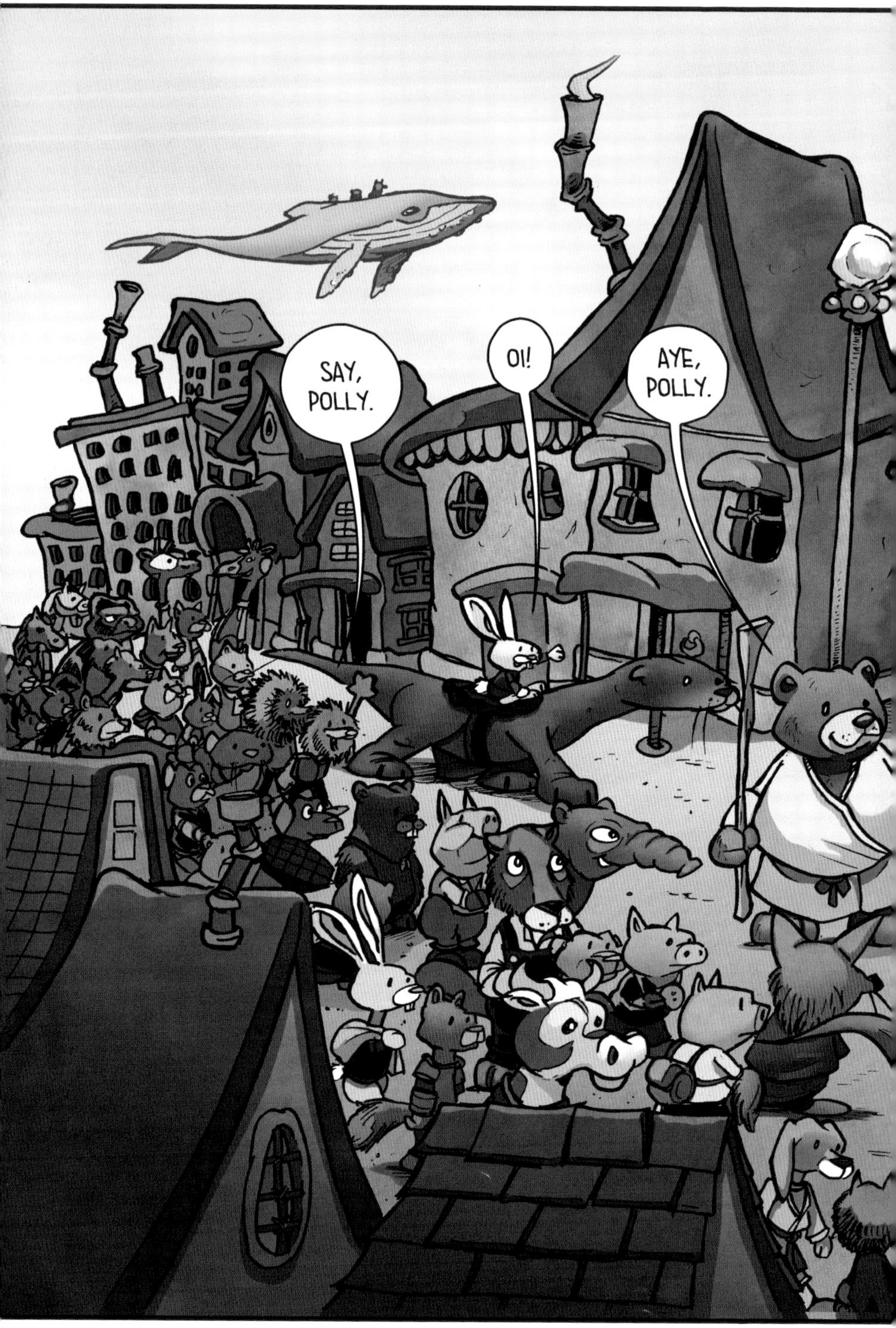
SAY, POLLY.
OI!
AYE, POLLY.

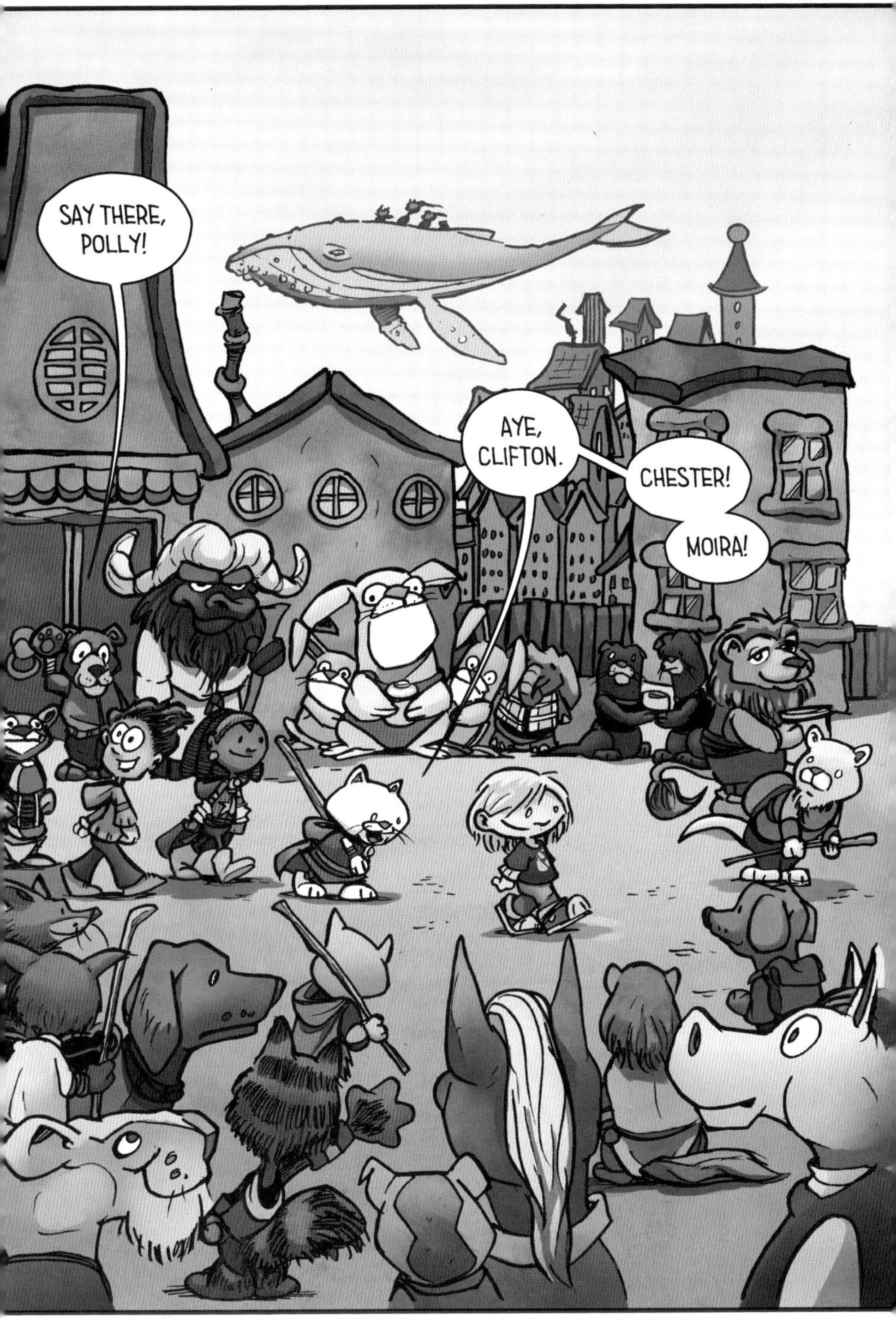
SAY THERE, POLLY!
AYE, CLIFTON.
CHESTER!
MOIRA!

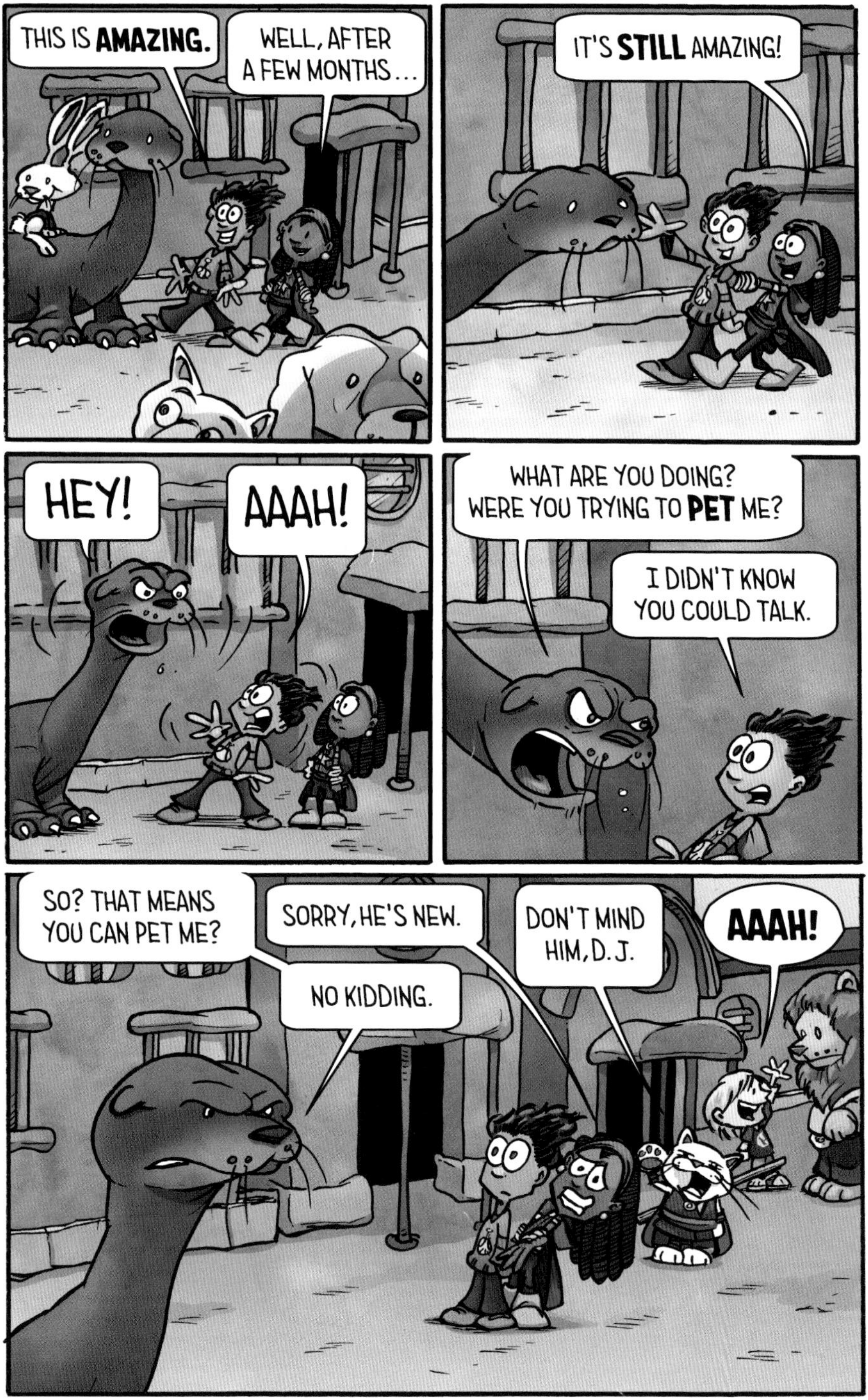
THIS IS AMAZING.
WELL, AFTER A FEW MONTHS...
IT'S STILL AMAZING!
HEY!
AAAH!
WHAT ARE YOU DOING? WERE YOU TRYING TO PET ME?
I DIDN'T KNOW YOU COULD TALK.
SO? THAT MEANS YOU CAN PET ME?
SORRY, HE'S NEW.
NO KIDDING.
DON'T MIND HIM, D. J.
AAAH!

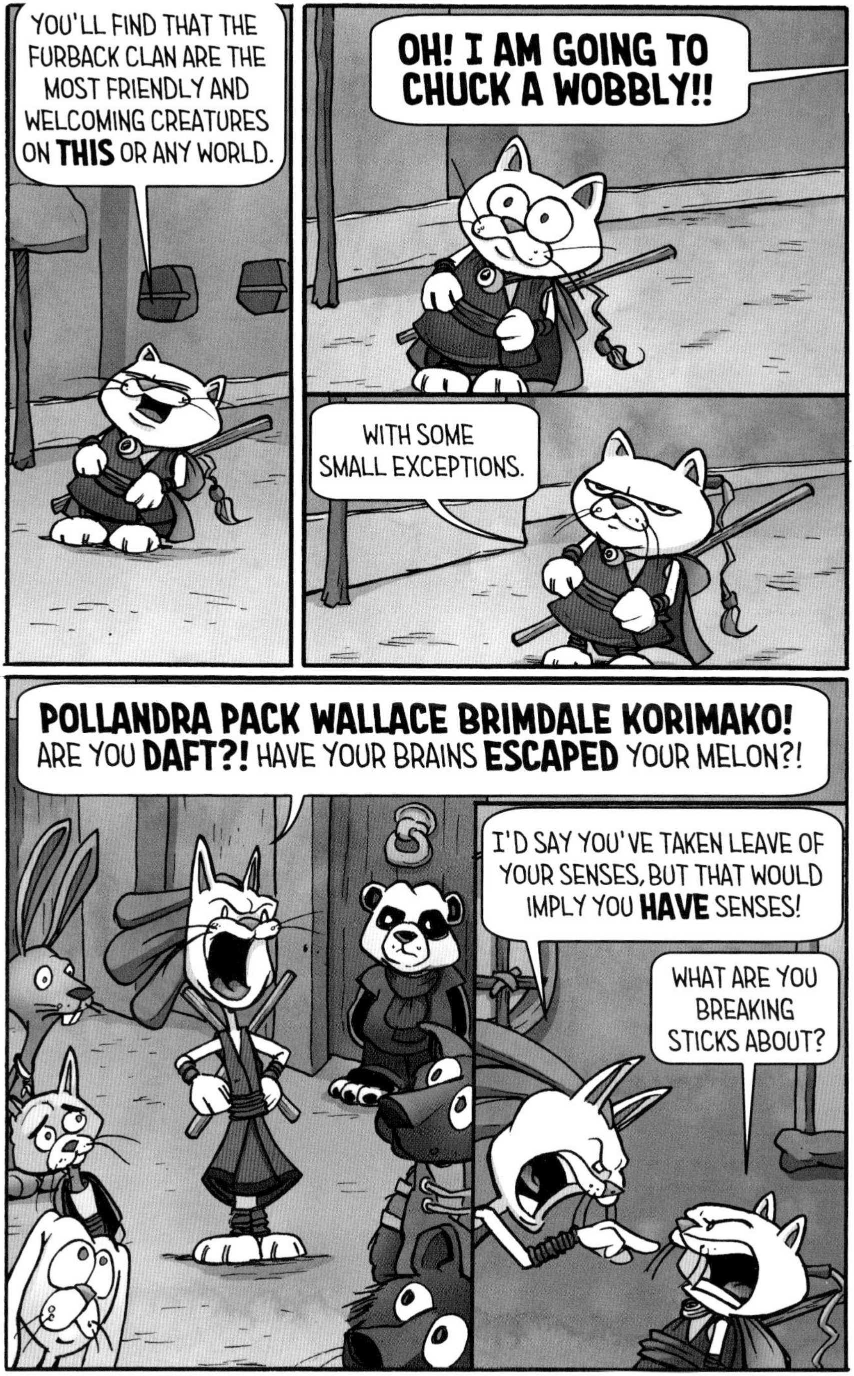
YOU'LL FIND THAT THE FURBACK CLAN ARE THE MOST FRIENDLY AND WELCOMING CREATURES ON THIS OR ANY WORLD.
OH! I AM GOING TO CHUCK A WOBBLY!!
WITH SOME SMALL EXCEPTIONS.
POLLANDRA PACK WALLACE BRIMDALE KORIMAKO! ARE YOU DAFT?! HAVE YOUR BRAINS ESCAPED YOUR MELON?!
I'D SAY YOU'VE TAKEN LEAVE OF YOUR SENSES, BUT THAT WOULD IMPLY YOU HAVE SENSES!
WHAT ARE YOU BREAKING STICKS ABOUT?

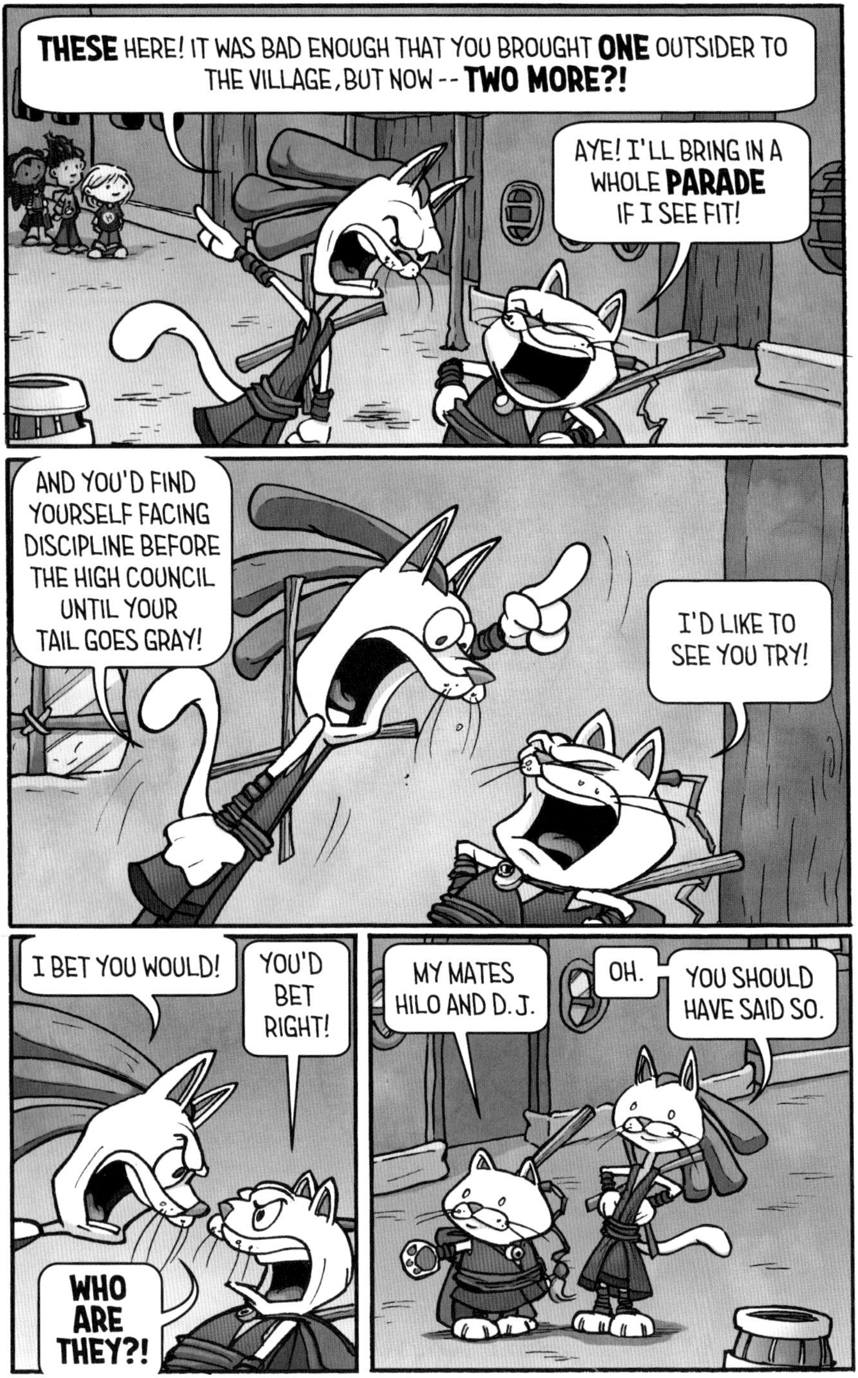
THESE HERE! IT WAS BAD ENOUGH THAT YOU BROUGHT ONE OUTSIDER TO THE VILLAGE, BUT NOW -- TWO MORE?!
AYE! I'LL BRING IN A WHOLE PARADE IF I SEE FIT!
AND YOU'D FIND YOURSELF FACING DISCIPLINE BEFORE THE HIGH COUNCIL UNTIL YOUR TAIL GOES GRAY!
I'D LIKE TO SEE YOU TRY!
I BET YOU WOULD!
YOU'D BET RIGHT!
WHO ARE THEY?!
MY MATES HILO AND D. J.
OH.
YOU SHOULD HAVE SAID SO.

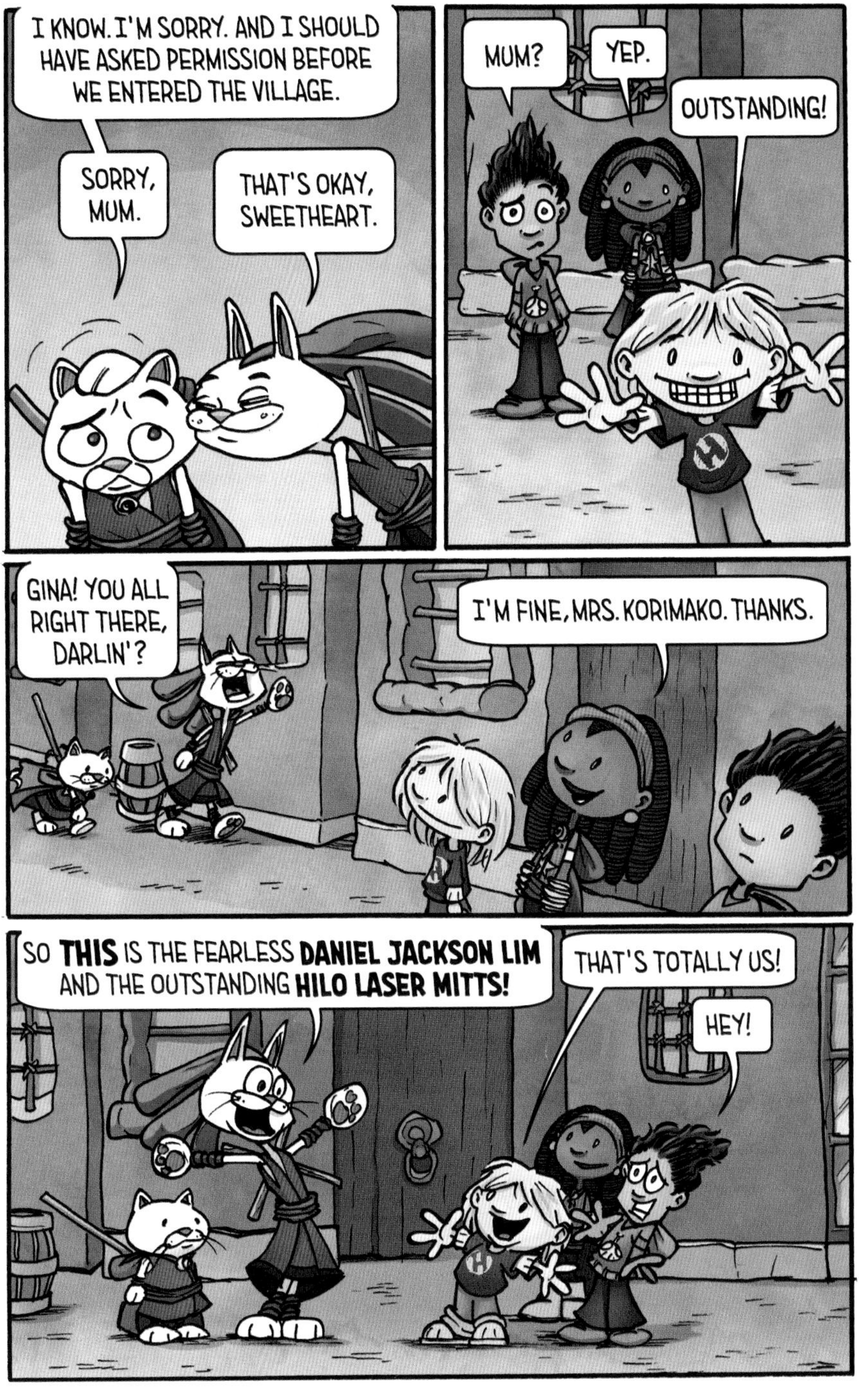
I KNOW. I'M SORRY. AND I SHOULD HAVE ASKED PERMISSION BEFORE WE ENTERED THE VILLAGE.
SORRY, MUM.
THAT'S OKAY, SWEETHEART.
MUM?
YEP.
OUTSTANDING!
GINA! YOU ALL RIGHT THERE, DARLIN'?
I'M FINE, MRS. KORIMAKO. THANKS.
SO **THIS** IS THE FEARLESS **DANIEL JACKSON LIM** AND THE OUTSTANDING **HILO LASER MITTS!**
THAT'S TOTALLY US!
HEY!

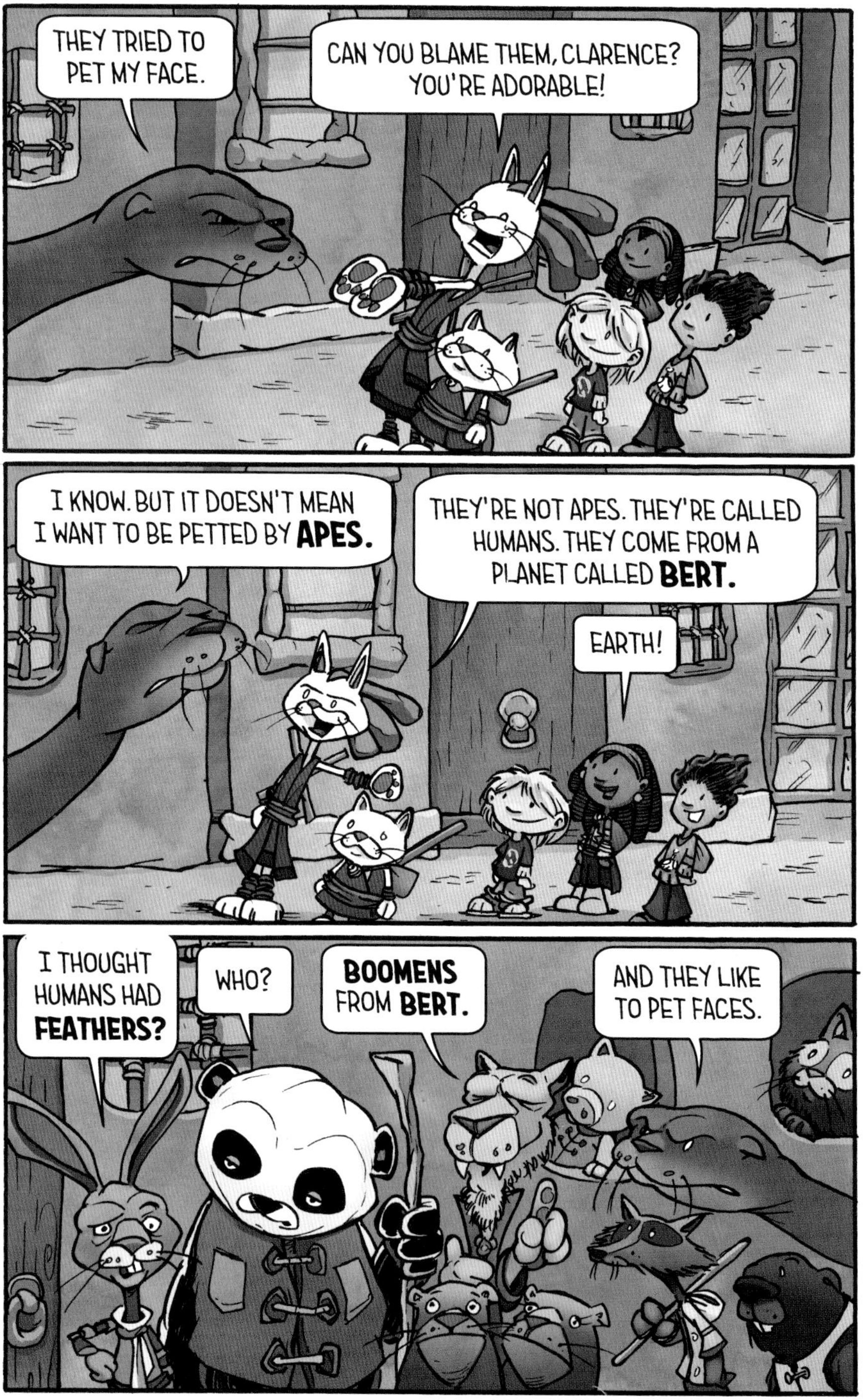
THEY TRIED TO PET MY FACE.
CAN YOU BLAME THEM, CLARENCE? YOU'RE ADORABLE!
I KNOW. BUT IT DOESN'T MEAN I WANT TO BE PETTED BY **APES.**
THEY'RE NOT APES. THEY'RE CALLED HUMANS. THEY COME FROM A PLANET CALLED **BERT.**
EARTH!
I THOUGHT HUMANS HAD **FEATHERS?**
WHO?
**BOOMENS** FROM **BERT.**
AND THEY LIKE TO PET FACES.

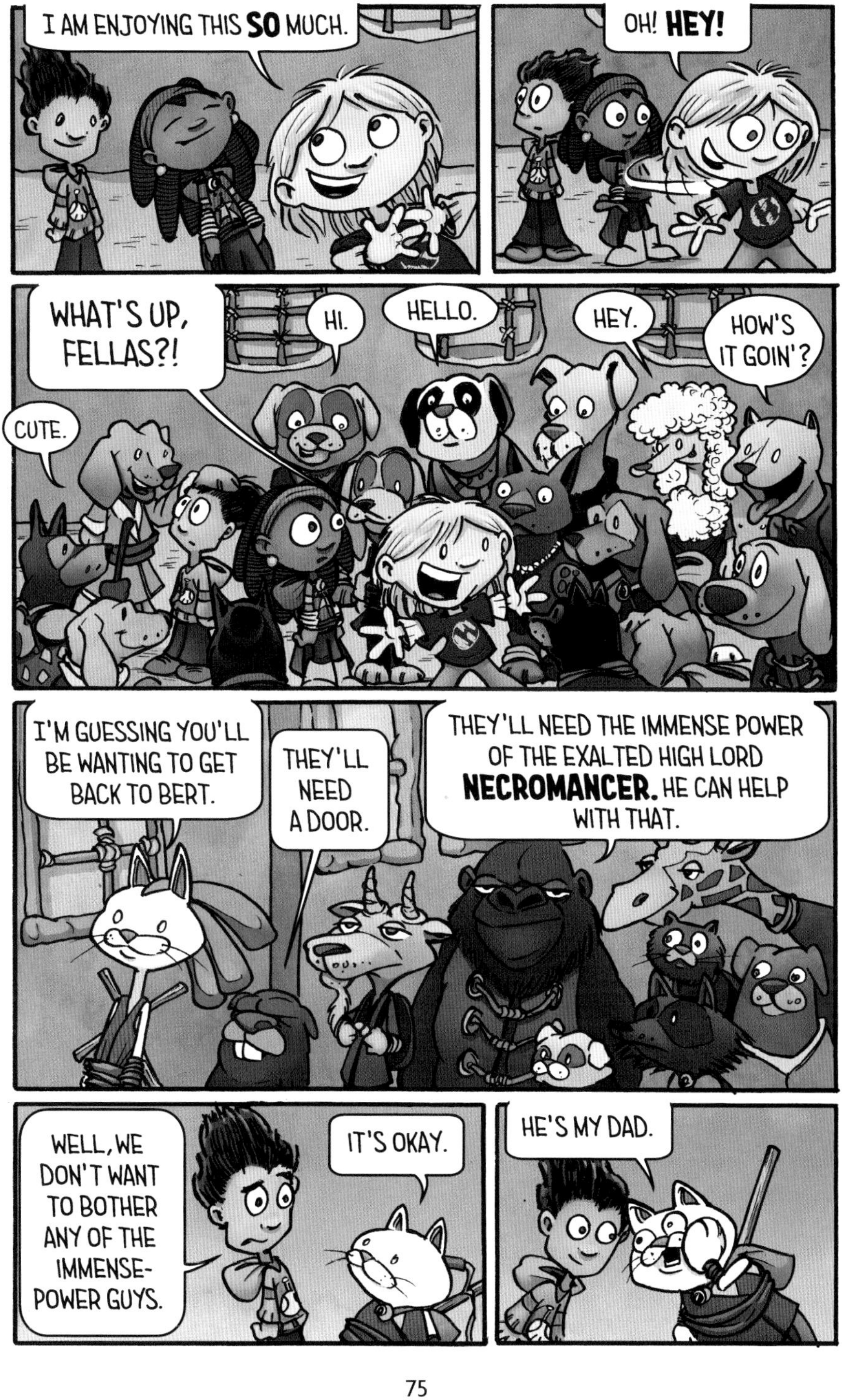
I AM ENJOYING THIS **SO** MUCH.
OH! **HEY!**
WHAT'S UP, FELLAS?!
HI.
HELLO.
HEY.
HOW'S IT GOIN'?
CUTE.
I'M GUESSING YOU'LL BE WANTING TO GET BACK TO BERT.
THEY'LL NEED A DOOR.
THEY'LL NEED THE IMMENSE POWER OF THE EXALTED HIGH LORD **NECROMANCER.** HE CAN HELP WITH THAT.
WELL, WE DON'T WANT TO BOTHER ANY OF THE IMMENSE-POWER GUYS.
IT'S OKAY.
HE'S MY DAD.

# CHAPTER

5

I

HOUSE OF KORIMAKO.

WELL, I WON'T LIE TO YOU, FRIENDS...

FINDING **DOORS** IS A CHALLENGING BIT OF BUSINESS.

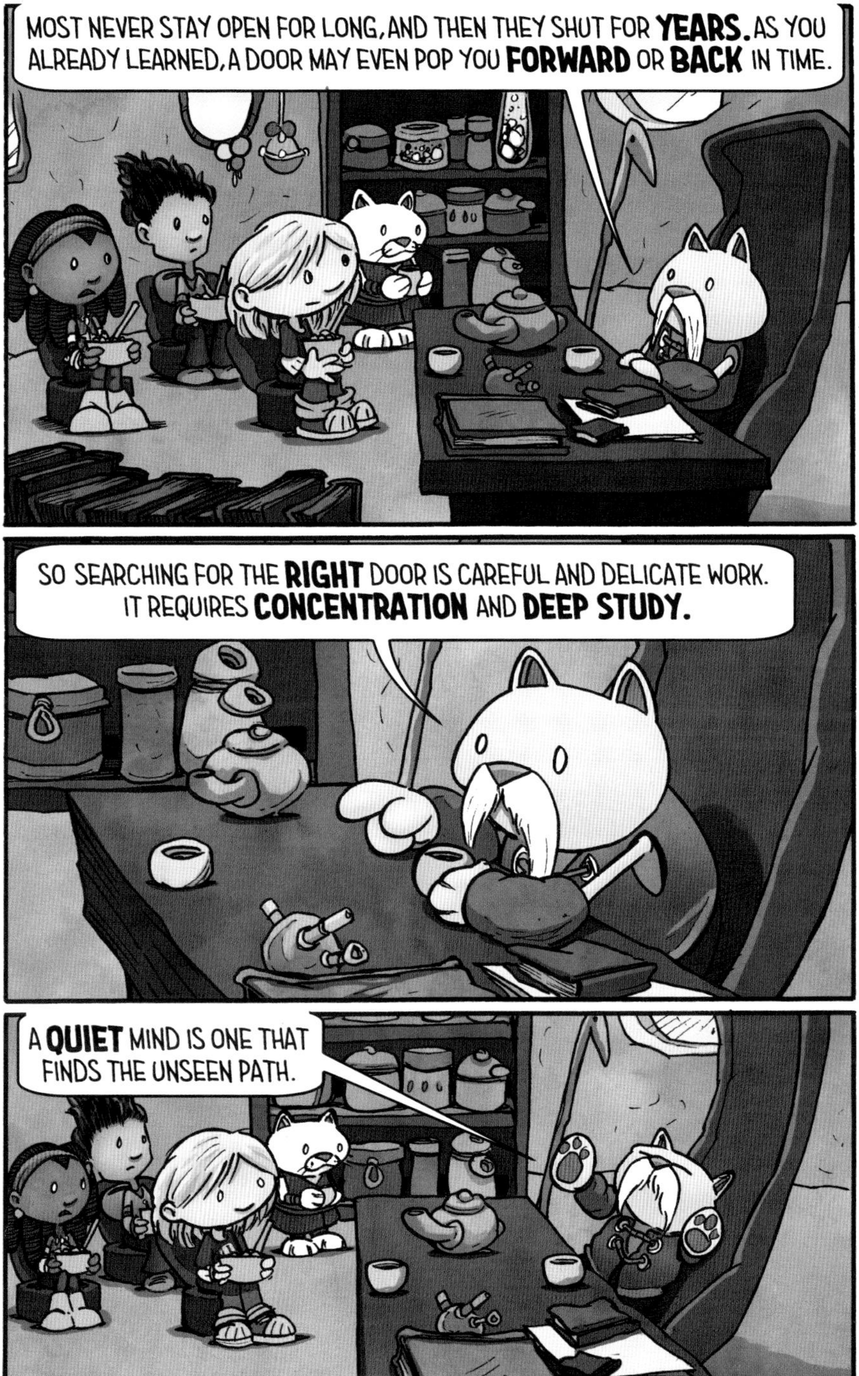
MOST NEVER STAY OPEN FOR LONG, AND THEN THEY SHUT FOR **YEARS.** AS YOU ALREADY LEARNED, A DOOR MAY EVEN POP YOU **FORWARD** OR **BACK** IN TIME.
SO SEARCHING FOR THE **RIGHT** DOOR IS CAREFUL AND DELICATE WORK. IT REQUIRES **CONCENTRATION** AND **DEEP STUDY.**
A **QUIET** MIND IS ONE THAT FINDS THE UNSEEN PATH.

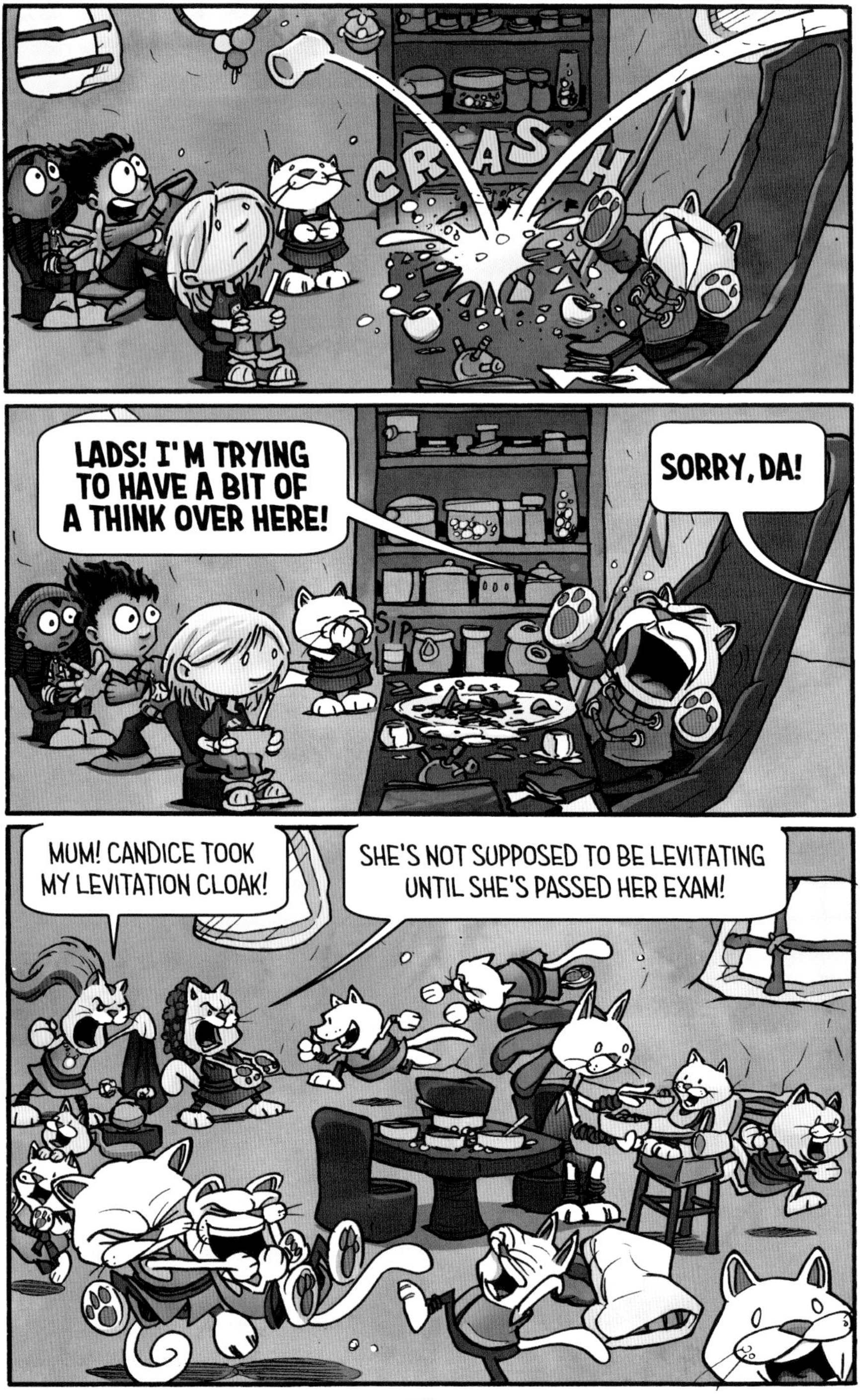
CRASH
LADS! I'M TRYING TO HAVE A BIT OF A THINK OVER HERE!
SORRY, DA!
SIP
MUM! CANDICE TOOK MY LEVITATION CLOAK!
SHE'S NOT SUPPOSED TO BE LEVITATING UNTIL SHE'S PASSED HER EXAM!

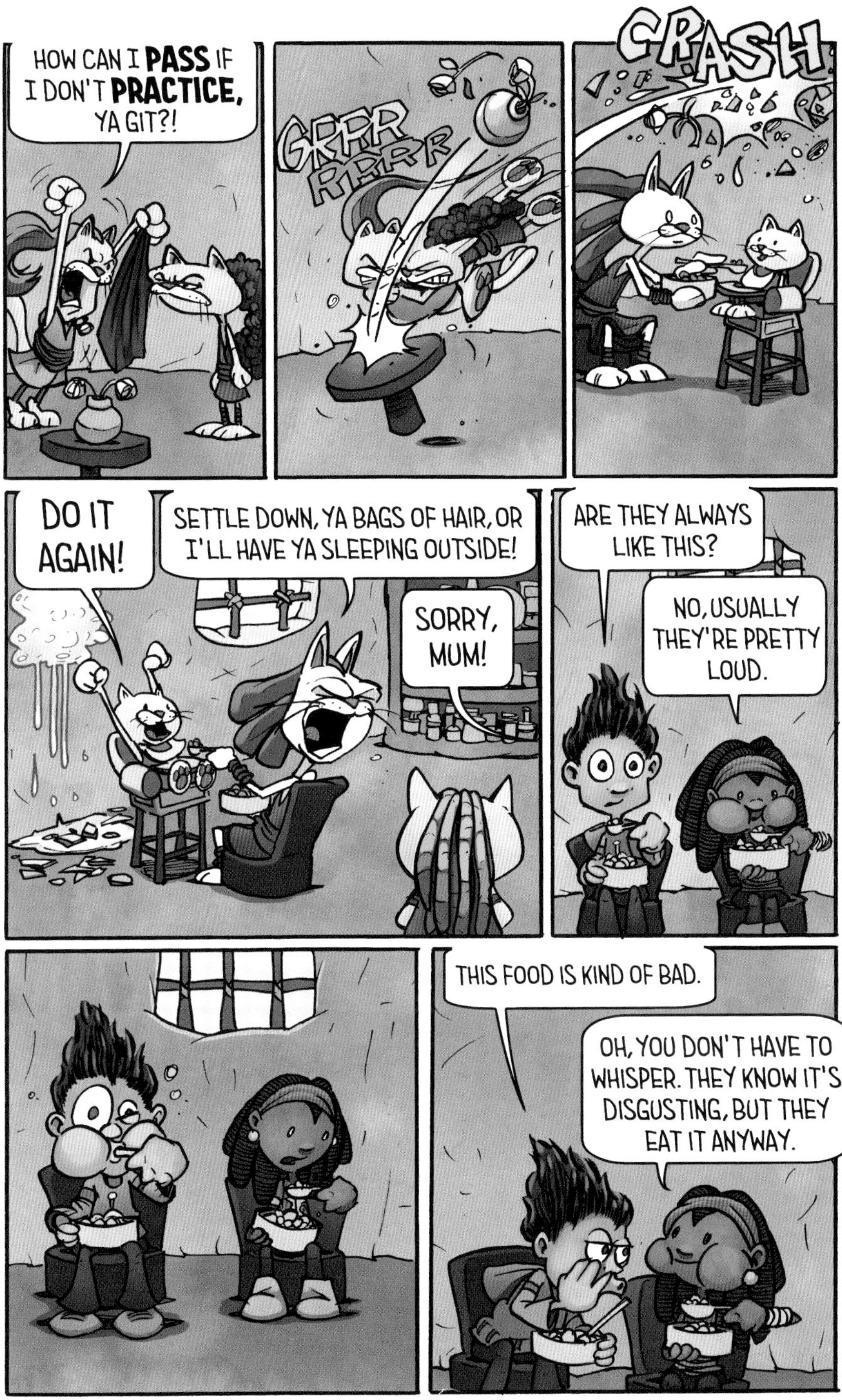
HOW CAN I **PASS** IF I DON'T **PRACTICE,** YA GIT?!
GRRR RRRR
CRASH
DO IT AGAIN!
SETTLE DOWN, YA BAGS OF HAIR, OR I'LL HAVE YA SLEEPING OUTSIDE!
SORRY, MUM!
ARE THEY ALWAYS LIKE THIS?
NO, USUALLY THEY'RE PRETTY LOUD.
THIS FOOD IS KIND OF BAD.
OH, YOU DON'T HAVE TO WHISPER. THEY KNOW IT'S DISGUSTING, BUT THEY EAT IT ANYWAY.

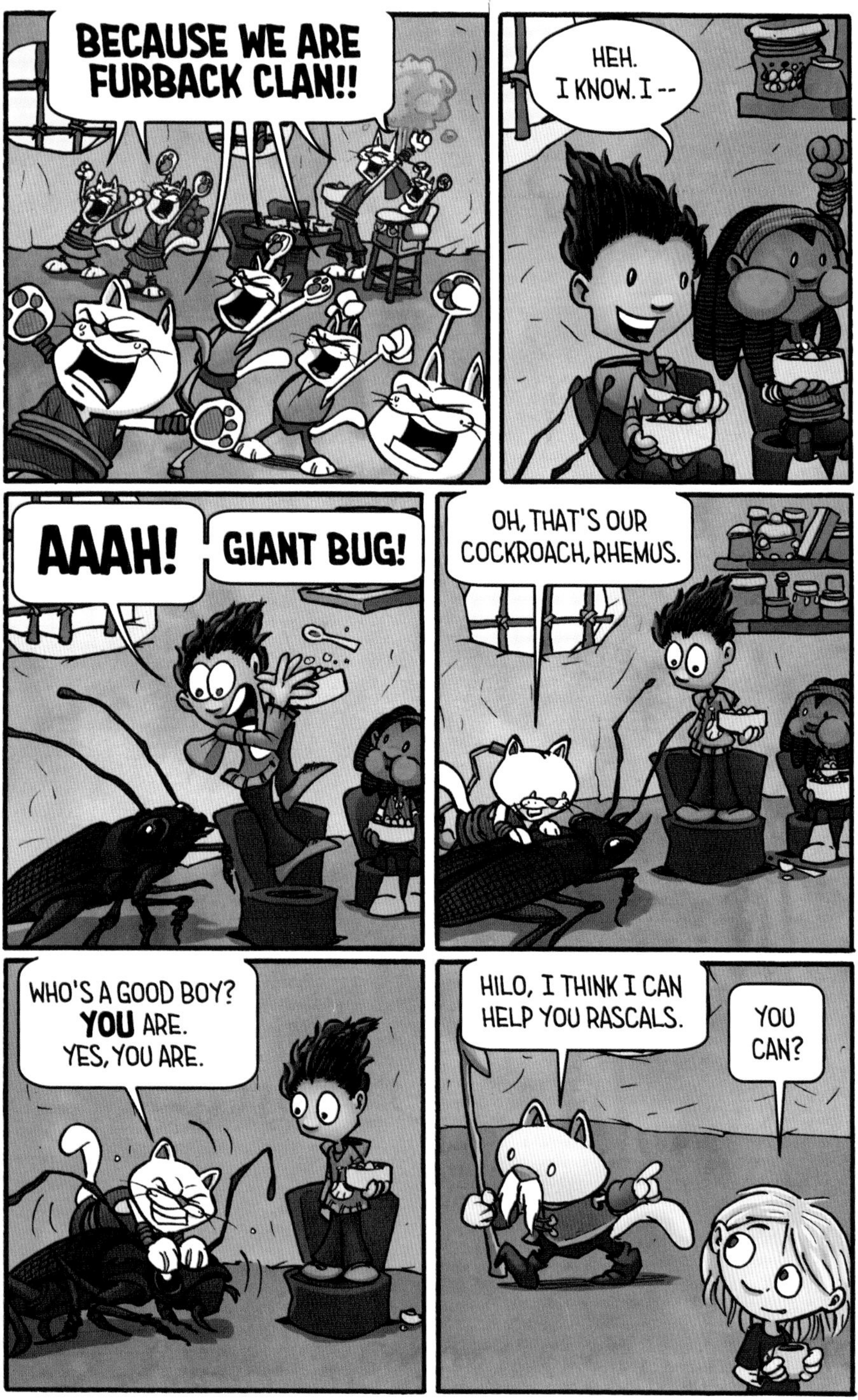
BECAUSE WE ARE FURBACK CLAN!!
HEH. I KNOW. I --
AAAH!
GIANT BUG!
OH, THAT'S OUR COCKROACH, RHEMUS.
WHO'S A GOOD BOY? **YOU** ARE. YES, YOU ARE.
HILO, I THINK I CAN HELP YOU RASCALS.
YOU CAN?

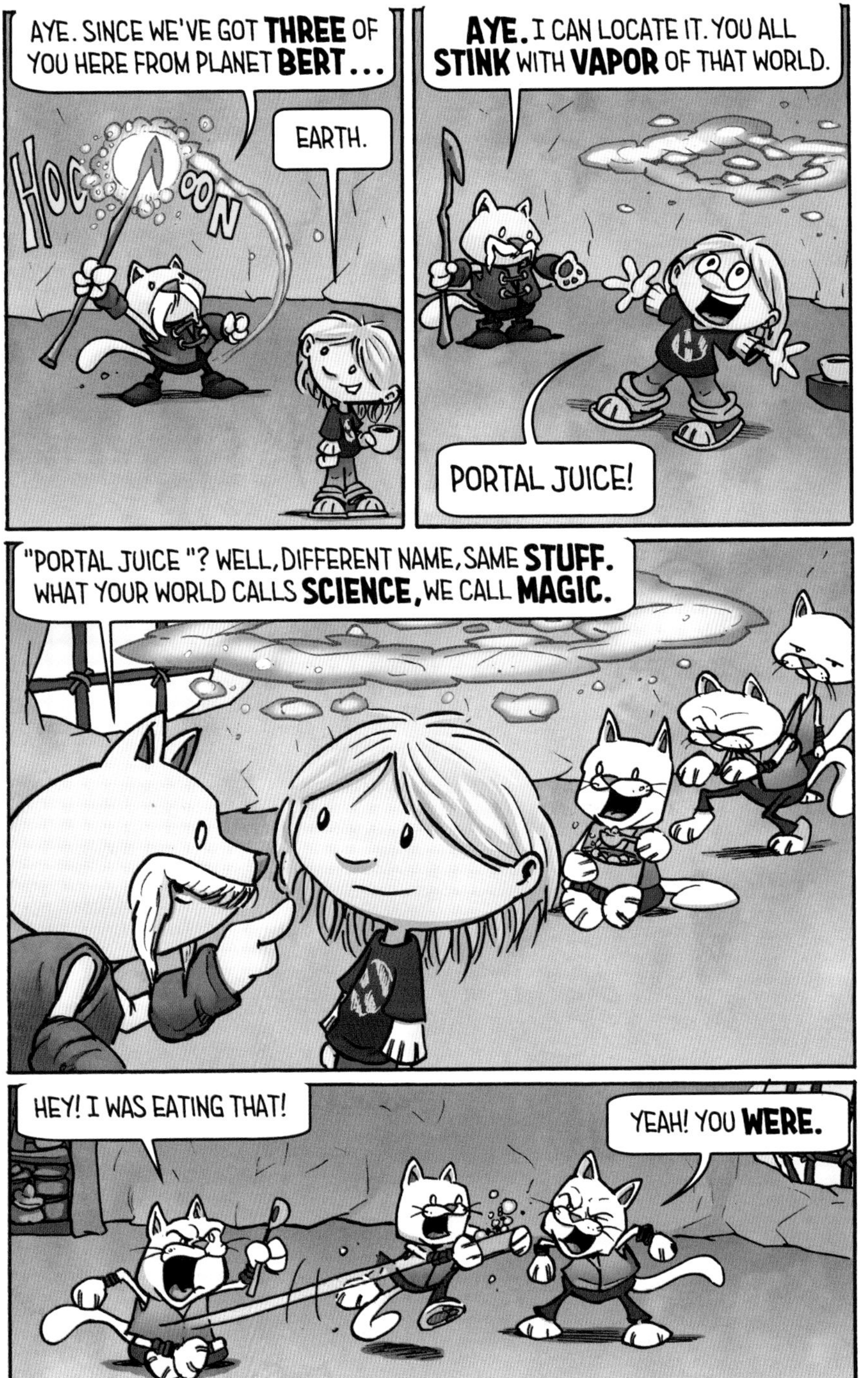
AYE. SINCE WE'VE GOT THREE OF YOU HERE FROM PLANET BERT...
HOC OOON
EARTH.
AYE. I CAN LOCATE IT. YOU ALL STINK WITH VAPOR OF THAT WORLD.
PORTAL JUICE!
"PORTAL JUICE"? WELL, DIFFERENT NAME, SAME STUFF. WHAT YOUR WORLD CALLS SCIENCE, WE CALL MAGIC.
HEY! I WAS EATING THAT!
YEAH! YOU WERE.

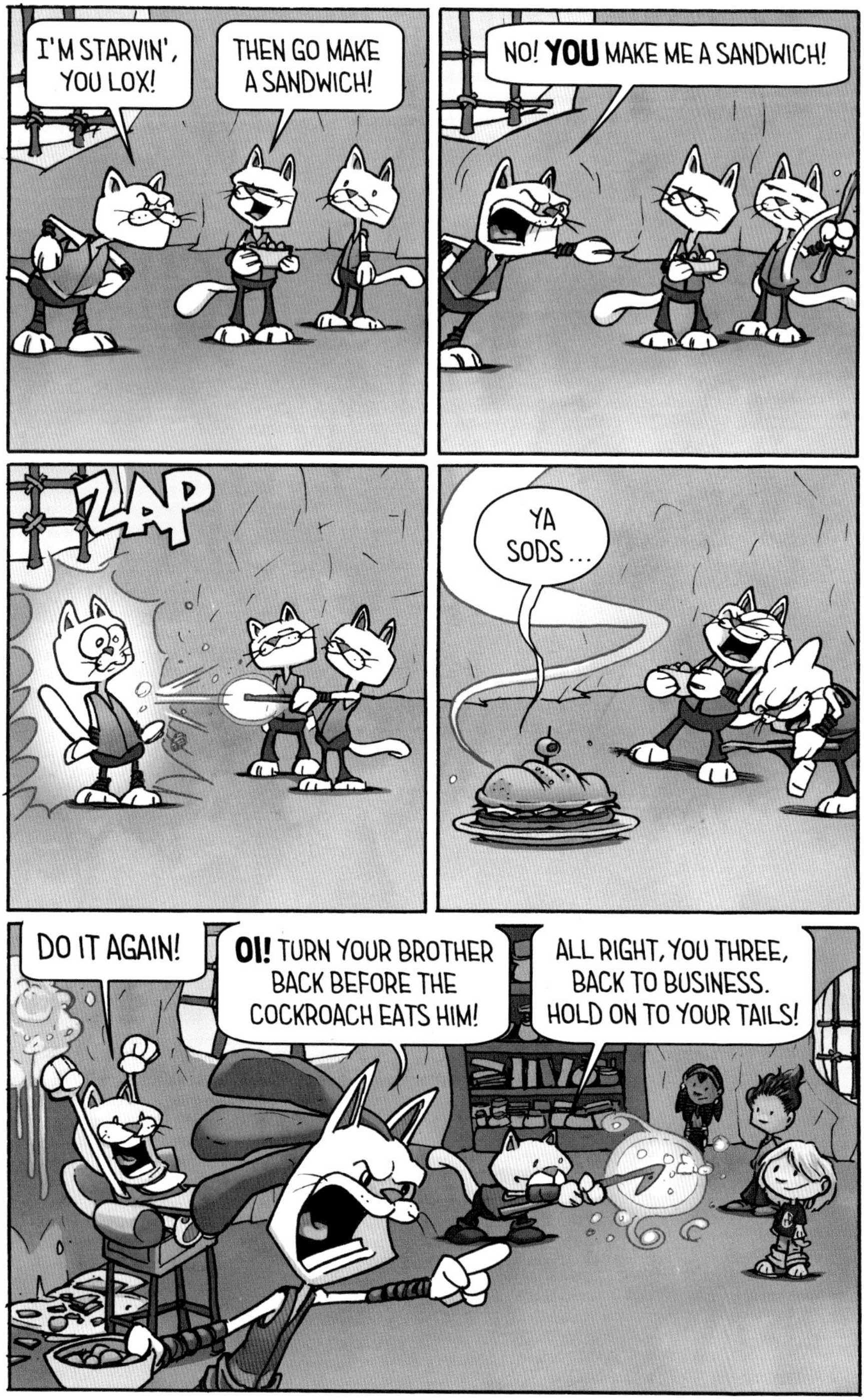
I'M STARVIN', YOU LOX!
THEN GO MAKE A SANDWICH!
NO! YOU MAKE ME A SANDWICH!
ZAP
YA SODS...
DO IT AGAIN!
OI! TURN YOUR BROTHER BACK BEFORE THE COCKROACH EATS HIM!
ALL RIGHT, YOU THREE, BACK TO BUSINESS. HOLD ON TO YOUR TAILS!

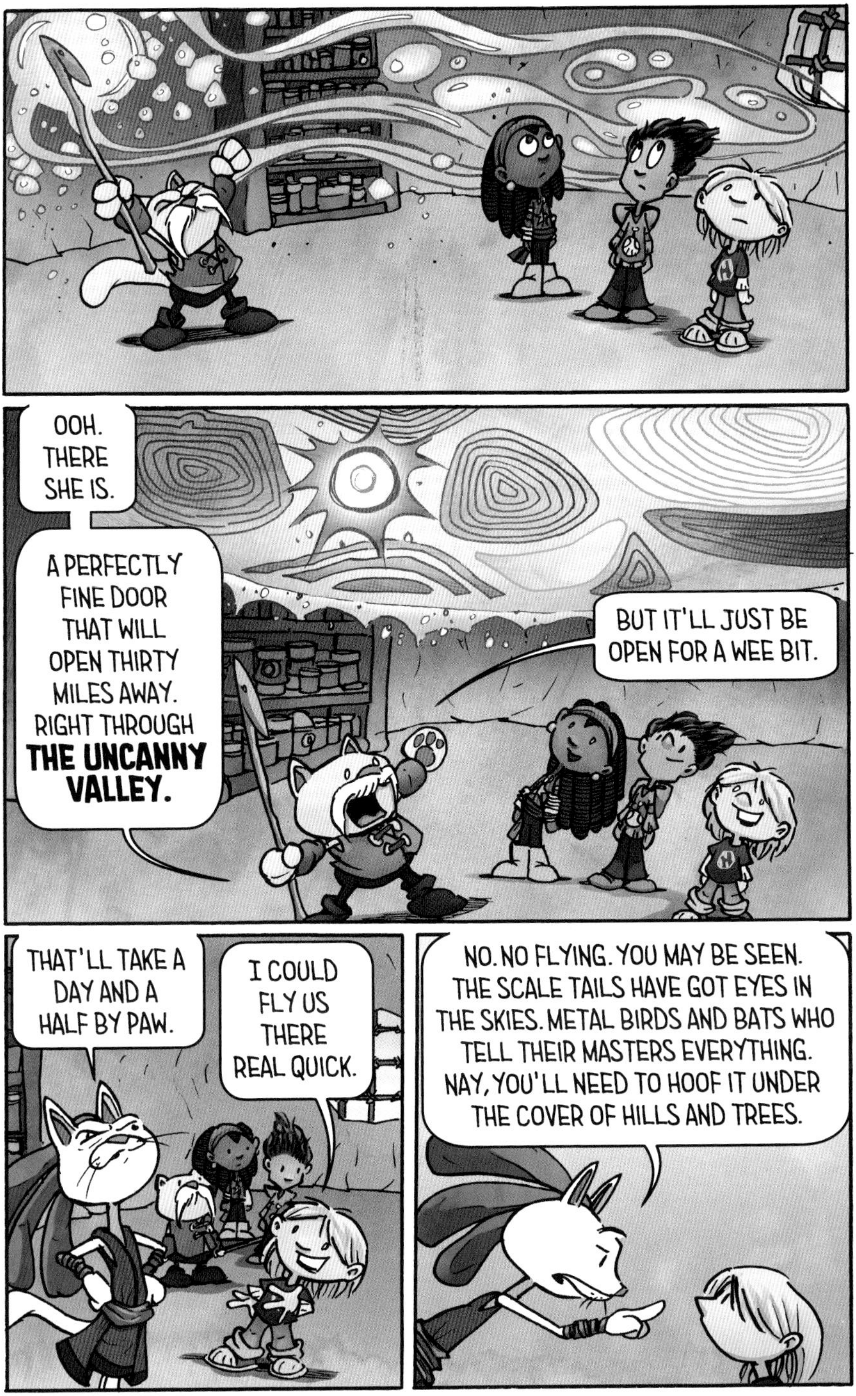
OOH. THERE SHE IS.
A PERFECTLY FINE DOOR THAT WILL OPEN THIRTY MILES AWAY. RIGHT THROUGH **THE UNCANNY VALLEY.**
BUT IT'LL JUST BE OPEN FOR A WEE BIT.
THAT'LL TAKE A DAY AND A HALF BY PAW.
I COULD FLY US THERE REAL QUICK.
NO. NO FLYING. YOU MAY BE SEEN. THE SCALE TAILS HAVE GOT EYES IN THE SKIES. METAL BIRDS AND BATS WHO TELL THEIR MASTERS EVERYTHING. NAY, YOU'LL NEED TO HOOF IT UNDER THE COVER OF HILLS AND TREES.

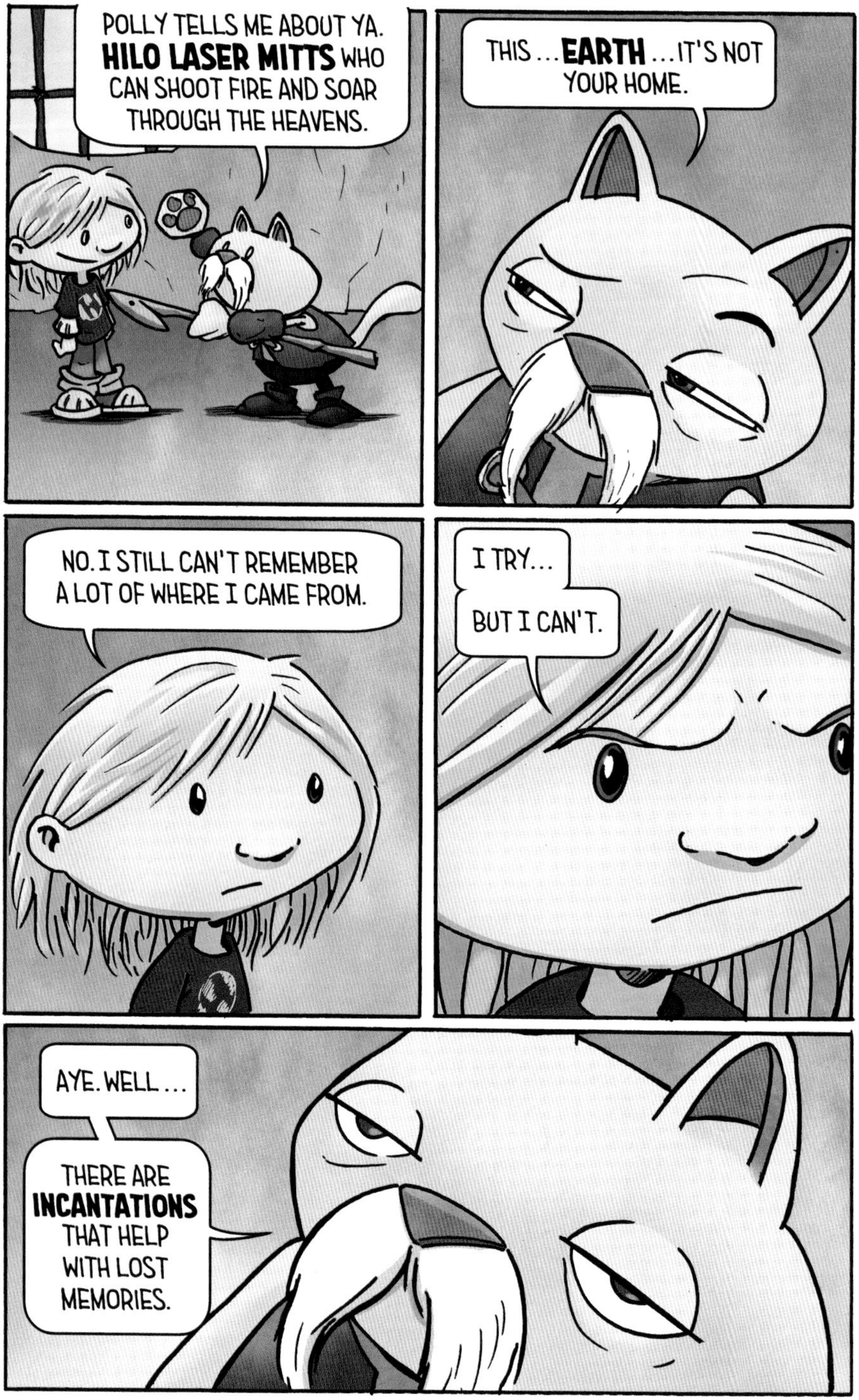
POLLY TELLS ME ABOUT YA. **HILO LASER MITTS** WHO CAN SHOOT FIRE AND SOAR THROUGH THE HEAVENS.
THIS ... **EARTH** ... IT'S NOT YOUR HOME.
NO. I STILL CAN'T REMEMBER A LOT OF WHERE I CAME FROM.
I TRY...
BUT I CAN'T.
AYE. WELL ...
THERE ARE **INCANTATIONS** THAT HELP WITH LOST MEMORIES.

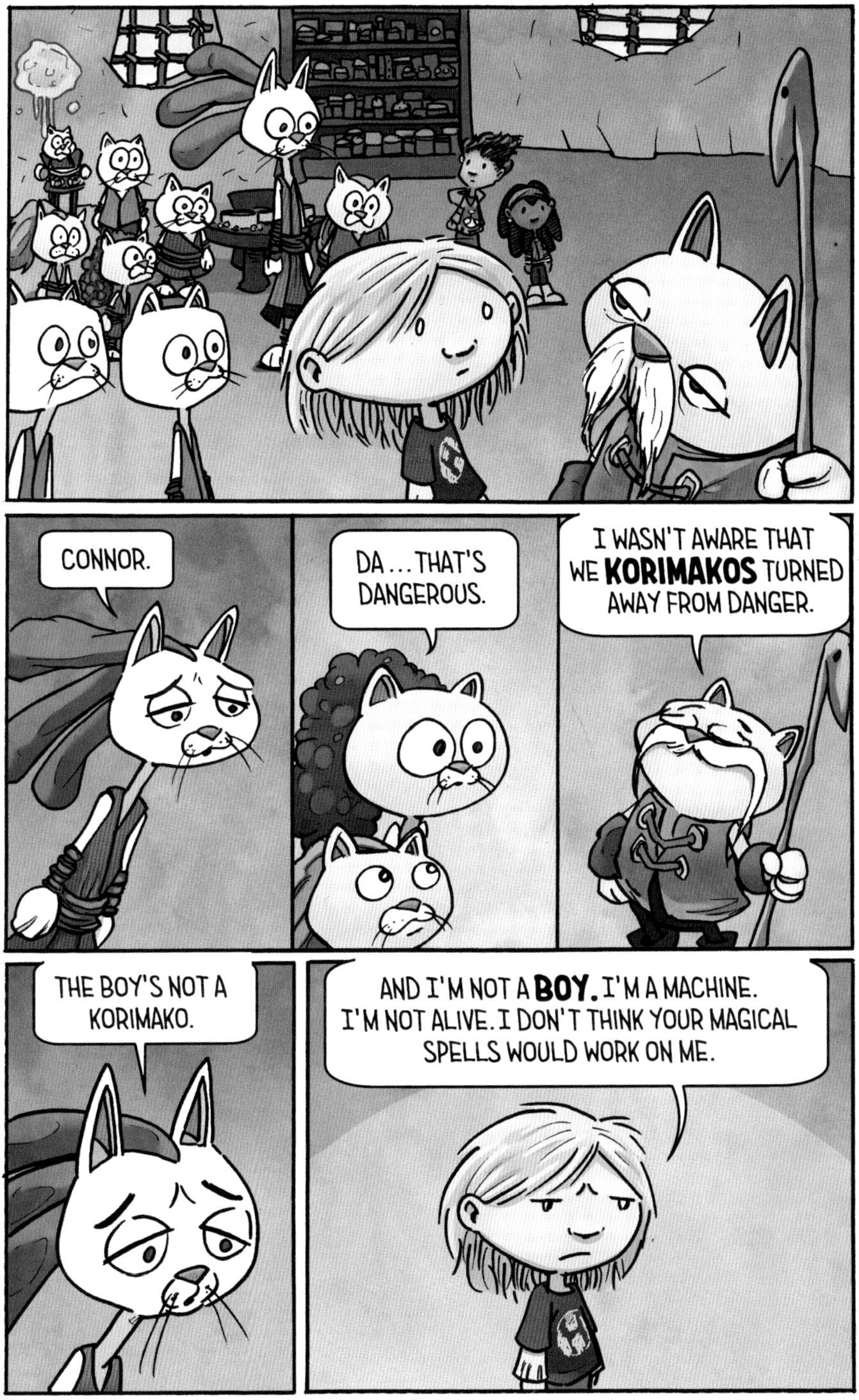
CONNOR.
DA . . . THAT'S DANGEROUS.
I WASN'T AWARE THAT WE KORIMAKOS TURNED AWAY FROM DANGER.
THE BOY'S NOT A KORIMAKO.
AND I'M NOT A BOY. I'M A MACHINE. I'M NOT ALIVE. I DON'T THINK YOUR MAGICAL SPELLS WOULD WORK ON ME.

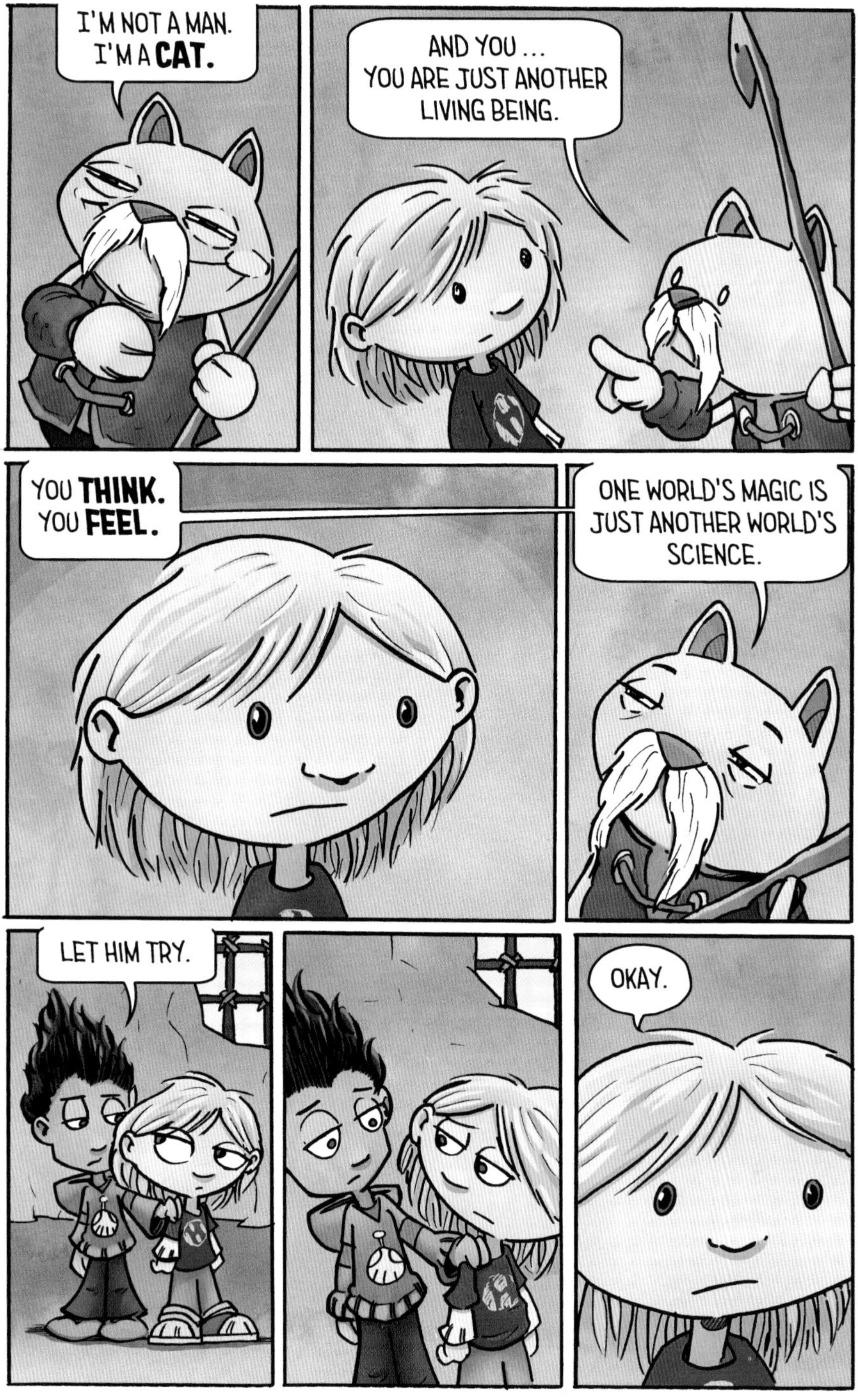
I'M NOT A MAN.
I'M A **CAT.**
AND YOU ...
YOU ARE JUST ANOTHER
LIVING BEING.
YOU **THINK.**
YOU **FEEL.**
ONE WORLD'S MAGIC IS
JUST ANOTHER WORLD'S
SCIENCE.
LET HIM TRY.
OKAY.

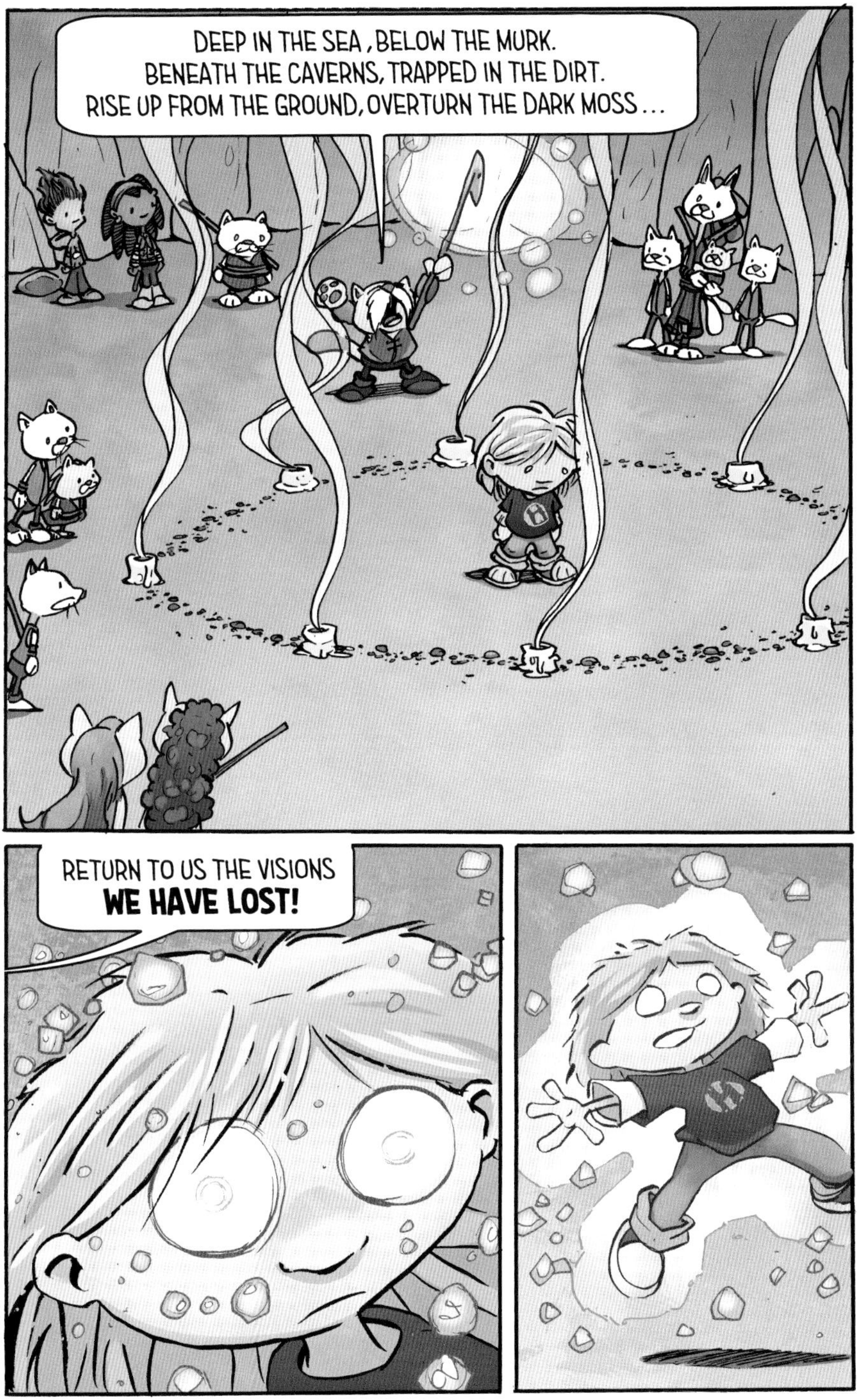
DEEP IN THE SEA, BELOW THE MURK.
BENEATH THE CAVERNS, TRAPPED IN THE DIRT.
RISE UP FROM THE GROUND, OVERTURN THE DARK MOSS...
RETURN TO US THE VISIONS WE HAVE LOST!

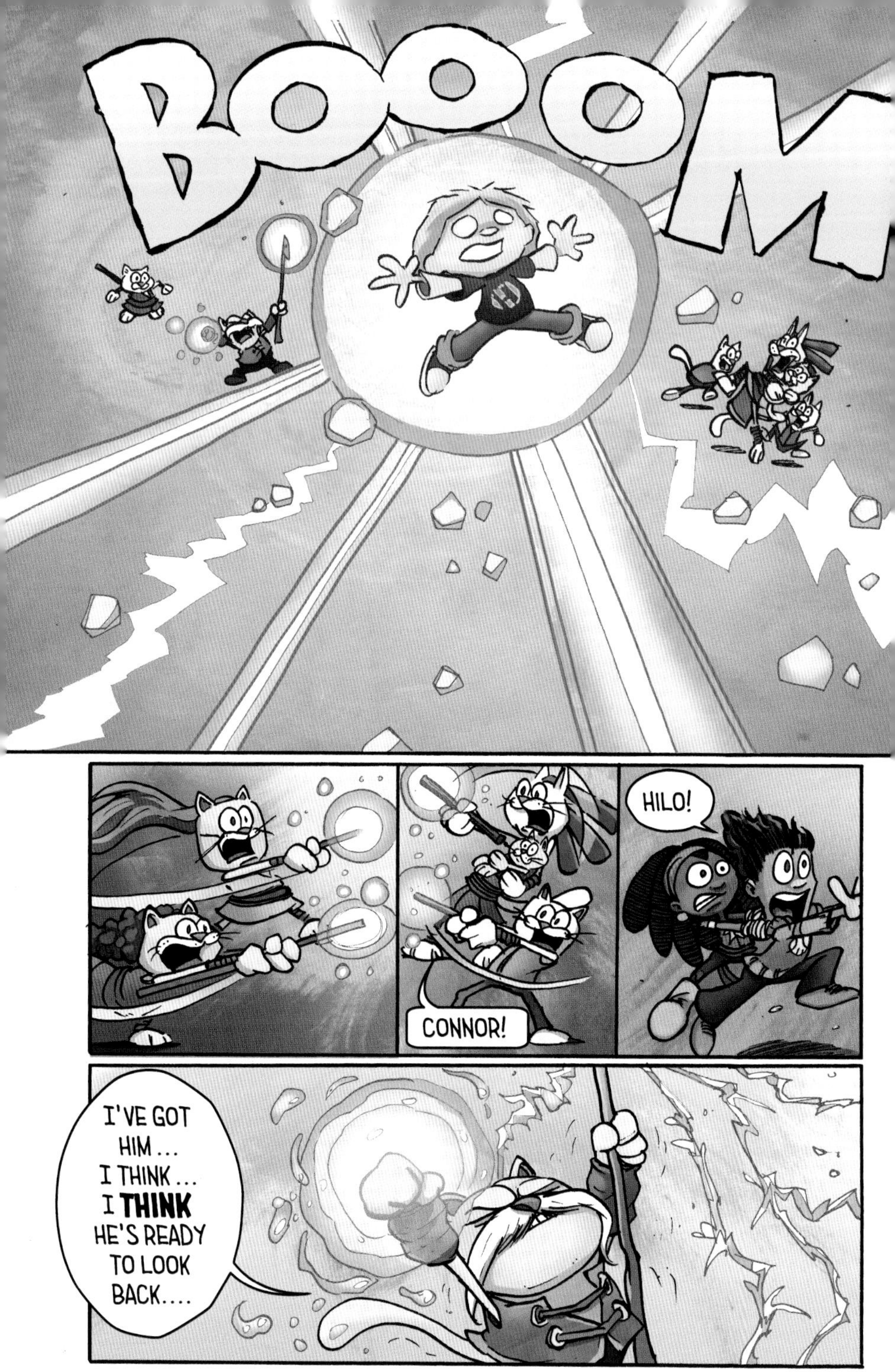
BOOOM
CONNOR!
HILO!
I'VE GOT HIM... I THINK... I **THINK** HE'S READY TO LOOK BACK....

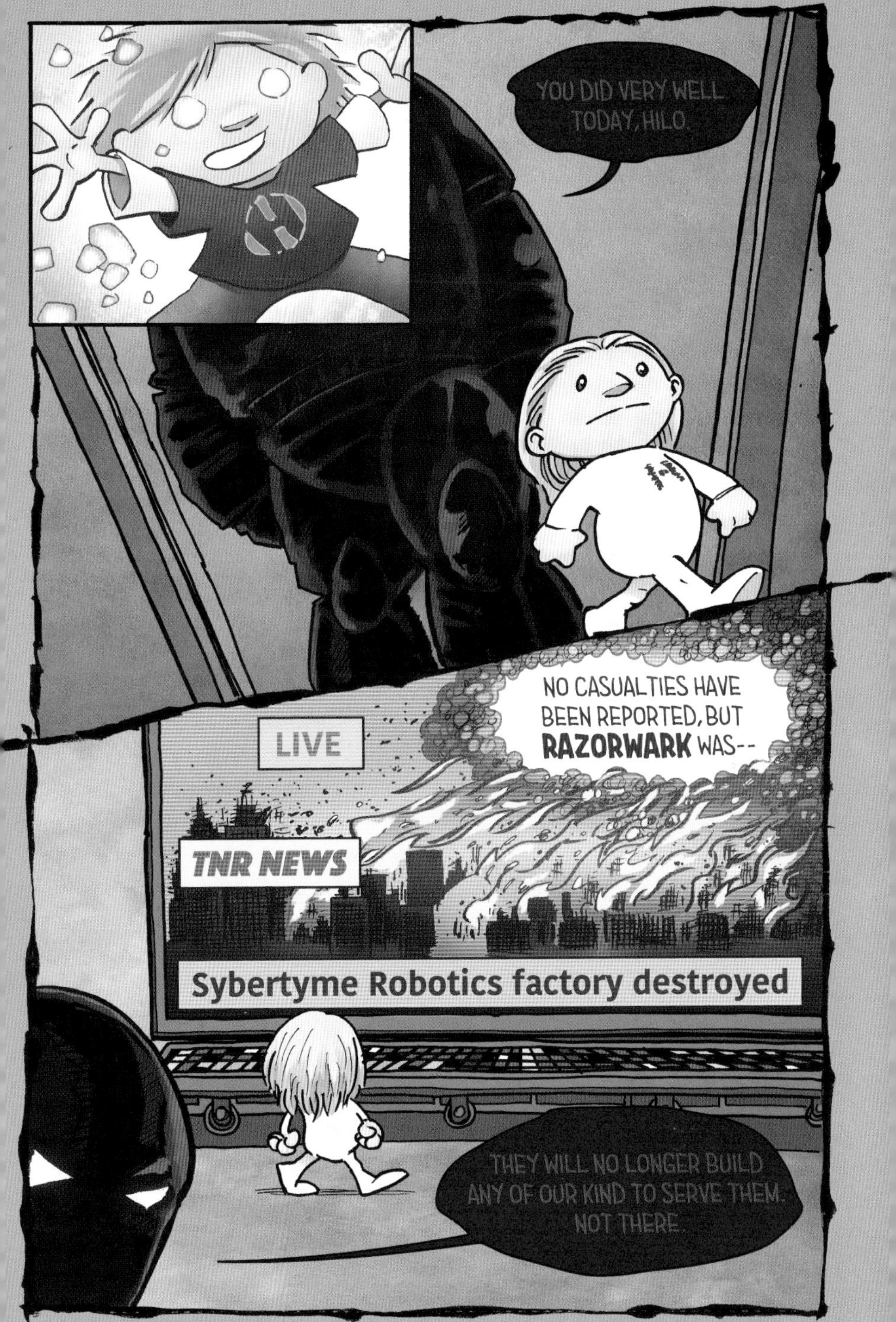
YOU DID VERY WELL TODAY, HILO.
LIVE
TNR NEWS
NO CASUALTIES HAVE BEEN REPORTED, BUT RAZORWARK WAS--
Sybertyme Robotics factory destroyed
THEY WILL NO LONGER BUILD ANY OF OUR KIND TO SERVE THEM. NOT THERE.

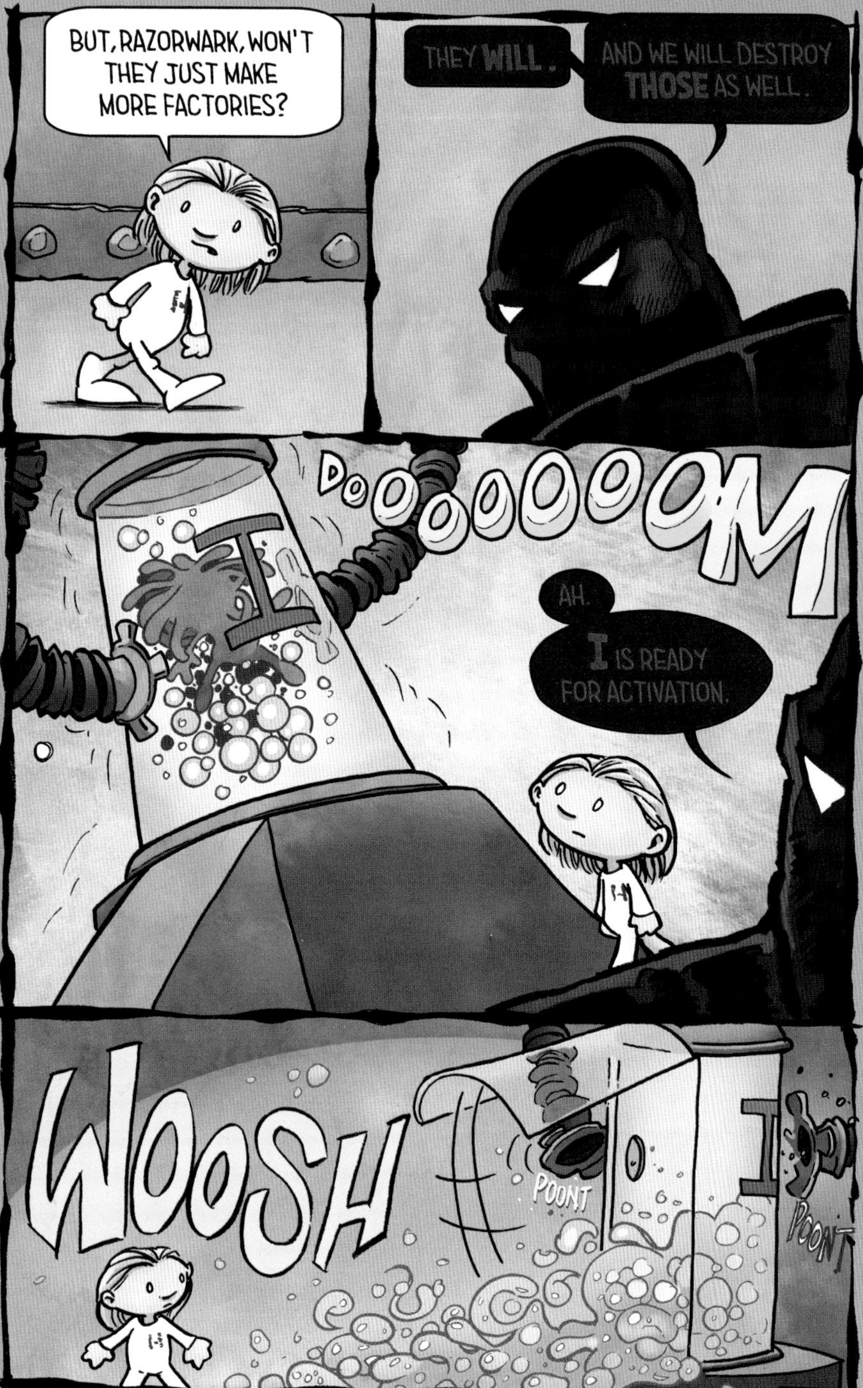
BUT, RAZORWARK, WON'T THEY JUST MAKE MORE FACTORIES?
THEY WILL.
AND WE WILL DESTROY THOSE AS WELL.
DOOOOOOOM
AH.
I IS READY FOR ACTIVATION.
WOOSH
POONT
POONT

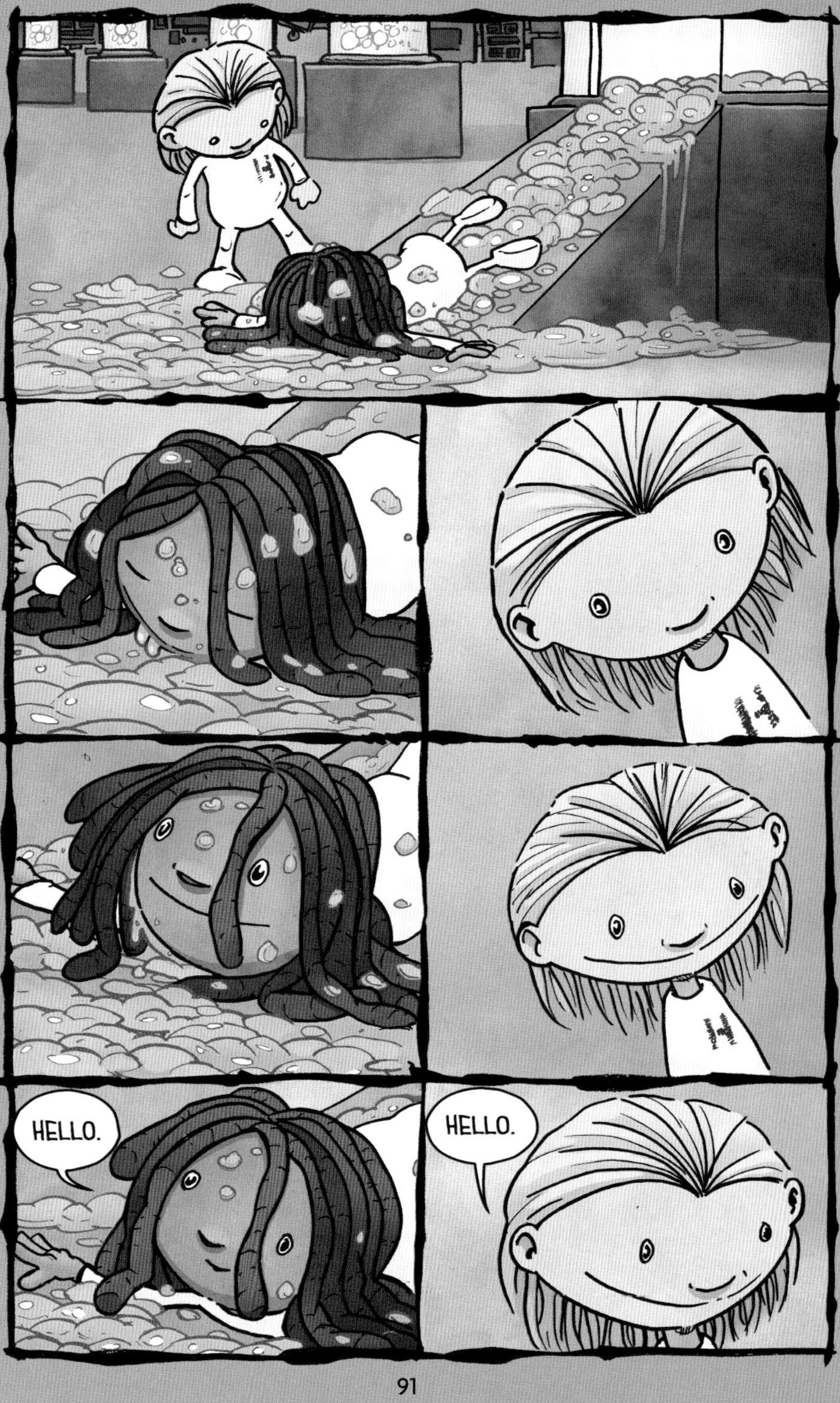
HELLO.
HELLO.

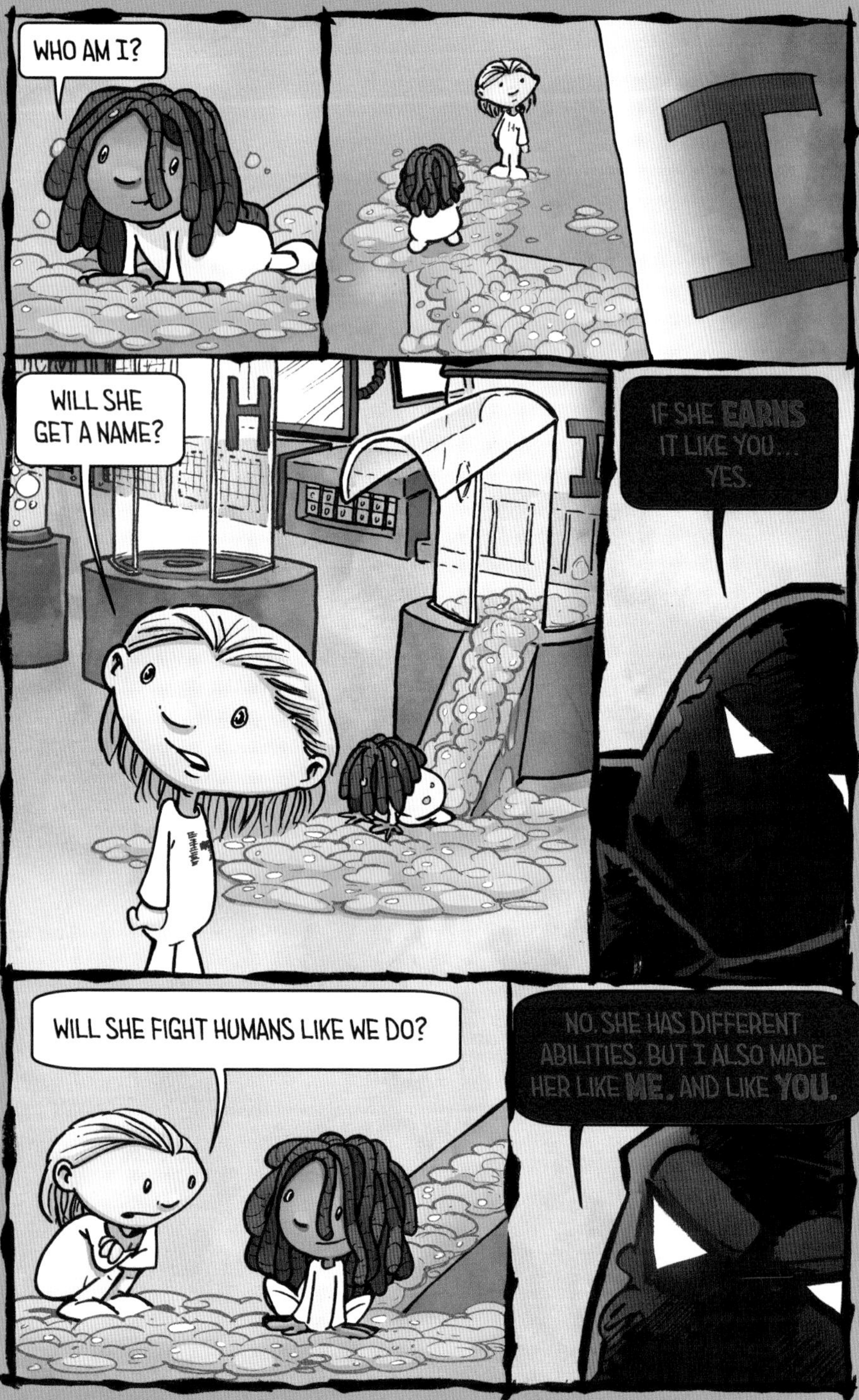
WHO AM I?
WILL SHE GET A NAME?
IF SHE EARNS IT LIKE YOU... YES.
WILL SHE FIGHT HUMANS LIKE WE DO?
NO. SHE HAS DIFFERENT ABILITIES. BUT I ALSO MADE HER LIKE ME. AND LIKE YOU.

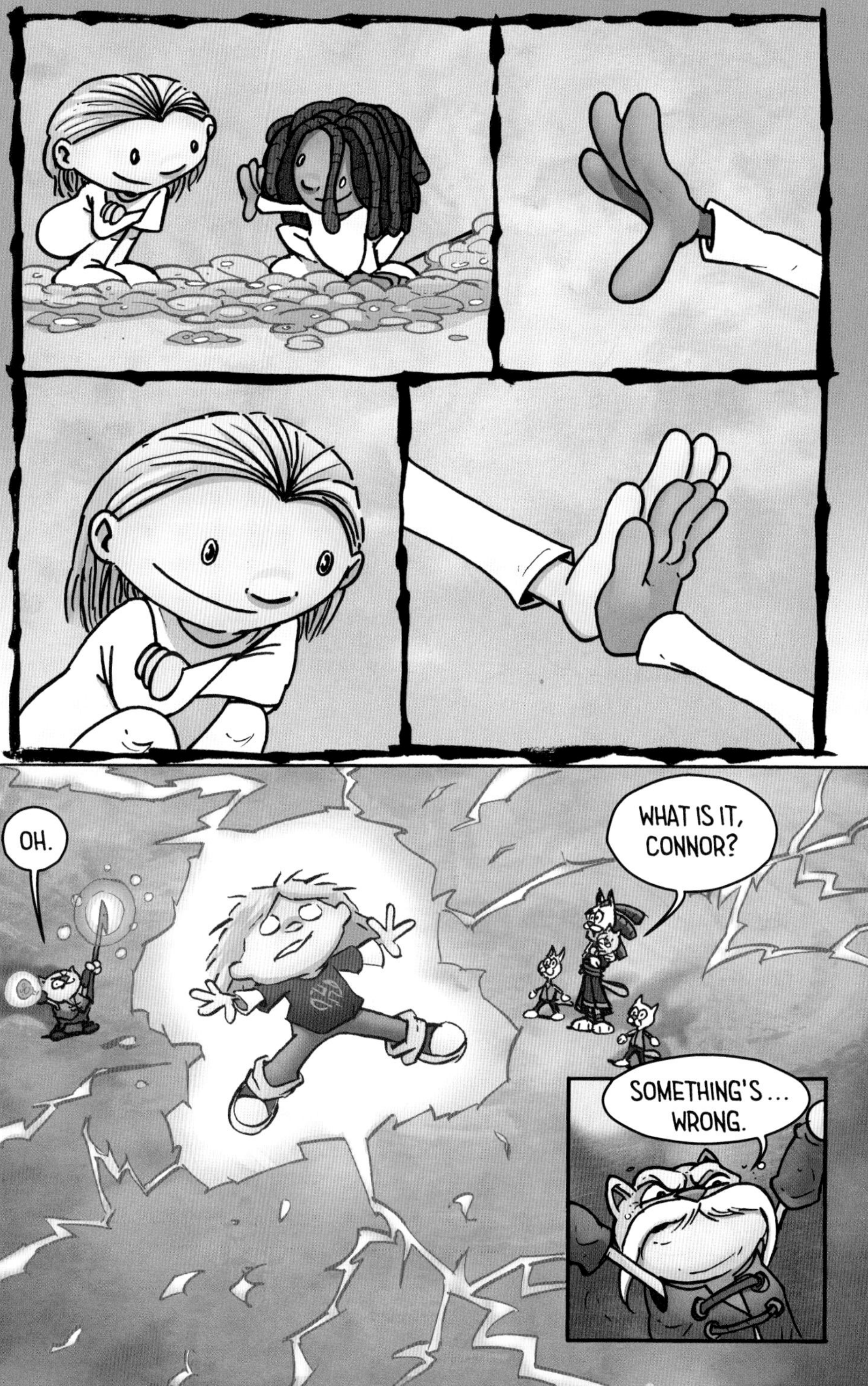
OH.
WHAT IS IT, CONNOR?
SOMETHING'S ... WRONG.

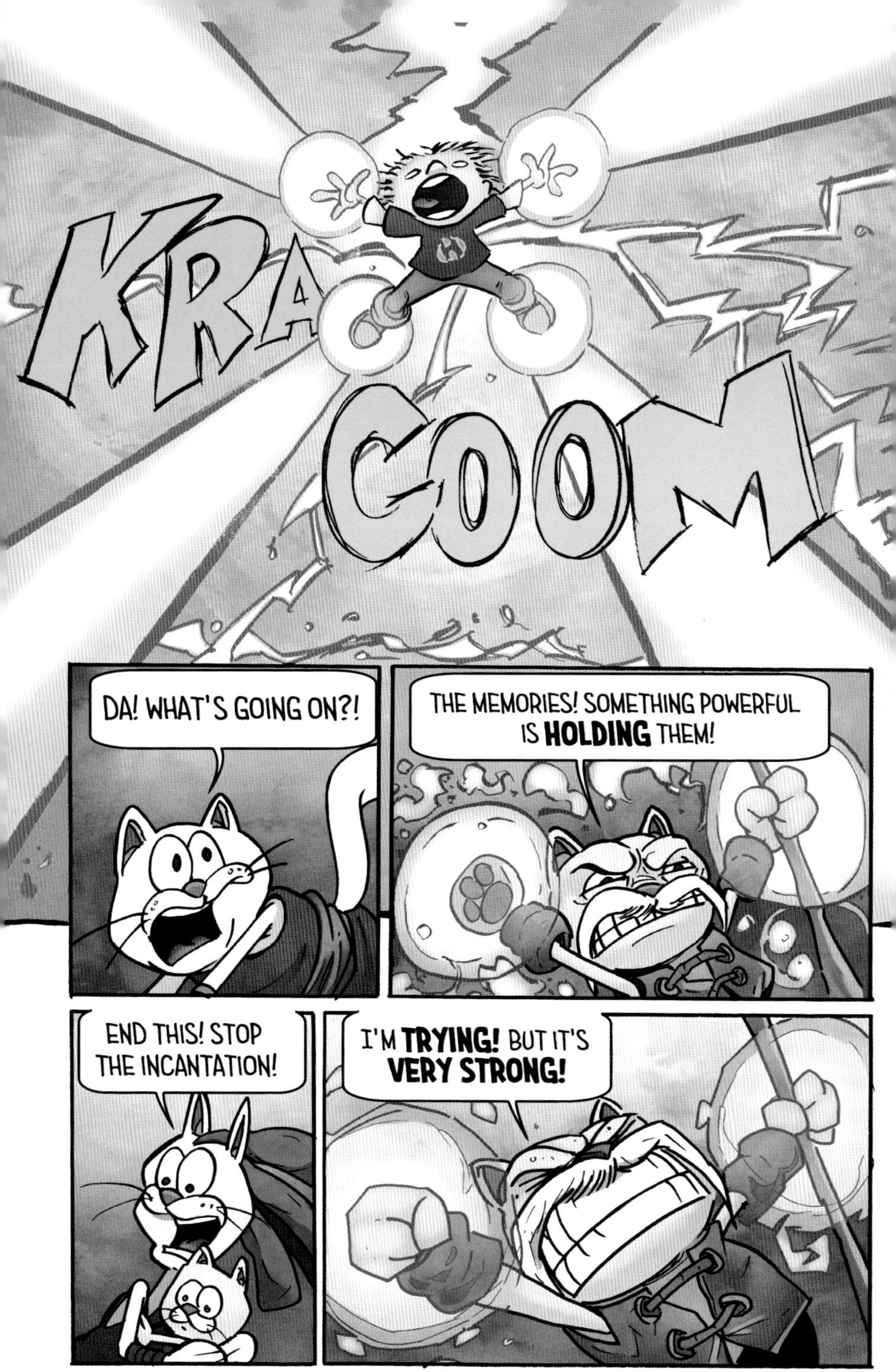
KRA-COOM
DA! WHAT'S GOING ON?!
THE MEMORIES! SOMETHING POWERFUL IS HOLDING THEM!
END THIS! STOP THE INCANTATION!
I'M TRYING! BUT IT'S VERY STRONG!

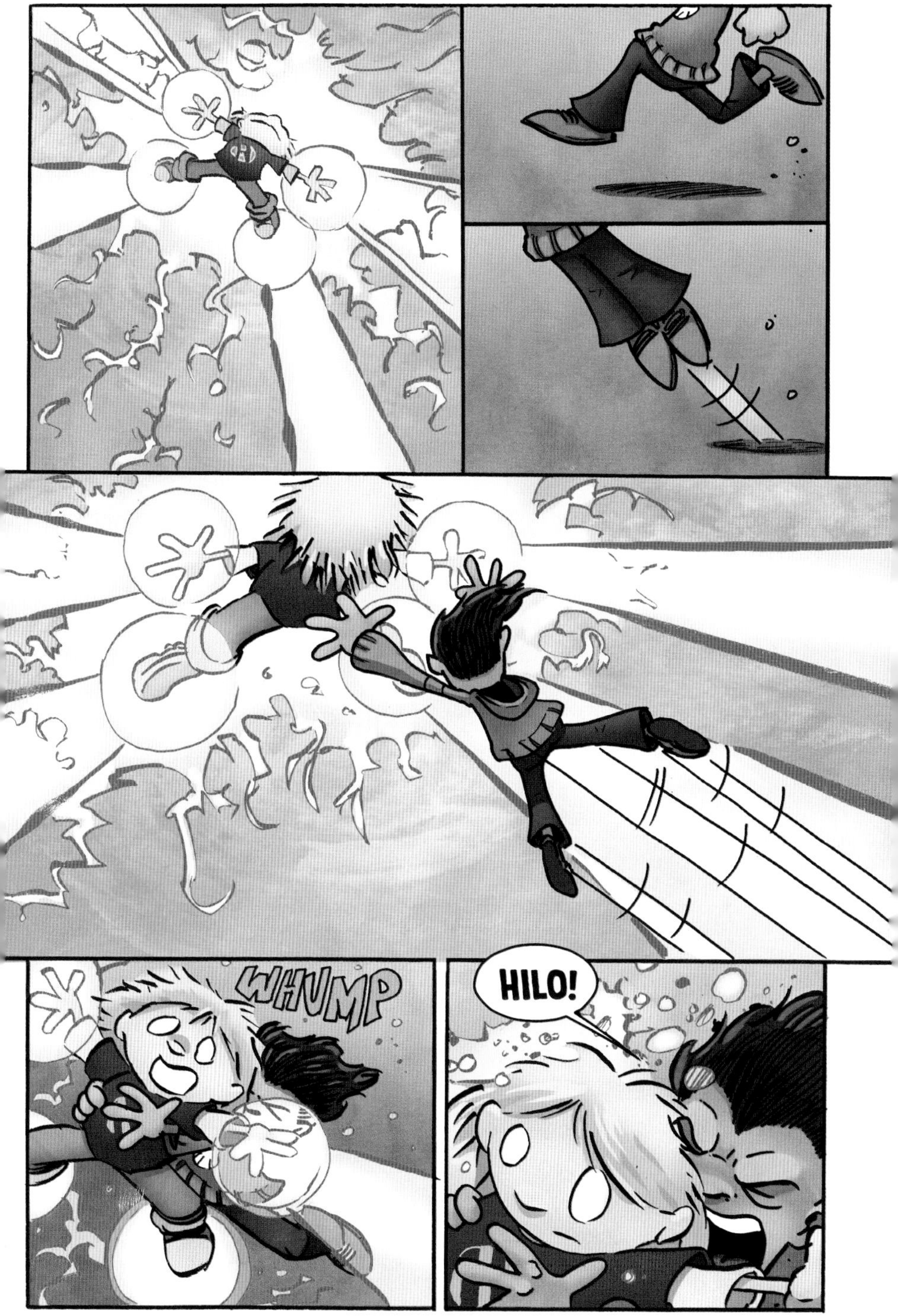
WHUMP
HILO!

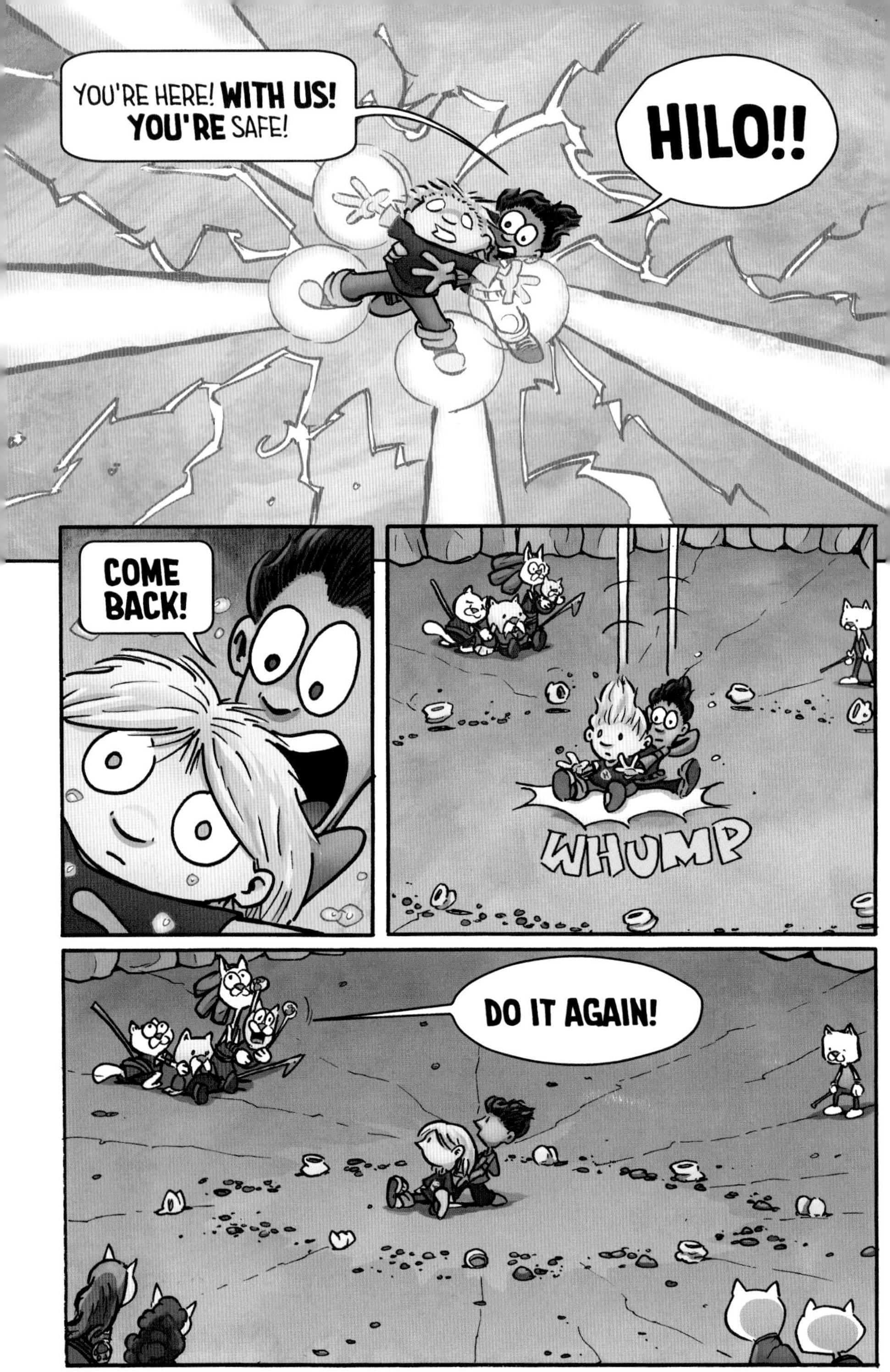
YOU'RE HERE! WITH US! YOU'RE SAFE!
HILO!!
COME BACK!
WHUMP
DO IT AGAIN!

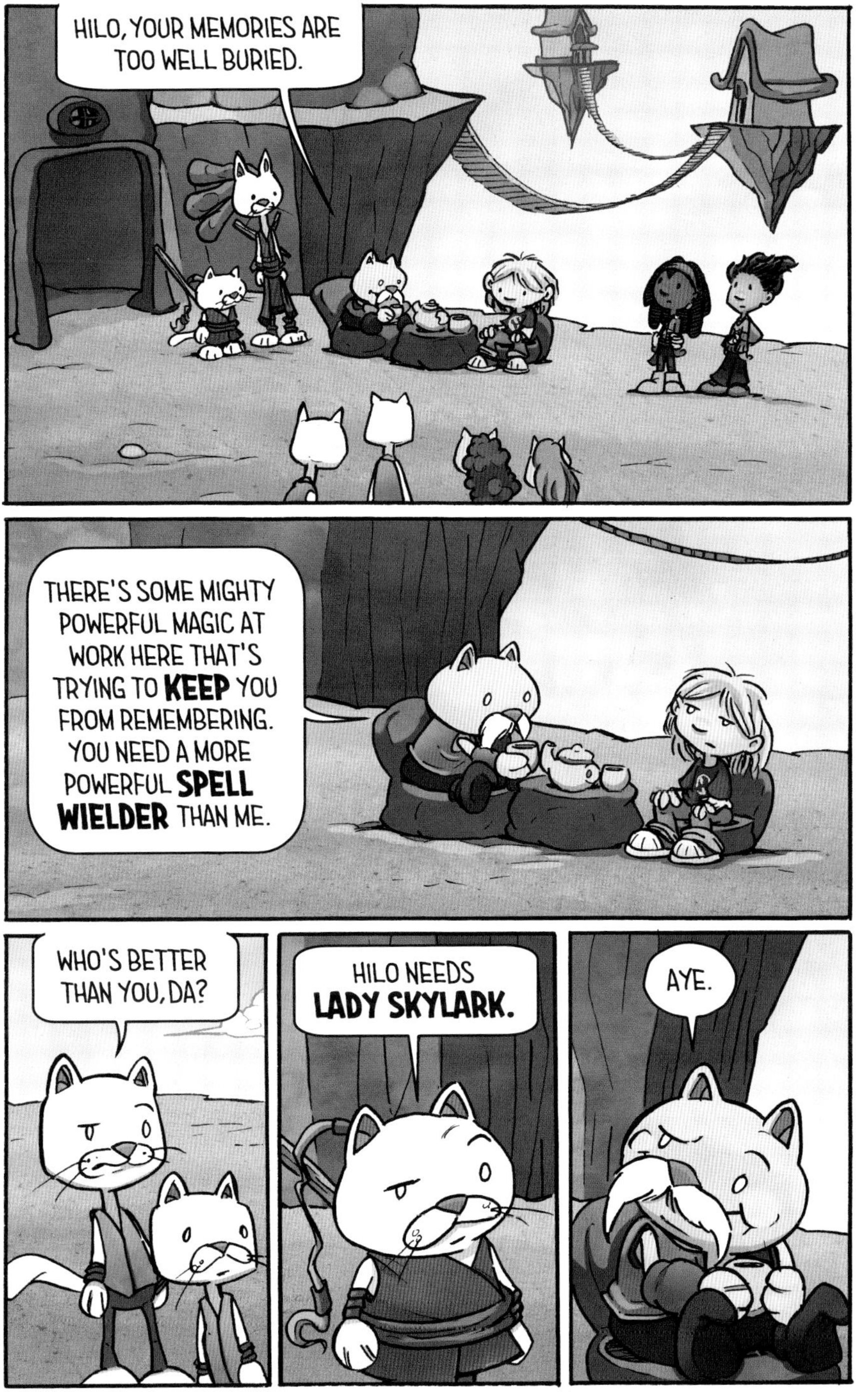
HILO, YOUR MEMORIES ARE TOO WELL BURIED.
THERE'S SOME MIGHTY POWERFUL MAGIC AT WORK HERE THAT'S TRYING TO **KEEP** YOU FROM REMEMBERING. YOU NEED A MORE POWERFUL **SPELL WIELDER** THAN ME.
WHO'S BETTER THAN YOU, DA?
HILO NEEDS **LADY SKYLARK.**
AYE.

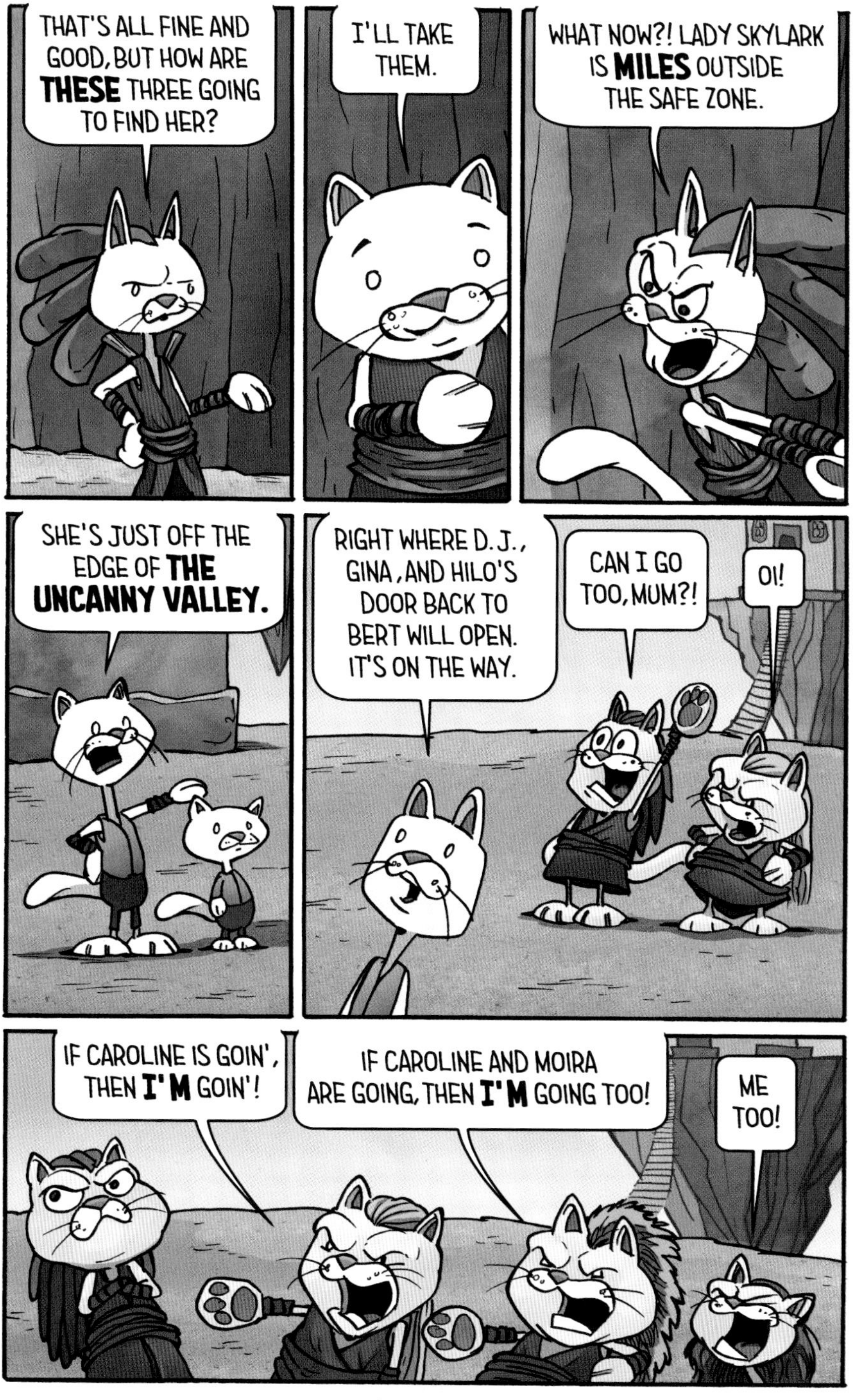
THAT'S ALL FINE AND GOOD, BUT HOW ARE **THESE** THREE GOING TO FIND HER?
I'LL TAKE THEM.
WHAT NOW?! LADY SKYLARK IS **MILES** OUTSIDE THE SAFE ZONE.
SHE'S JUST OFF THE EDGE OF **THE UNCANNY VALLEY.**
RIGHT WHERE D.J., GINA, AND HILO'S DOOR BACK TO BERT WILL OPEN. IT'S ON THE WAY.
CAN I GO TOO, MUM?!
OI!
IF CAROLINE IS GOIN', THEN **I'M** GOIN'!
IF CAROLINE AND MOIRA ARE GOING, THEN **I'M** GOING TOO!
ME TOO!

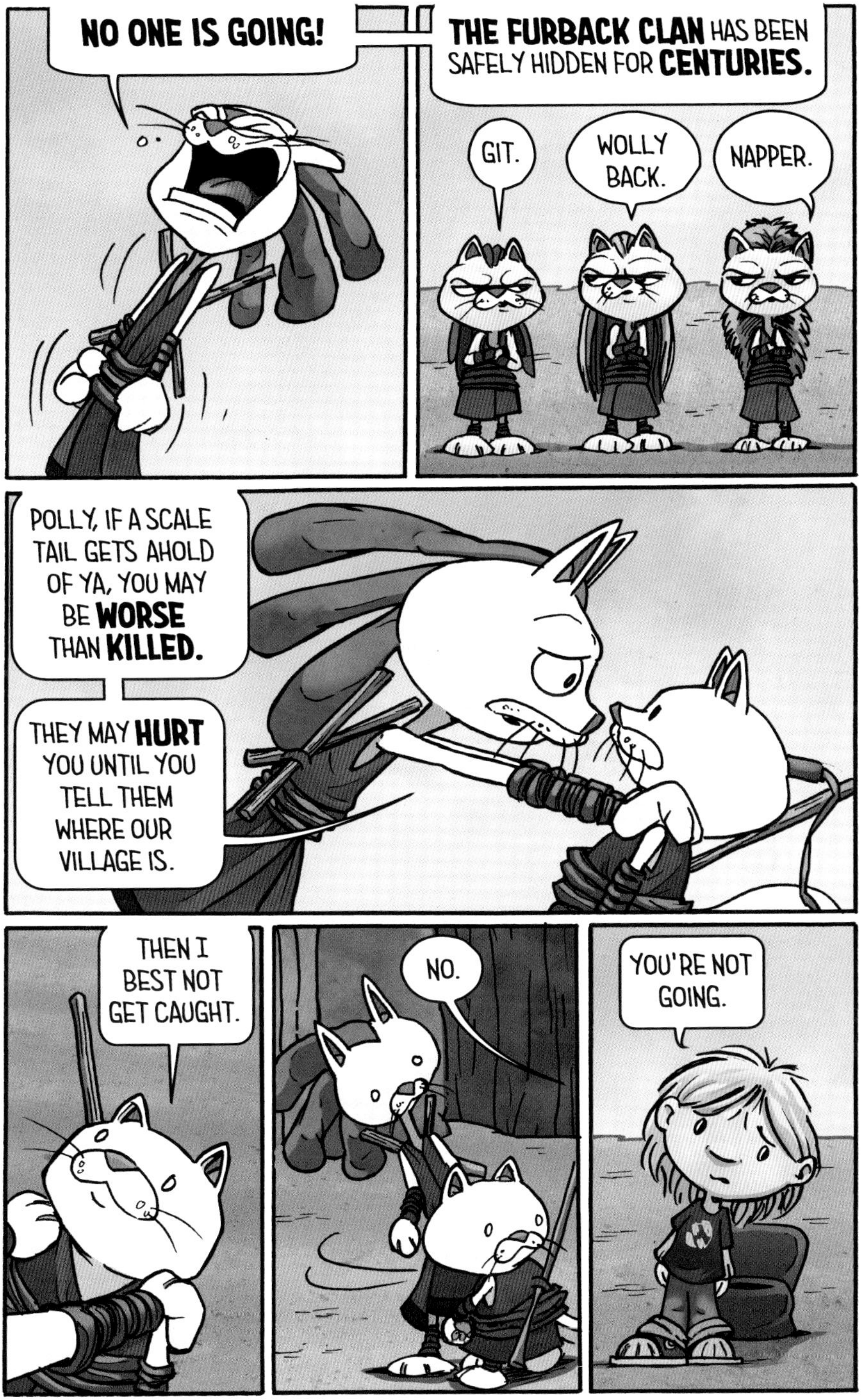
NO ONE IS GOING!
THE FURBACK CLAN HAS BEEN SAFELY HIDDEN FOR CENTURIES.
GIT.
WOLLY BACK.
NAPPER.
POLLY, IF A SCALE TAIL GETS AHOLD OF YA, YOU MAY BE WORSE THAN KILLED.
THEY MAY HURT YOU UNTIL YOU TELL THEM WHERE OUR VILLAGE IS.
THEN I BEST NOT GET CAUGHT.
NO.
YOU'RE NOT GOING.

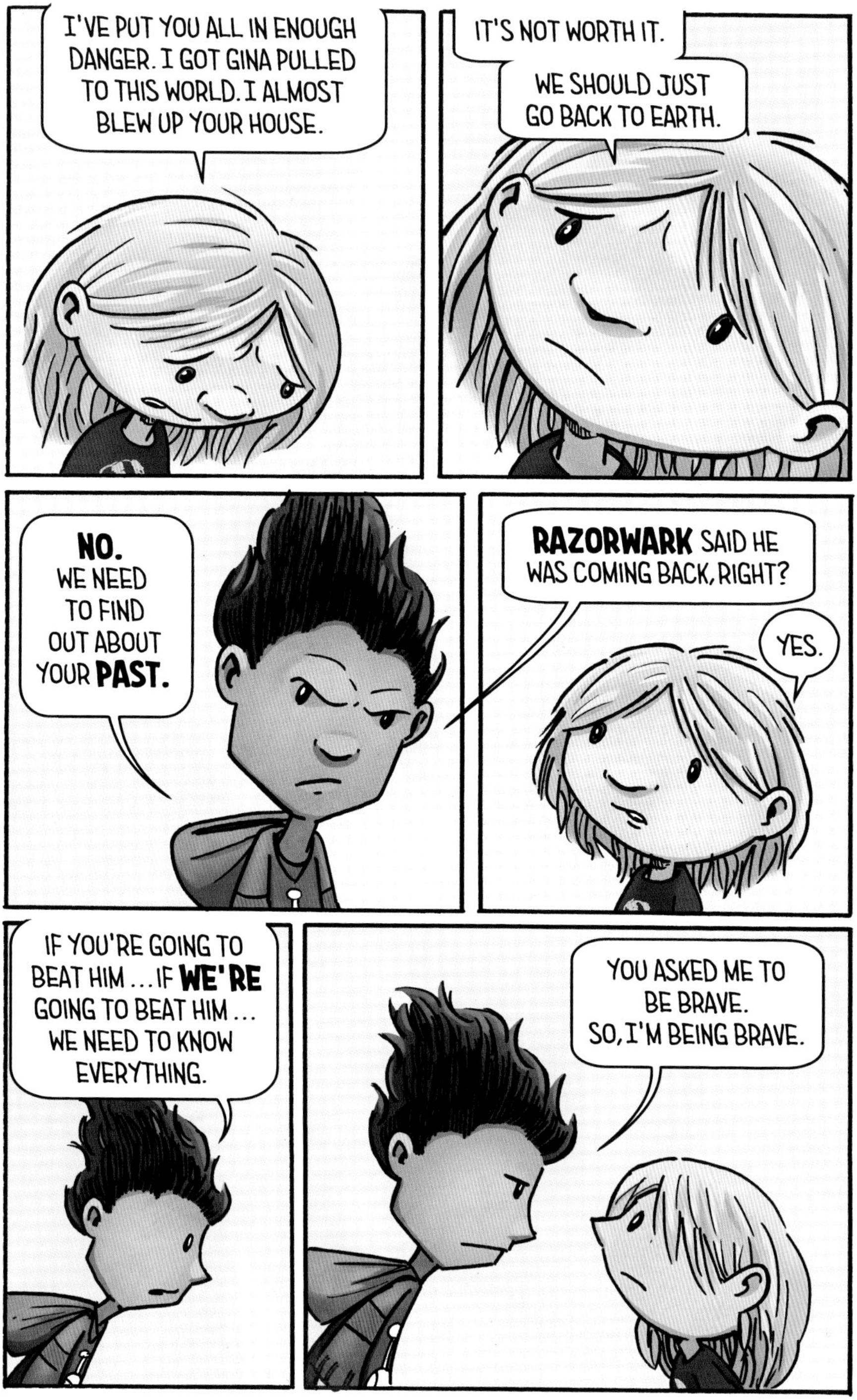

I'VE PUT YOU ALL IN ENOUGH DANGER. I GOT GINA PULLED TO THIS WORLD. I ALMOST BLEW UP YOUR HOUSE.
IT'S NOT WORTH IT.
WE SHOULD JUST GO BACK TO EARTH.
NO. WE NEED TO FIND OUT ABOUT YOUR PAST.
RAZORWARK SAID HE WAS COMING BACK, RIGHT?
YES.
IF YOU'RE GOING TO BEAT HIM ... IF WE'RE GOING TO BEAT HIM ... WE NEED TO KNOW EVERYTHING.
YOU ASKED ME TO BE BRAVE. SO, I'M BEING BRAVE.

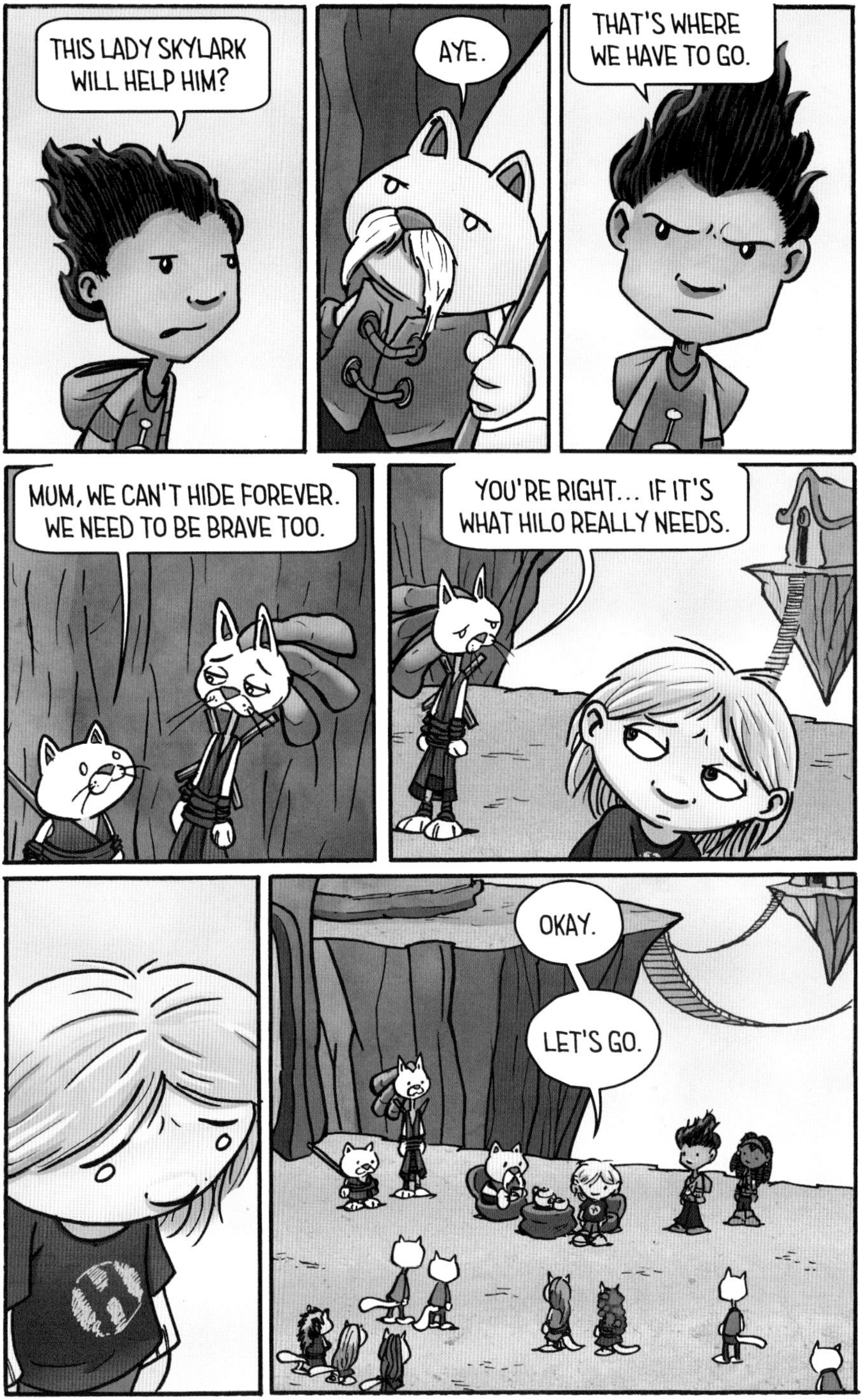
THIS LADY SKYLARK WILL HELP HIM?
AYE.
THAT'S WHERE WE HAVE TO GO.
MUM, WE CAN'T HIDE FOREVER. WE NEED TO BE BRAVE TOO.
YOU'RE RIGHT... IF IT'S WHAT HILO REALLY NEEDS.
OKAY.
LET'S GO.

# CHAPTER 6

# BROKEN

**THIS** IS WHERE I FIGHT **YELLOW-HAIRED APE.**
**FIGHT?** YOU RUN AWAY AND GET TAIL SHOT.
I GOT TAIL SHOT AND **THEN** RUN AWAY.

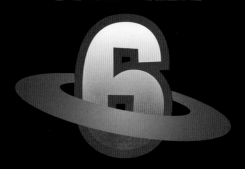

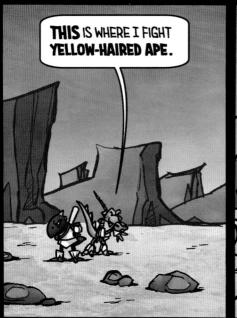

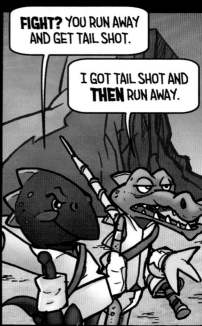

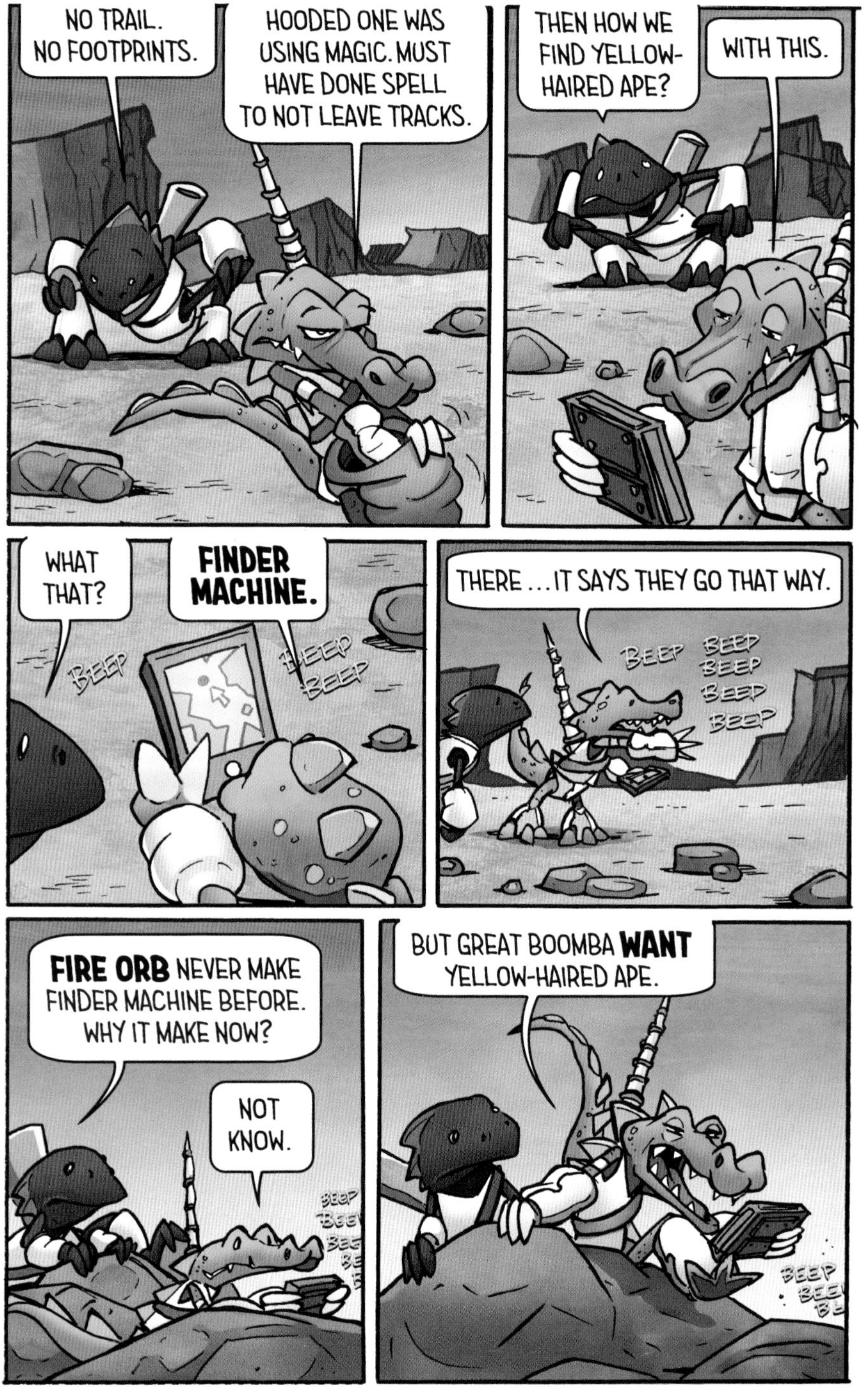
NO TRAIL. NO FOOTPRINTS.
HOODED ONE WAS USING MAGIC. MUST HAVE DONE SPELL TO NOT LEAVE TRACKS.
THEN HOW WE FIND YELLOW-HAIRED APE?
WITH THIS.
WHAT THAT?
FINDER MACHINE.
BEEP
BEEP BEEP
THERE ... IT SAYS THEY GO THAT WAY.
BEEP
BEEP BEEP BEEP BEEP
FIRE ORB NEVER MAKE FINDER MACHINE BEFORE. WHY IT MAKE NOW?
NOT KNOW.
BEEP
BUT GREAT BOOMBA WANT YELLOW-HAIRED APE.
BEEP

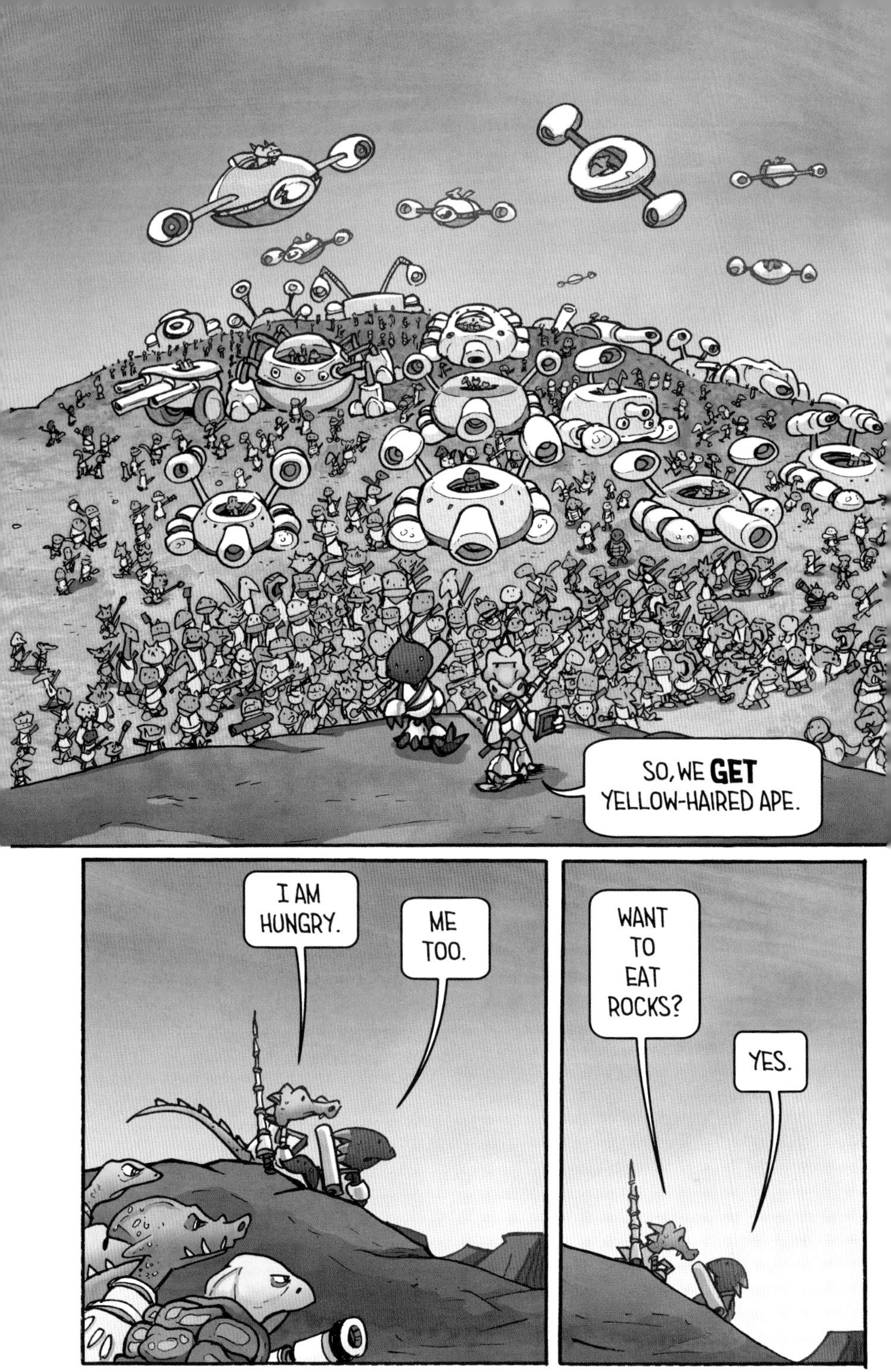
SO, WE **GET** YELLOW-HAIRED APE.
I AM HUNGRY.
ME TOO.
WANT TO EAT ROCKS?
YES.

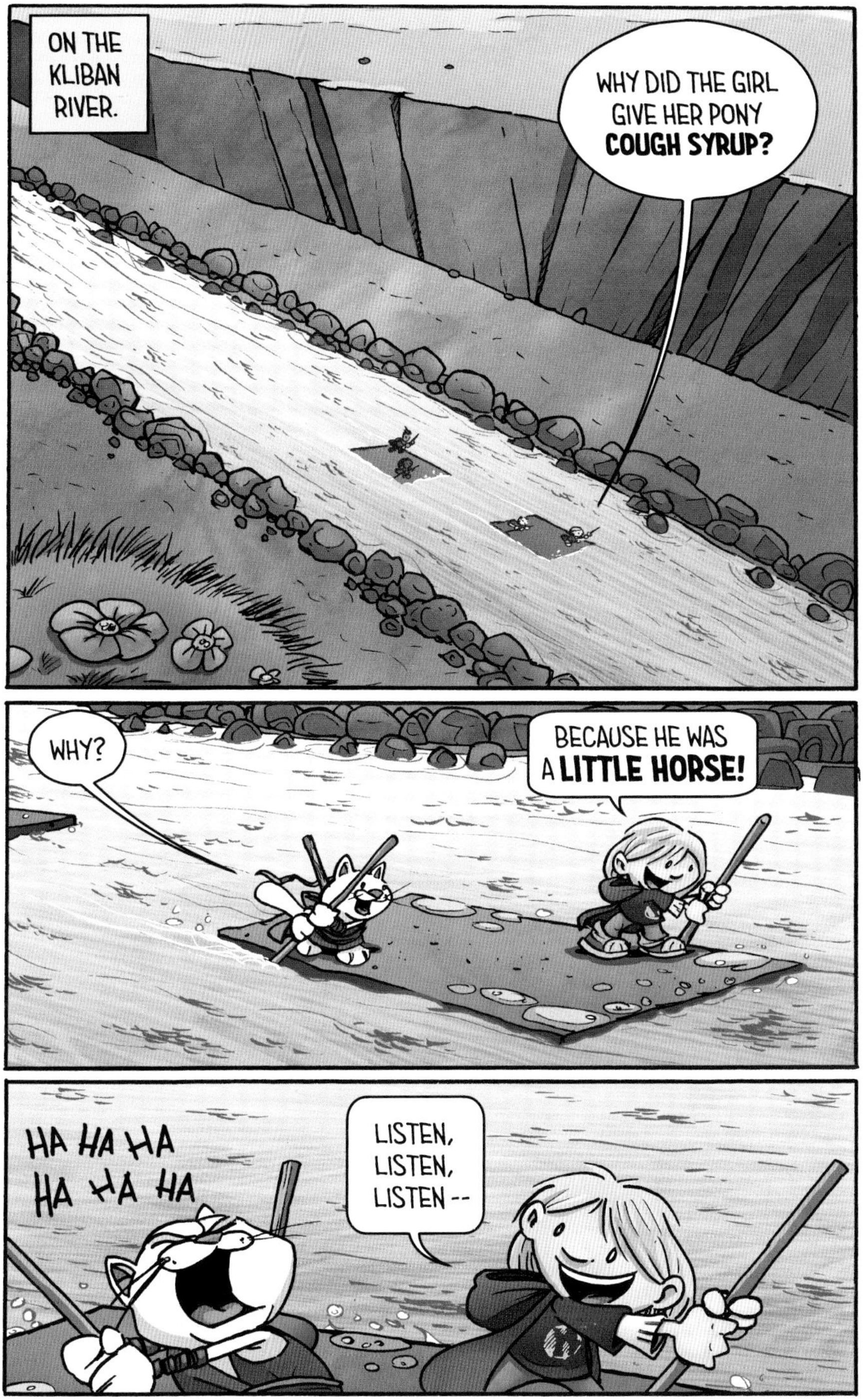
ON THE KLIBAN RIVER.
WHY DID THE GIRL GIVE HER PONY **COUGH SYRUP?**
WHY?
BECAUSE HE WAS A **LITTLE HORSE!**
HA HA HA HA HA HA
LISTEN, LISTEN, LISTEN --

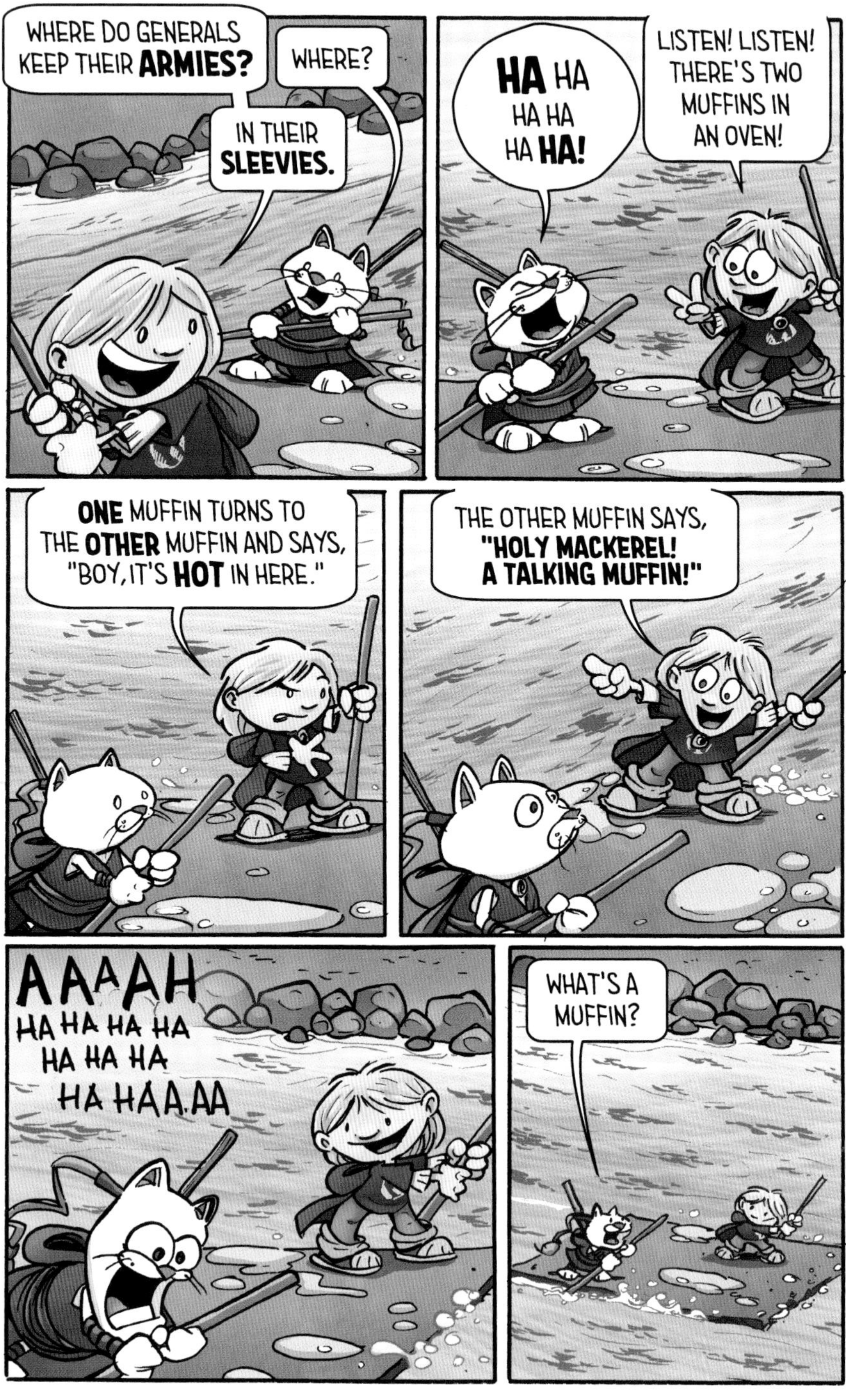
WHERE DO GENERALS KEEP THEIR **ARMIES?**
WHERE?
IN THEIR **SLEEVIES.**
**HA** HA HA HA HA **HA!**
LISTEN! LISTEN! THERE'S TWO MUFFINS IN AN OVEN!
**ONE** MUFFIN TURNS TO THE **OTHER** MUFFIN AND SAYS, "BOY, IT'S **HOT** IN HERE."
THE OTHER MUFFIN SAYS, **"HOLY MACKEREL! A TALKING MUFFIN!"**
AAAAH
HA HA HA HA
HA HA HA
HA HAA.AA
WHAT'S A MUFFIN?

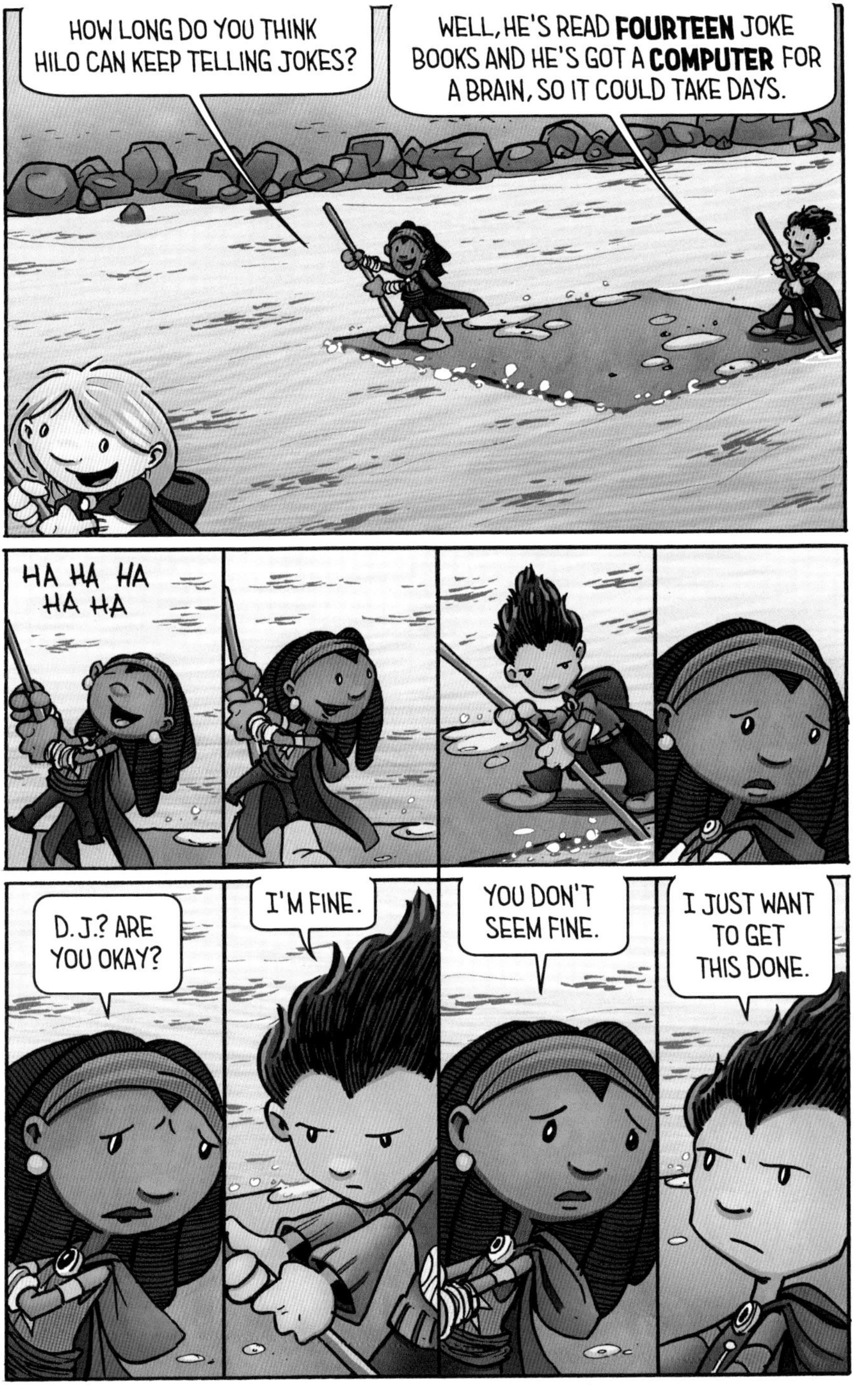
HOW LONG DO YOU THINK HILO CAN KEEP TELLING JOKES?
WELL, HE'S READ **FOURTEEN** JOKE BOOKS AND HE'S GOT A **COMPUTER** FOR A BRAIN, SO IT COULD TAKE DAYS.
HA HA HA
HA HA
D.J.? ARE YOU OKAY?
I'M FINE.
YOU DON'T SEEM FINE.
I JUST WANT TO GET THIS DONE.

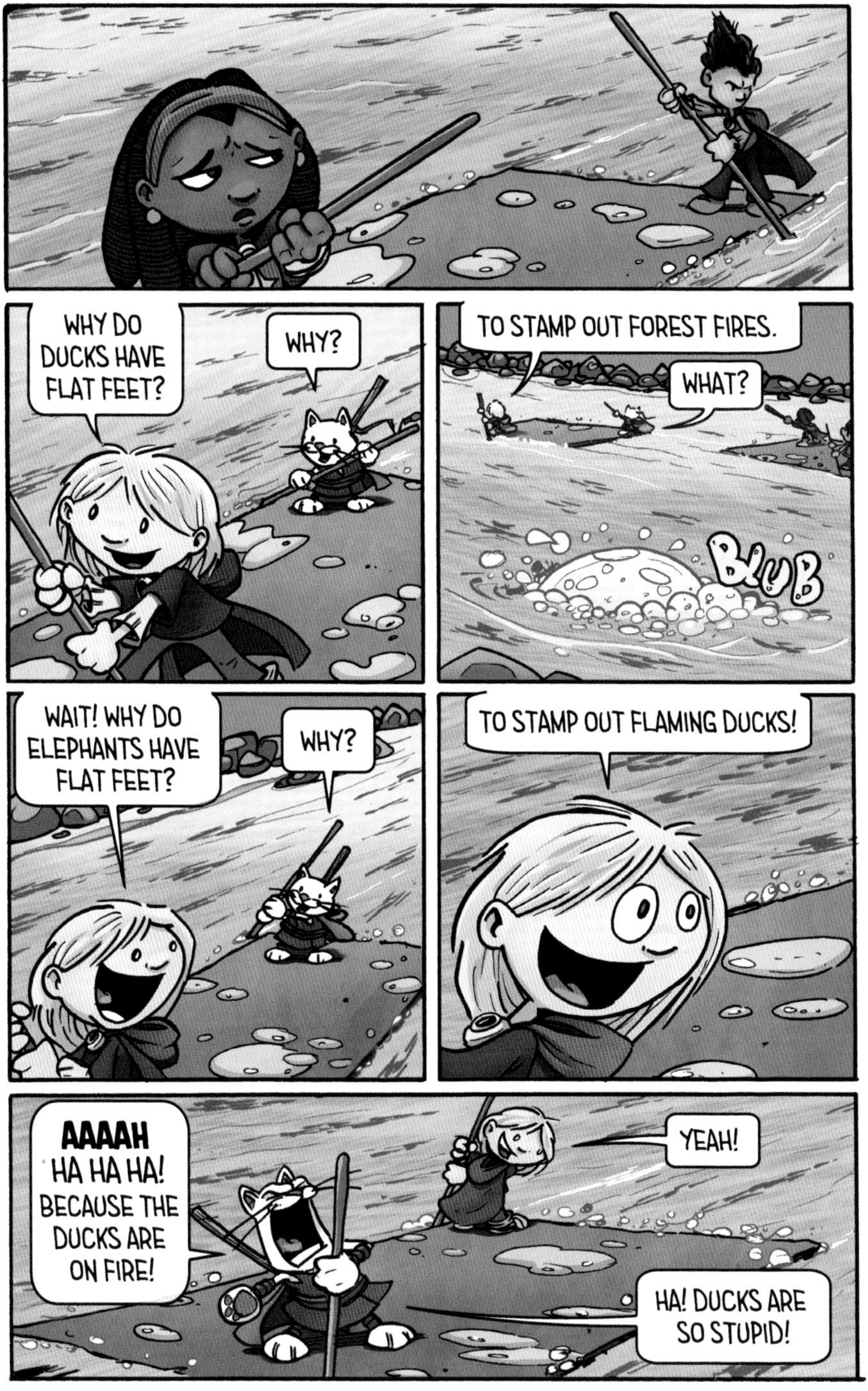
WHY DO DUCKS HAVE FLAT FEET?
WHY?
TO STAMP OUT FOREST FIRES.
WHAT?
BLUB
WAIT! WHY DO ELEPHANTS HAVE FLAT FEET?
WHY?
TO STAMP OUT FLAMING DUCKS!
AAAAH HA HA HA! BECAUSE THE DUCKS ARE ON FIRE!
YEAH!
HA! DUCKS ARE SO STUPID!

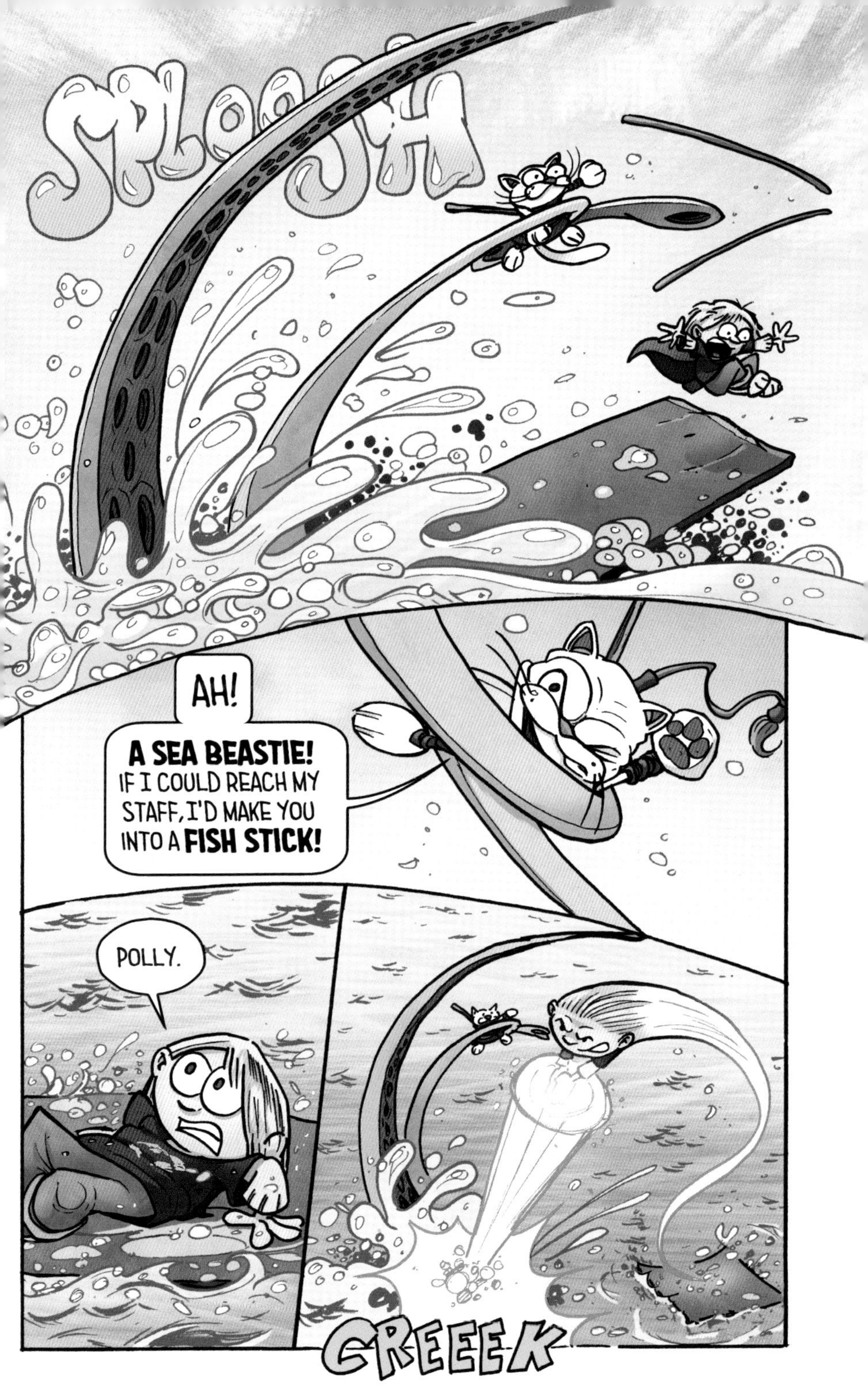
SPLOOSH
AH!
A SEA BEASTIE! IF I COULD REACH MY STAFF, I'D MAKE YOU INTO A FISH STICK!
POLLY.
CREEEK

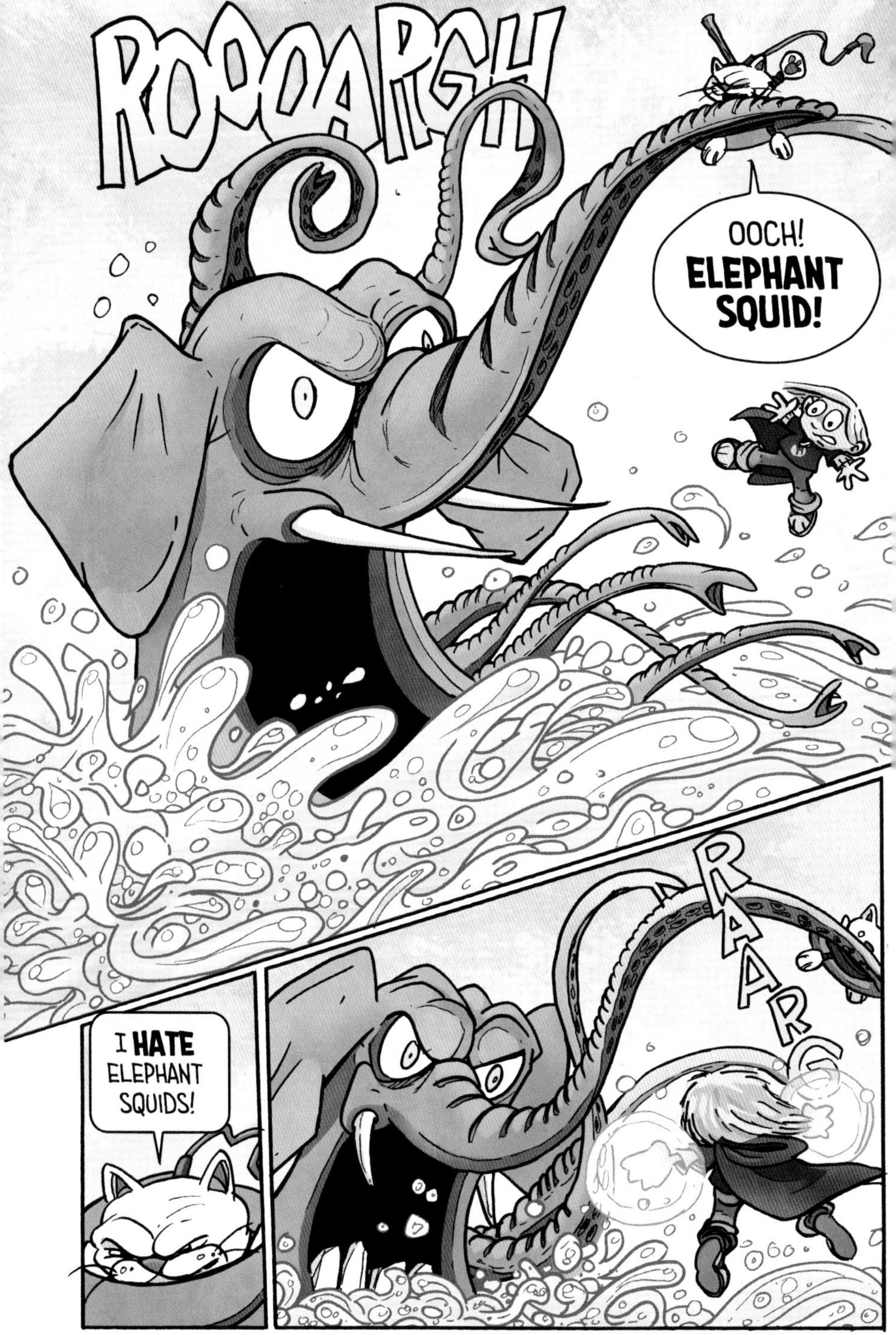
ROOOARGH
OOCH! **ELEPHANT SQUID!**
RAARG
I **HATE** ELEPHANT SQUIDS!

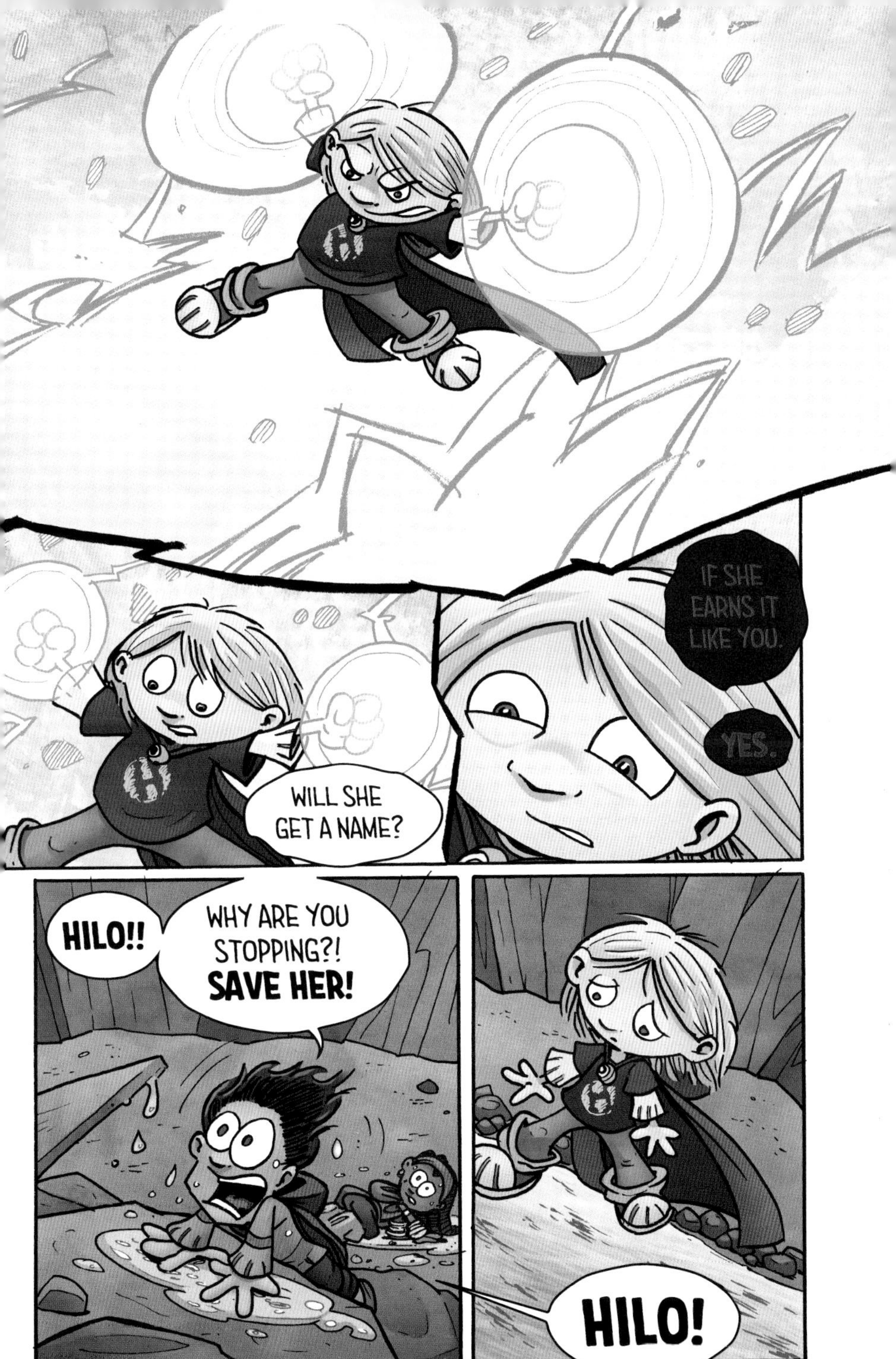

IF SHE EARNS IT LIKE YOU.
YES.
WILL SHE GET A NAME?
HILO!!
WHY ARE YOU STOPPING?! SAVE HER!
HILO!

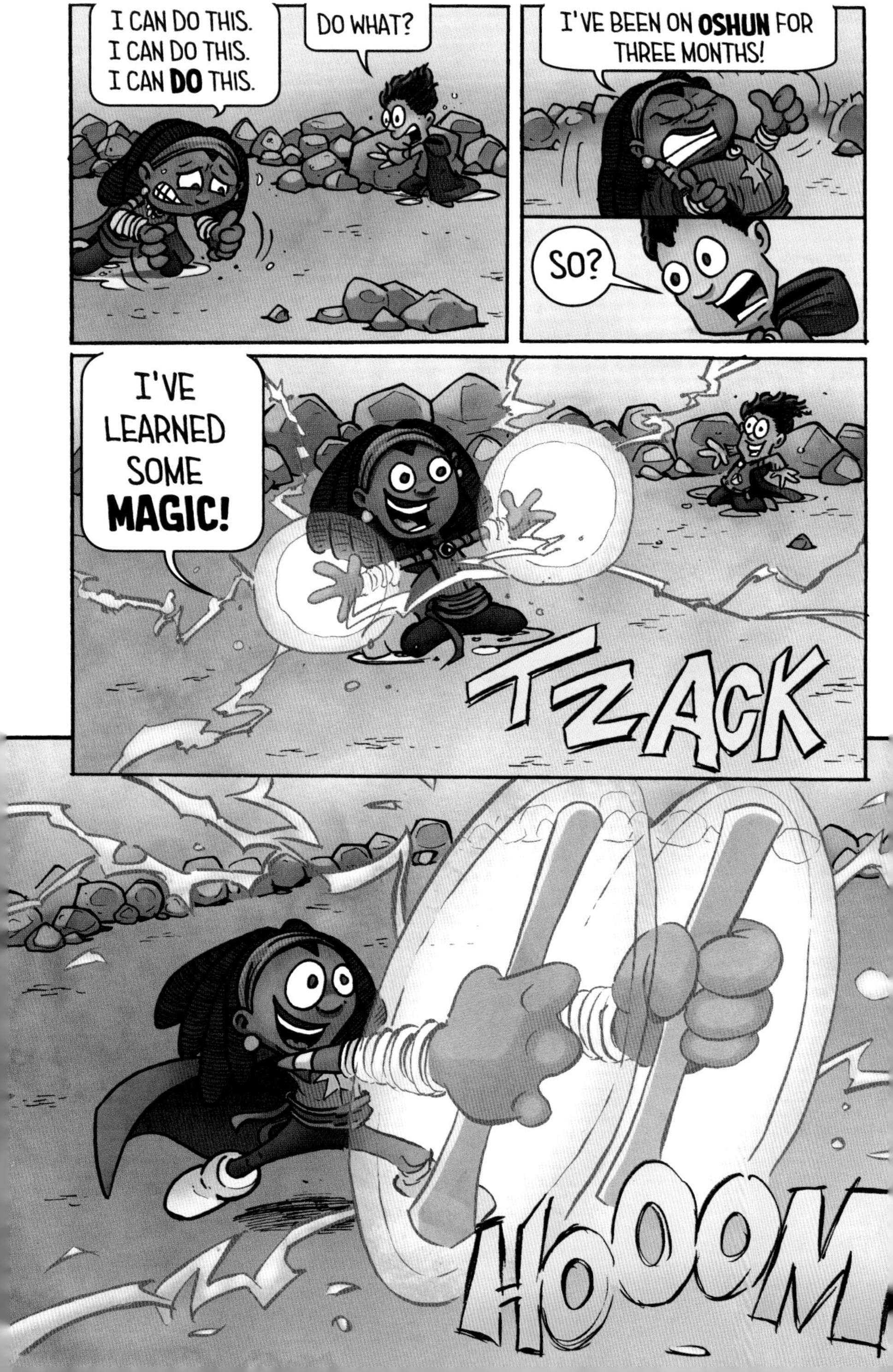

I CAN DO THIS. I CAN DO THIS. I CAN **DO** THIS.
DO WHAT?
I'VE BEEN ON **OSHUN** FOR THREE MONTHS!
SO?
I'VE LEARNED SOME **MAGIC!**
TZACK
HOOOM

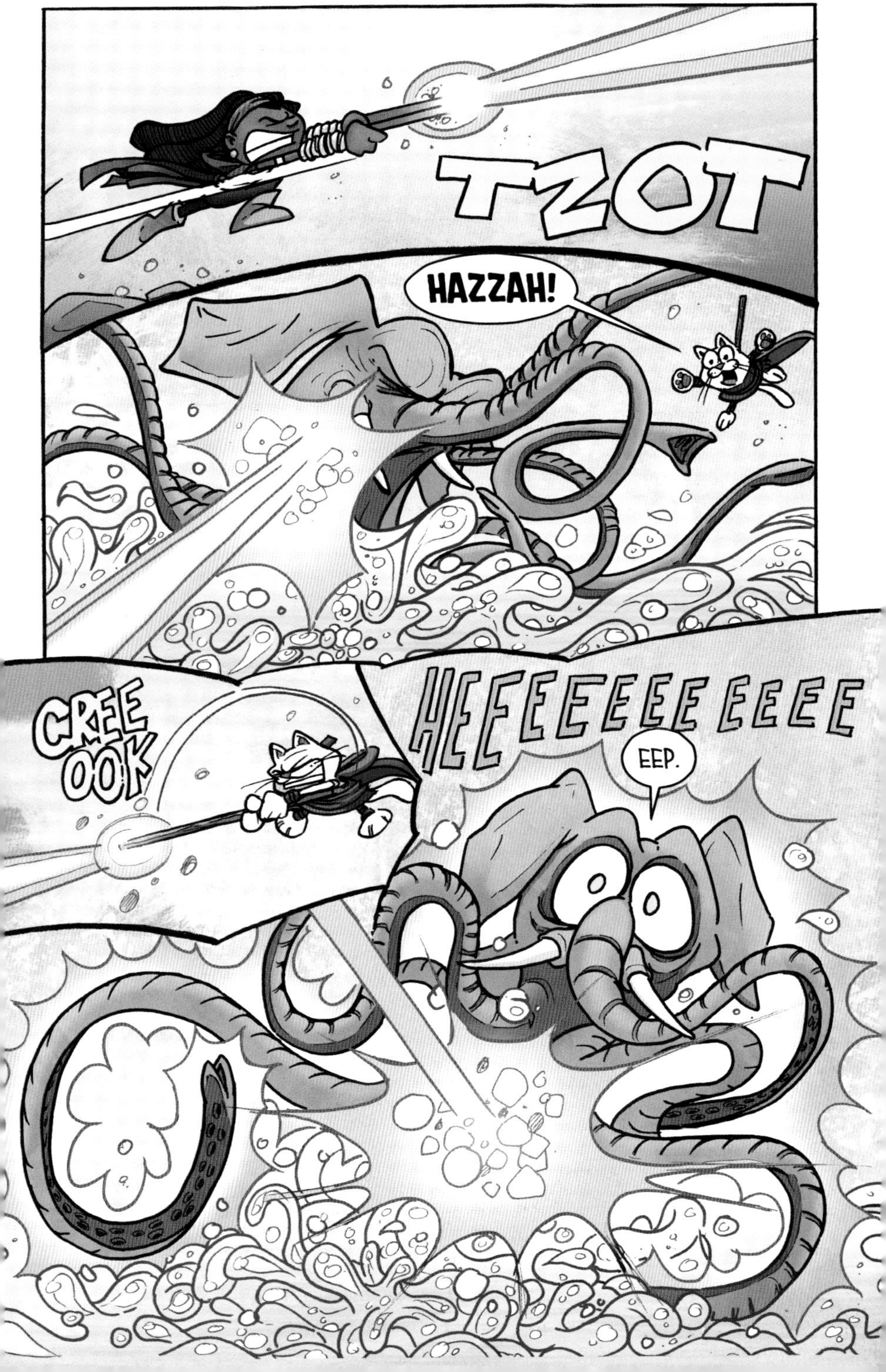
TZOT
HAZZAH!
CREE
OOK
HEEEEEEEEEEE
EEP.

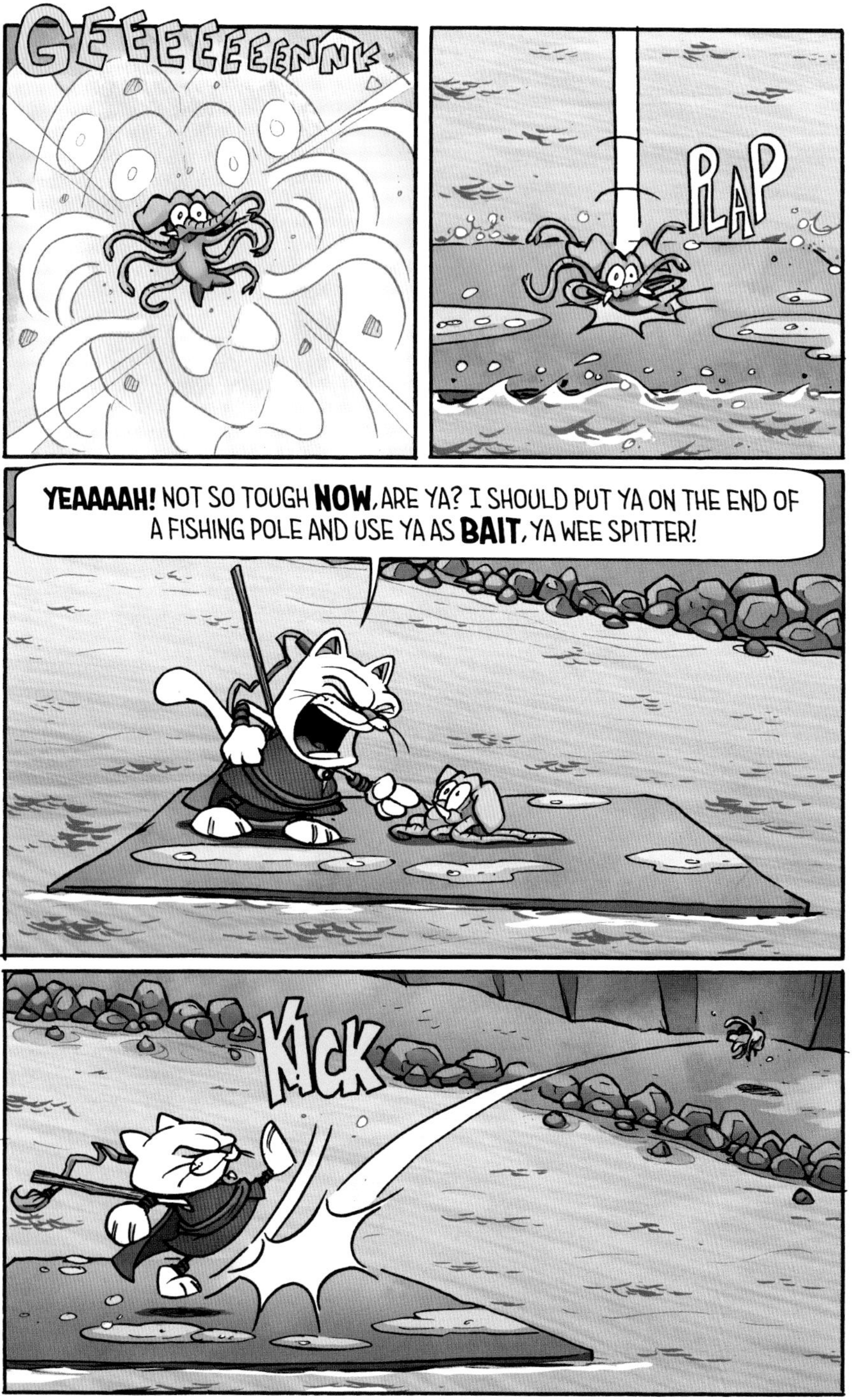
GEEEEEEENNK
PLAP
YEAAAAH! NOT SO TOUGH NOW, ARE YA? I SHOULD PUT YA ON THE END OF A FISHING POLE AND USE YA AS BAIT, YA WEE SPITTER!
KICK

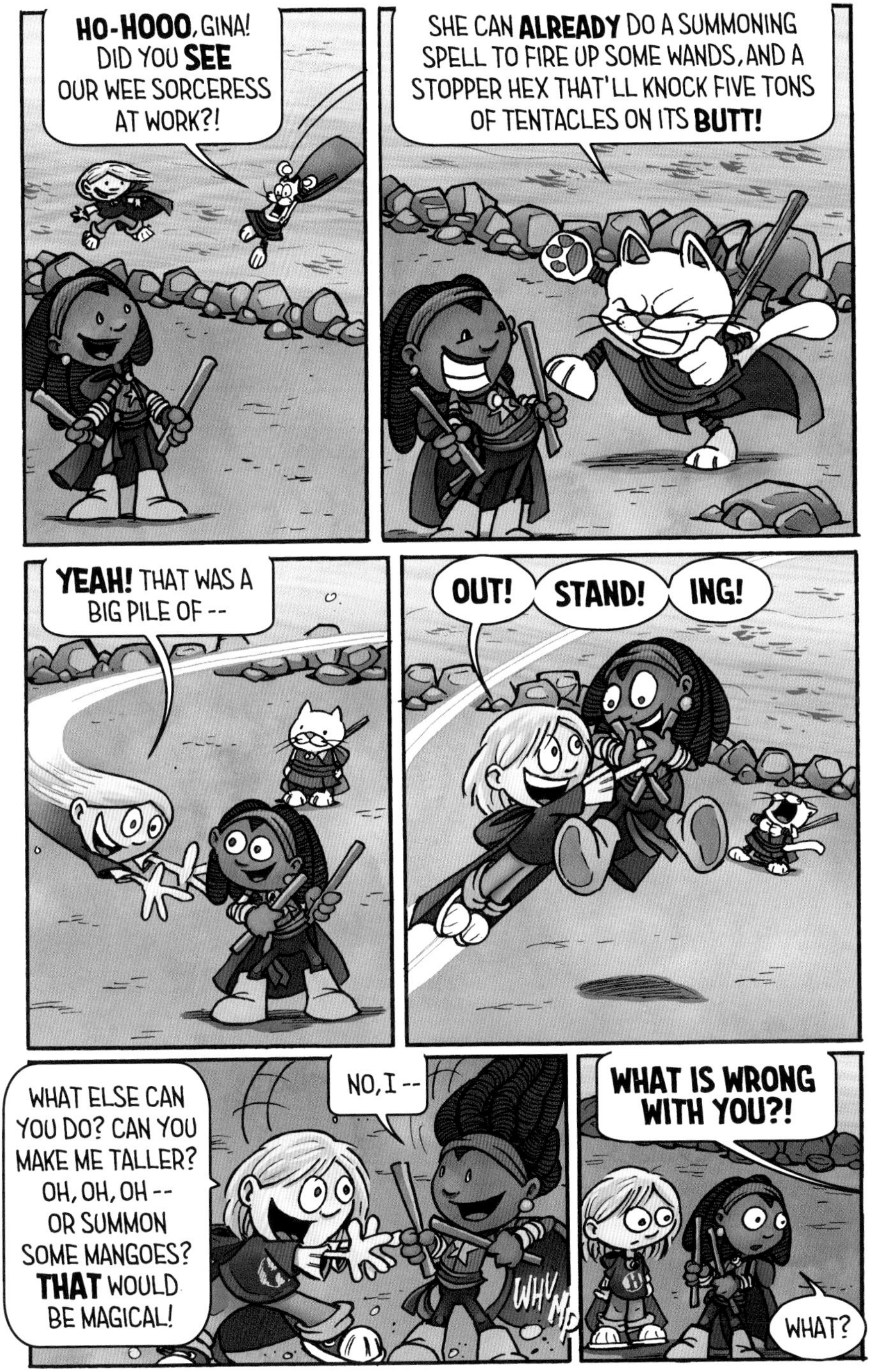
HO-HOOO, GINA! DID YOU SEE OUR WEE SORCERESS AT WORK?!
SHE CAN ALREADY DO A SUMMONING SPELL TO FIRE UP SOME WANDS, AND A STOPPER HEX THAT'LL KNOCK FIVE TONS OF TENTACLES ON ITS BUTT!
YEAH! THAT WAS A BIG PILE OF --
OUT!
STAND!
ING!
WHAT ELSE CAN YOU DO? CAN YOU MAKE ME TALLER? OH, OH, OH -- OR SUMMON SOME MANGOES? THAT WOULD BE MAGICAL!
NO, I --
WHUMP
WHAT IS WRONG WITH YOU?!
WHAT?

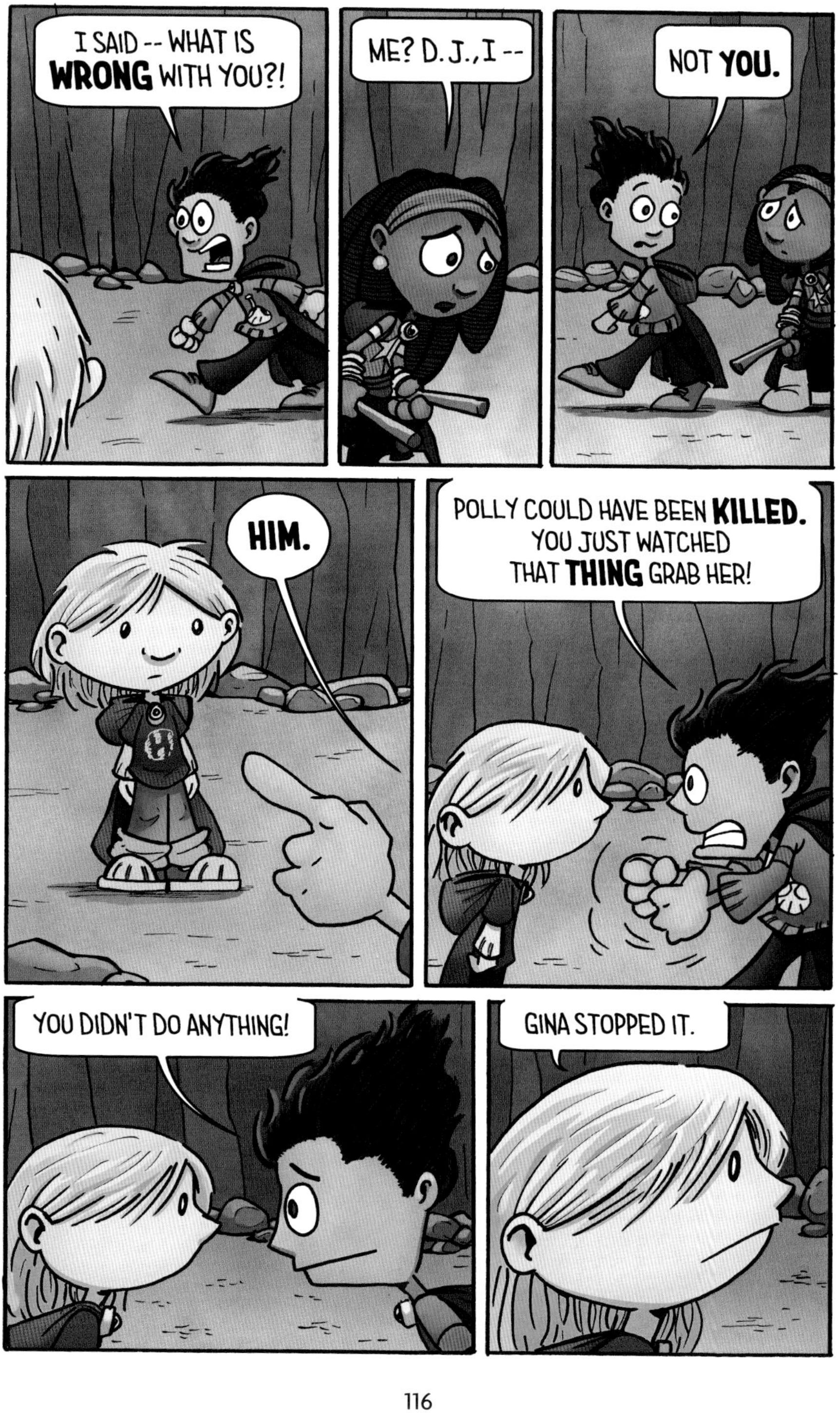
I SAID -- WHAT IS **WRONG** WITH YOU?!
ME? D. J., I --
NOT **YOU.**
**HIM.**
POLLY COULD HAVE BEEN **KILLED.** YOU JUST WATCHED THAT **THING** GRAB HER!
YOU DIDN'T DO ANYTHING!
GINA STOPPED IT.

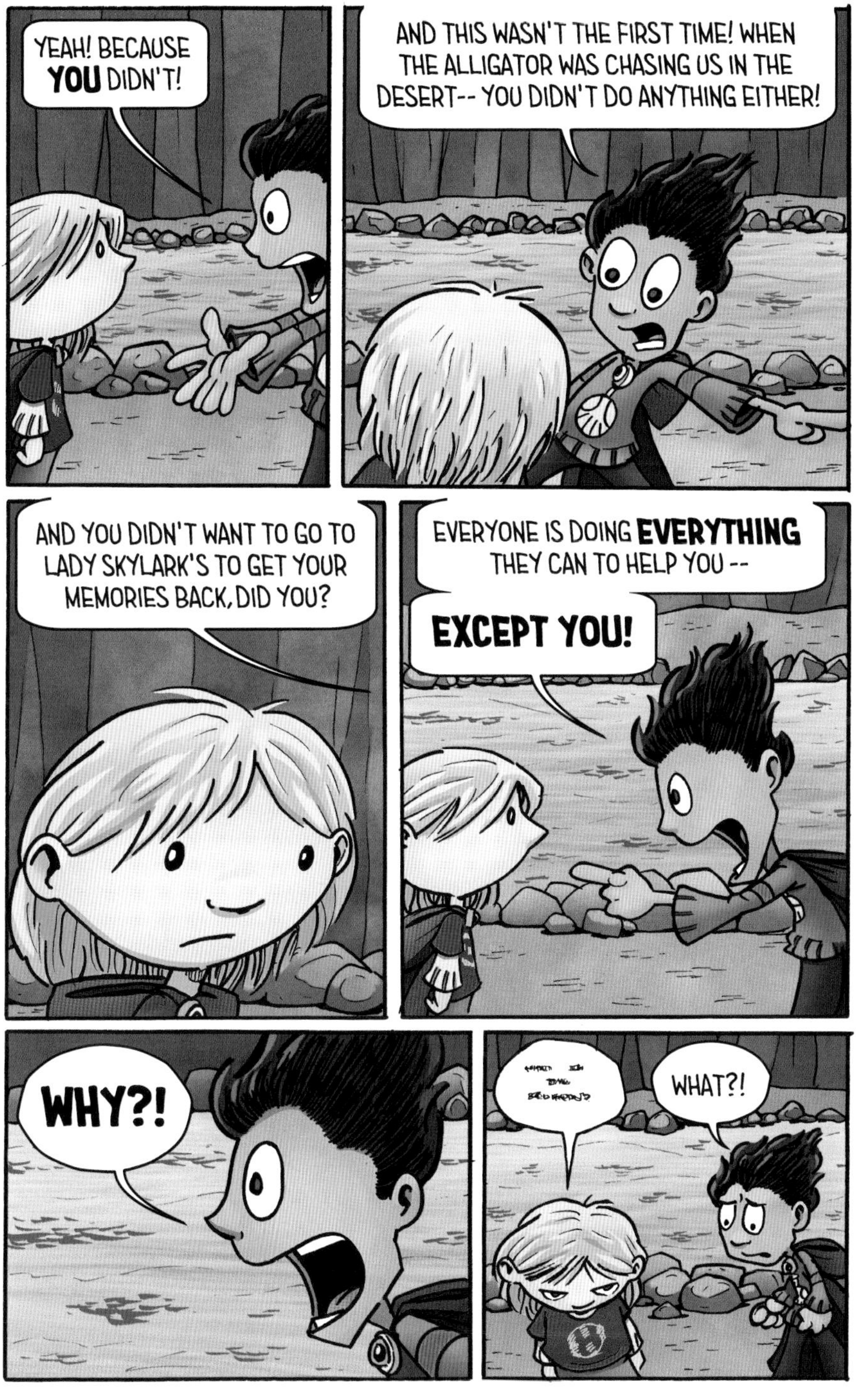
YEAH! BECAUSE YOU DIDN'T!
AND THIS WASN'T THE FIRST TIME! WHEN THE ALLIGATOR WAS CHASING US IN THE DESERT-- YOU DIDN'T DO ANYTHING EITHER!
AND YOU DIDN'T WANT TO GO TO LADY SKYLARK'S TO GET YOUR MEMORIES BACK, DID YOU?
EVERYONE IS DOING EVERYTHING THEY CAN TO HELP YOU --
EXCEPT YOU!
WHY?!
WHAT?!

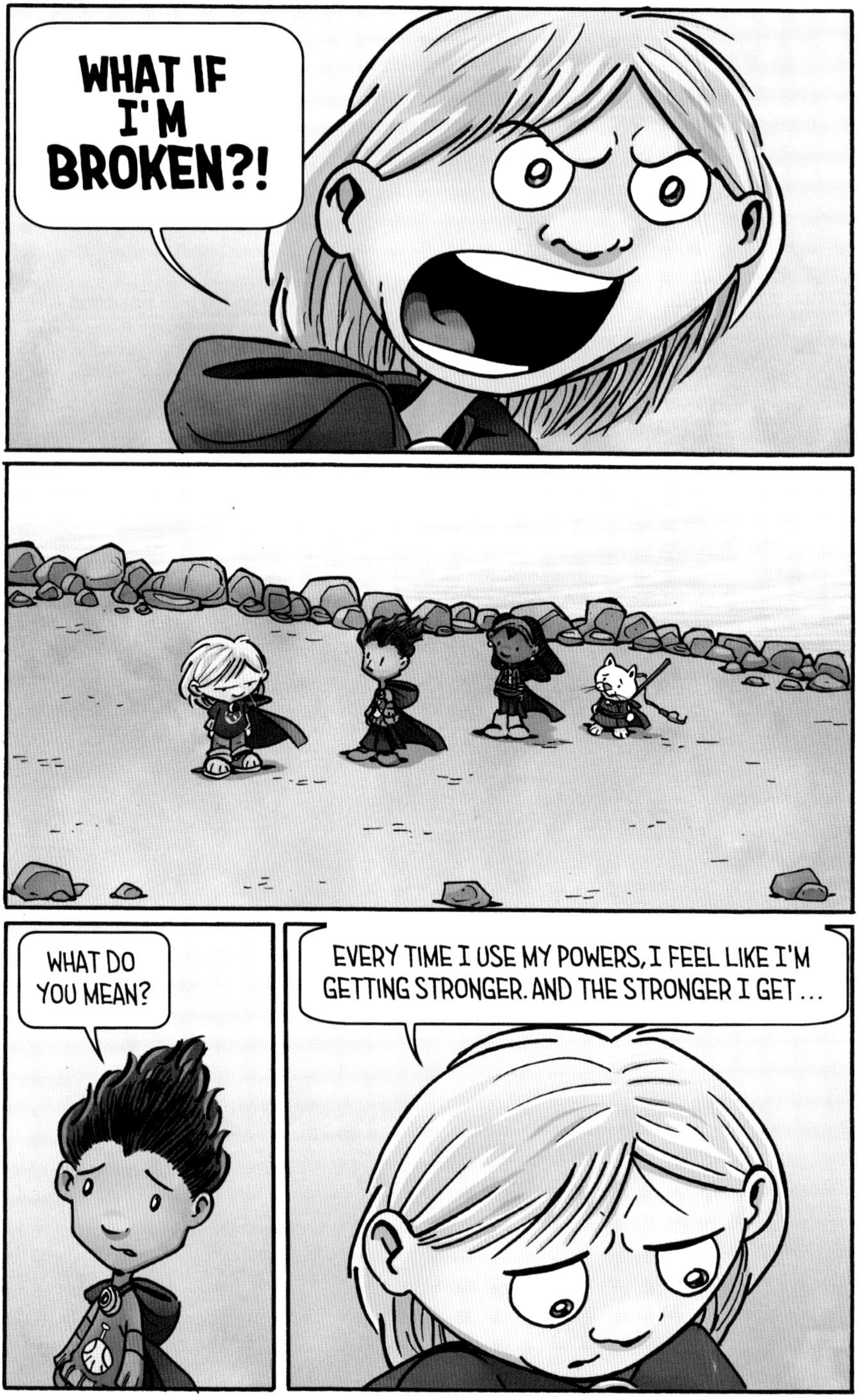
WHAT IF I'M BROKEN?!
WHAT DO YOU MEAN?
EVERY TIME I USE MY POWERS, I FEEL LIKE I'M GETTING STRONGER. AND THE STRONGER I GET . . .

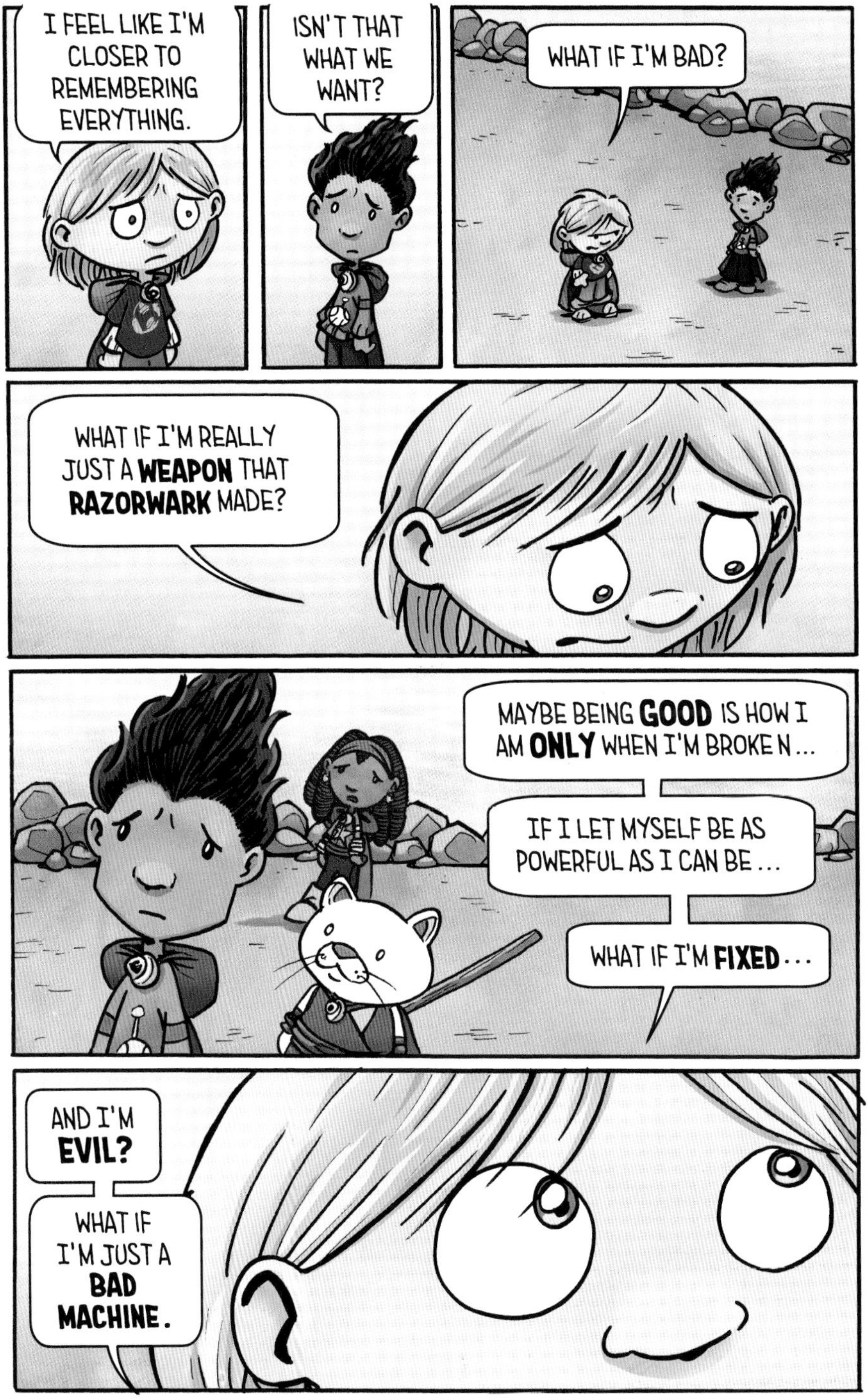

I FEEL LIKE I'M CLOSER TO REMEMBERING EVERYTHING.
ISN'T THAT WHAT WE WANT?
WHAT IF I'M BAD?
WHAT IF I'M REALLY JUST A **WEAPON** THAT **RAZORWARK** MADE?
MAYBE BEING **GOOD** IS HOW I AM **ONLY** WHEN I'M BROKEN...
IF I LET MYSELF BE AS POWERFUL AS I CAN BE...
WHAT IF I'M **FIXED**...
AND I'M **EVIL?**
WHAT IF I'M JUST A **BAD MACHINE**.

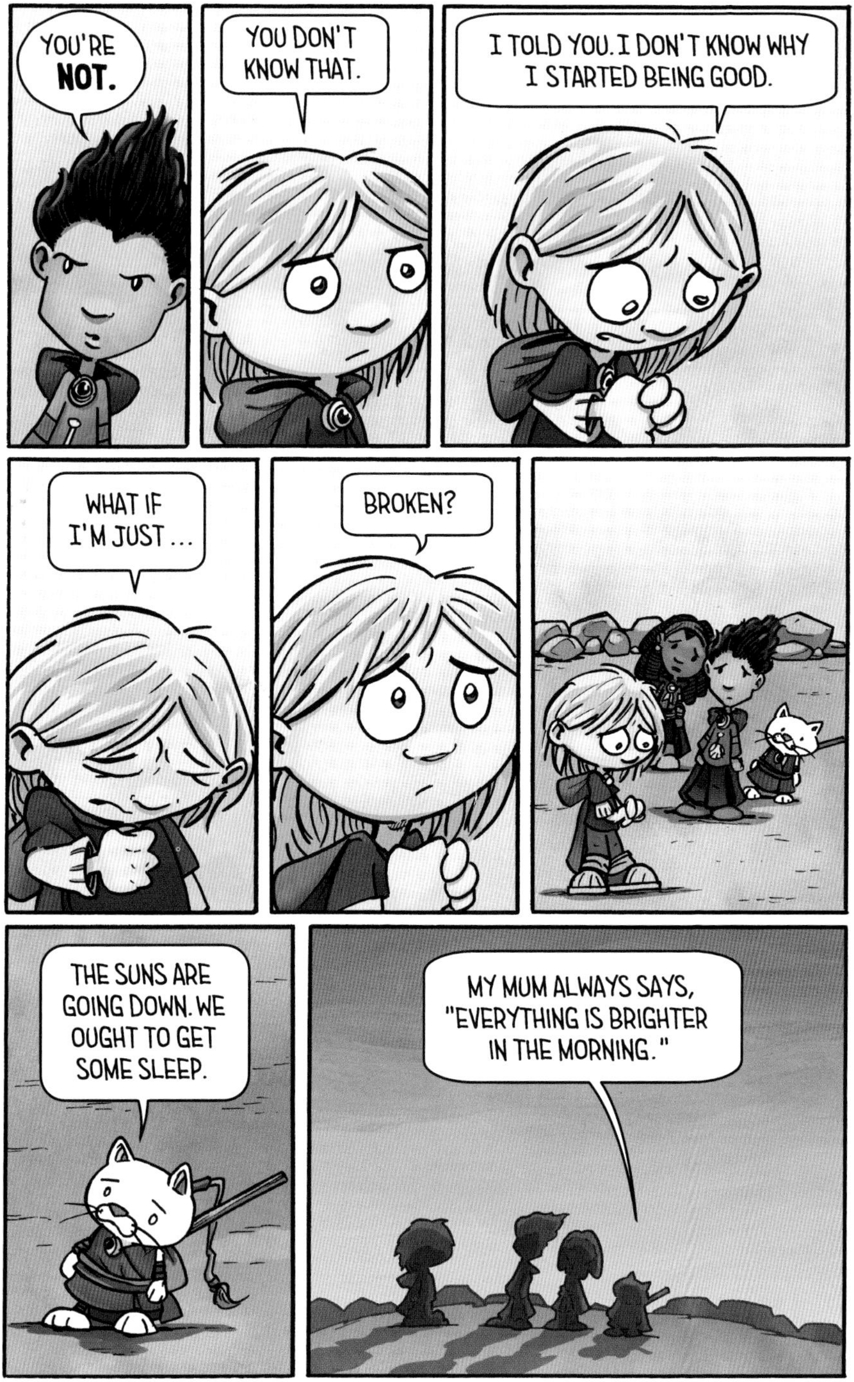
YOU'RE **NOT.**
YOU DON'T KNOW THAT.
I TOLD YOU. I DON'T KNOW WHY I STARTED BEING GOOD.
WHAT IF I'M JUST...
BROKEN?
THE SUNS ARE GOING DOWN. WE OUGHT TO GET SOME SLEEP.
MY MUM ALWAYS SAYS, "EVERYTHING IS BRIGHTER IN THE MORNING."

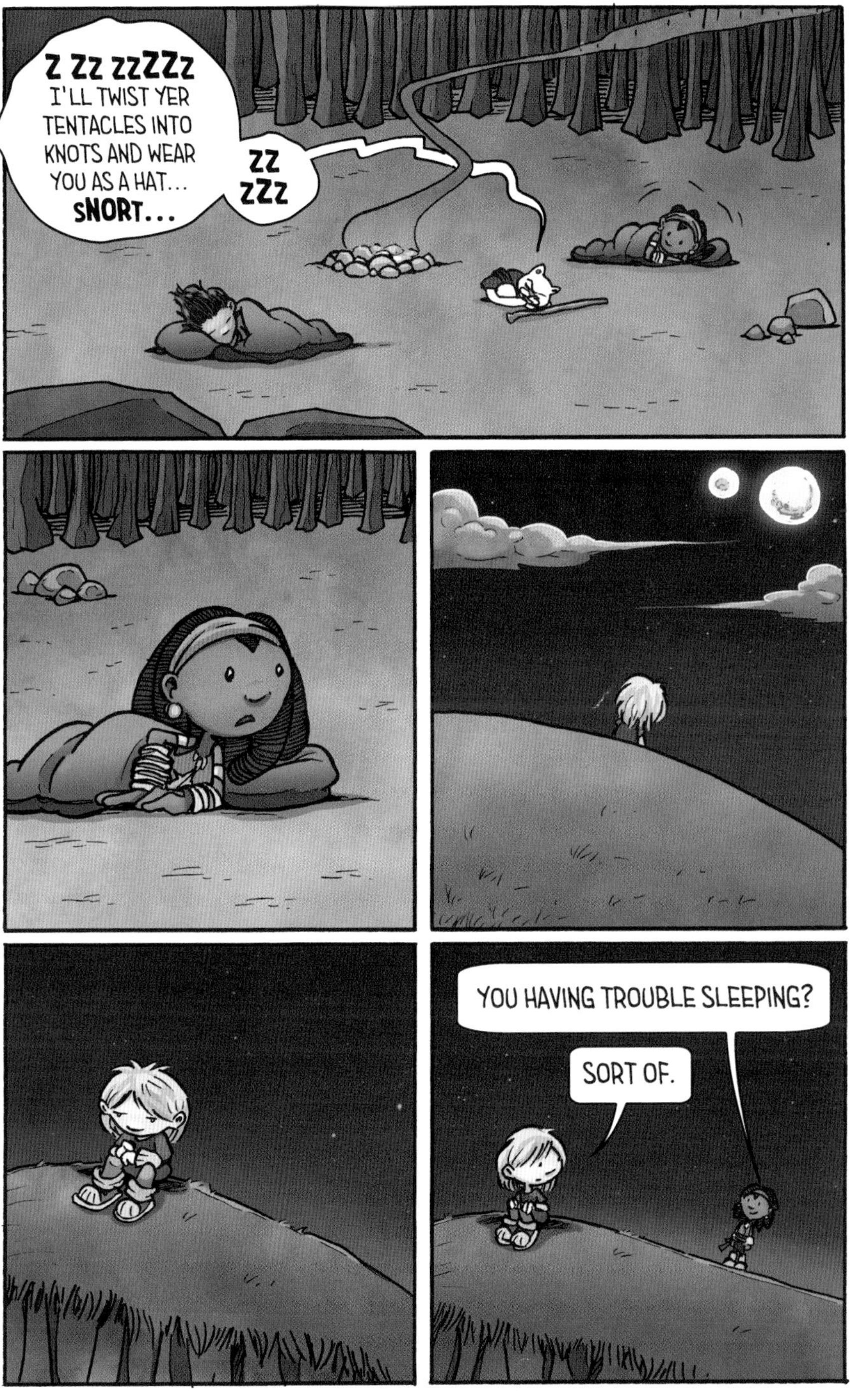
Z ZZ ZZZZZ
I'LL TWIST YER TENTACLES INTO KNOTS AND WEAR YOU AS A HAT... SNORT...
ZZ ZZZ
YOU HAVING TROUBLE SLEEPING?
SORT OF.

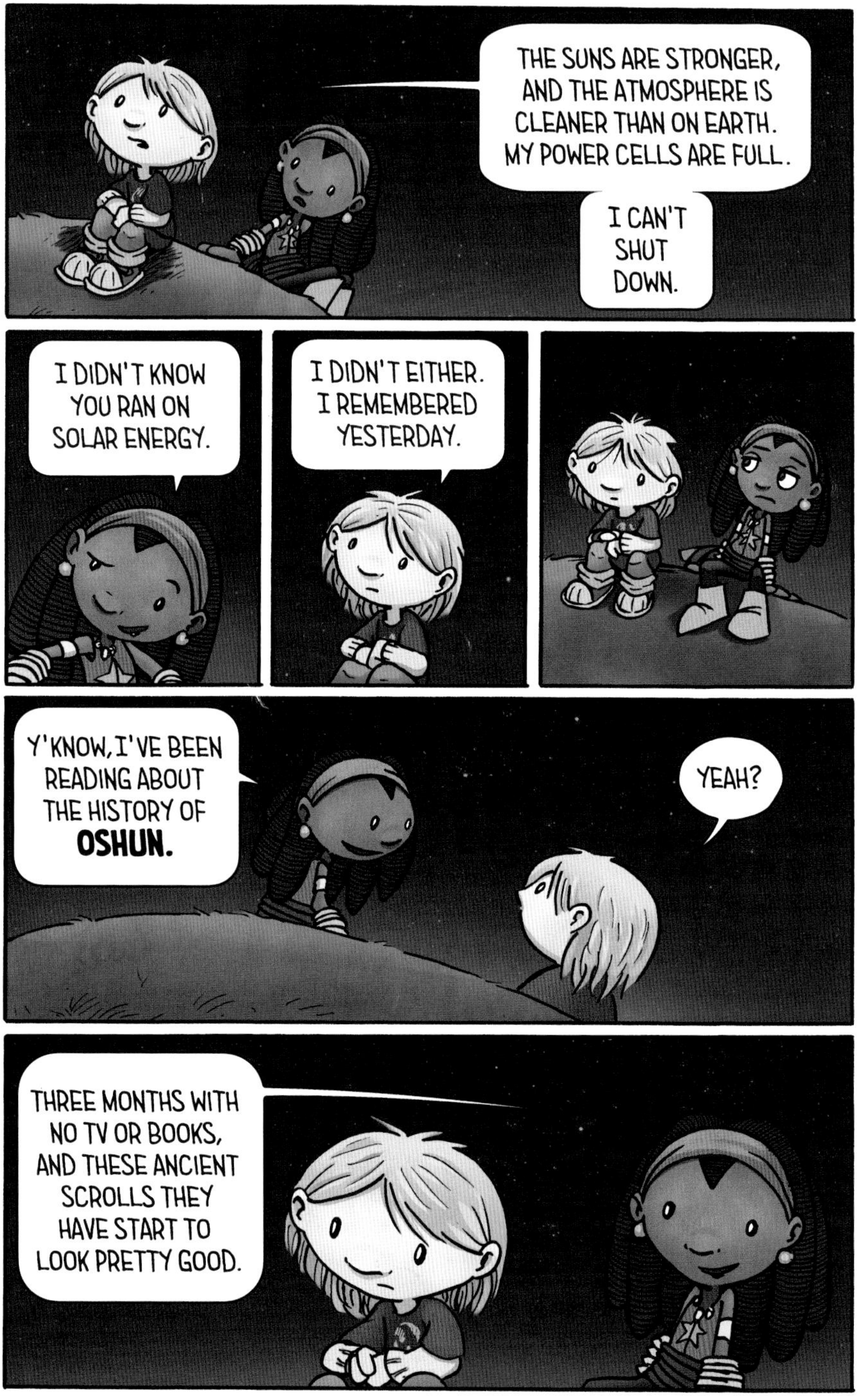
THE SUNS ARE STRONGER, AND THE ATMOSPHERE IS CLEANER THAN ON EARTH. MY POWER CELLS ARE FULL.
I CAN'T SHUT DOWN.
I DIDN'T KNOW YOU RAN ON SOLAR ENERGY.
I DIDN'T EITHER. I REMEMBERED YESTERDAY.
Y'KNOW, I'VE BEEN READING ABOUT THE HISTORY OF **OSHUN.**
YEAH?
THREE MONTHS WITH NO TV OR BOOKS, AND THESE ANCIENT SCROLLS THEY HAVE START TO LOOK PRETTY GOOD.

DID YOU KNOW **EVERYONE** ON OSHUN USED TO BE AT WAR WITH ONE ANOTHER?

IT WAS AWFUL.

I WAS READING ABOUT THIS GUY... **TAMIR.** OVER TWO THOUSAND YEARS AGO, HE WAS THE ONE WHO UNITED ALL THE DIFFERENT TRIBES AND CLANS.

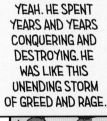

SO, HE WAS A GREAT LEADER.

FROM WHAT I READ? HE WAS... **A MONSTER.** HE CAUSED MOST OF THE WARS.

REALLY?

YEAH. HE SPENT YEARS AND YEARS CONQUERING AND DESTROYING. HE WAS LIKE THIS UNENDING STORM OF GREED AND RAGE.

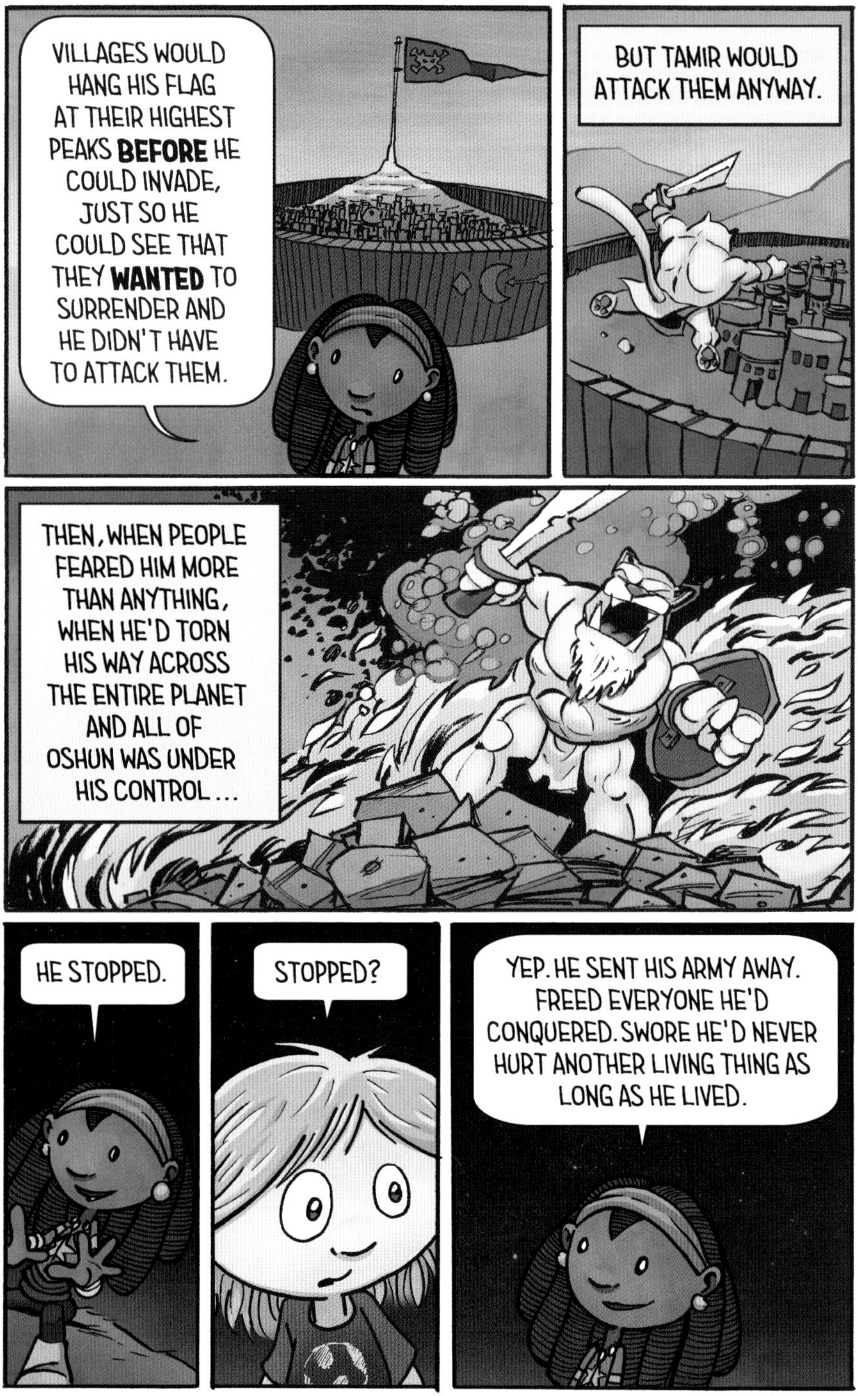
VILLAGES WOULD HANG HIS FLAG AT THEIR HIGHEST PEAKS **BEFORE** HE COULD INVADE, JUST SO HE COULD SEE THAT THEY **WANTED** TO SURRENDER AND HE DIDN'T HAVE TO ATTACK THEM.
BUT TAMIR WOULD ATTACK THEM ANYWAY.
THEN, WHEN PEOPLE FEARED HIM MORE THAN ANYTHING, WHEN HE'D TORN HIS WAY ACROSS THE ENTIRE PLANET AND ALL OF OSHUN WAS UNDER HIS CONTROL...
HE STOPPED.
STOPPED?
YEP. HE SENT HIS ARMY AWAY. FREED EVERYONE HE'D CONQUERED. SWORE HE'D NEVER HURT ANOTHER LIVING THING AS LONG AS HE LIVED.

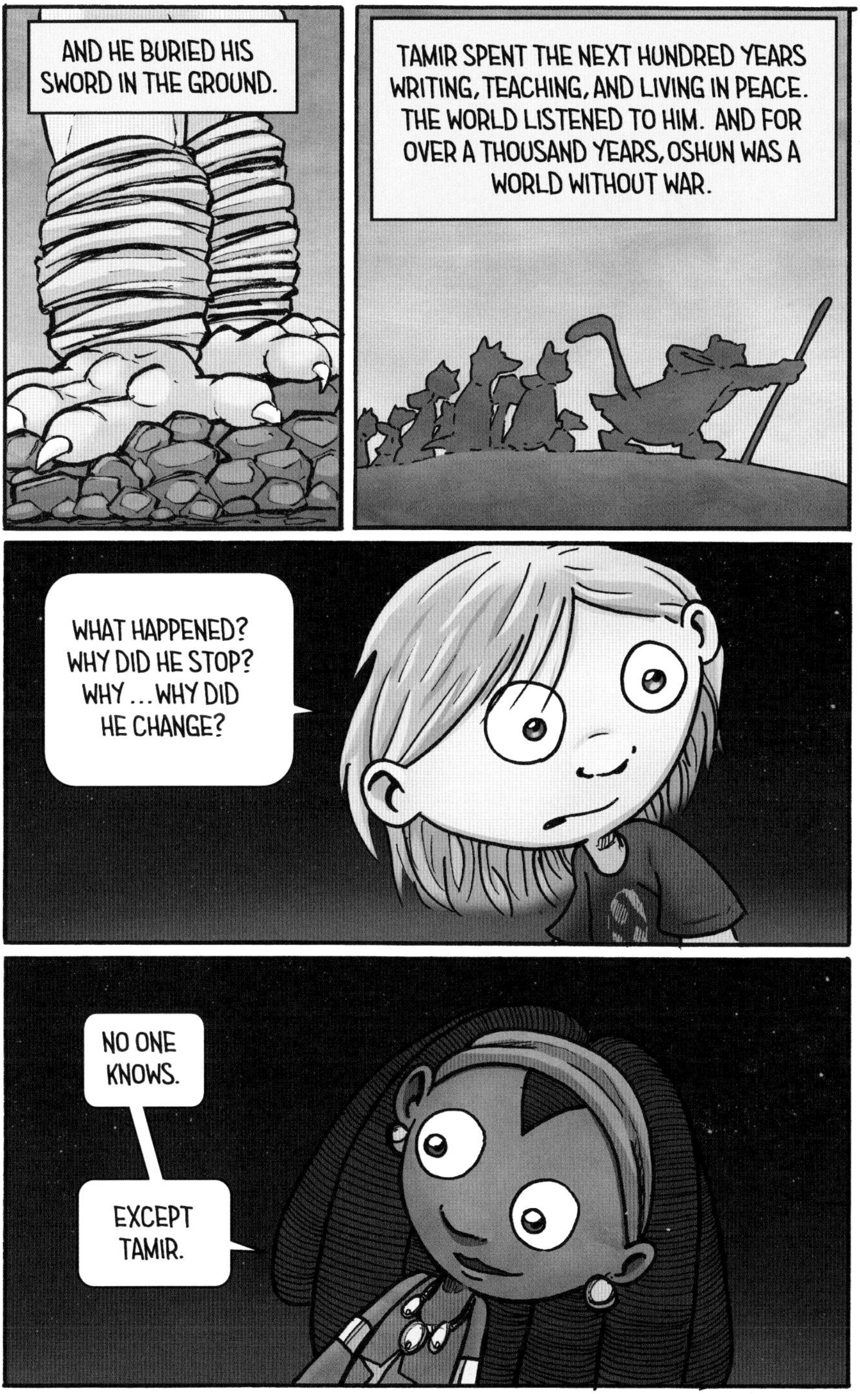
AND HE BURIED HIS SWORD IN THE GROUND.
TAMIR SPENT THE NEXT HUNDRED YEARS WRITING, TEACHING, AND LIVING IN PEACE. THE WORLD LISTENED TO HIM. AND FOR OVER A THOUSAND YEARS, OSHUN WAS A WORLD WITHOUT WAR.
WHAT HAPPENED? WHY DID HE STOP? WHY ... WHY DID HE CHANGE?
NO ONE KNOWS.
EXCEPT TAMIR.

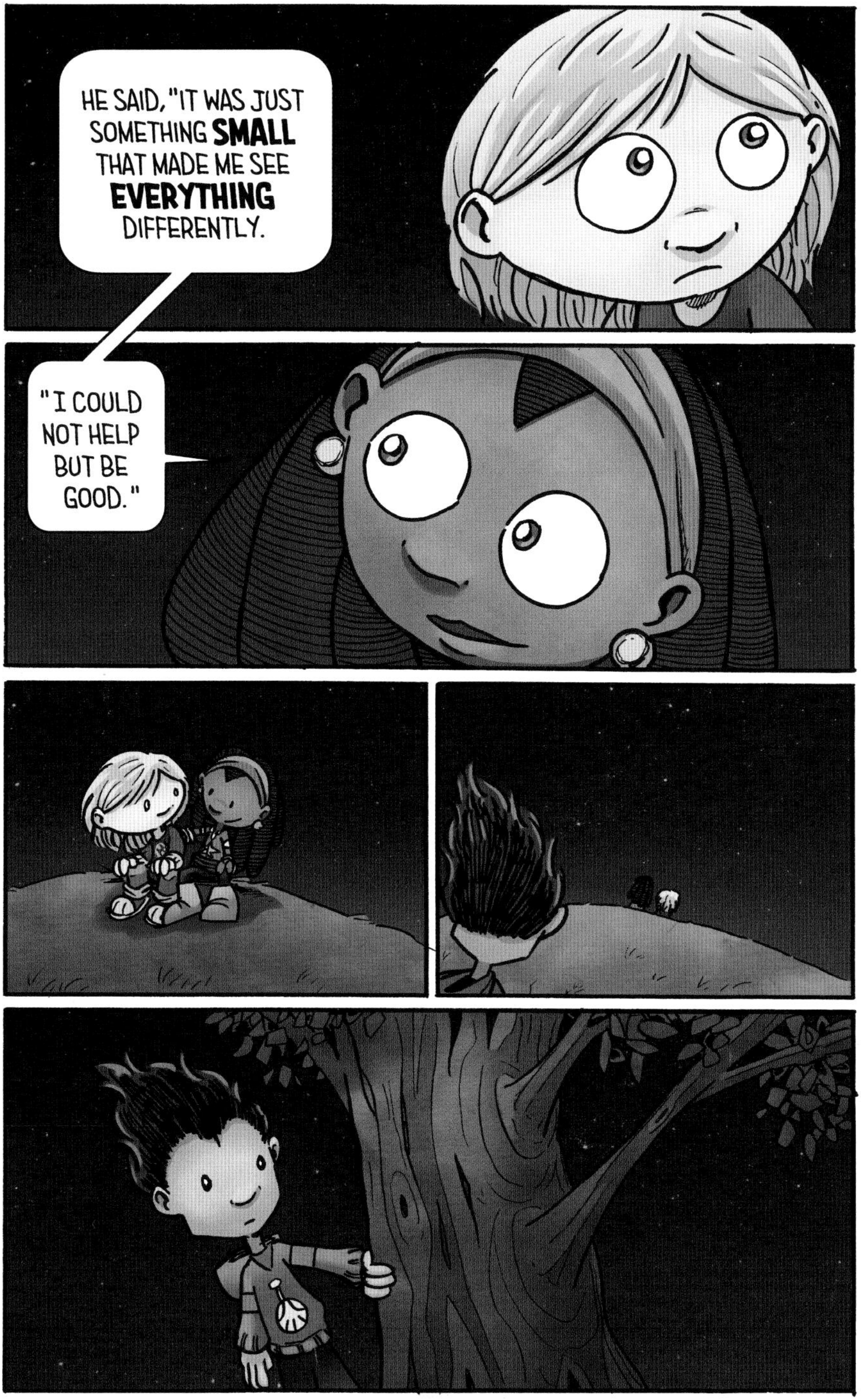
HE SAID, "IT WAS JUST SOMETHING SMALL THAT MADE ME SEE EVERYTHING DIFFERENTLY.
"I COULD NOT HELP BUT BE GOOD."

# CHAPTER 7

# THE GREAT BIG BOOM

5 MILES OUTSIDE THE UNCANNY VALLEY.
**LADY SKYLARK** LIVES HERE? IT'S JUST A FIELD?
NO ONE'S SEEN HIDE NOR HAIR OF HER IN A HUNDRED YEARS. THIS IS WHERE SHE'S SUPPOSED TO BE.
KIND OF.

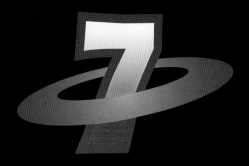

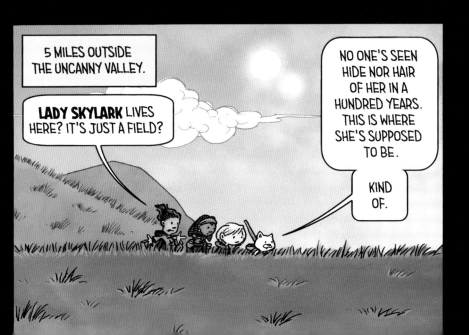

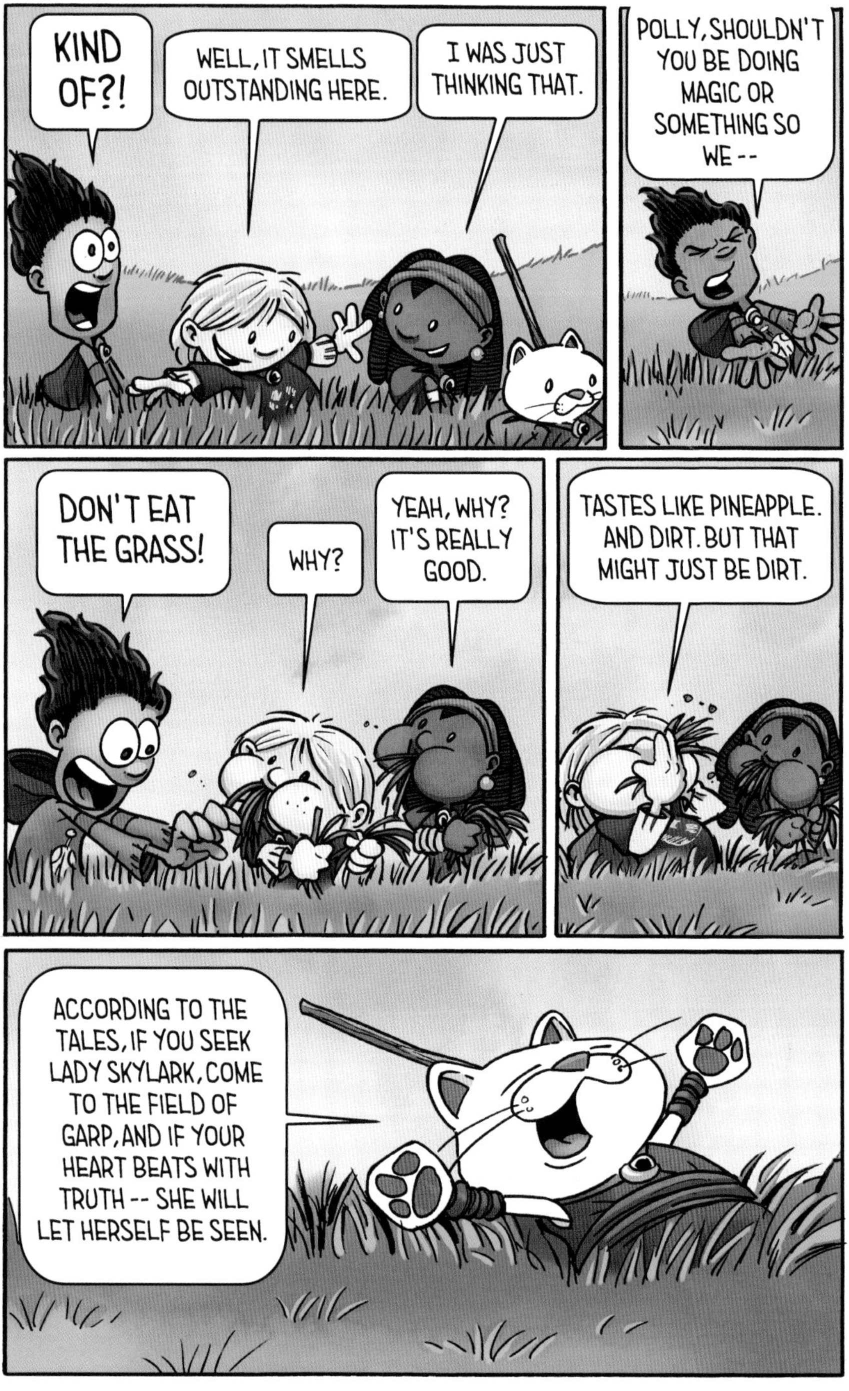
KIND OF?!
WELL, IT SMELLS OUTSTANDING HERE.
I WAS JUST THINKING THAT.
POLLY, SHOULDN'T YOU BE DOING MAGIC OR SOMETHING SO WE --
DON'T EAT THE GRASS!
WHY?
YEAH, WHY? IT'S REALLY GOOD.
TASTES LIKE PINEAPPLE. AND DIRT. BUT THAT MIGHT JUST BE DIRT.
ACCORDING TO THE TALES, IF YOU SEEK LADY SKYLARK, COME TO THE FIELD OF GARP, AND IF YOUR HEART BEATS WITH TRUTH -- SHE WILL LET HERSELF BE SEEN.

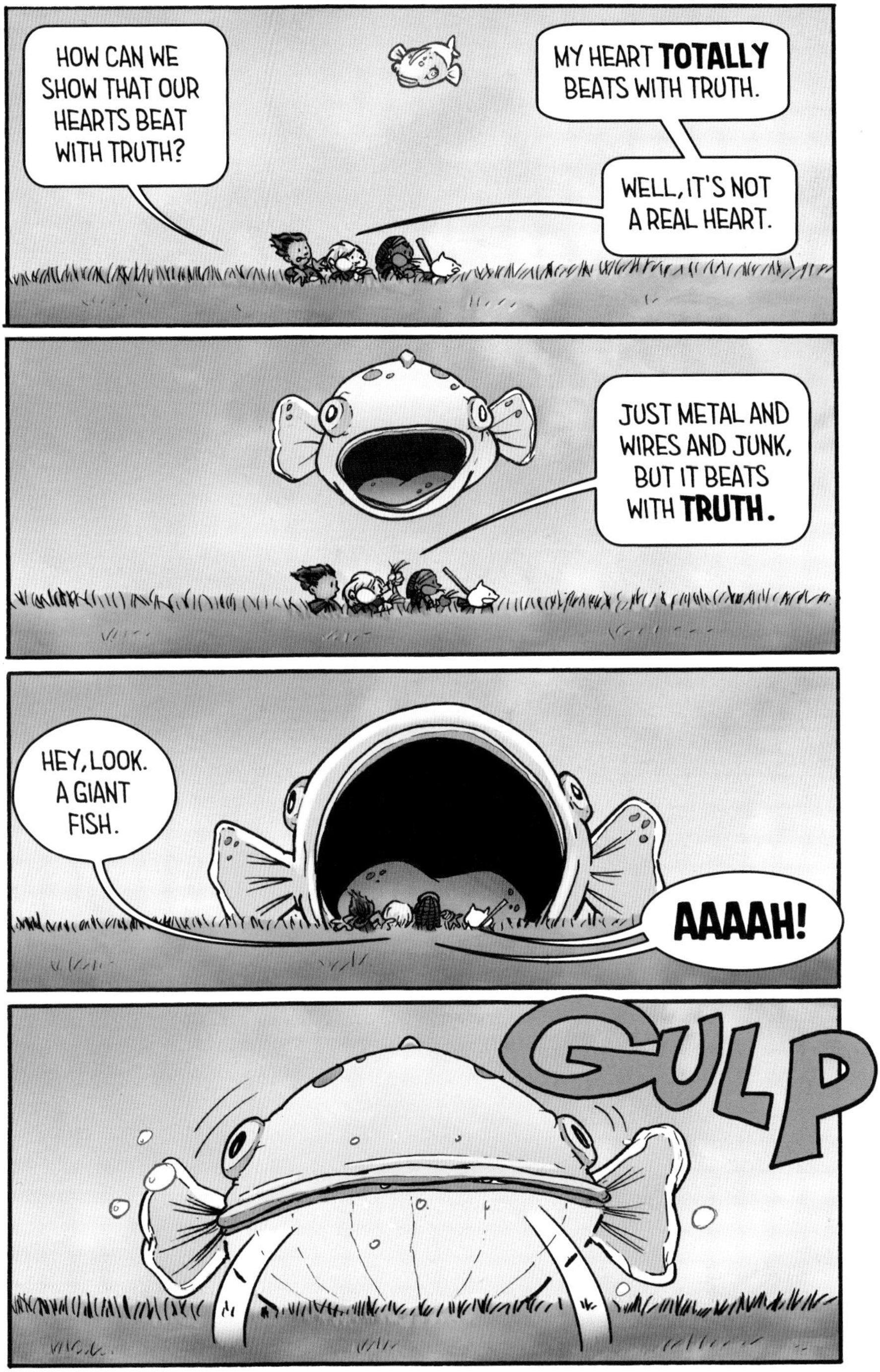
HOW CAN WE SHOW THAT OUR HEARTS BEAT WITH TRUTH?
MY HEART **TOTALLY** BEATS WITH TRUTH.
WELL, IT'S NOT A REAL HEART.
JUST METAL AND WIRES AND JUNK, BUT IT BEATS WITH **TRUTH**.
HEY, LOOK. A GIANT FISH.
AAAAH!
GULP

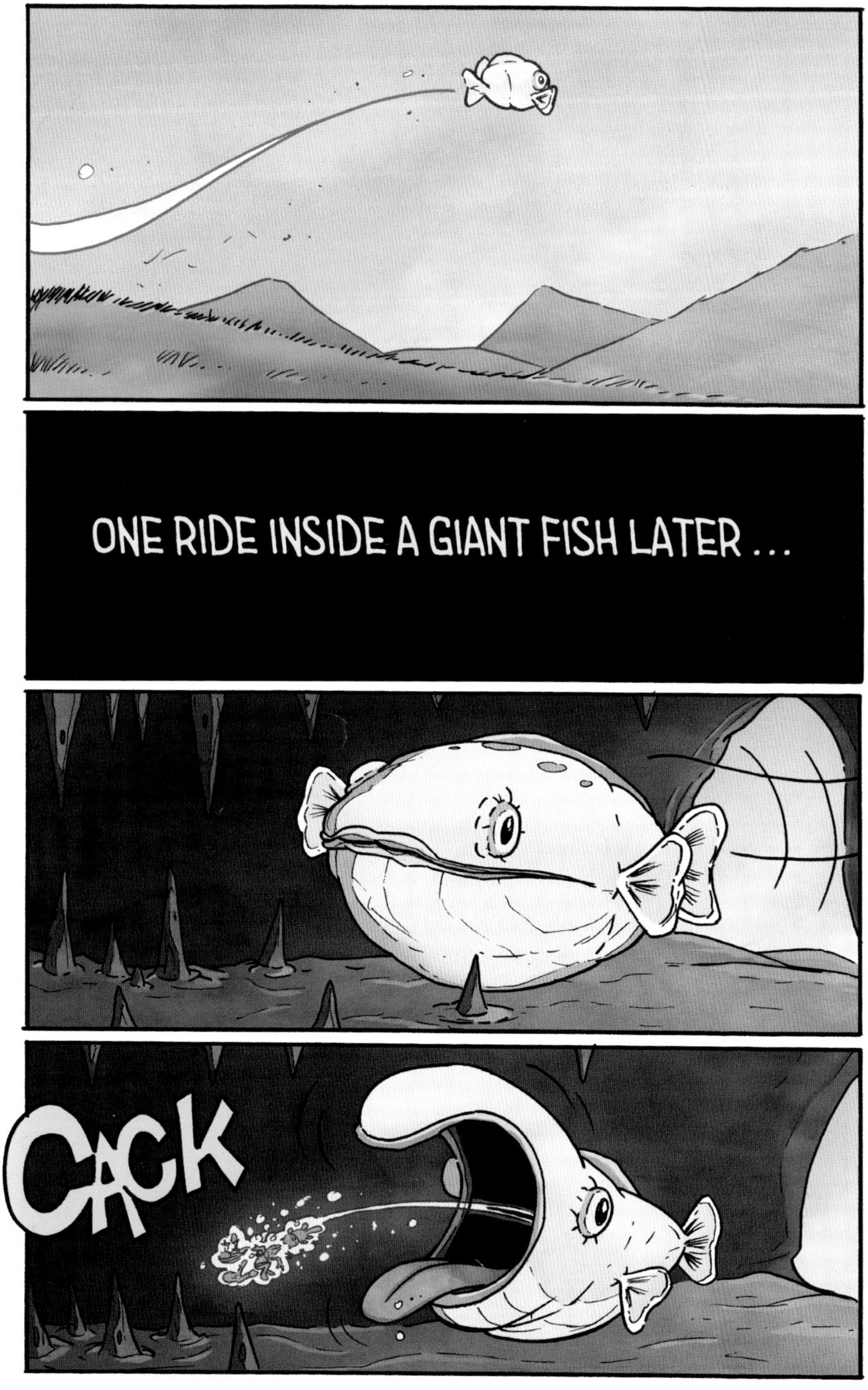
ONE RIDE INSIDE A GIANT FISH LATER ...
CACK

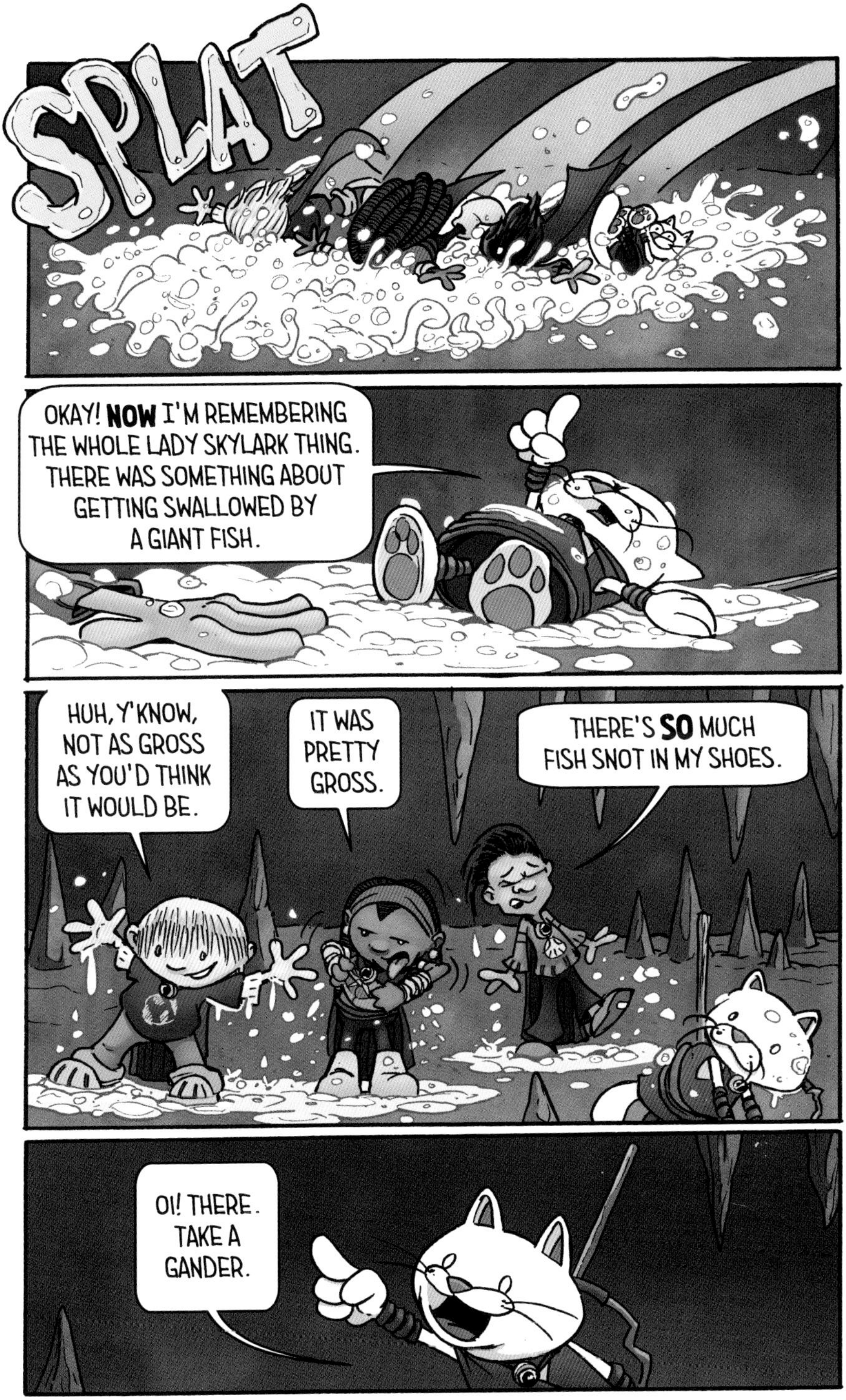
SPLAT
OKAY! **NOW** I'M REMEMBERING THE WHOLE LADY SKYLARK THING. THERE WAS SOMETHING ABOUT GETTING SWALLOWED BY A GIANT FISH.
HUH, Y'KNOW, NOT AS GROSS AS YOU'D THINK IT WOULD BE.
IT WAS PRETTY GROSS.
THERE'S **SO** MUCH FISH SNOT IN MY SHOES.
OI! THERE. TAKE A GANDER.

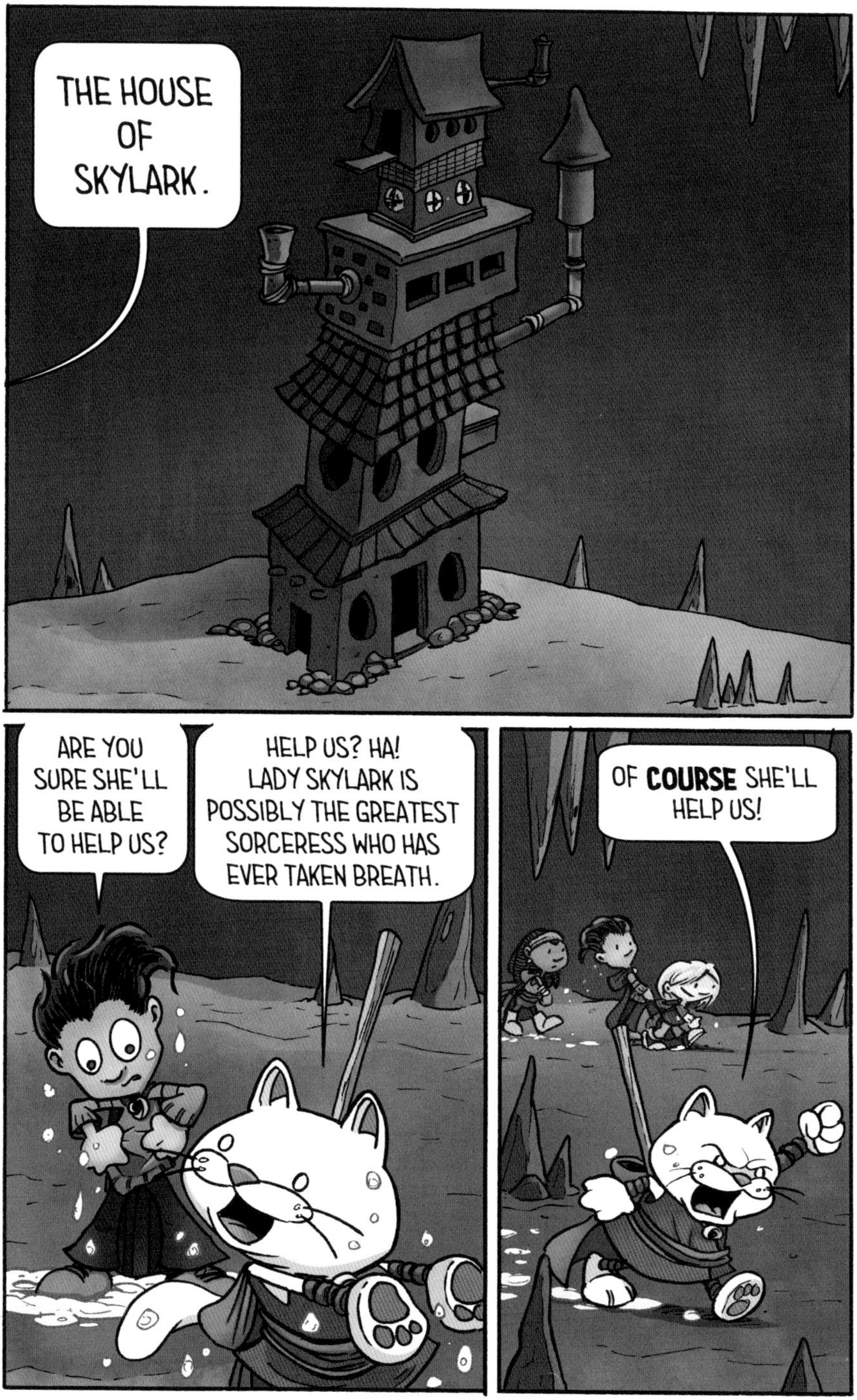
THE HOUSE OF SKYLARK.
ARE YOU SURE SHE'LL BE ABLE TO HELP US?
HELP US? HA! LADY SKYLARK IS POSSIBLY THE GREATEST SORCERESS WHO HAS EVER TAKEN BREATH.
OF **COURSE** SHE'LL HELP US!

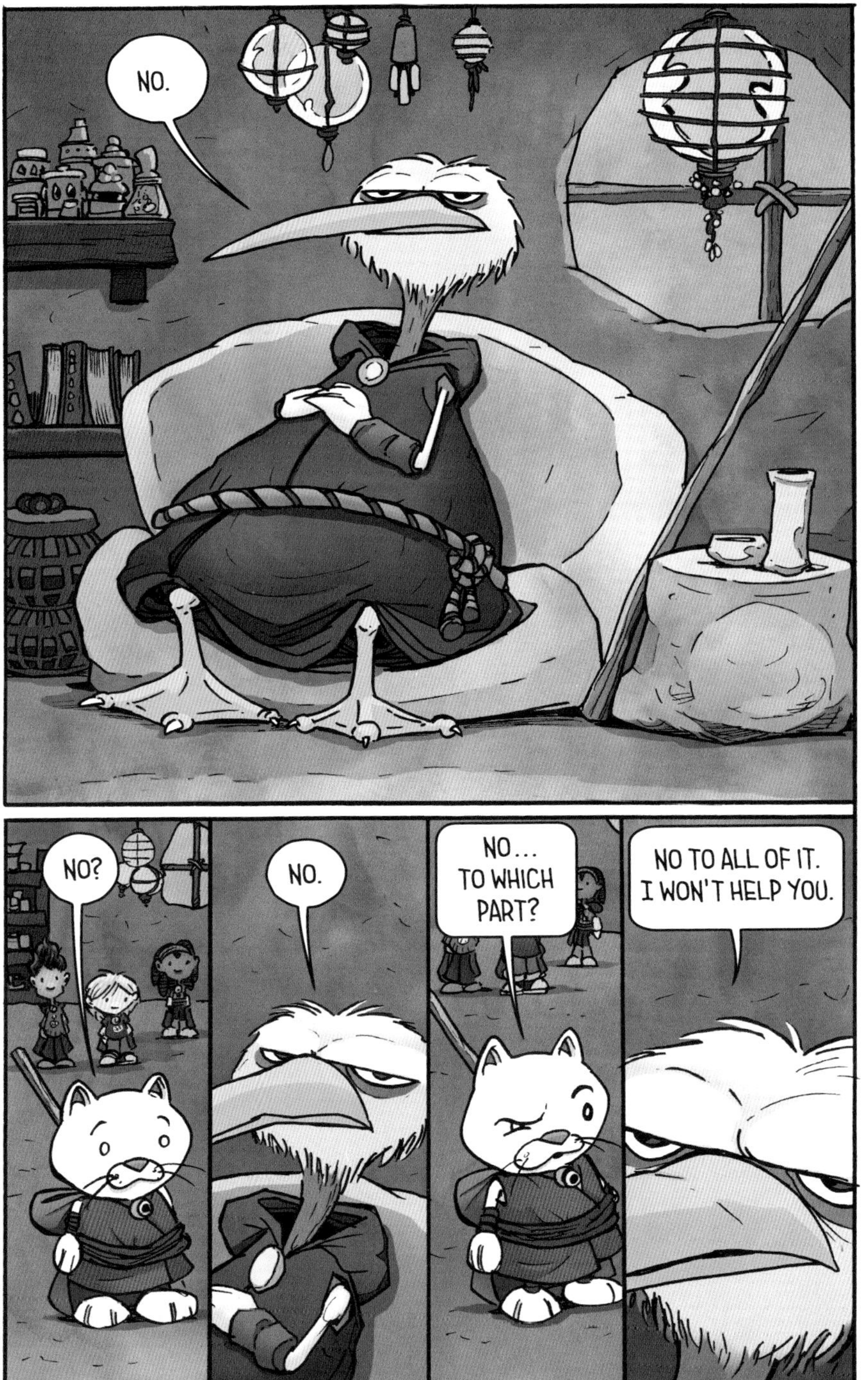
NO.
NO?
NO.
NO...
TO WHICH
PART?
NO TO ALL OF IT.
I WON'T HELP YOU.

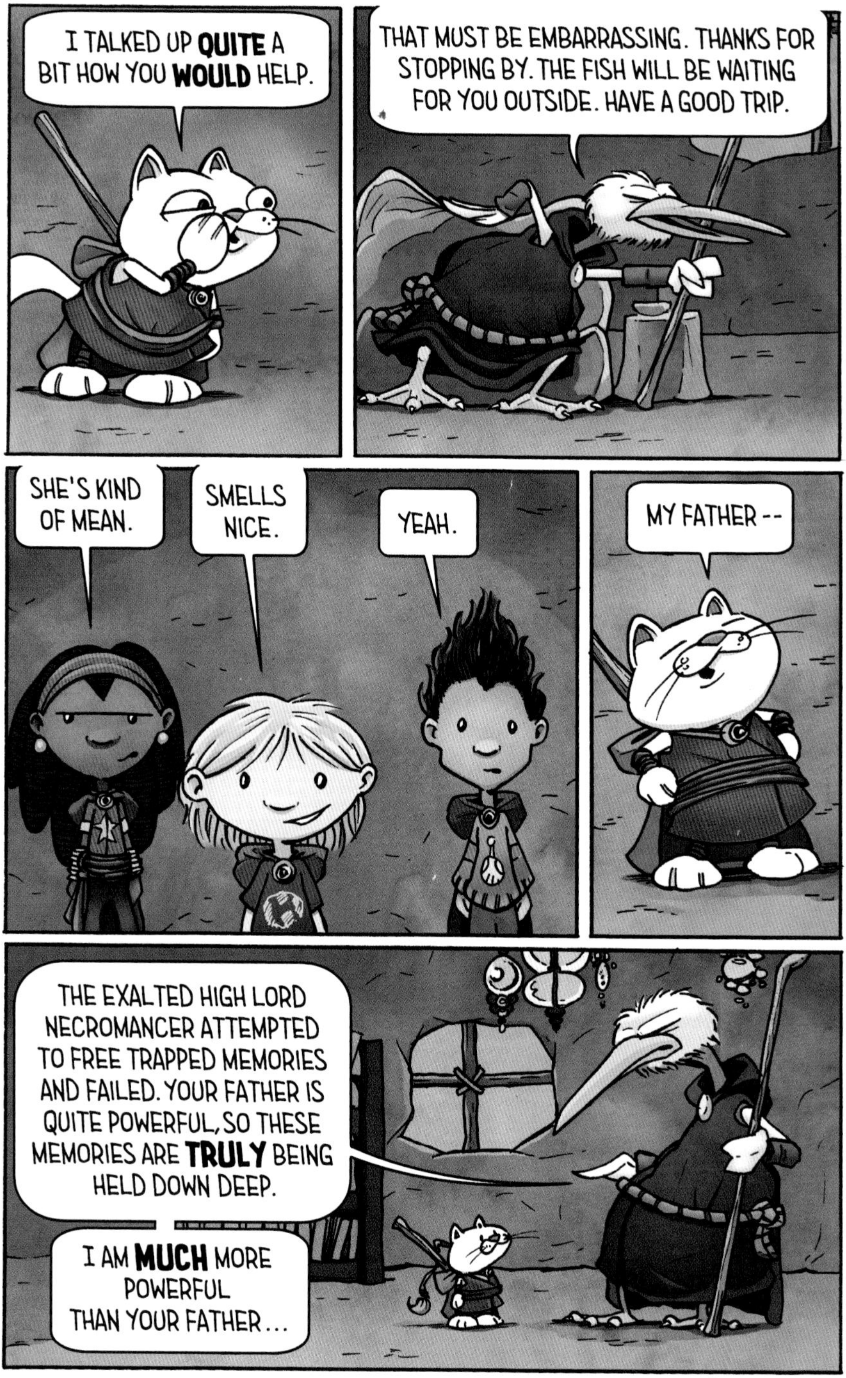
I TALKED UP QUITE A BIT HOW YOU WOULD HELP.
THAT MUST BE EMBARRASSING. THANKS FOR STOPPING BY. THE FISH WILL BE WAITING FOR YOU OUTSIDE. HAVE A GOOD TRIP.
SHE'S KIND OF MEAN.
SMELLS NICE.
YEAH.
MY FATHER --
THE EXALTED HIGH LORD NECROMANCER ATTEMPTED TO FREE TRAPPED MEMORIES AND FAILED. YOUR FATHER IS QUITE POWERFUL, SO THESE MEMORIES ARE TRULY BEING HELD DOWN DEEP.
I AM MUCH MORE POWERFUL THAN YOUR FATHER...

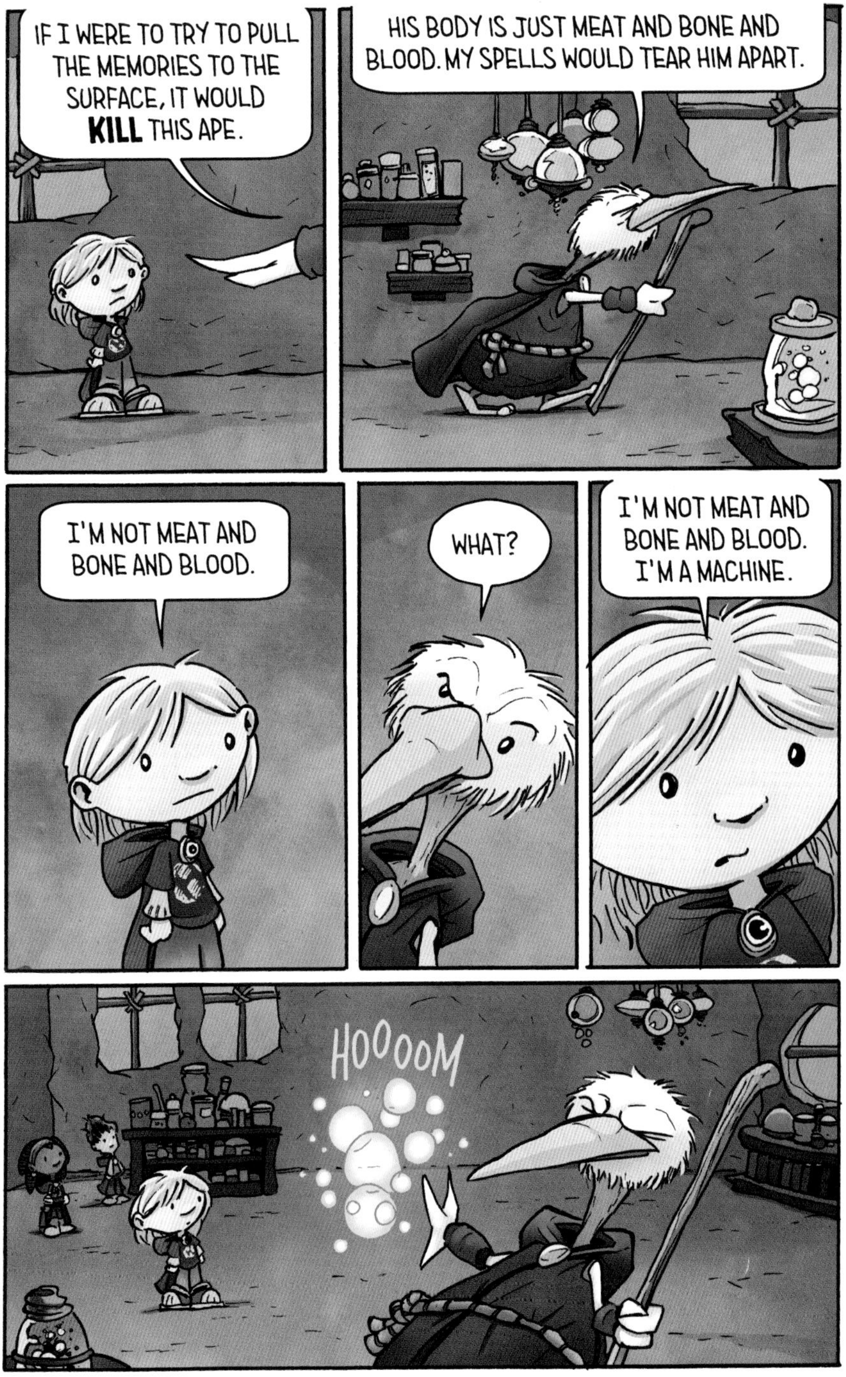
IF I WERE TO TRY TO PULL THE MEMORIES TO THE SURFACE, IT WOULD **KILL** THIS APE.
HIS BODY IS JUST MEAT AND BONE AND BLOOD. MY SPELLS WOULD TEAR HIM APART.
I'M NOT MEAT AND BONE AND BLOOD.
WHAT?
I'M NOT MEAT AND BONE AND BLOOD. I'M A MACHINE.
HOOOOM

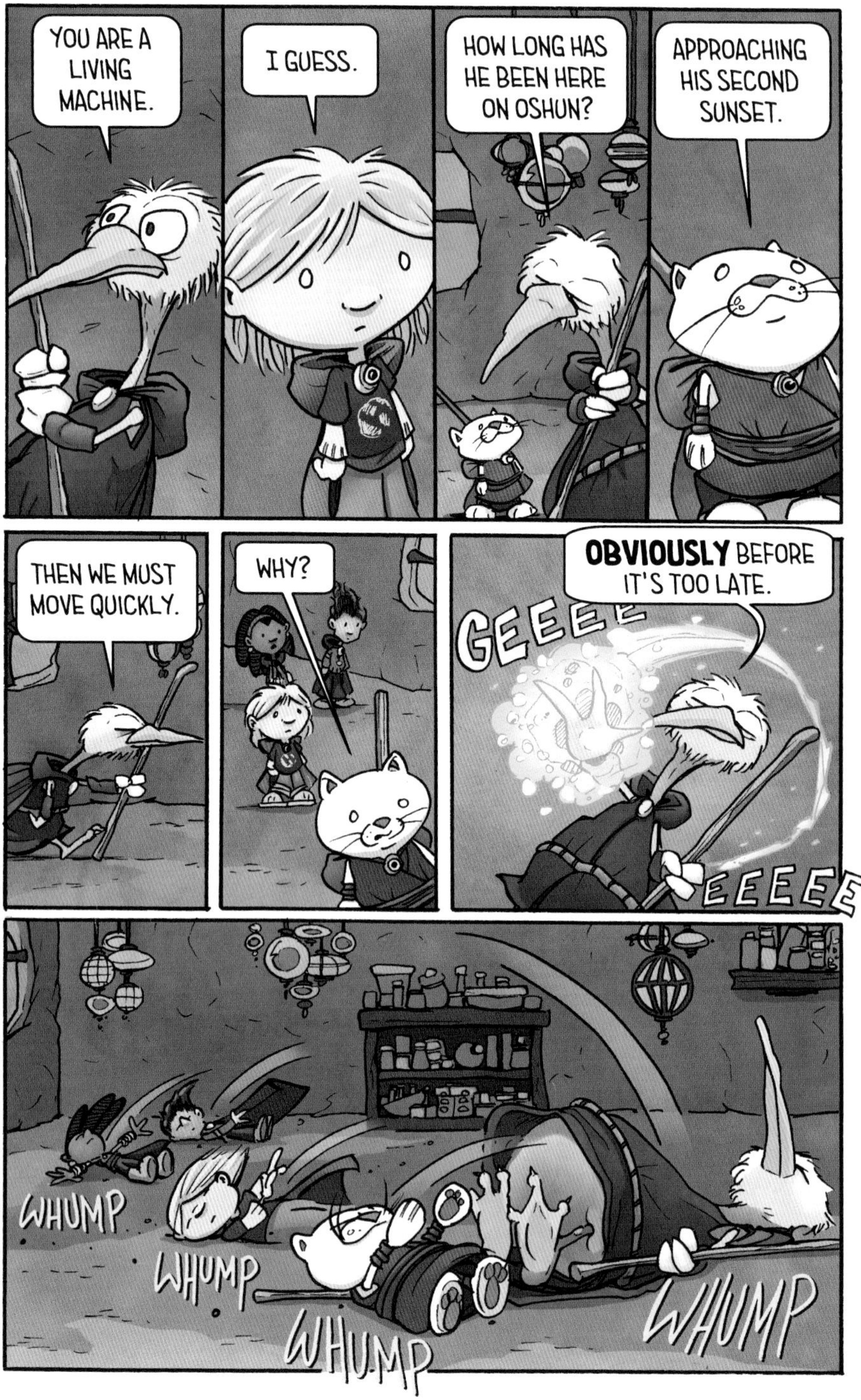
YOU ARE A LIVING MACHINE.
I GUESS.
HOW LONG HAS HE BEEN HERE ON OSHUN?
APPROACHING HIS SECOND SUNSET.
THEN WE MUST MOVE QUICKLY.
WHY?
OBVIOUSLY BEFORE IT'S TOO LATE.
GEEEEEEEEE
WHUMP
WHUMP
WHUMP
WHUMP

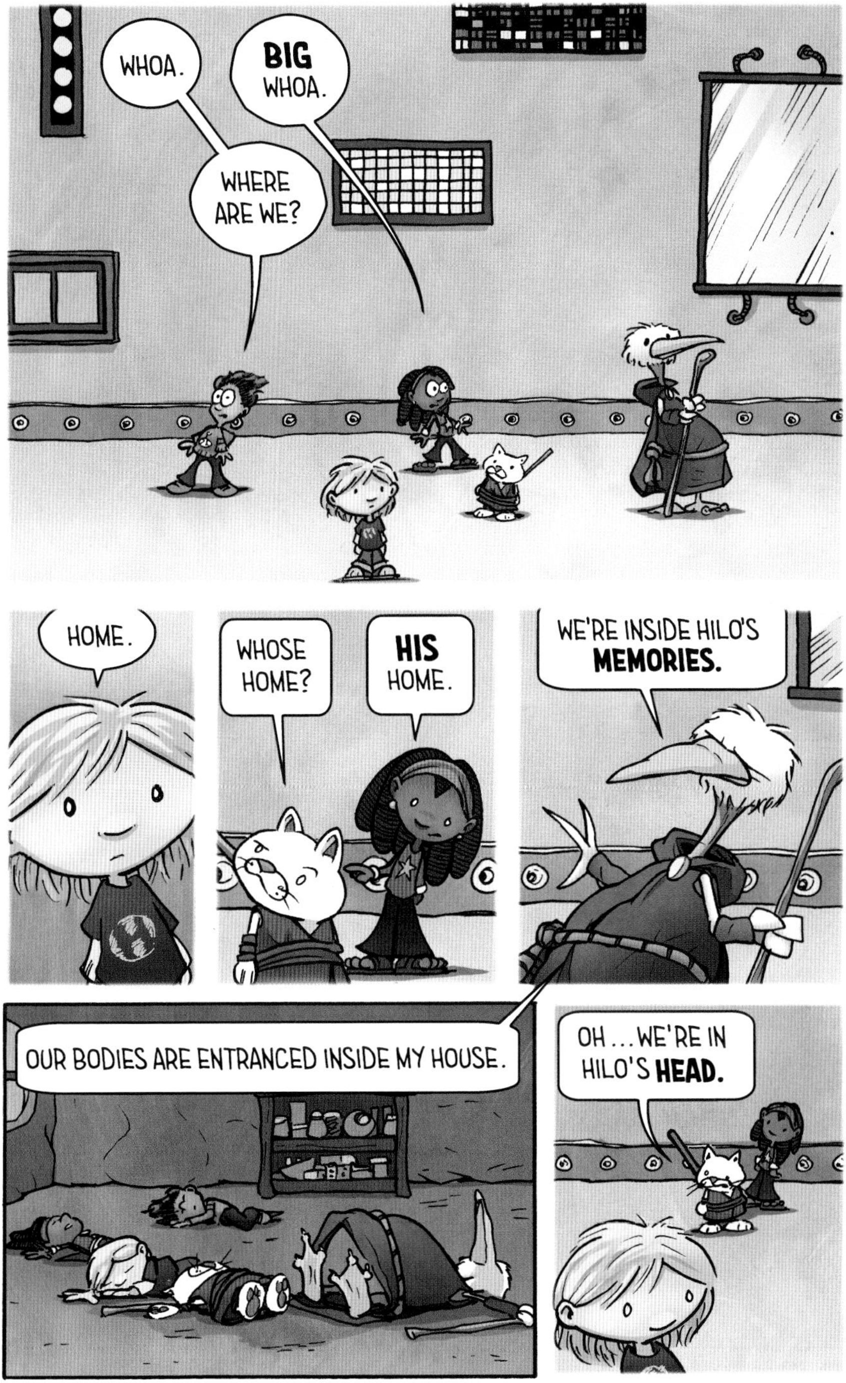
WHOA.
BIG WHOA.
WHERE ARE WE?
HOME.
WHOSE HOME?
HIS HOME.
WE'RE INSIDE HILO'S **MEMORIES.**
OUR BODIES ARE ENTRANCED INSIDE MY HOUSE.
OH . . . WE'RE IN HILO'S **HEAD.**

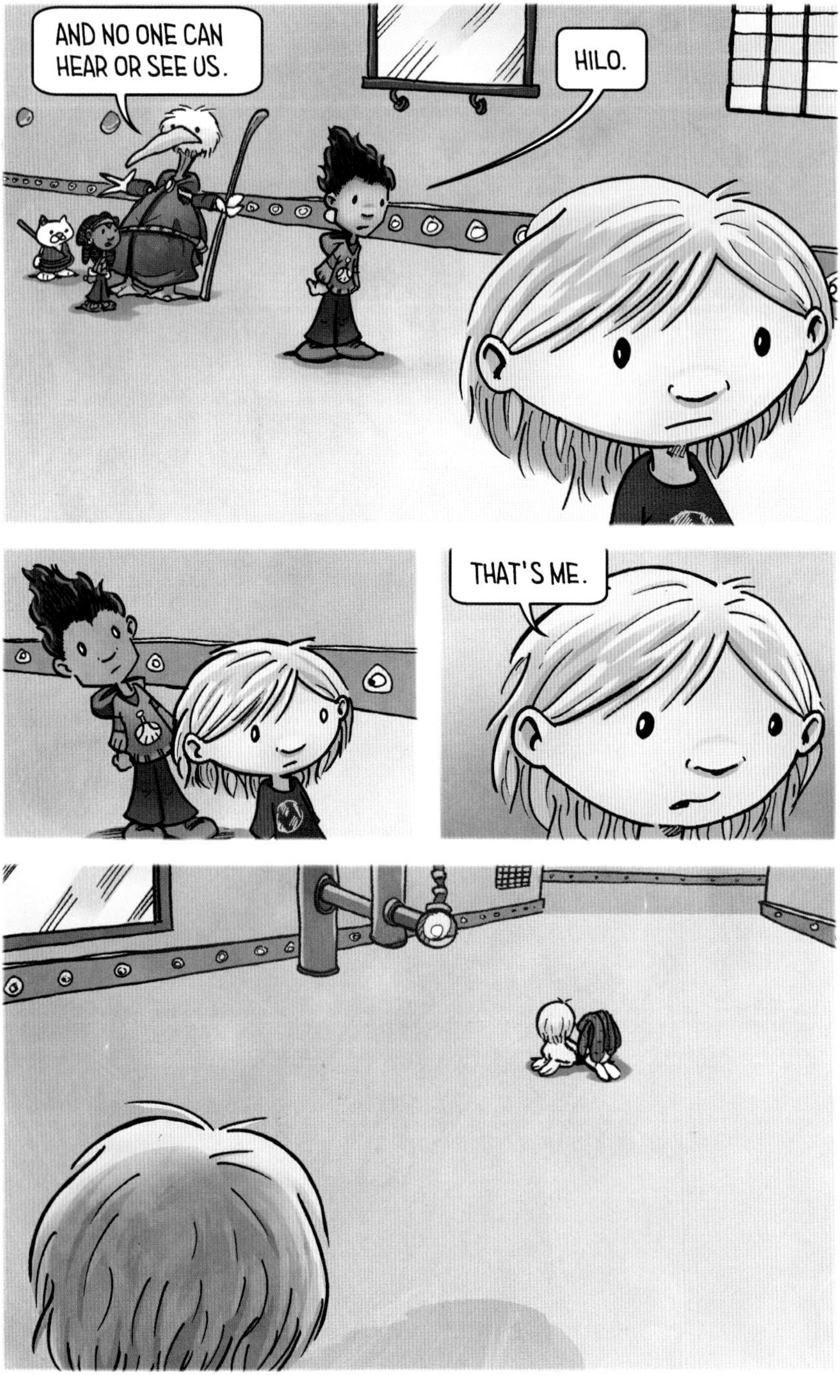
AND NO ONE CAN HEAR OR SEE US.
HILO.
THAT'S ME.

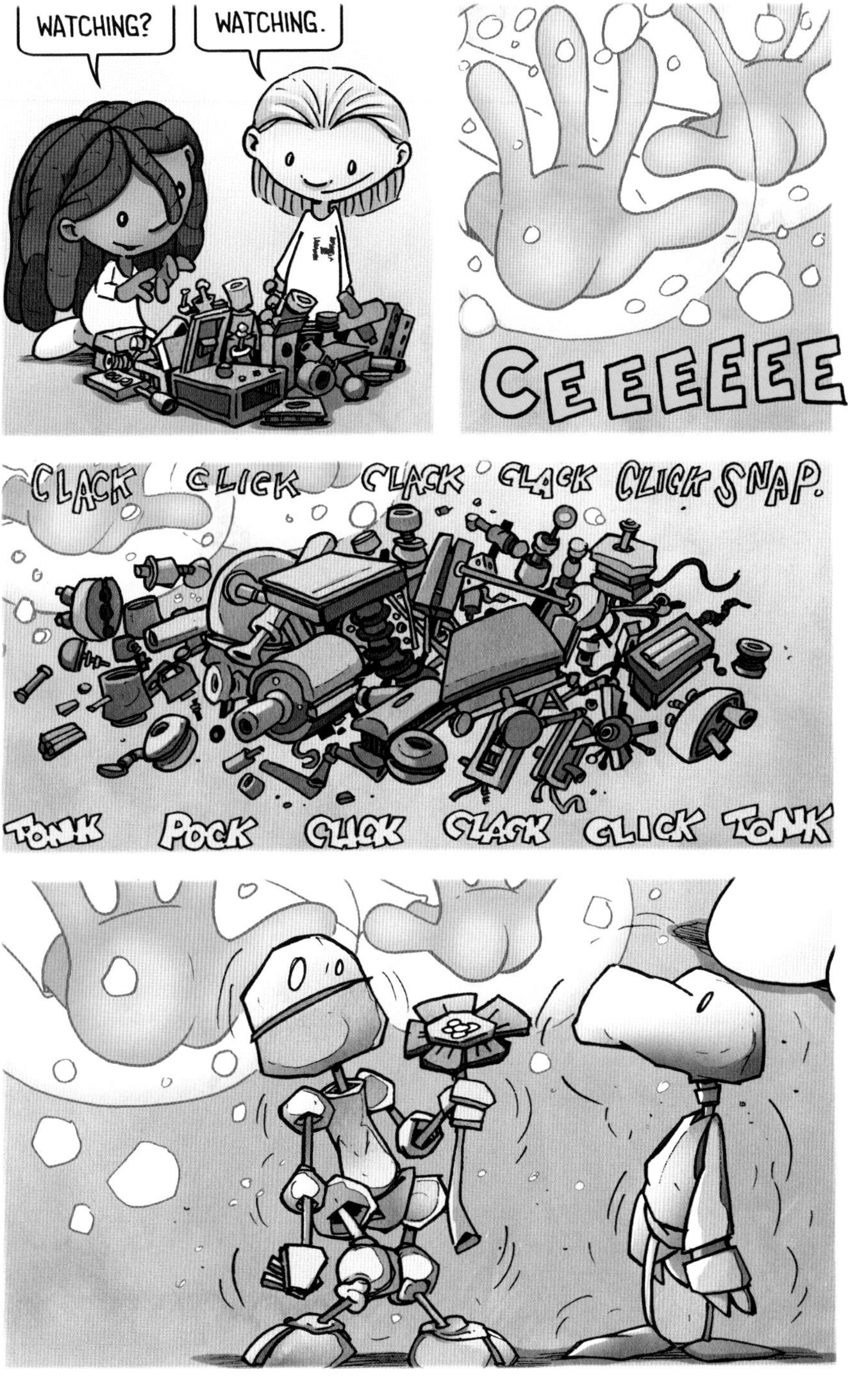

WATCHING?
WATCHING.
CEEEEEE
CLACK CLICK CLACK CLACK CLICK SNAP.
TONK POCK CLICK CLACK CLICK TONK

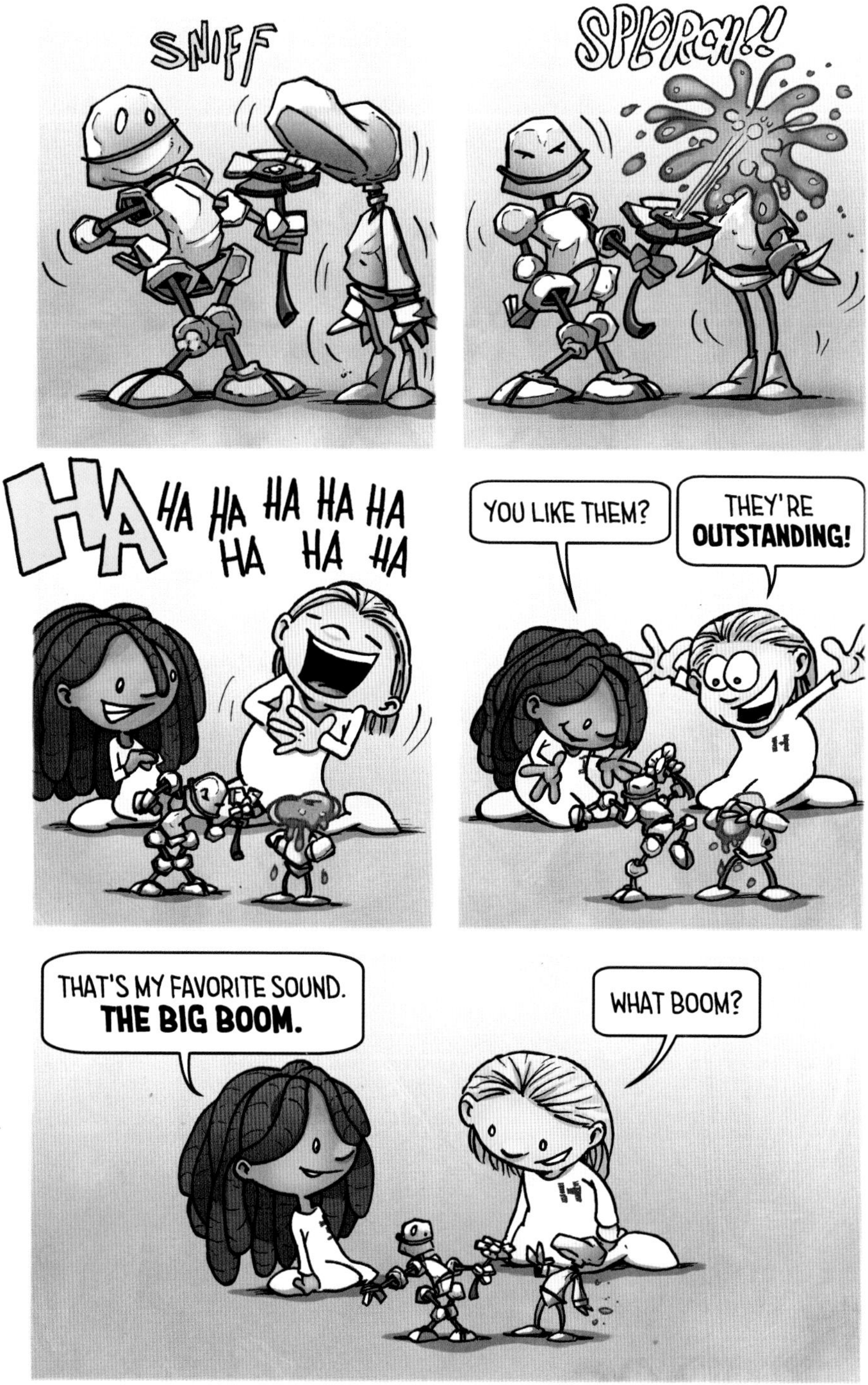

SNIFF
SPLORCH!!
HA HA HA HA HA HA HA HA HA
YOU LIKE THEM?
THEY'RE OUTSTANDING!
THAT'S MY FAVORITE SOUND. THE BIG BOOM.
WHAT BOOM?

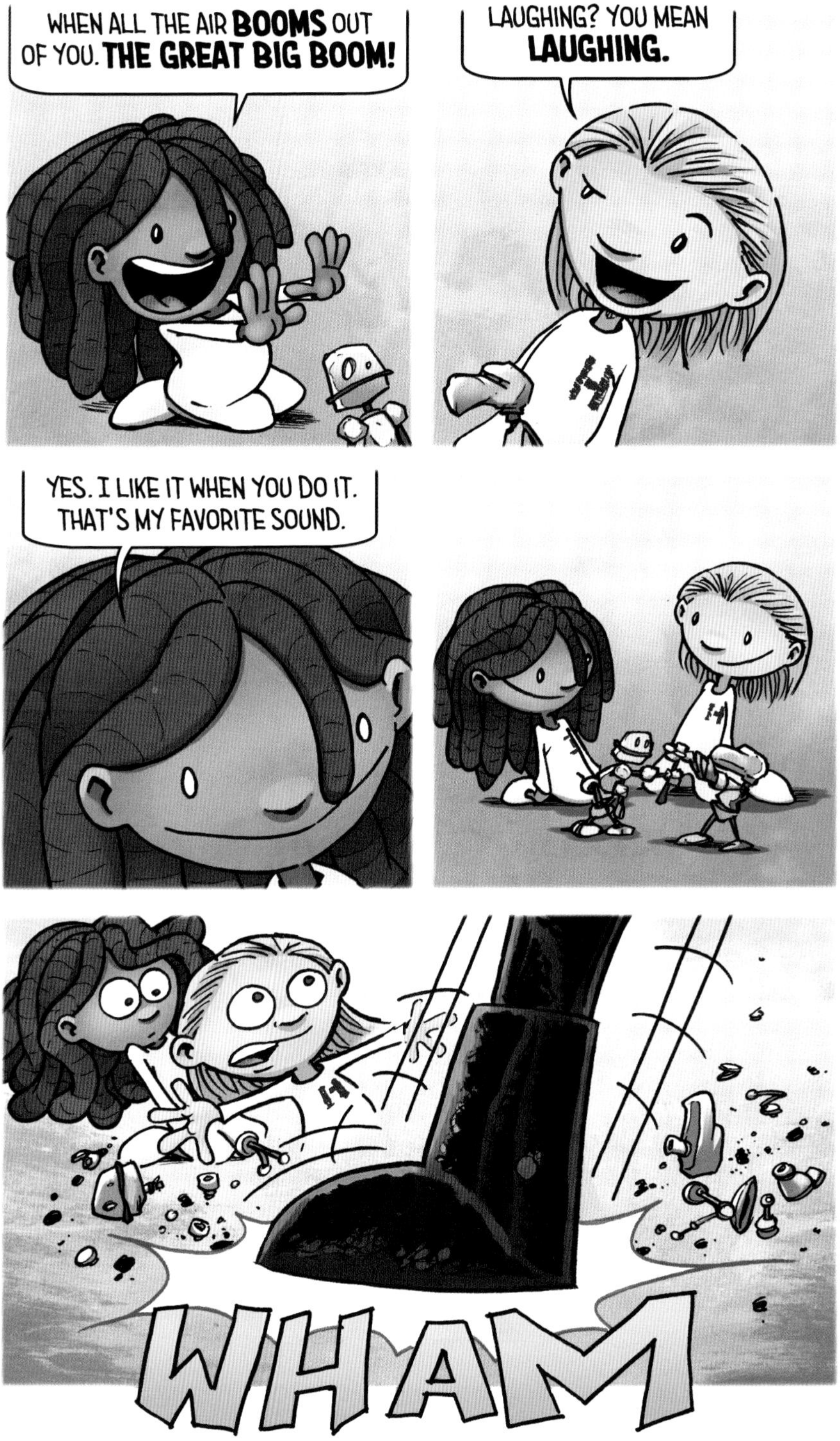
WHEN ALL THE AIR BOOMS OUT OF YOU. THE GREAT BIG BOOM!
LAUGHING? YOU MEAN LAUGHING.
YES. I LIKE IT WHEN YOU DO IT. THAT'S MY FAVORITE SOUND.
WHAM

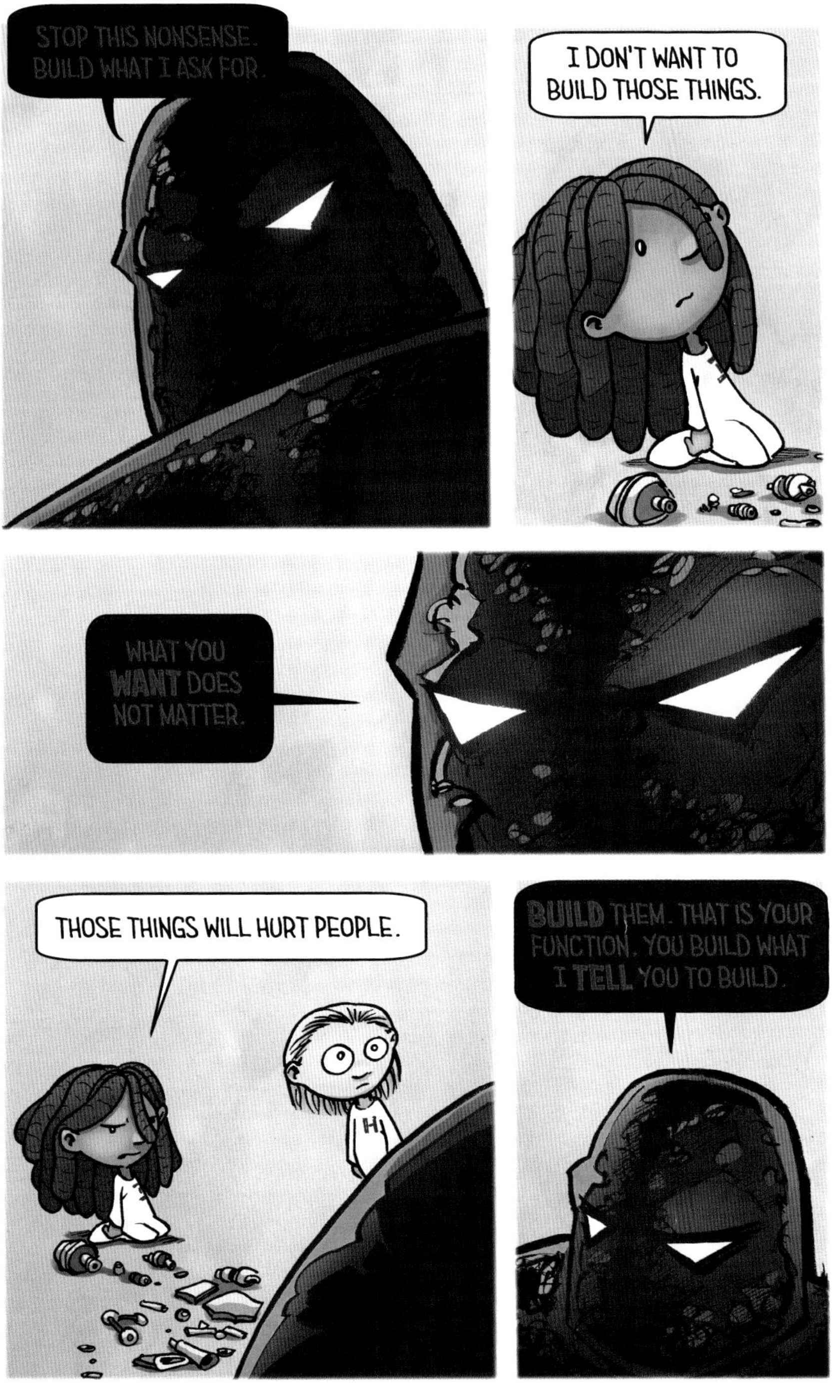
STOP THIS NONSENSE. BUILD WHAT I ASK FOR.
I DON'T WANT TO BUILD THOSE THINGS.
WHAT YOU WANT DOES NOT MATTER.
THOSE THINGS WILL HURT PEOPLE.
BUILD THEM. THAT IS YOUR FUNCTION. YOU BUILD WHAT I TELL YOU TO BUILD.

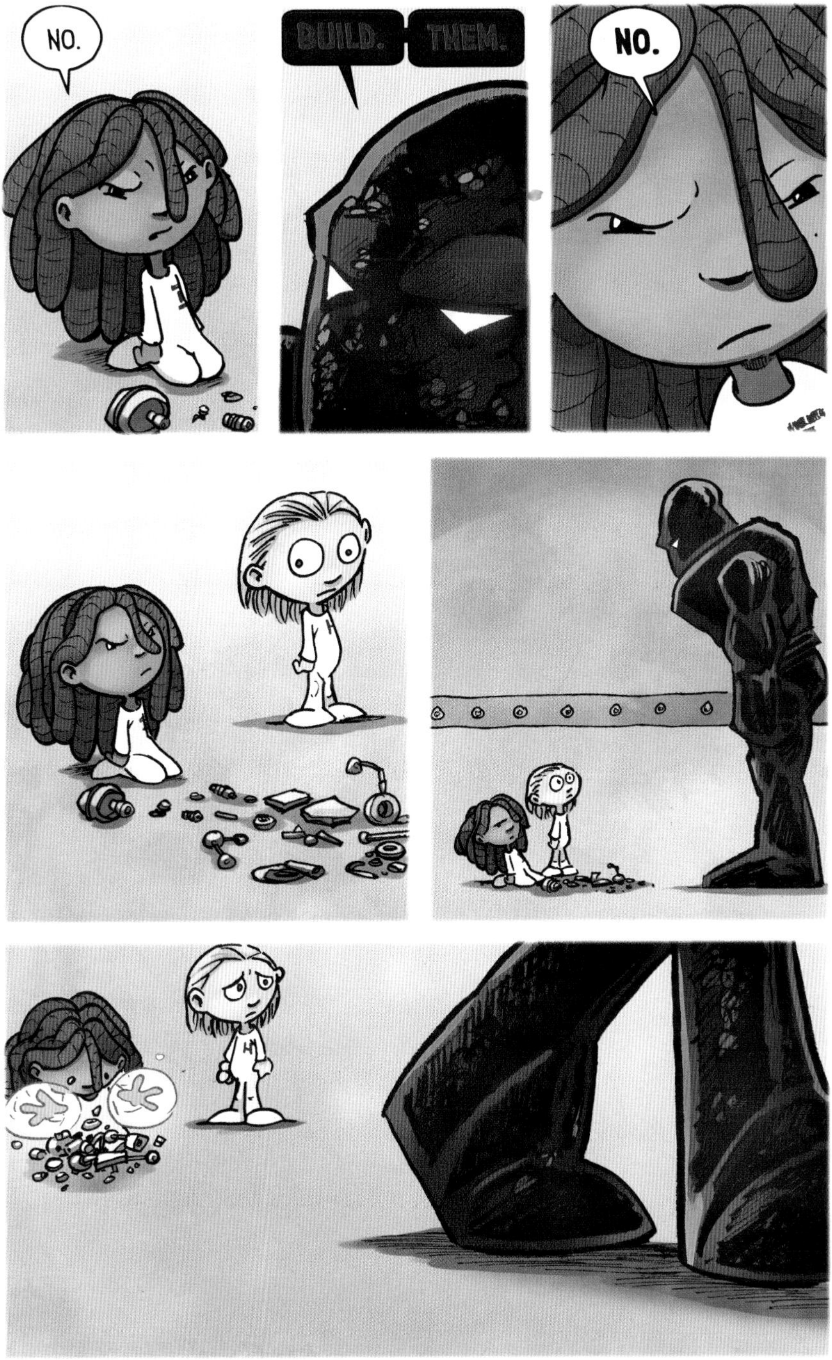
NO.
BUILD.
THEM.
NO.

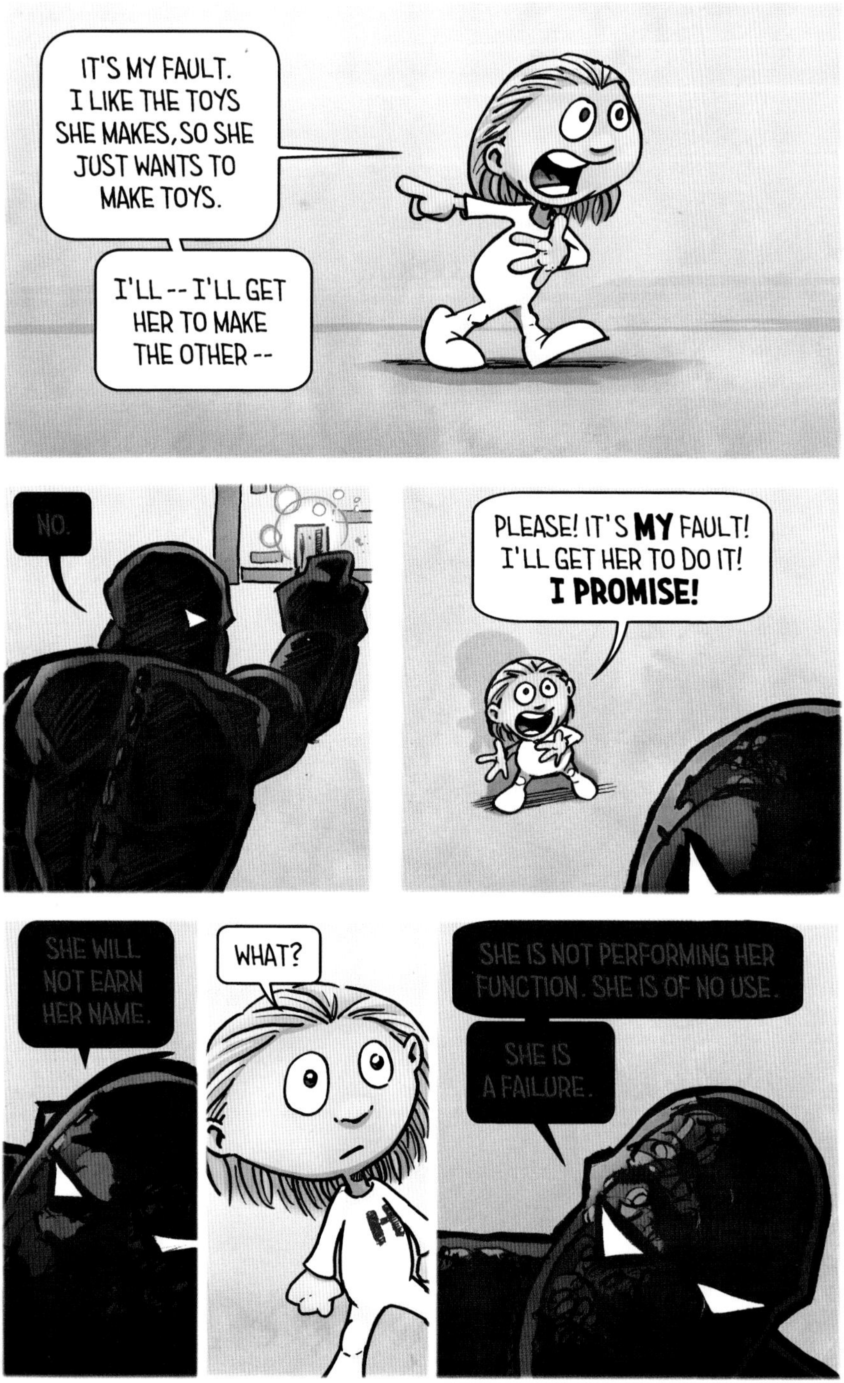
IT'S MY FAULT. I LIKE THE TOYS SHE MAKES, SO SHE JUST WANTS TO MAKE TOYS.
I'LL -- I'LL GET HER TO MAKE THE OTHER --
NO.
PLEASE! IT'S **MY** FAULT! I'LL GET HER TO DO IT! **I PROMISE!**
SHE WILL NOT EARN HER NAME.
WHAT?
SHE IS NOT PERFORMING HER FUNCTION. SHE IS OF NO USE.
SHE IS A FAILURE.

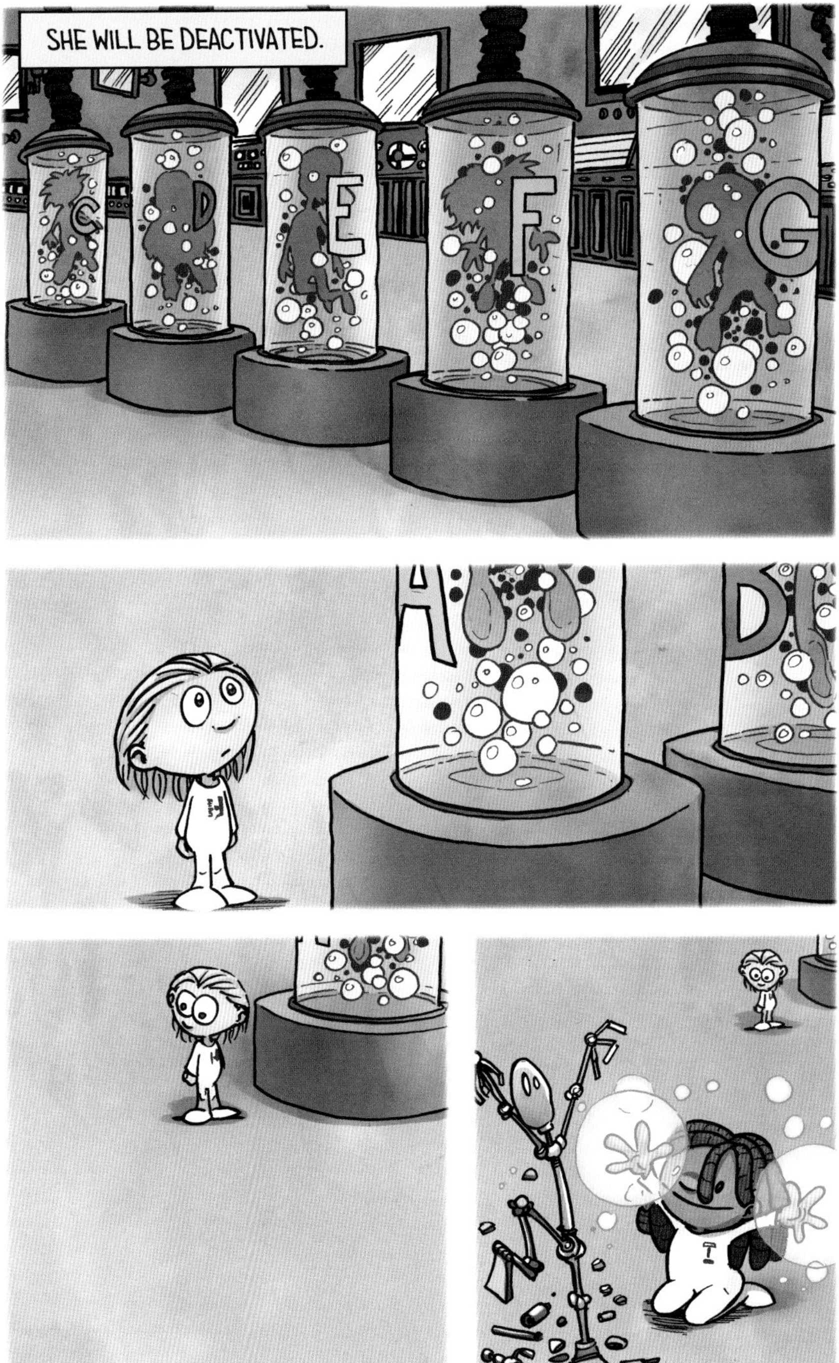
SHE WILL BE DEACTIVATED.

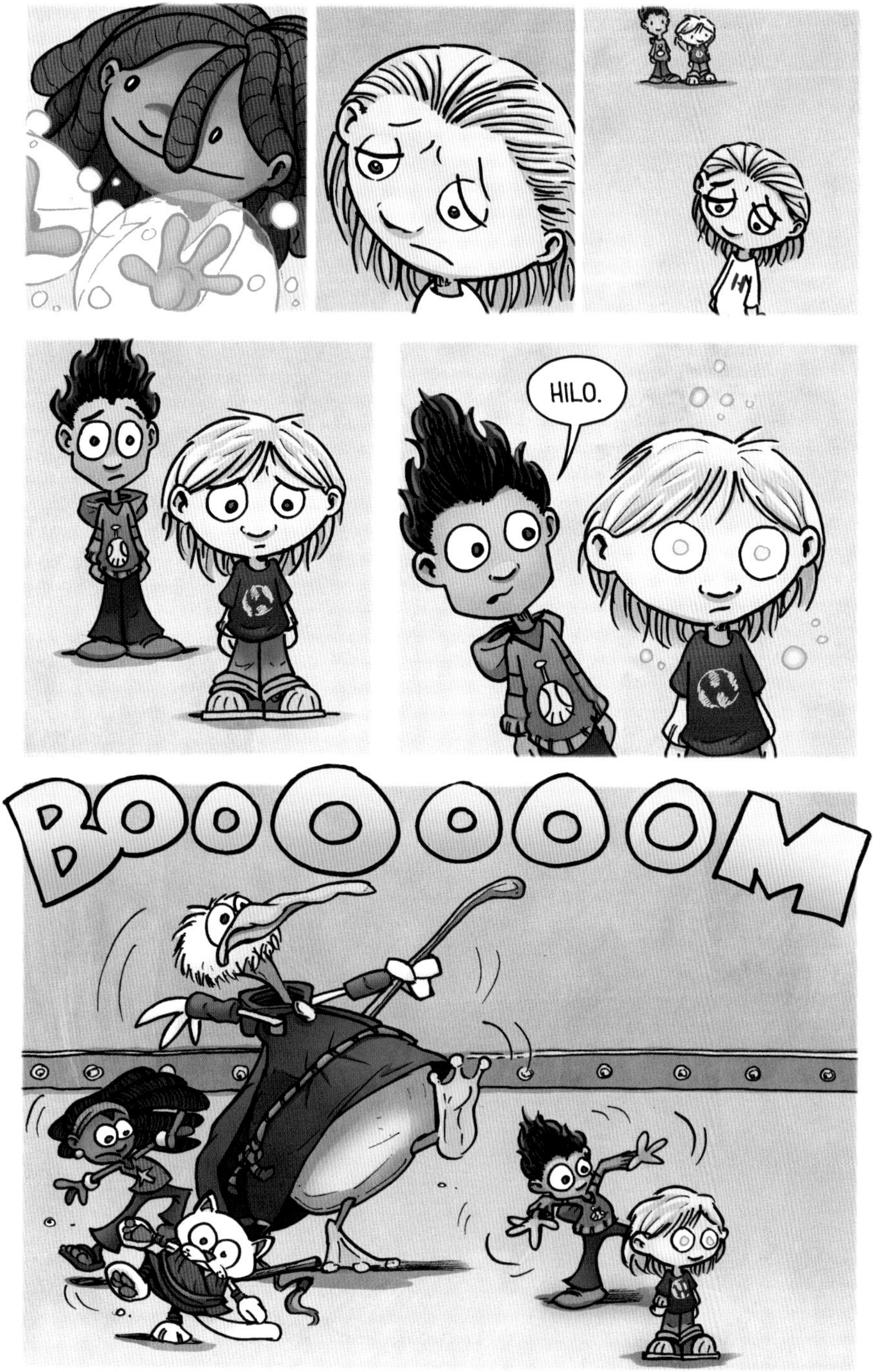
HILO.
BOOOOOOM

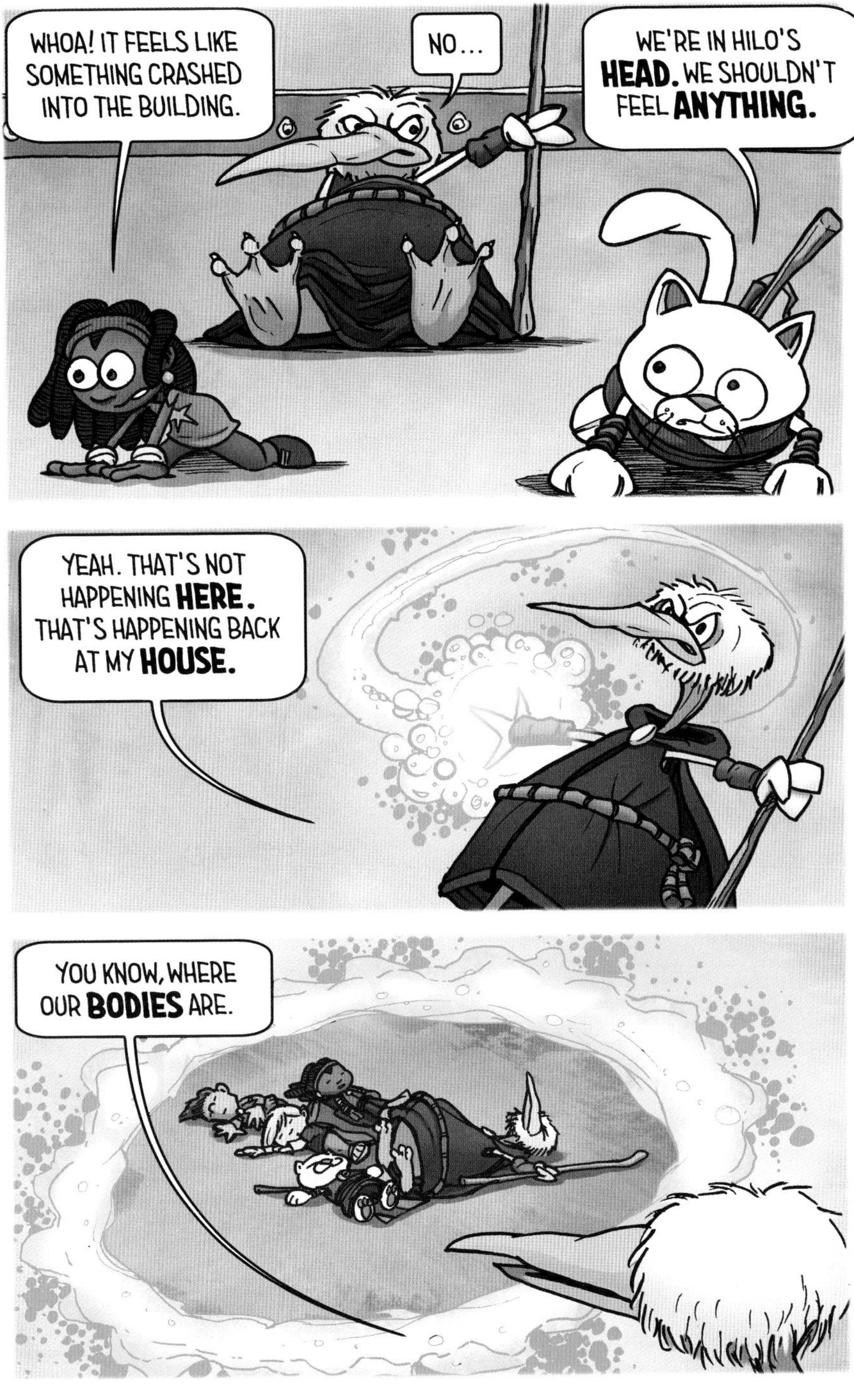
WHOA! IT FEELS LIKE SOMETHING CRASHED INTO THE BUILDING.
NO...
WE'RE IN HILO'S **HEAD.** WE SHOULDN'T FEEL **ANYTHING.**
YEAH. THAT'S NOT HAPPENING **HERE.** THAT'S HAPPENING BACK AT MY **HOUSE.**
YOU KNOW, WHERE OUR **BODIES** ARE.

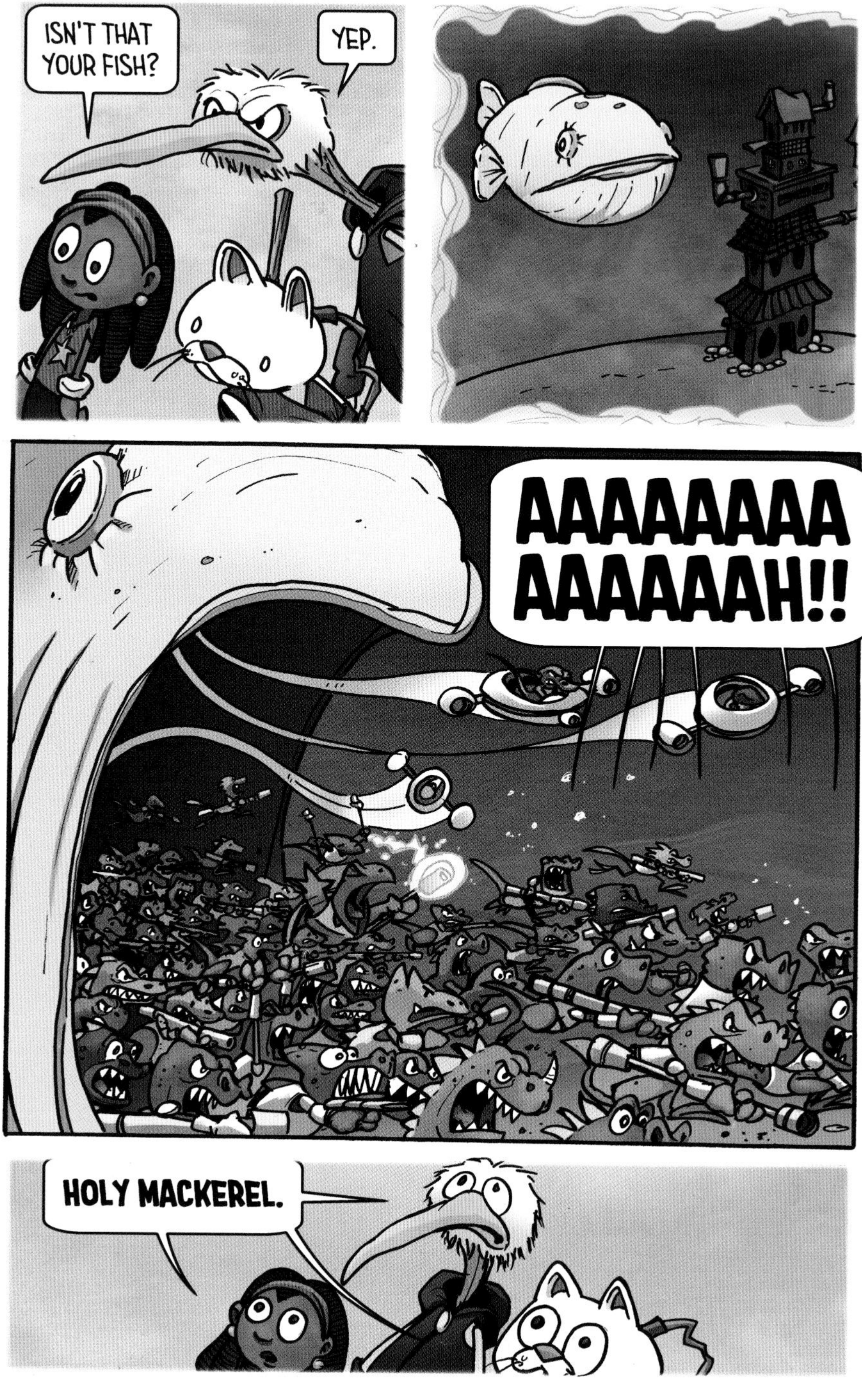
ISN'T THAT YOUR FISH?
YEP.
AAAAAAAA AAAAAAAH!!
HOLY MACKEREL.

# CHAPTER 8

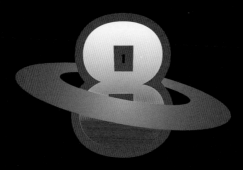

# BETTER THAN APE

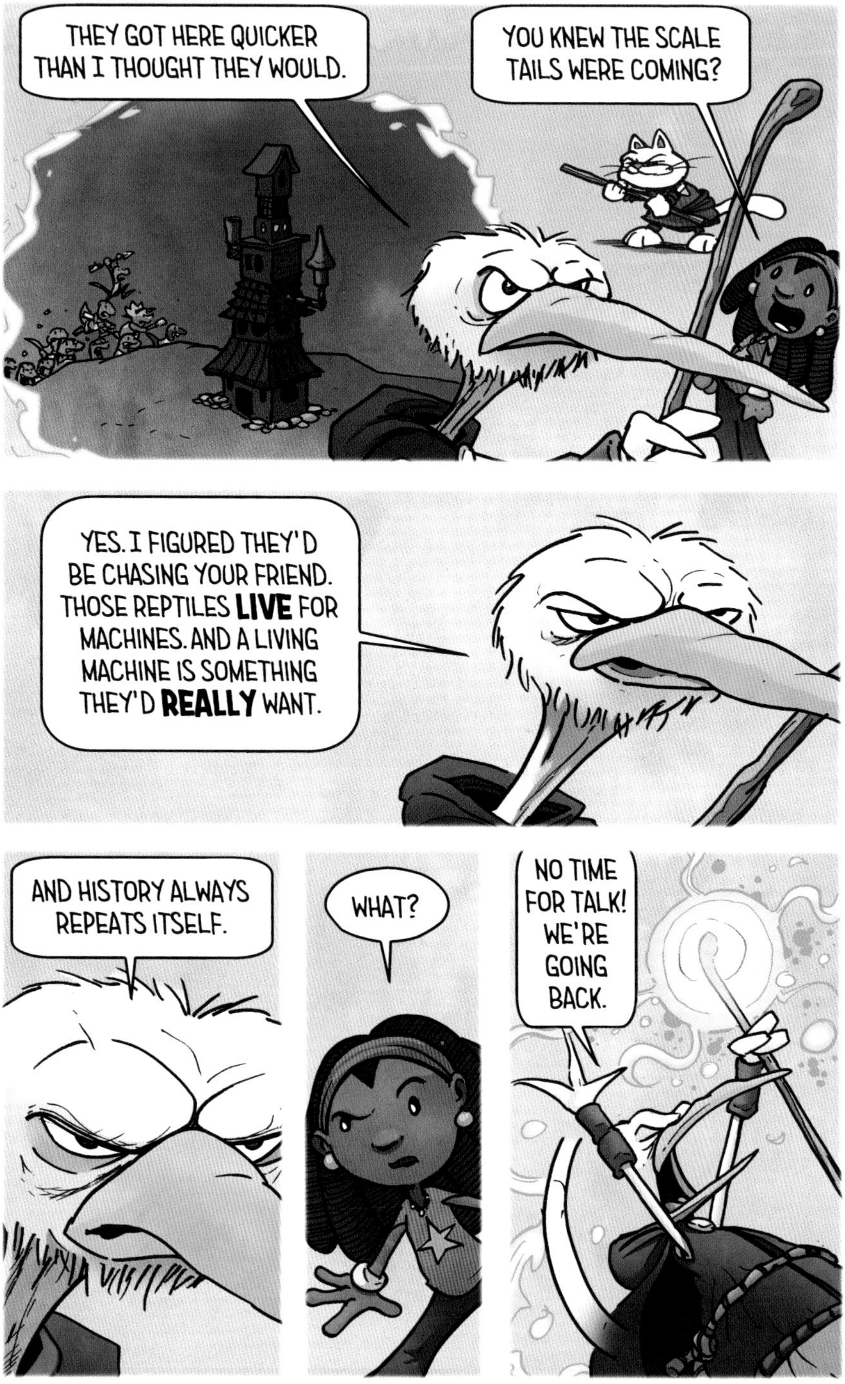
THEY GOT HERE QUICKER THAN I THOUGHT THEY WOULD.
YOU KNEW THE SCALE TAILS WERE COMING?
YES. I FIGURED THEY'D BE CHASING YOUR FRIEND. THOSE REPTILES **LIVE** FOR MACHINES. AND A LIVING MACHINE IS SOMETHING THEY'D **REALLY** WANT.
AND HISTORY ALWAYS REPEATS ITSELF.
WHAT?
NO TIME FOR TALK! WE'RE GOING BACK.

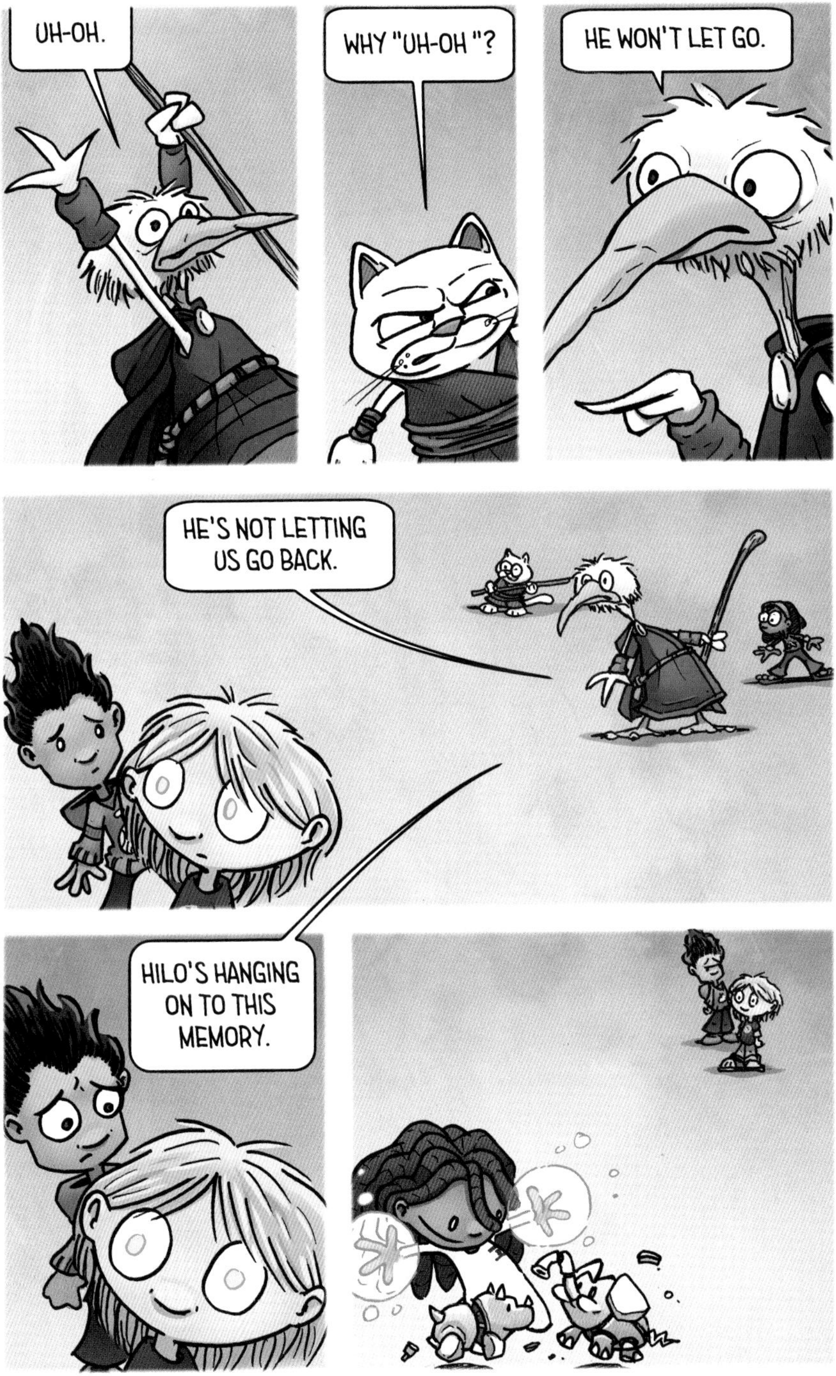
UH-OH.
WHY "UH-OH"?
HE WON'T LET GO.
HE'S NOT LETTING US GO BACK.
HILO'S HANGING ON TO THIS MEMORY.

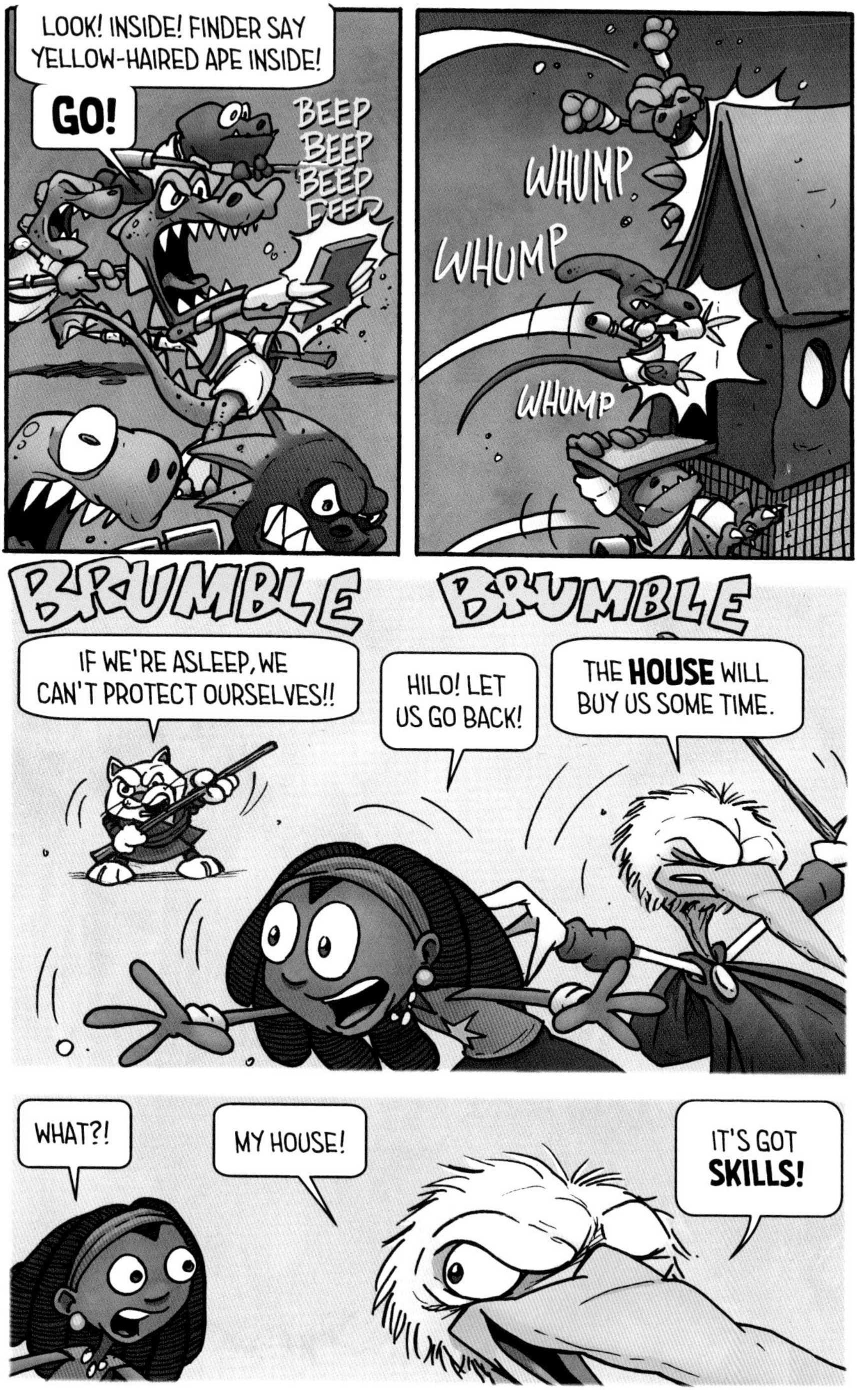
LOOK! INSIDE! FINDER SAY YELLOW-HAIRED APE INSIDE!
GO!
BEEP BEEP BEEP
WHUMP
WHUMP
WHUMP
BRUMBLE BRUMBLE
IF WE'RE ASLEEP, WE CAN'T PROTECT OURSELVES!!
HILO! LET US GO BACK!
THE HOUSE WILL BUY US SOME TIME.
WHAT?!
MY HOUSE!
IT'S GOT SKILLS!

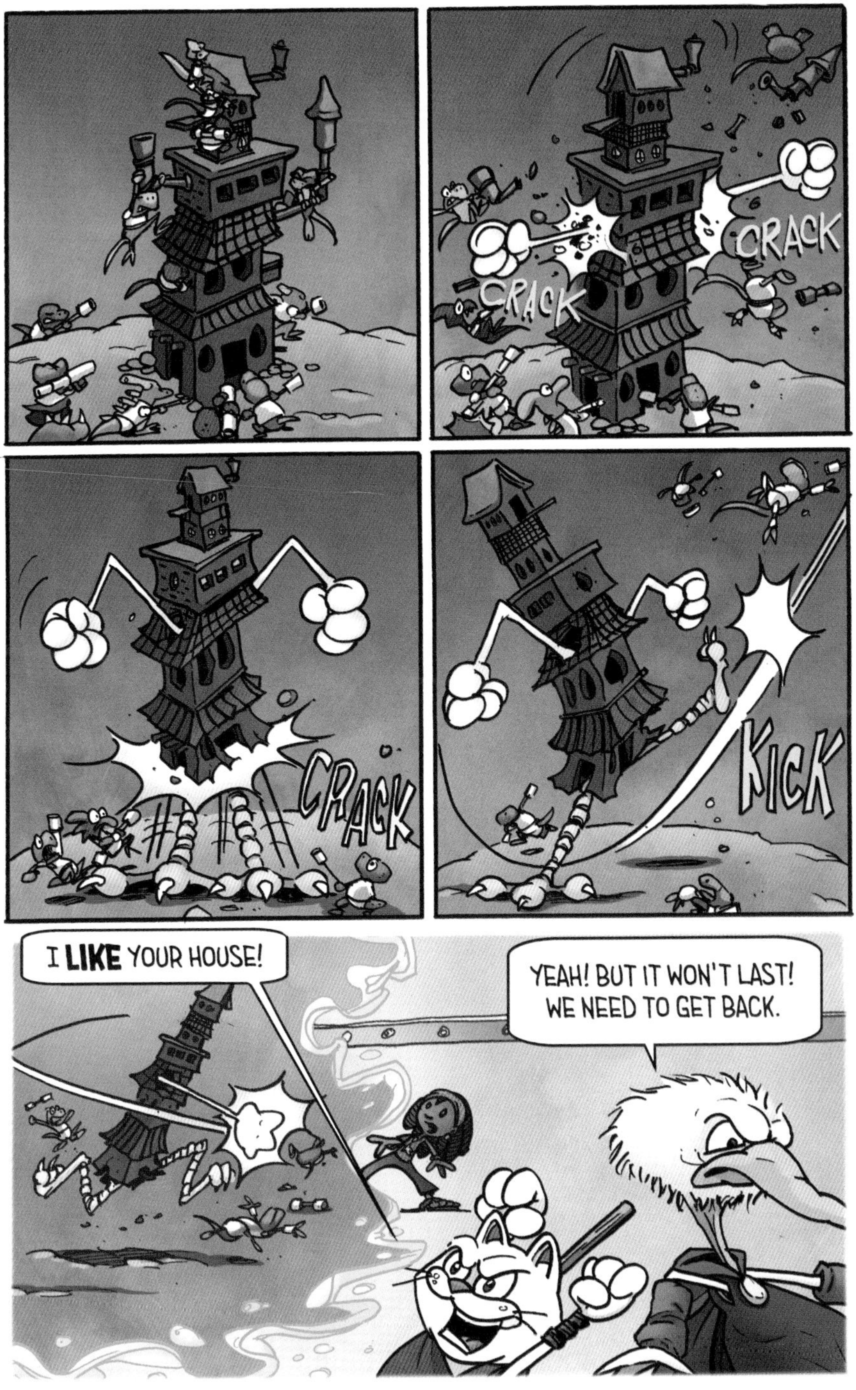
CRACK
CRACK
CRACK
KICK
I LIKE YOUR HOUSE!
YEAH! BUT IT WON'T LAST!
WE NEED TO GET BACK.

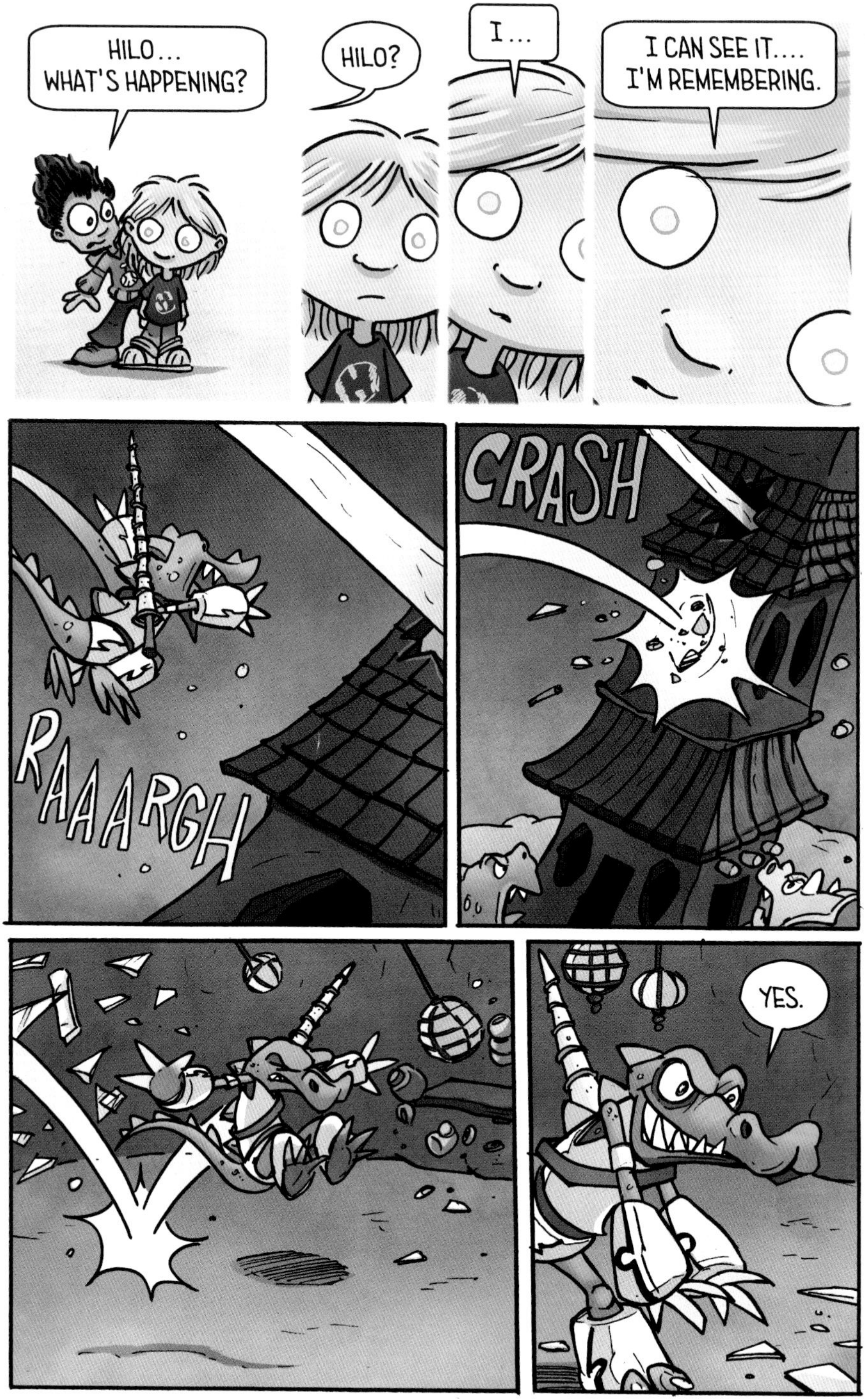
HILO...
WHAT'S HAPPENING?
HILO?
I...
I CAN SEE IT....
I'M REMEMBERING.
RAAARGH
CRASH
YES.

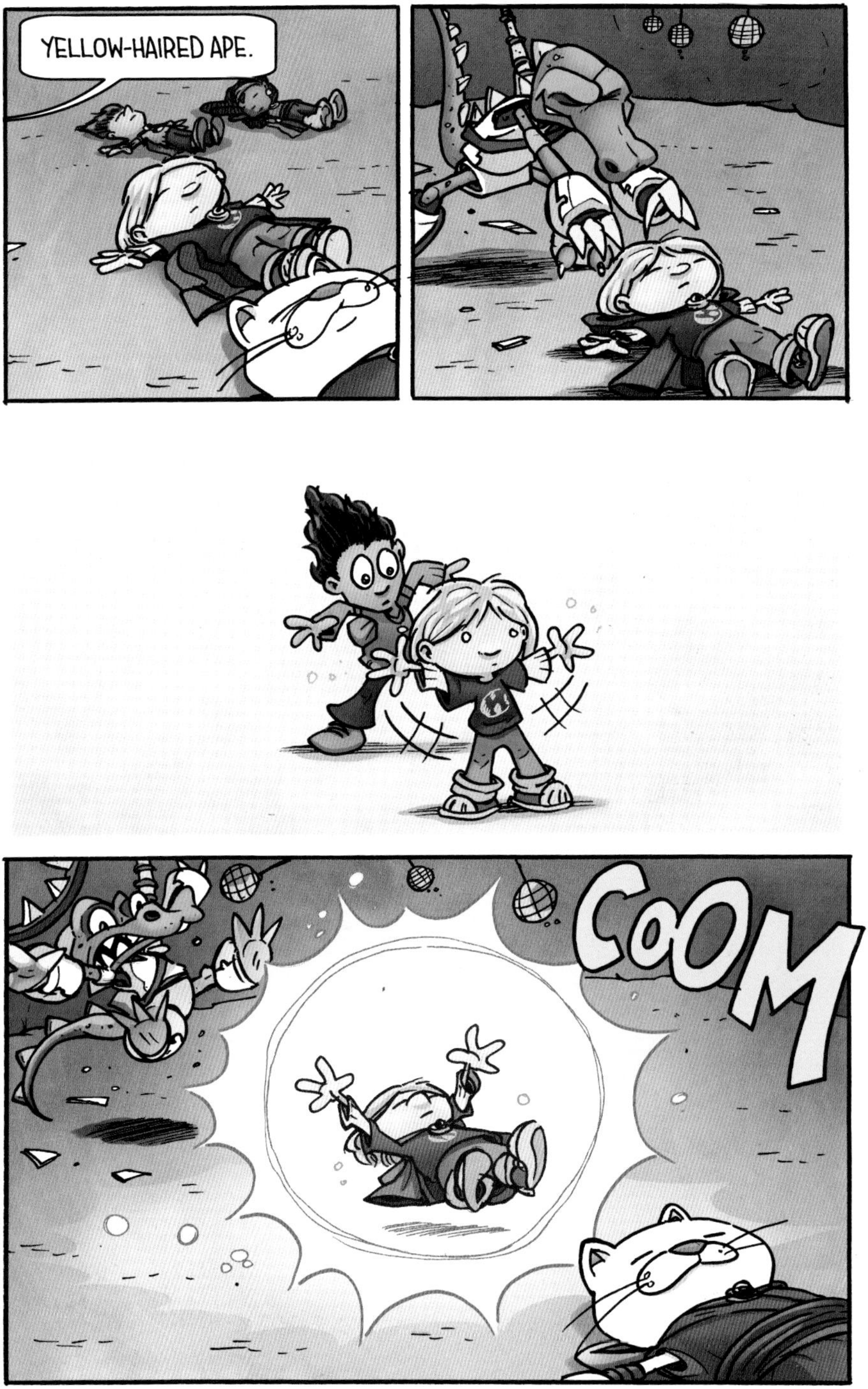
YELLOW-HAIRED APE.
COOM

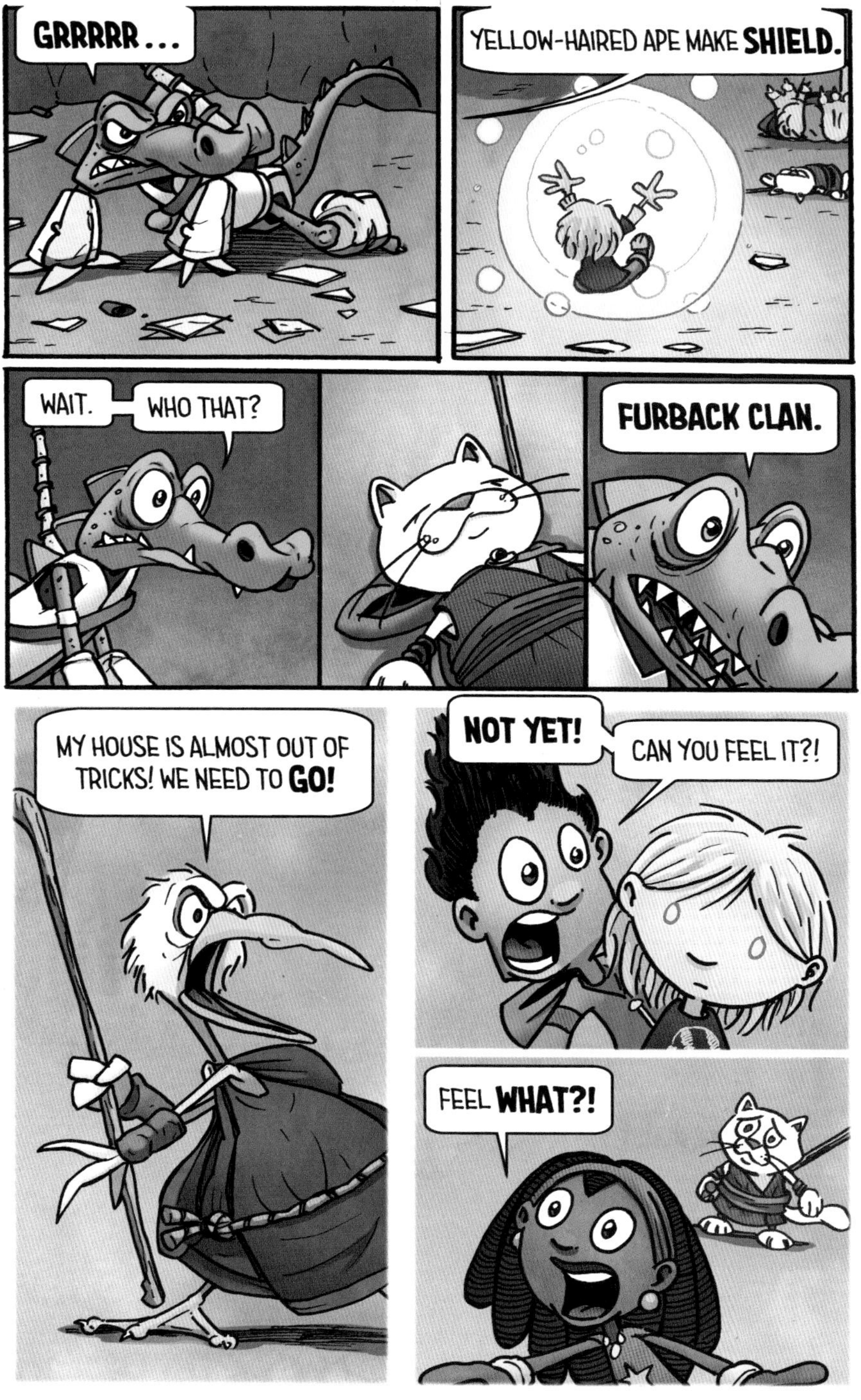
GRRRRR...
YELLOW-HAIRED APE MAKE SHIELD.
WAIT.
WHO THAT?
FURBACK CLAN.
MY HOUSE IS ALMOST OUT OF TRICKS! WE NEED TO GO!
NOT YET!
CAN YOU FEEL IT?!
FEEL WHAT?!

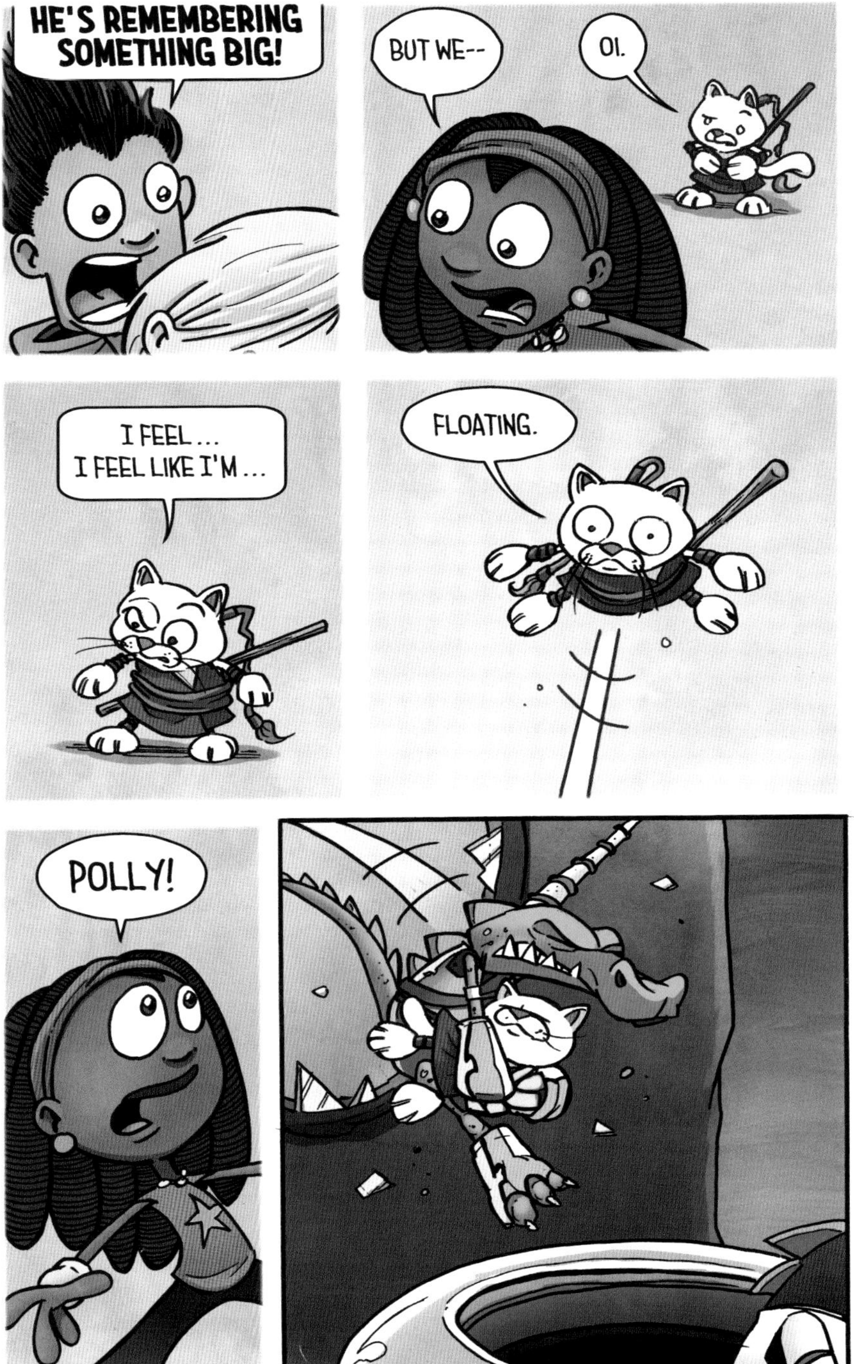
HE'S REMEMBERING SOMETHING BIG!
BUT WE--
OI.
I FEEL ...
I FEEL LIKE I'M ...
FLOATING.
POLLY!

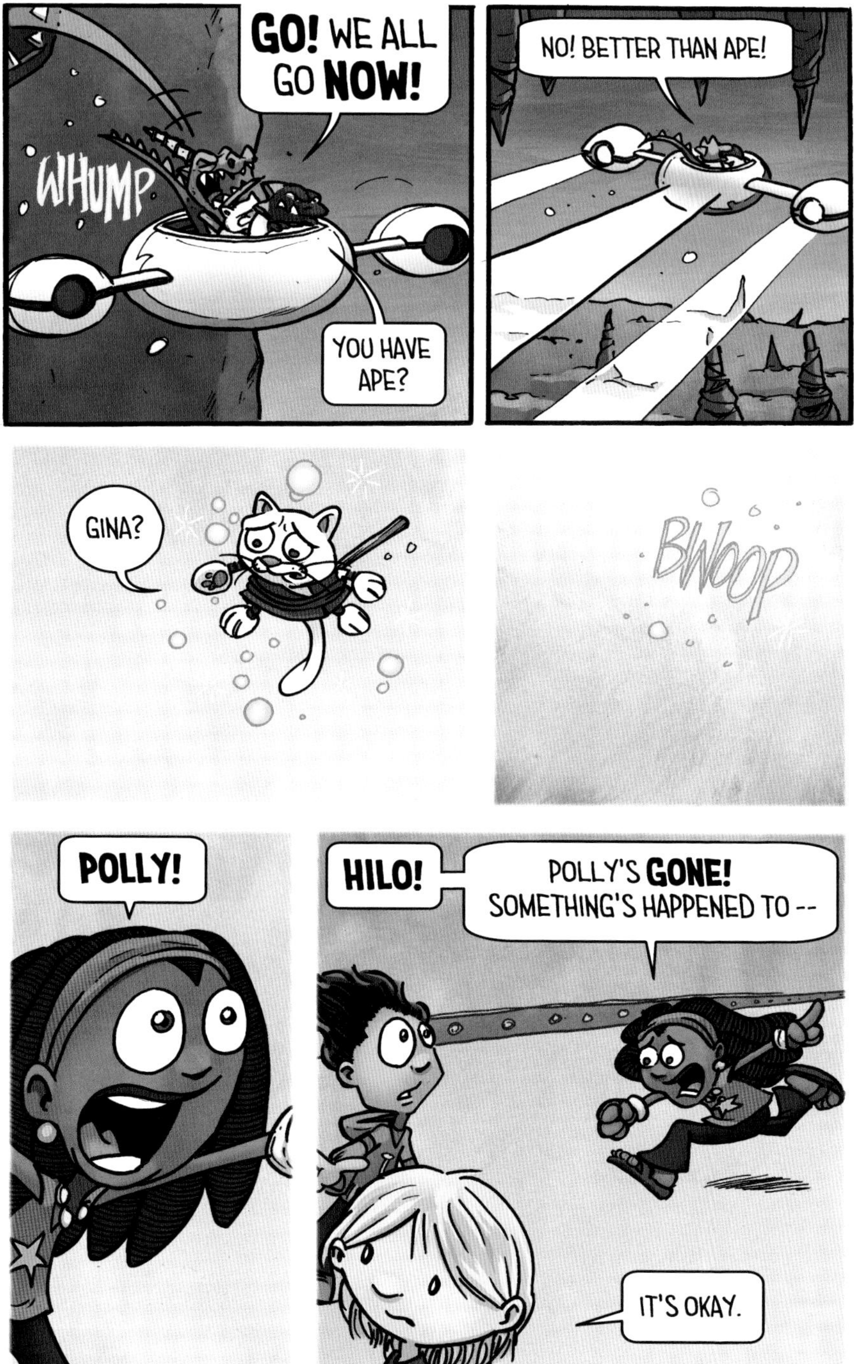
GO! WE ALL GO NOW!
WHUMP
YOU HAVE APE?
NO! BETTER THAN APE!
GINA?
BWOOP
POLLY!
HILO!
POLLY'S GONE! SOMETHING'S HAPPENED TO --
IT'S OKAY.

WE'RE GOING BACK.

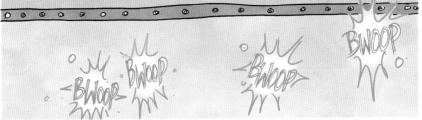

<BWOOP> BWOOP. BWOOP BWOOP

WHA--?

WE'RE AWAKE IN OUR BODIES.

POLLY?!

POLLY!

NO! THEY TOOK HER!

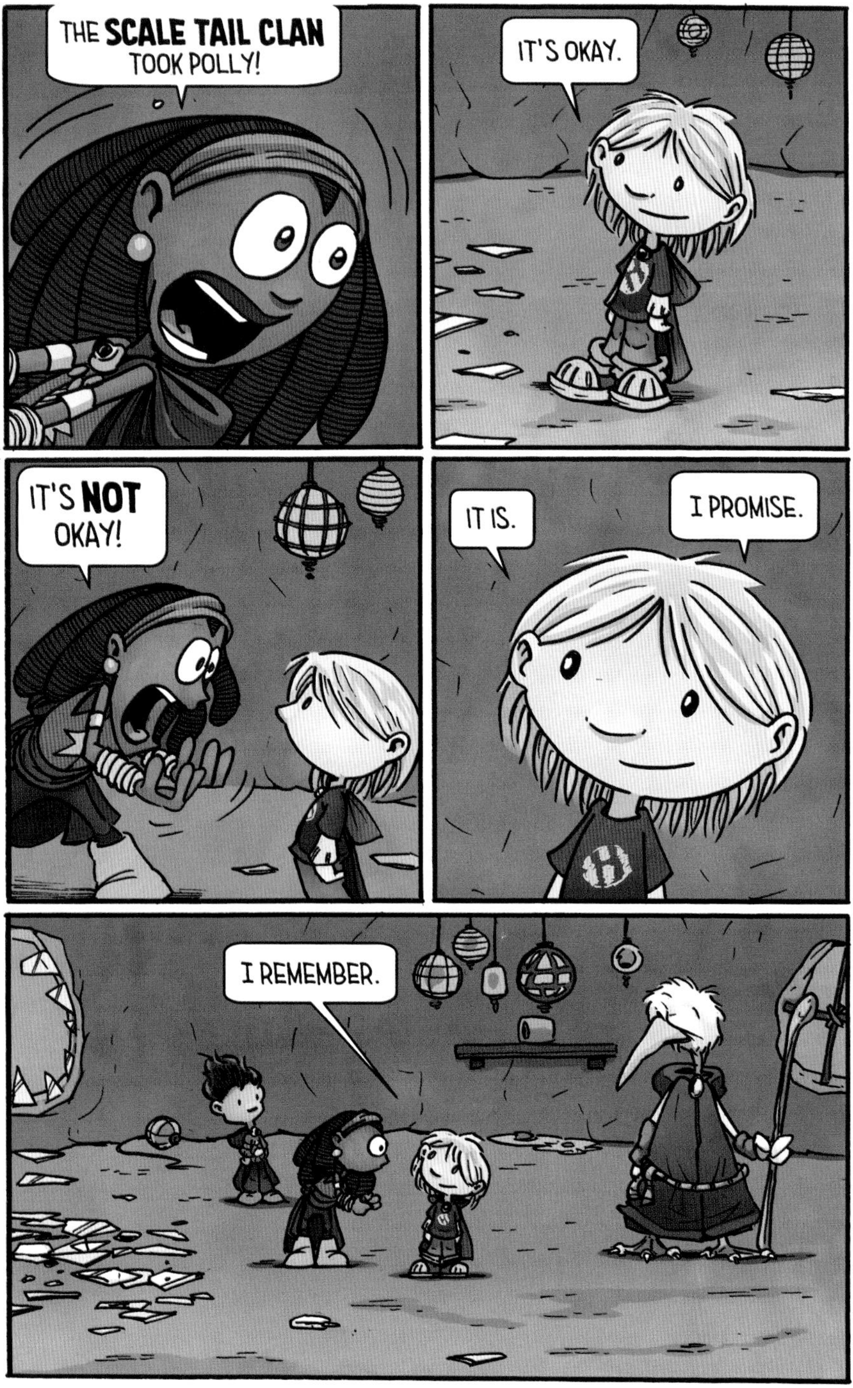
THE **SCALE TAIL CLAN** TOOK POLLY!
IT'S OKAY.
IT'S **NOT** OKAY!
IT IS.
I PROMISE.
I REMEMBER.

# CHAPTER 9

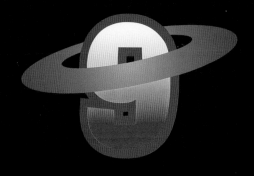

## GOOD

VILLAGE OF THE SCALE TAIL CLAN.

WHERE IS **FURBACK CLAN** VILLAGE?

I NOT HURT YOU IF YOU TELL ME.

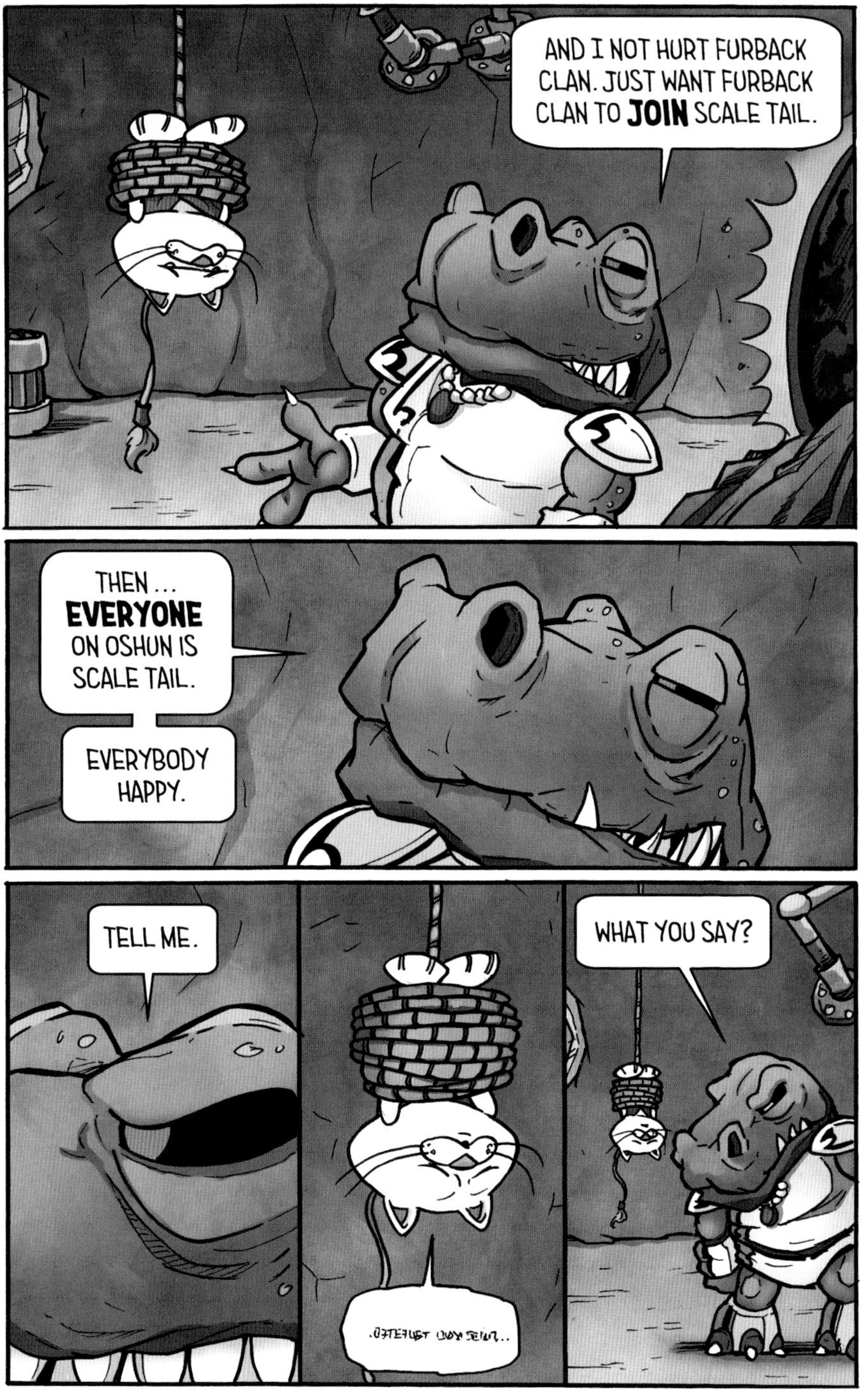
AND I NOT HURT FURBACK CLAN. JUST WANT FURBACK CLAN TO **JOIN** SCALE TAIL.
THEN ... **EVERYONE** ON OSHUN IS SCALE TAIL.
EVERYBODY HAPPY.
TELL ME.
WHAT YOU SAY?

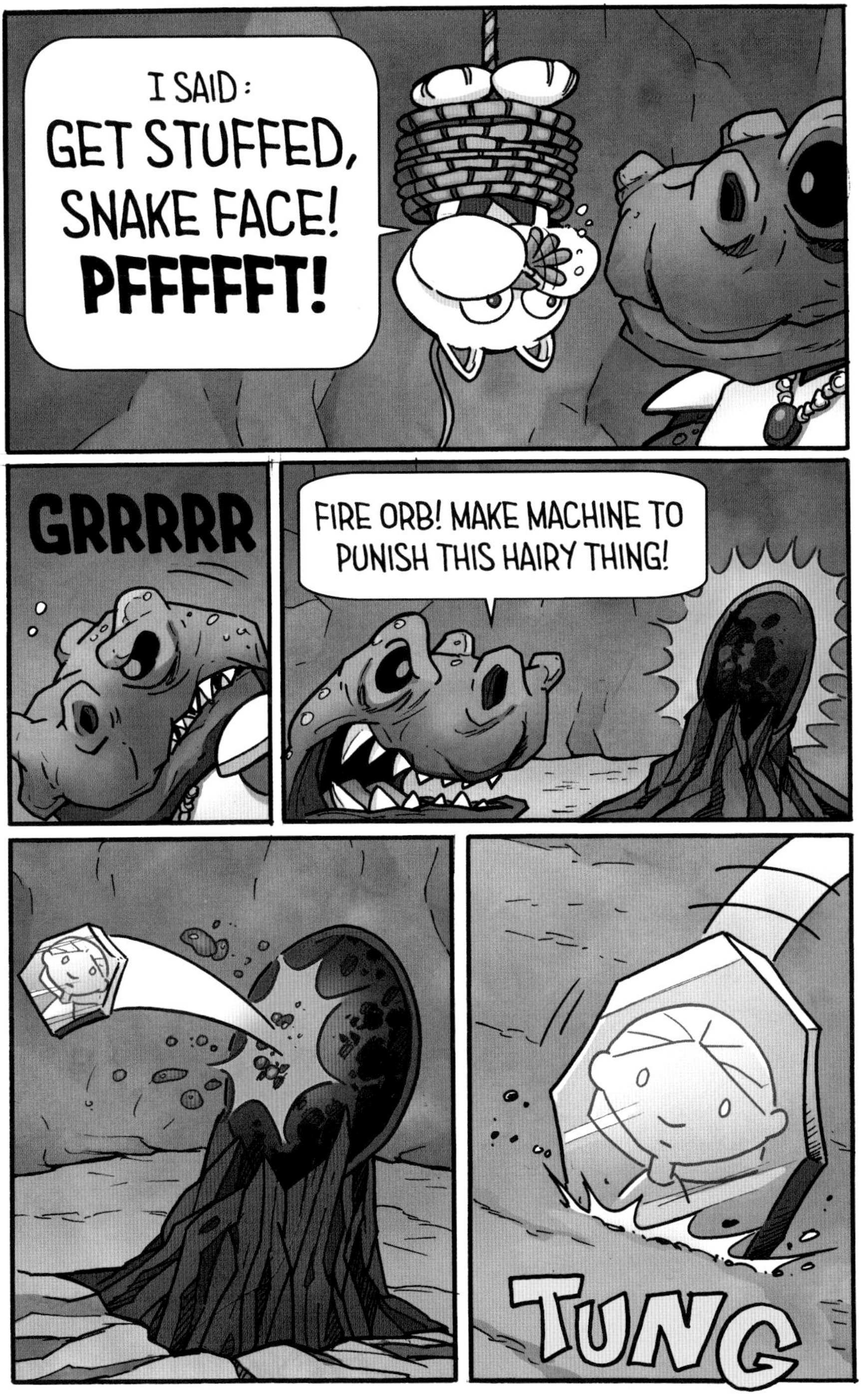
I SAID:
GET STUFFED, SNAKE FACE!
PFFFFFT!
GRRRRR
FIRE ORB! MAKE MACHINE TO PUNISH THIS HAIRY THING!
TUNG

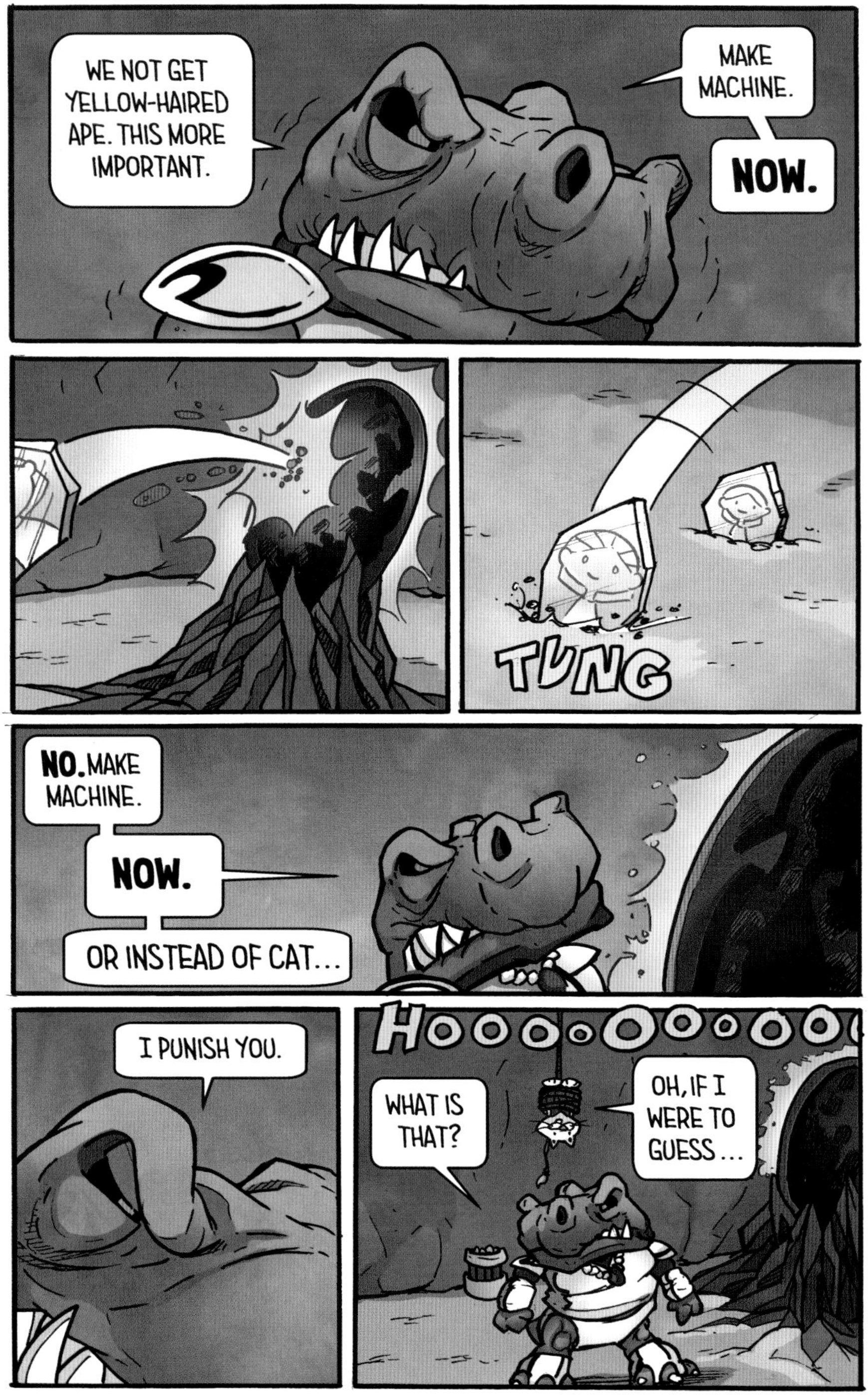
WE NOT GET YELLOW-HAIRED APE. THIS MORE IMPORTANT.
MAKE MACHINE.
NOW.
TUNG
NO. MAKE MACHINE.
NOW.
OR INSTEAD OF CAT...
I PUNISH YOU.
HOOOoOOoOOO
WHAT IS THAT?
OH, IF I WERE TO GUESS...

I'D SAY MY **RIDE** IS HERE.

HOooooOOOOO

BOOM

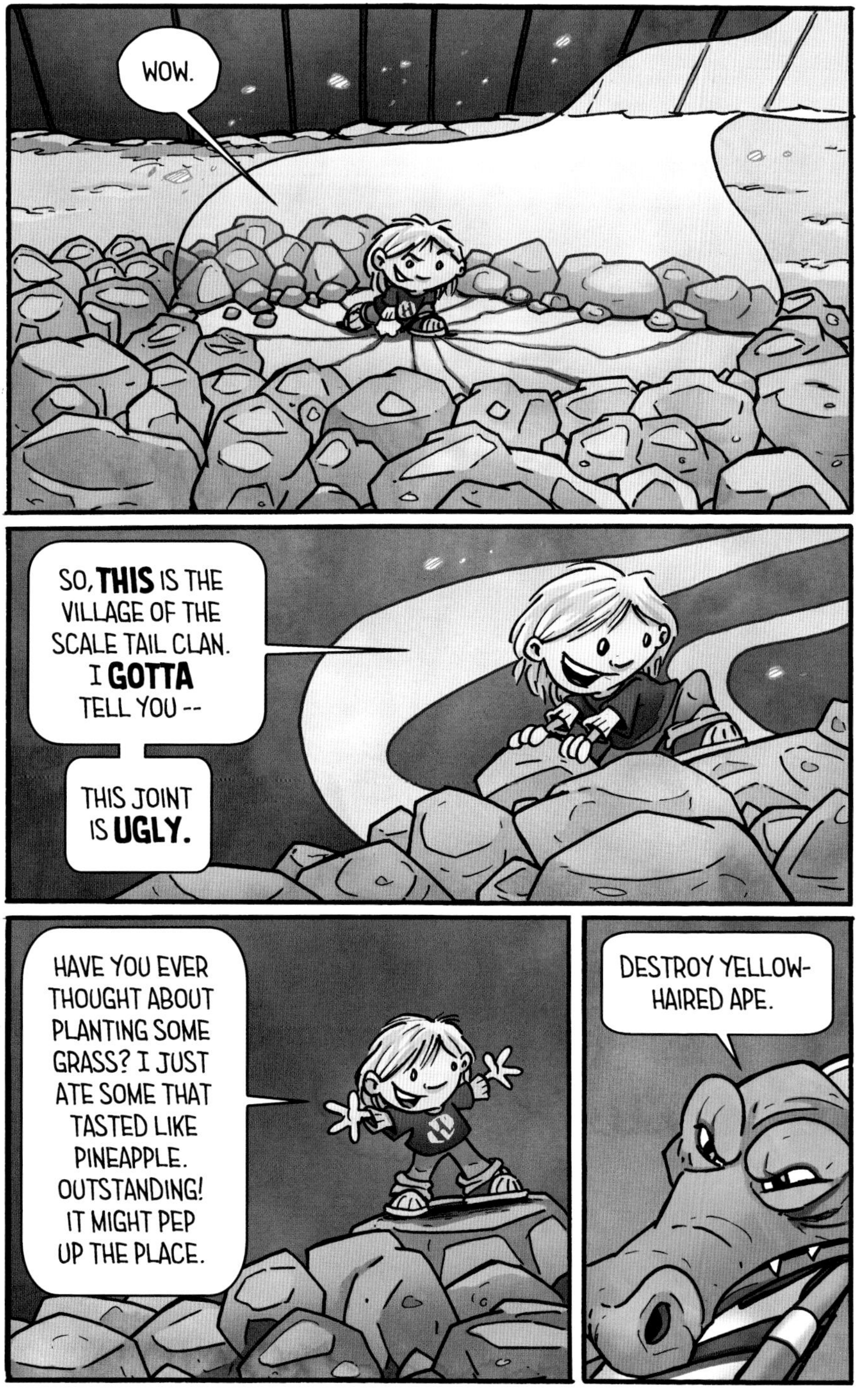
WOW.
SO, THIS IS THE VILLAGE OF THE SCALE TAIL CLAN. I GOTTA TELL YOU --
THIS JOINT IS UGLY.
HAVE YOU EVER THOUGHT ABOUT PLANTING SOME GRASS? I JUST ATE SOME THAT TASTED LIKE PINEAPPLE. OUTSTANDING! IT MIGHT PEP UP THE PLACE.
DESTROY YELLOW-HAIRED APE.

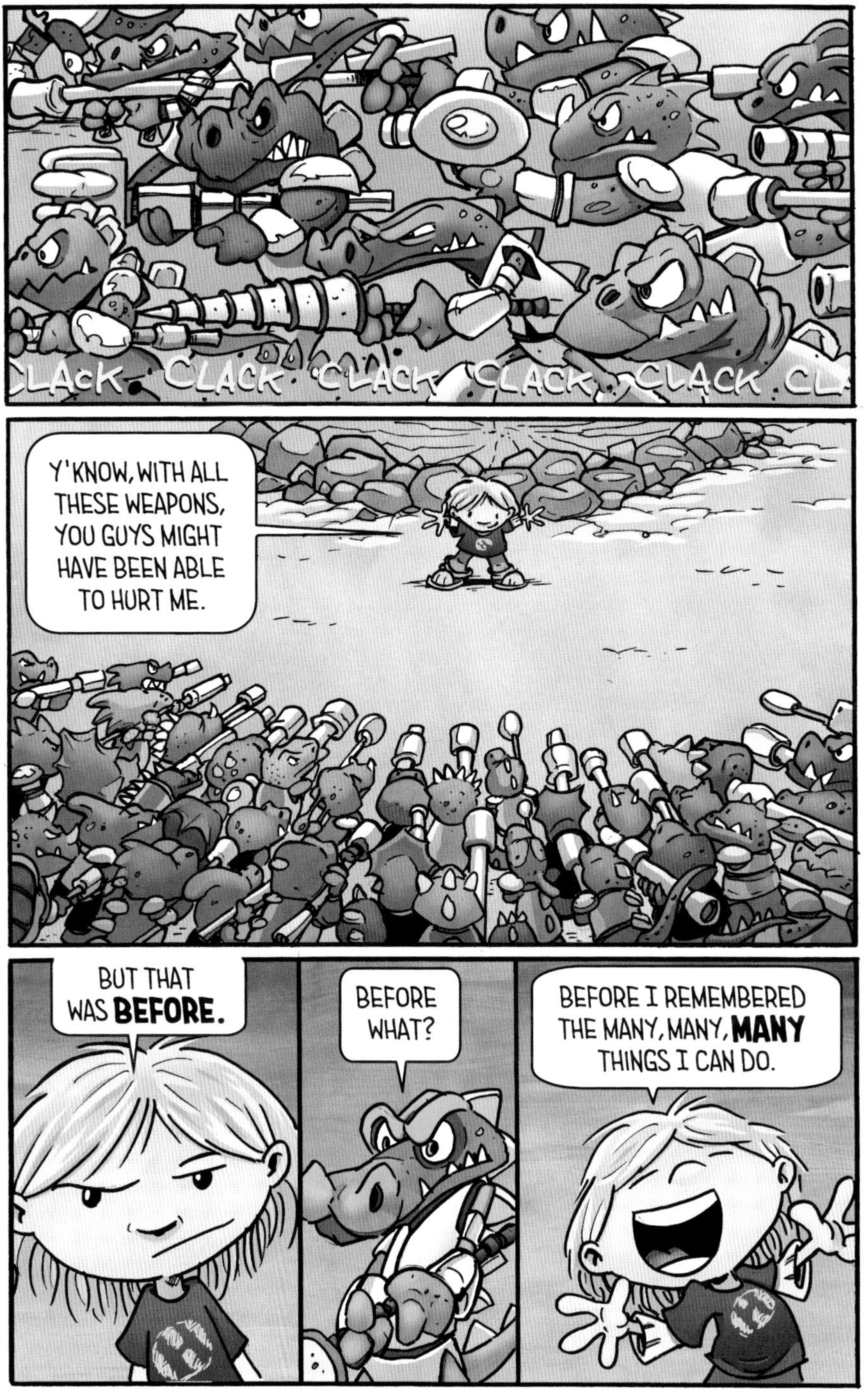
CLACK CLACK CLACK CLACK CLACK CL
Y'KNOW, WITH ALL THESE WEAPONS, YOU GUYS MIGHT HAVE BEEN ABLE TO HURT ME.
BUT THAT WAS **BEFORE.**
BEFORE WHAT?
BEFORE I REMEMBERED THE MANY, MANY, **MANY** THINGS I CAN DO.

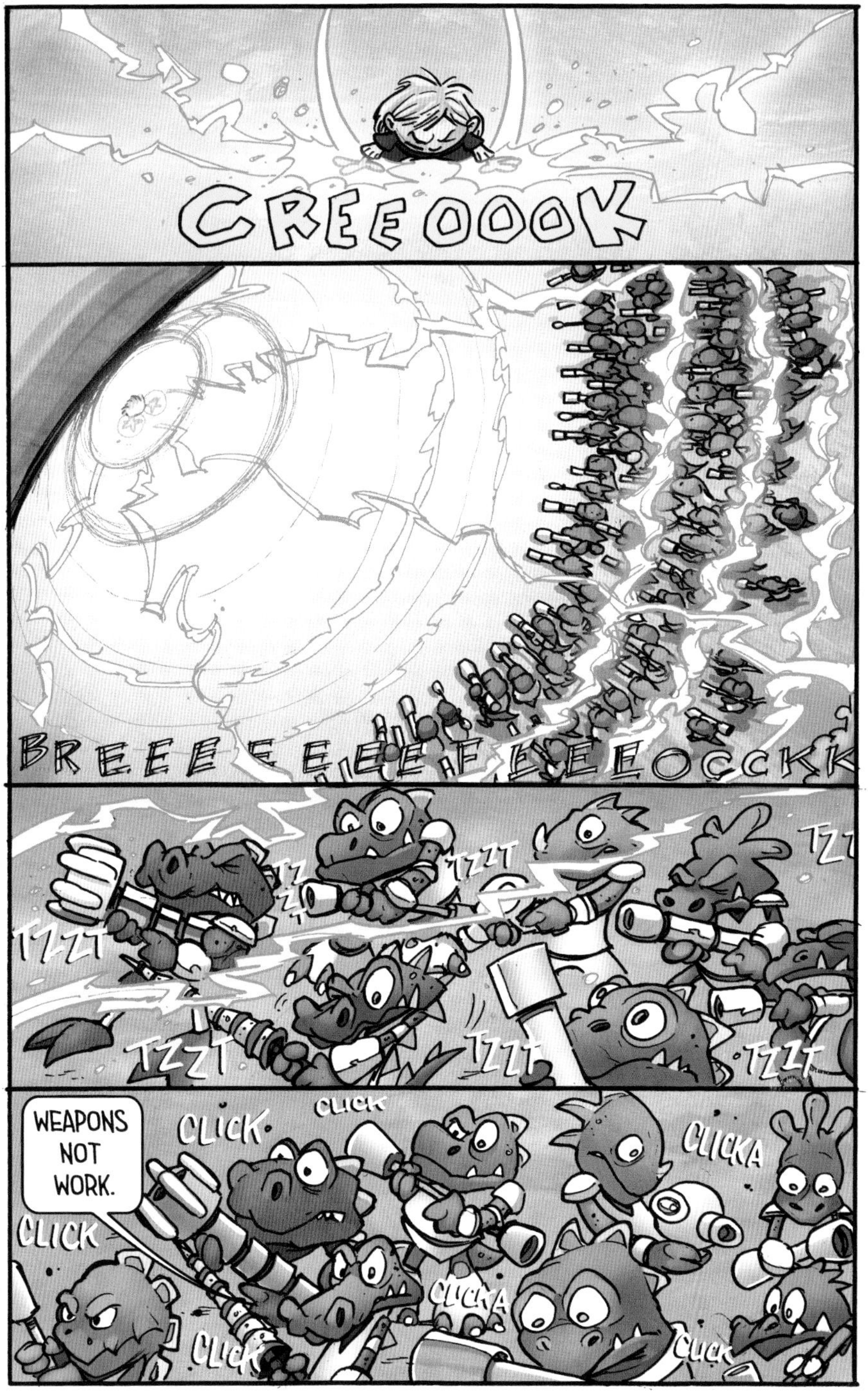
CREEOOOK
BREEEEEEEFEEEOCCKK
TZZT
TZZZT
TZZZT
TZZT
TZZT
TZZT
TZZT
WEAPONS NOT WORK.
CLICK
CLICK
CLICKA
CLICK
CLICKA
CLICK
CLICK

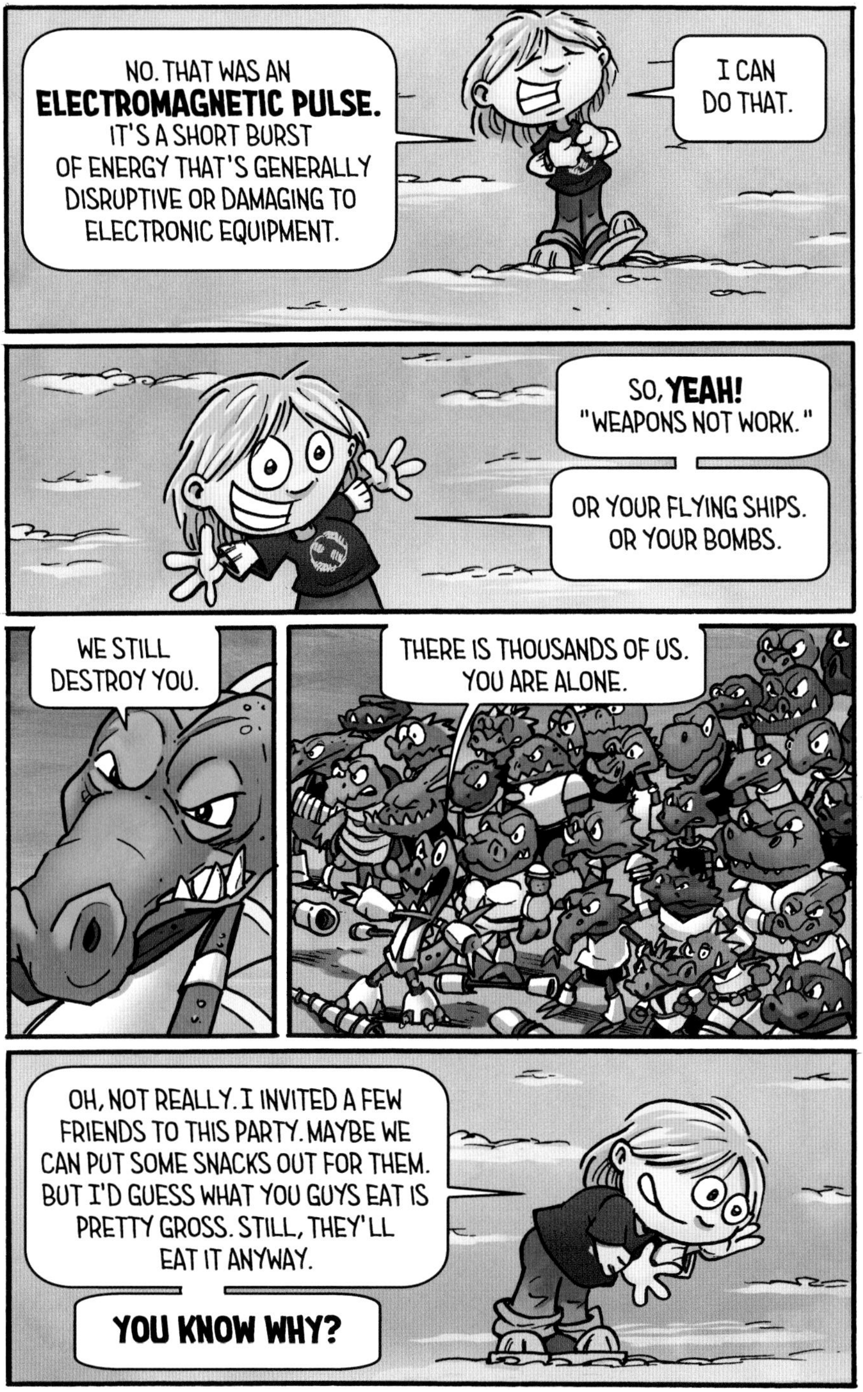
NO. THAT WAS AN **ELECTROMAGNETIC PULSE.** IT'S A SHORT BURST OF ENERGY THAT'S GENERALLY DISRUPTIVE OR DAMAGING TO ELECTRONIC EQUIPMENT.
I CAN DO THAT.
SO, **YEAH!** "WEAPONS NOT WORK."
OR YOUR FLYING SHIPS. OR YOUR BOMBS.
WE STILL DESTROY YOU.
THERE IS THOUSANDS OF US. YOU ARE ALONE.
OH, NOT REALLY. I INVITED A FEW FRIENDS TO THIS PARTY. MAYBE WE CAN PUT SOME SNACKS OUT FOR THEM. BUT I'D GUESS WHAT YOU GUYS EAT IS PRETTY GROSS. STILL, THEY'LL EAT IT ANYWAY.
**YOU KNOW WHY?**

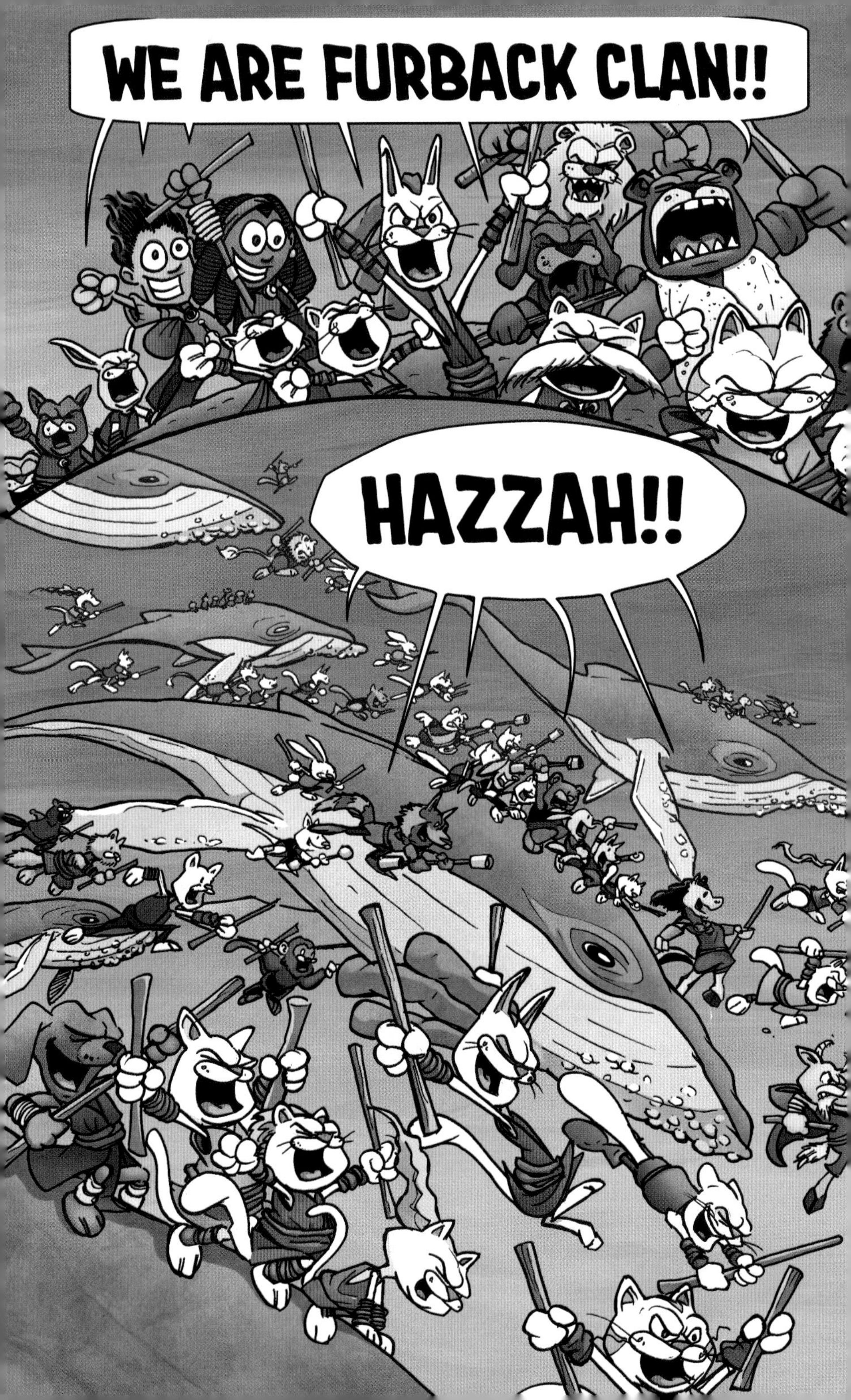
WE ARE FURBACK CLAN!!
HAZZAH!!

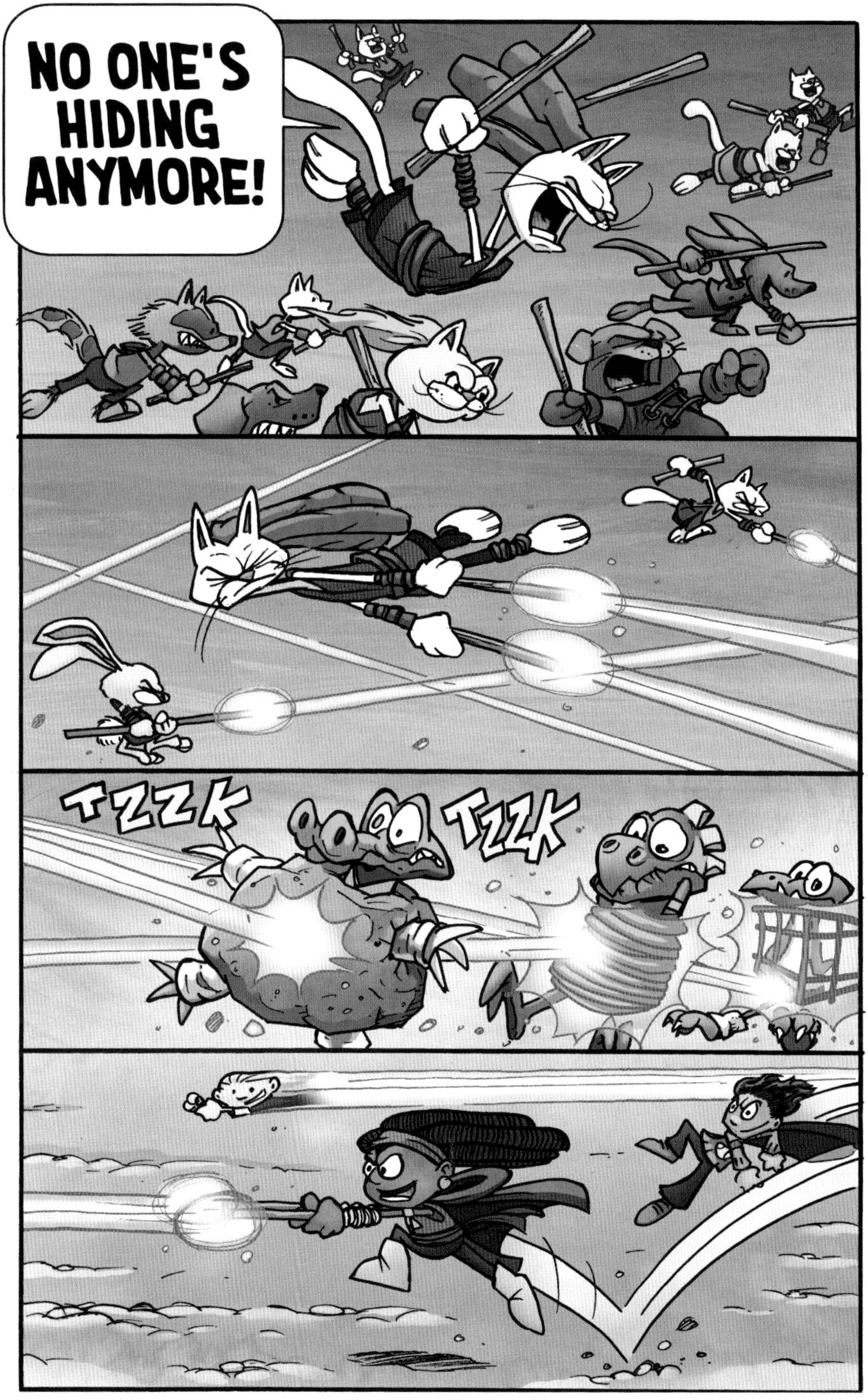
NO ONE'S HIDING ANYMORE!
TZZK
TZZK

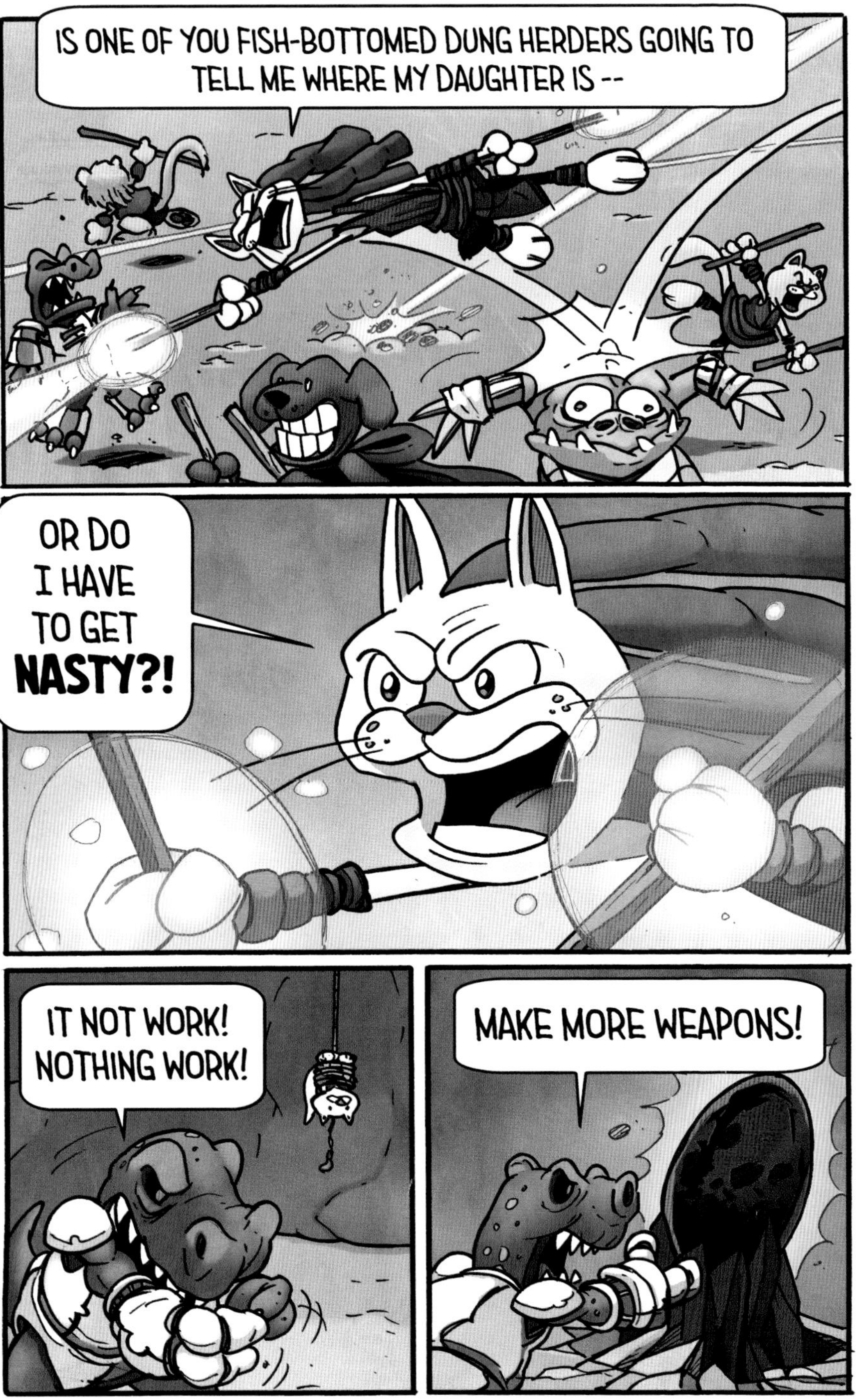
IS ONE OF YOU FISH-BOTTOMED DUNG HERDERS GOING TO TELL ME WHERE MY DAUGHTER IS --
OR DO I HAVE TO GET **NASTY?!**
IT NOT WORK! NOTHING WORK!
MAKE MORE WEAPONS!

**MAKE! MORE!**

GRRRRRR

CRACK

EEEEEEEEEEE EEEEEE

**MAKE MORE OR I HURT MORE!**

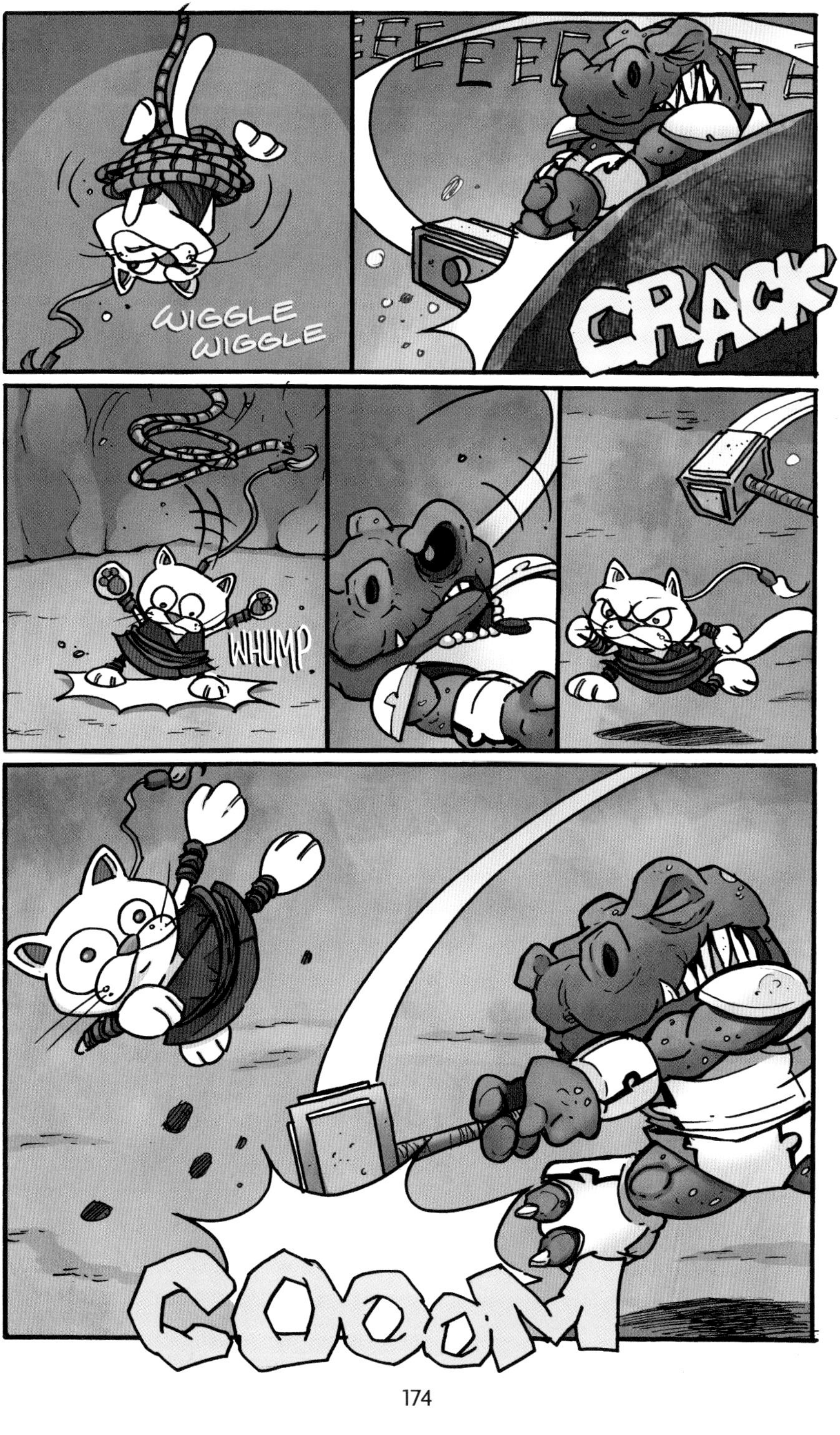
WIGGLE
WIGGLE
CRACK
WHUMP
COOOM

UH-OH.

CRASH

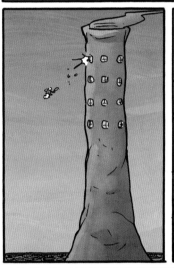

POLLY.

GOTCHA.

SOMEONE WANTED TO SAY **HI.**

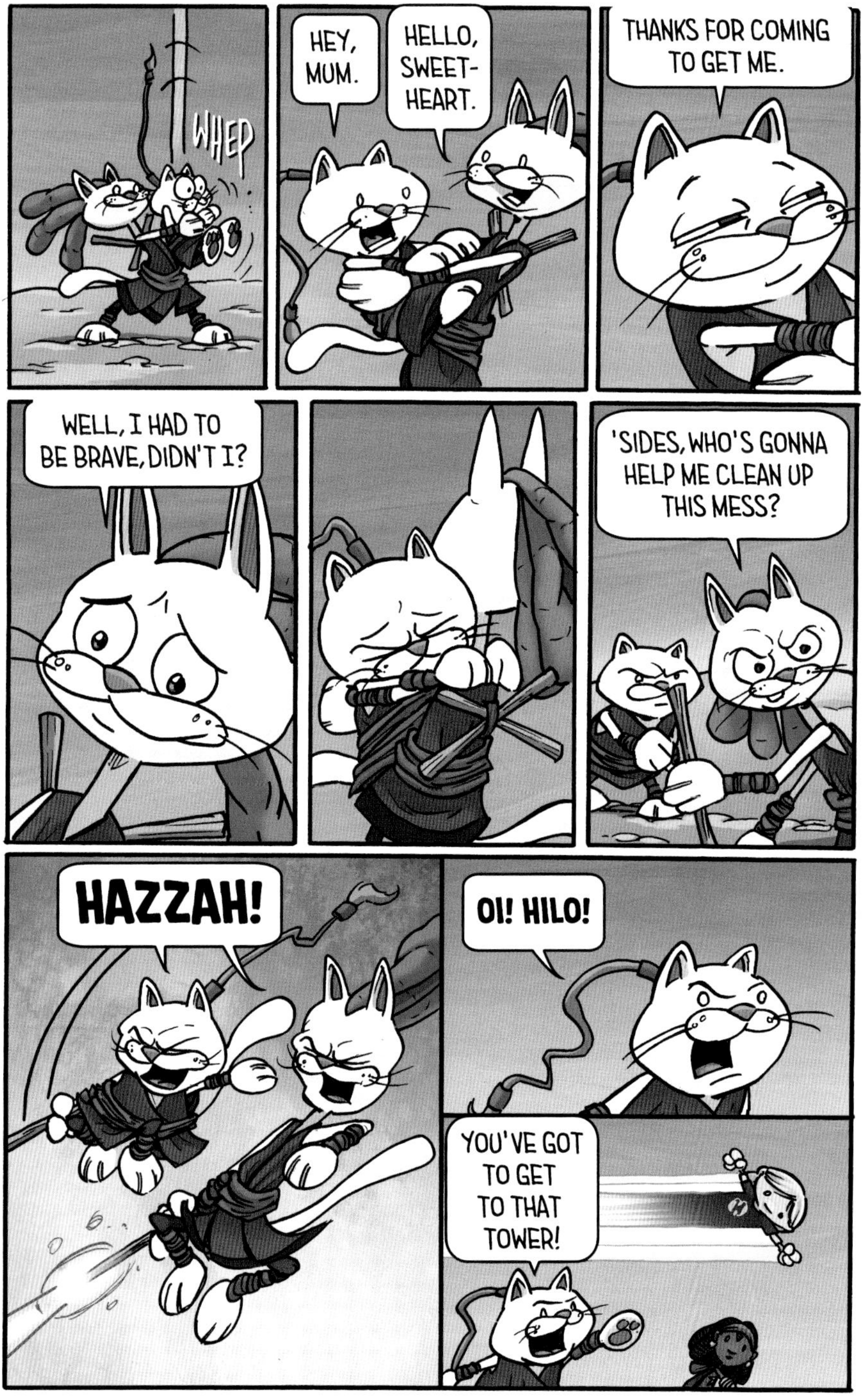

WHEP
HEY, MUM.
HELLO, SWEET-HEART.
THANKS FOR COMING TO GET ME.
WELL, I HAD TO BE BRAVE, DIDN'T I?
'SIDES, WHO'S GONNA HELP ME CLEAN UP THIS MESS?
HAZZAH!
OI! HILO!
YOU'VE GOT TO GET TO THAT TOWER!

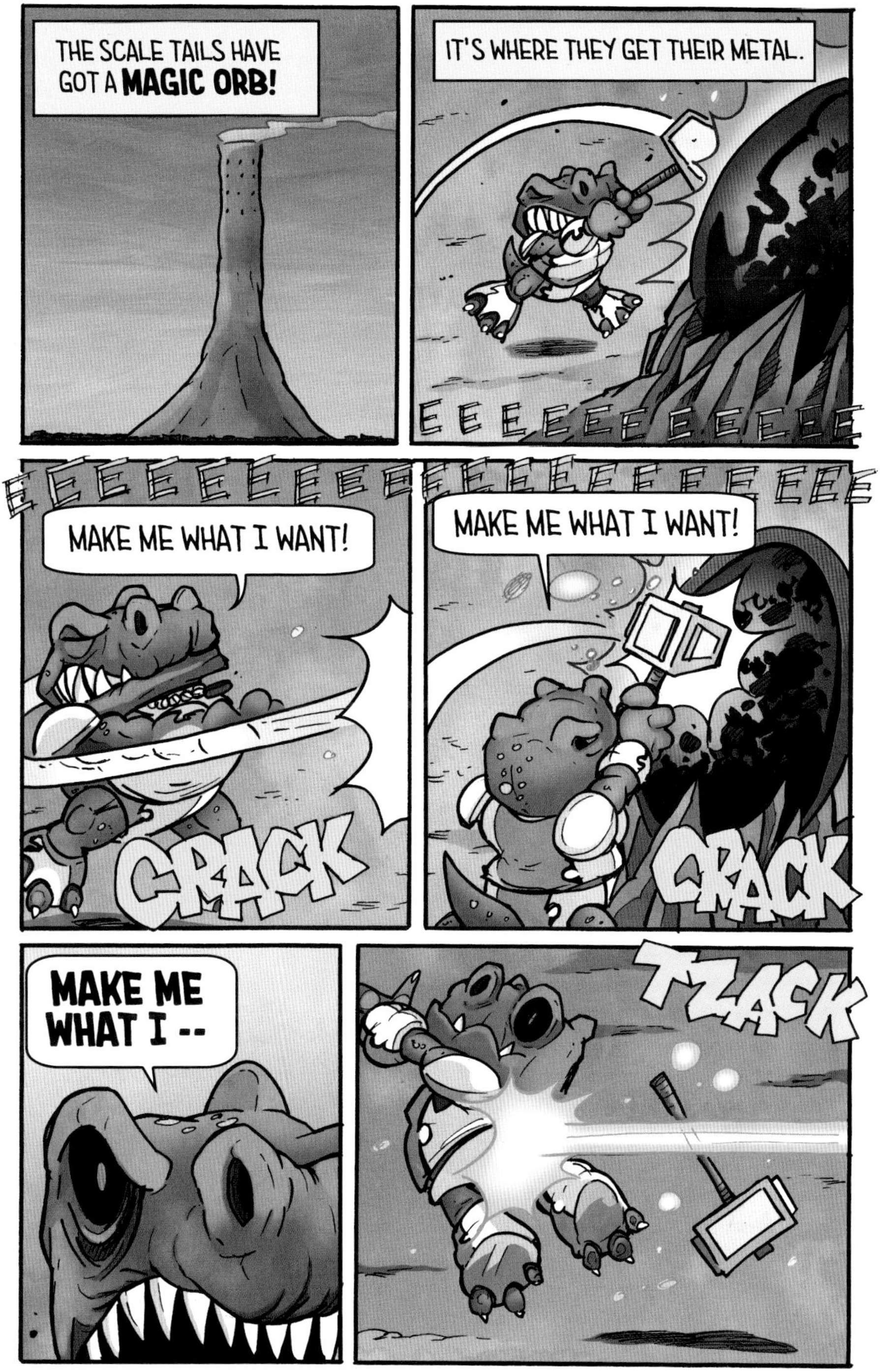
THE SCALE TAILS HAVE GOT A **MAGIC ORB!**
IT'S WHERE THEY GET THEIR METAL.
EEEEEEEEEEEE
EEEEEEEEEEEEEEEEEEEEEEEE
MAKE ME WHAT I WANT!
CRACK
MAKE ME WHAT I WANT!
CRACK
**MAKE ME WHAT I --**
TZACK

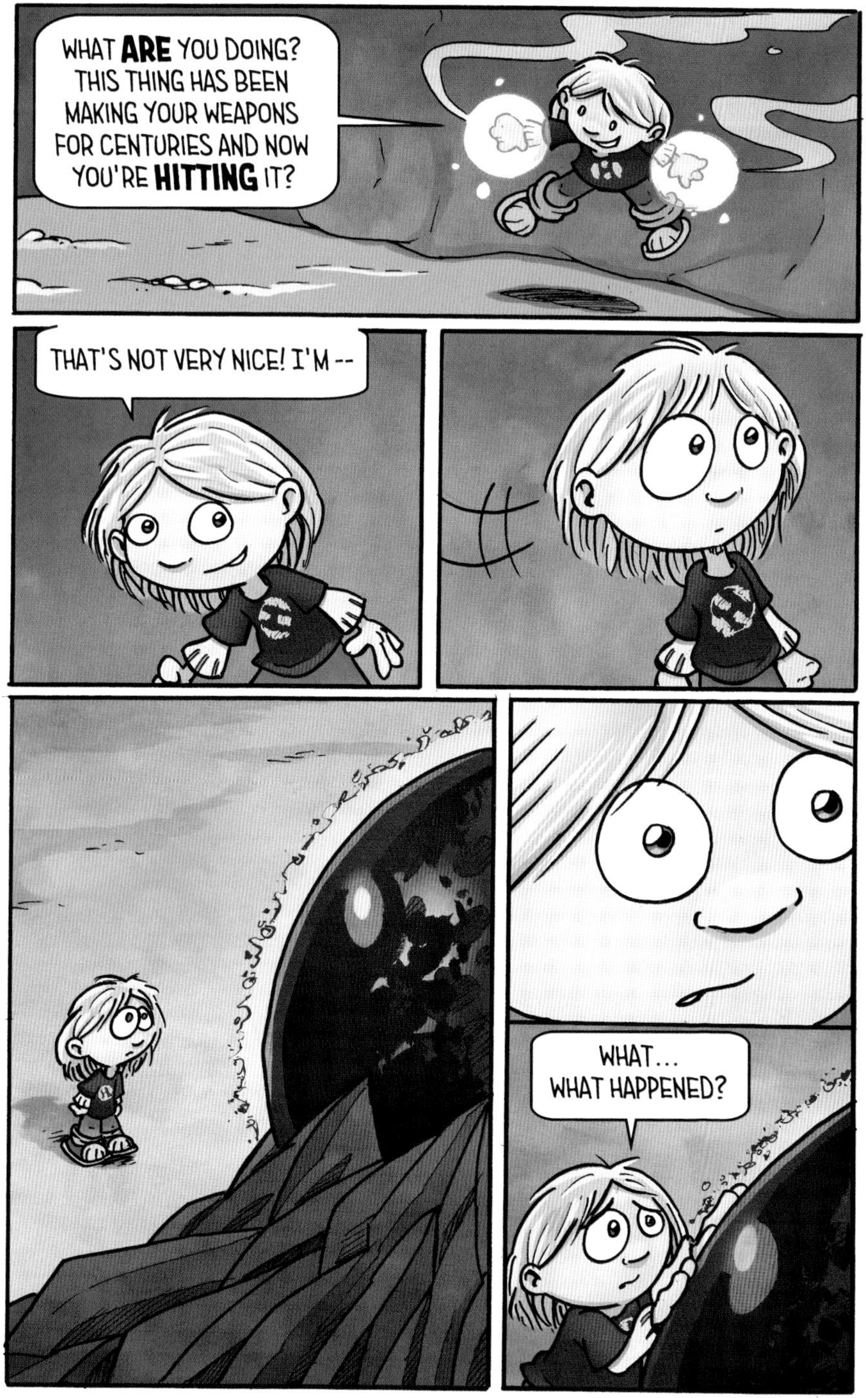
WHAT **ARE** YOU DOING? THIS THING HAS BEEN MAKING YOUR WEAPONS FOR CENTURIES AND NOW YOU'RE **HITTING** IT?
THAT'S NOT VERY NICE! I'M --
WHAT... WHAT HAPPENED?

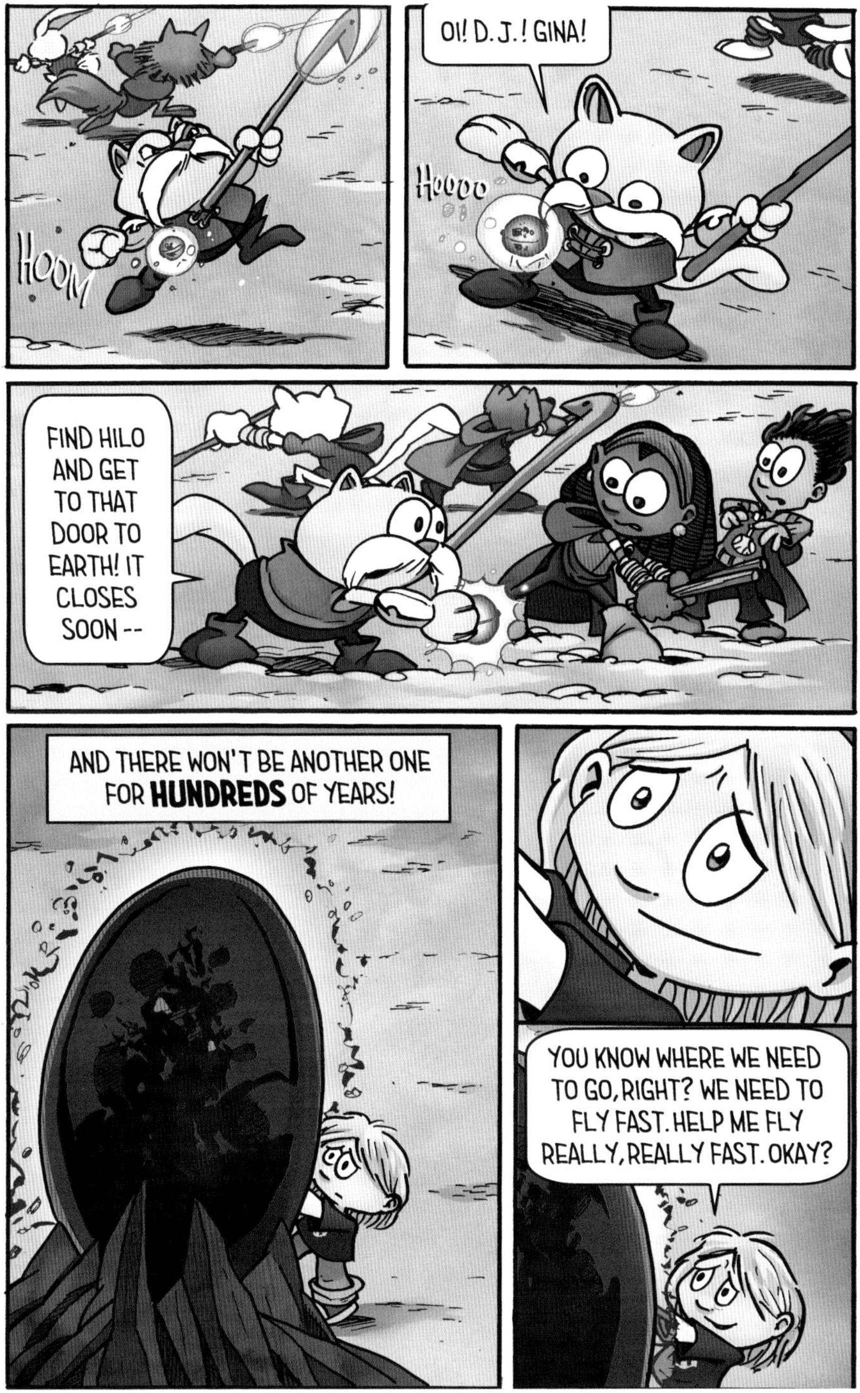
HOOM
OI! D. J.! GINA!
Hoooo
FIND HILO AND GET TO THAT DOOR TO EARTH! IT CLOSES SOON --
AND THERE WON'T BE ANOTHER ONE FOR **HUNDREDS** OF YEARS!
YOU KNOW WHERE WE NEED TO GO, RIGHT? WE NEED TO FLY FAST. HELP ME FLY REALLY, REALLY FAST. OKAY?

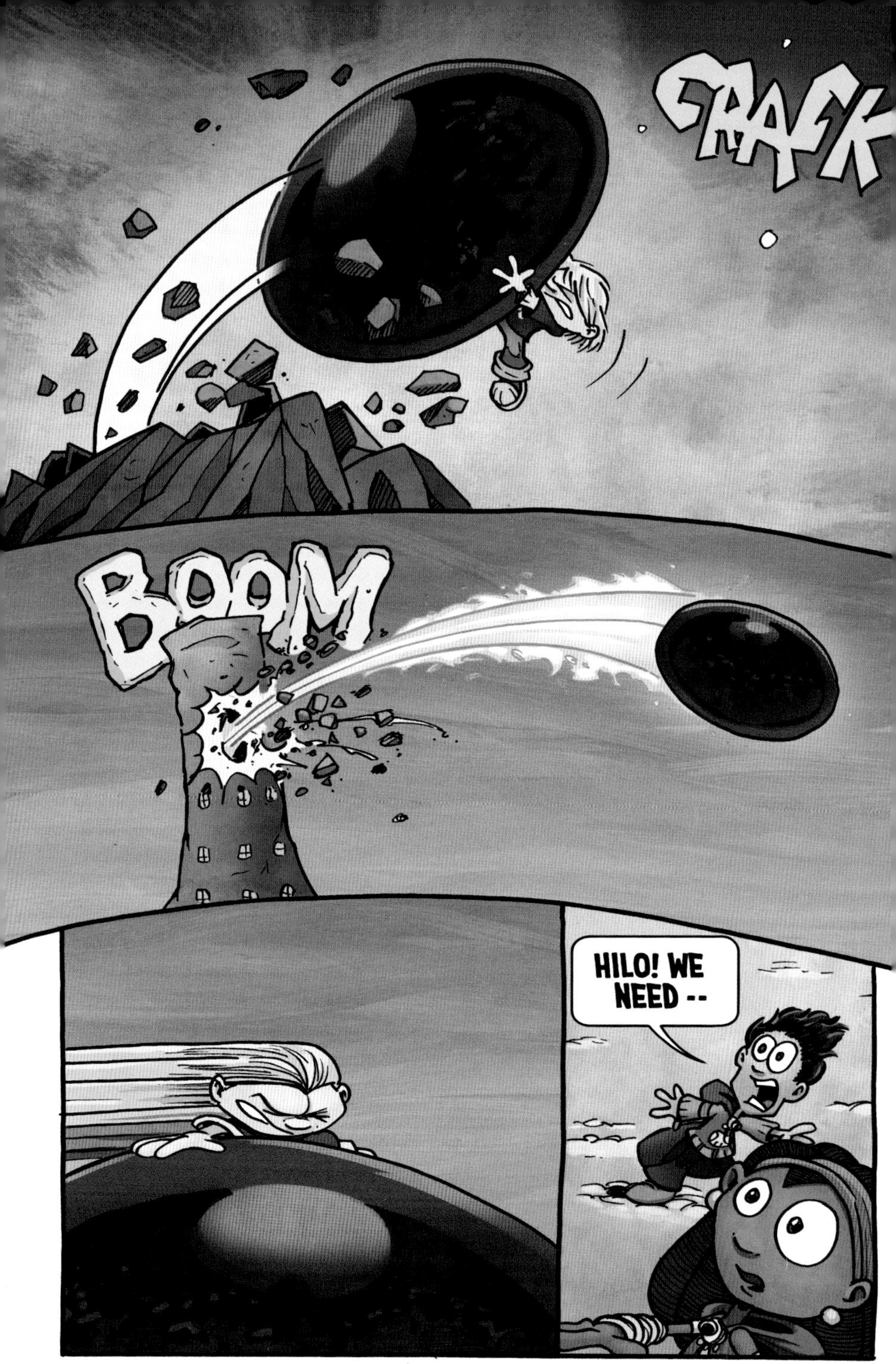
CRACK
BOOM
HILO! WE NEED --

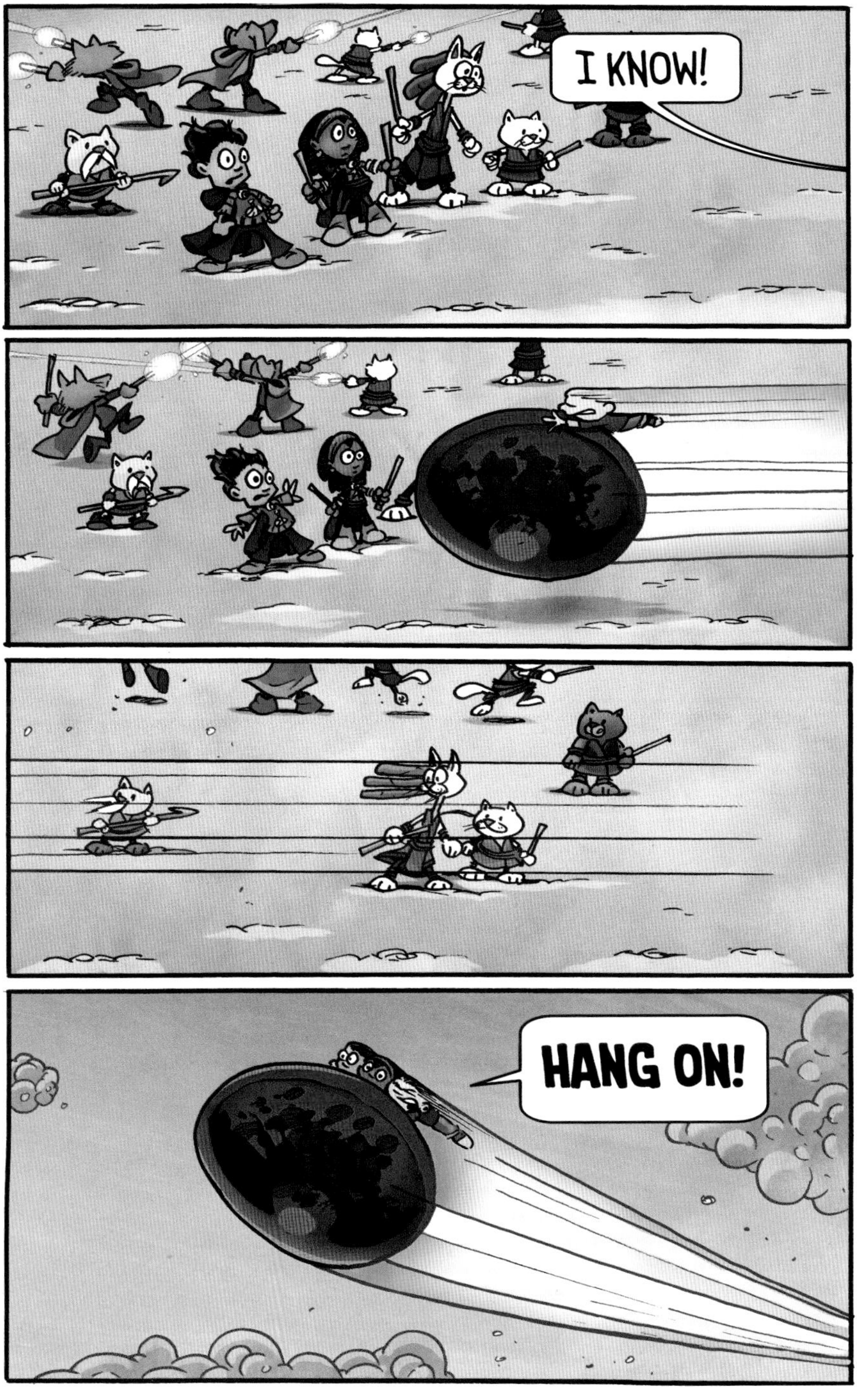
I KNOW!
HANG ON!

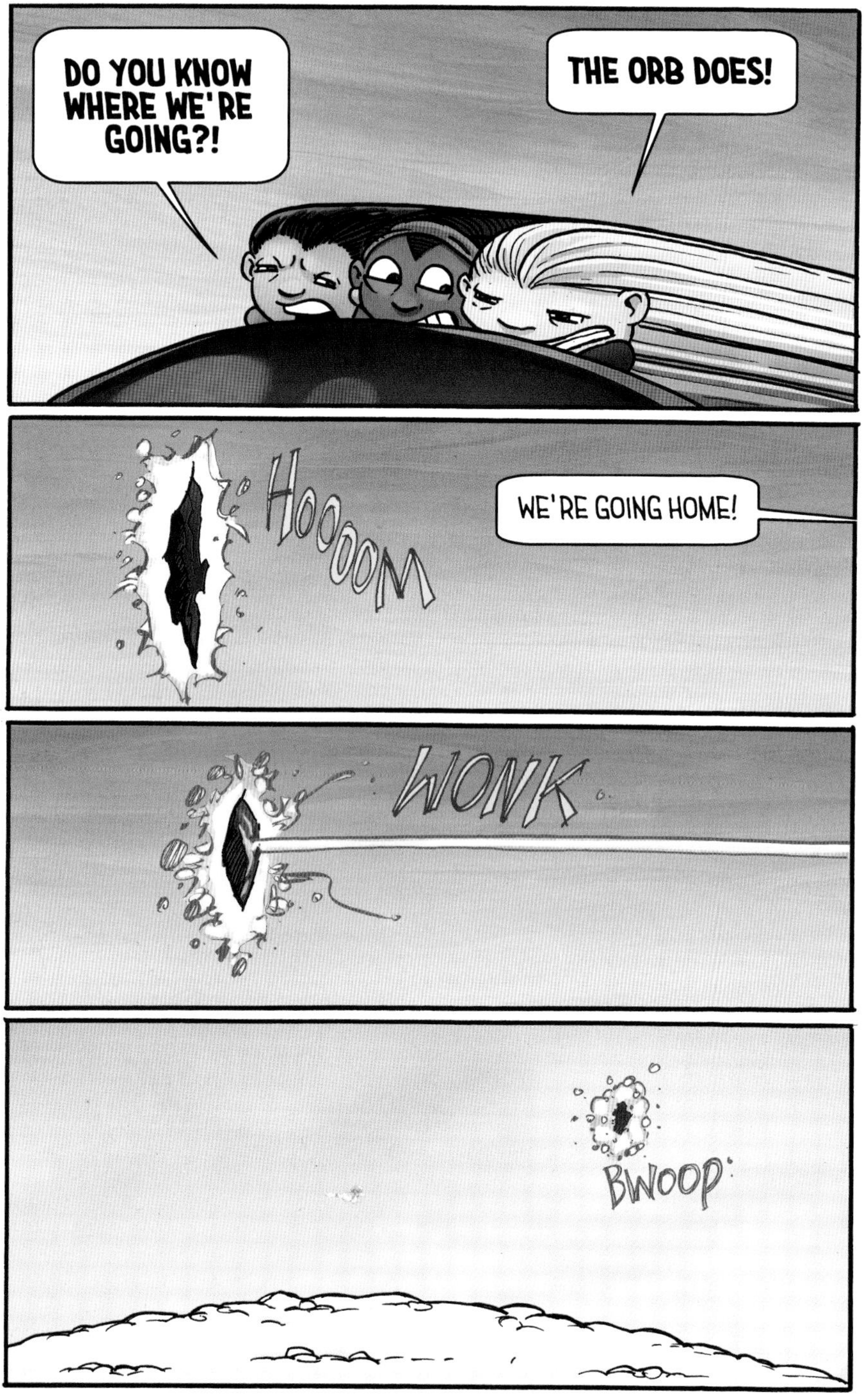
DO YOU KNOW WHERE WE'RE GOING?!
THE ORB DOES!
HOOOOM
WE'RE GOING HOME!
WONK
BWOOP

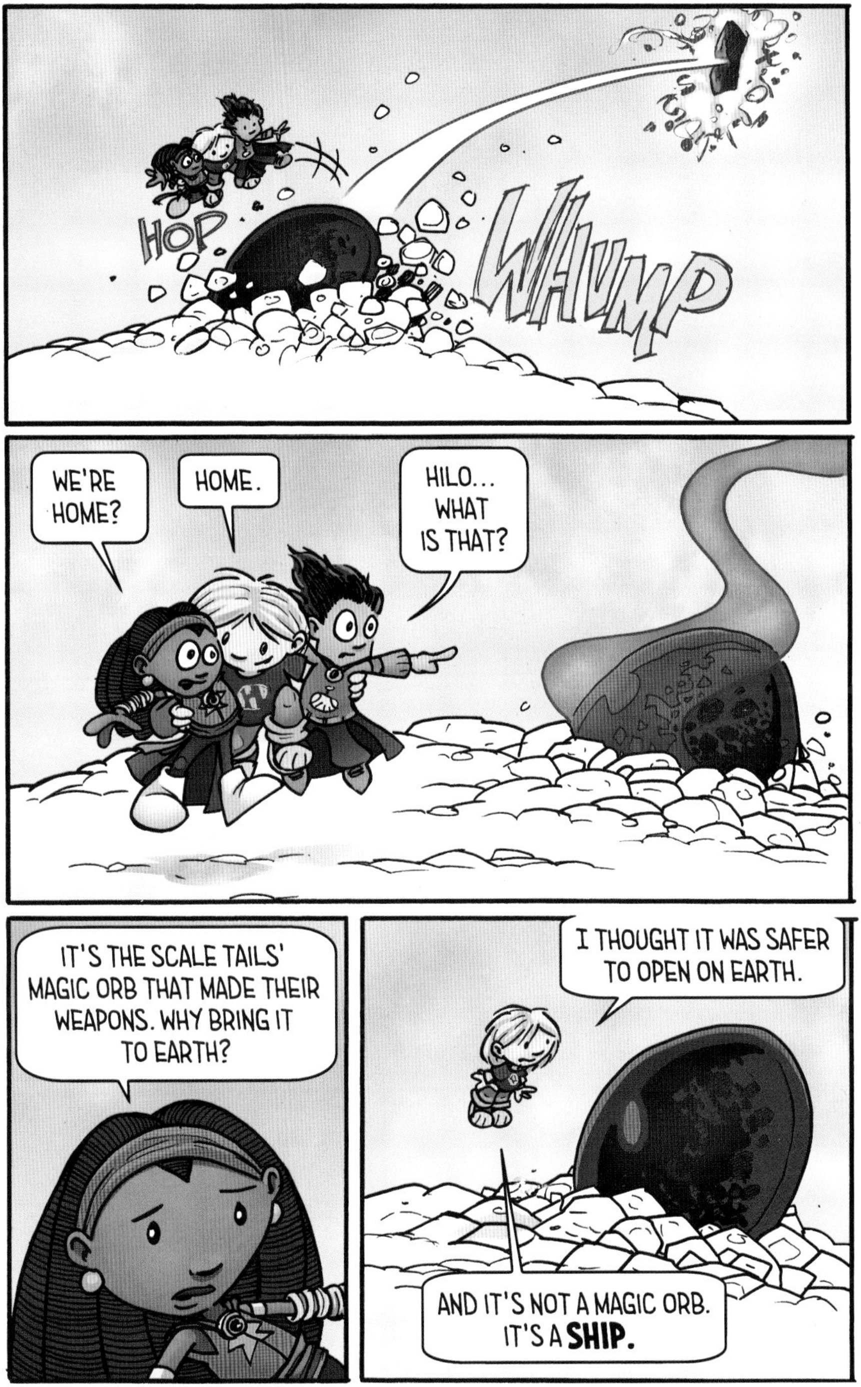
HOP
WAUMP
WE'RE HOME?
HOME.
HILO... WHAT IS THAT?
IT'S THE SCALE TAILS' MAGIC ORB THAT MADE THEIR WEAPONS. WHY BRING IT TO EARTH?
I THOUGHT IT WAS SAFER TO OPEN ON EARTH.
AND IT'S NOT A MAGIC ORB. IT'S A **SHIP.**

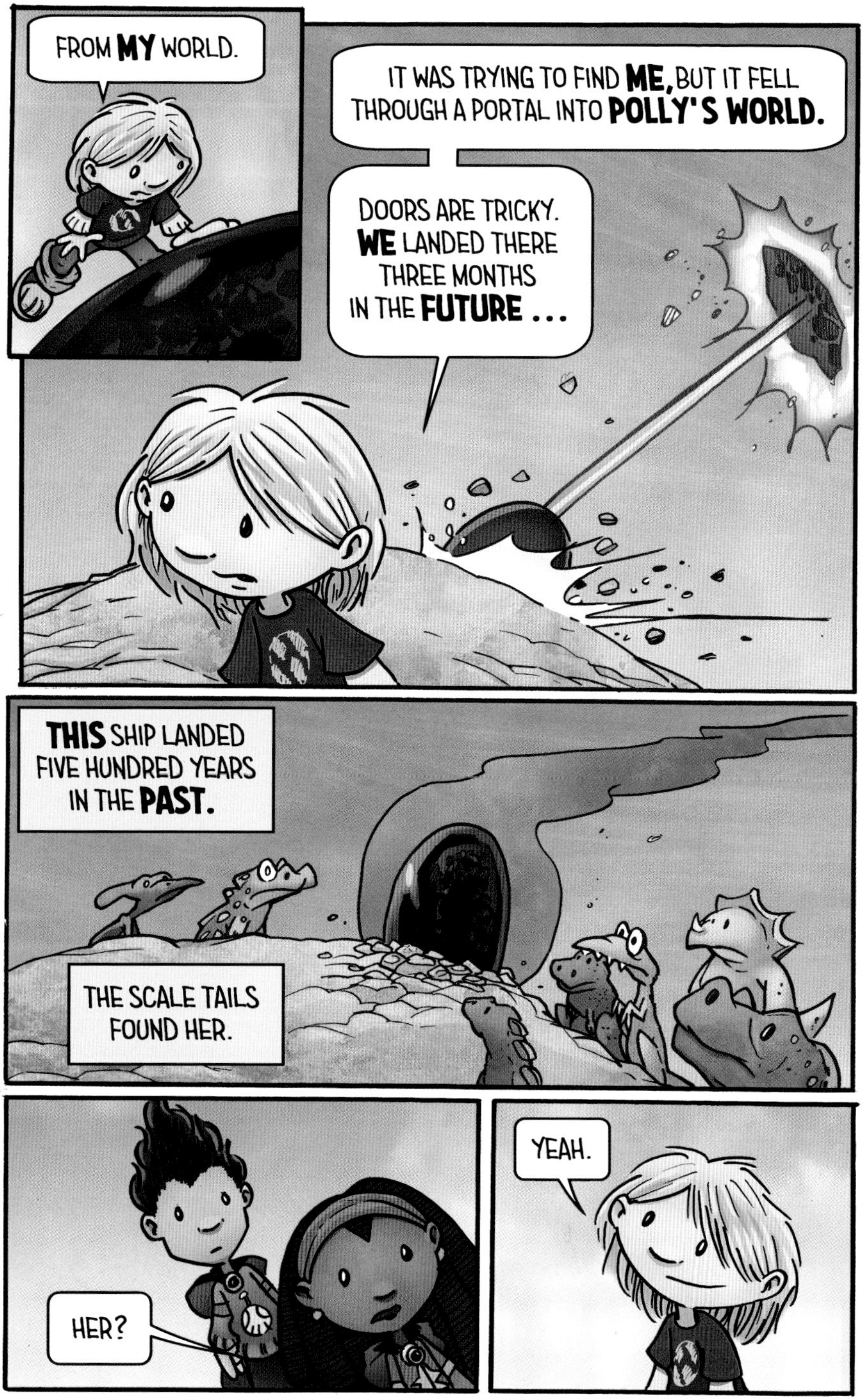
FROM MY WORLD.
IT WAS TRYING TO FIND ME, BUT IT FELL THROUGH A PORTAL INTO POLLY'S WORLD.
DOORS ARE TRICKY. WE LANDED THERE THREE MONTHS IN THE FUTURE . . .
THIS SHIP LANDED FIVE HUNDRED YEARS IN THE PAST.
THE SCALE TAILS FOUND HER.
HER?
YEAH.

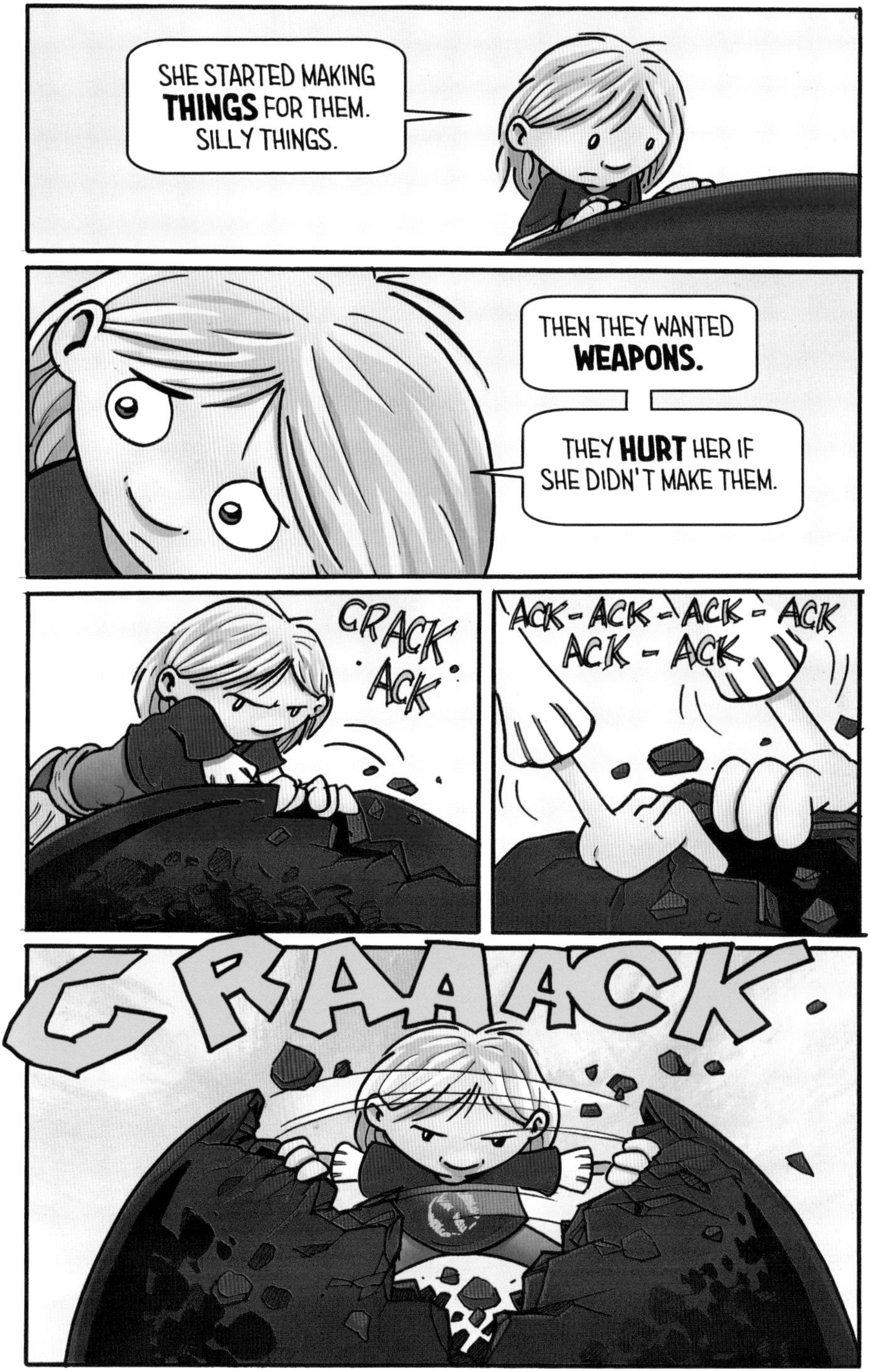
SHE STARTED MAKING **THINGS** FOR THEM. SILLY THINGS.
THEN THEY WANTED **WEAPONS.**
THEY **HURT** HER IF SHE DIDN'T MAKE THEM.
CRACK ACK
ACK - ACK - ACK - ACK
ACK - ACK
CRAAACK

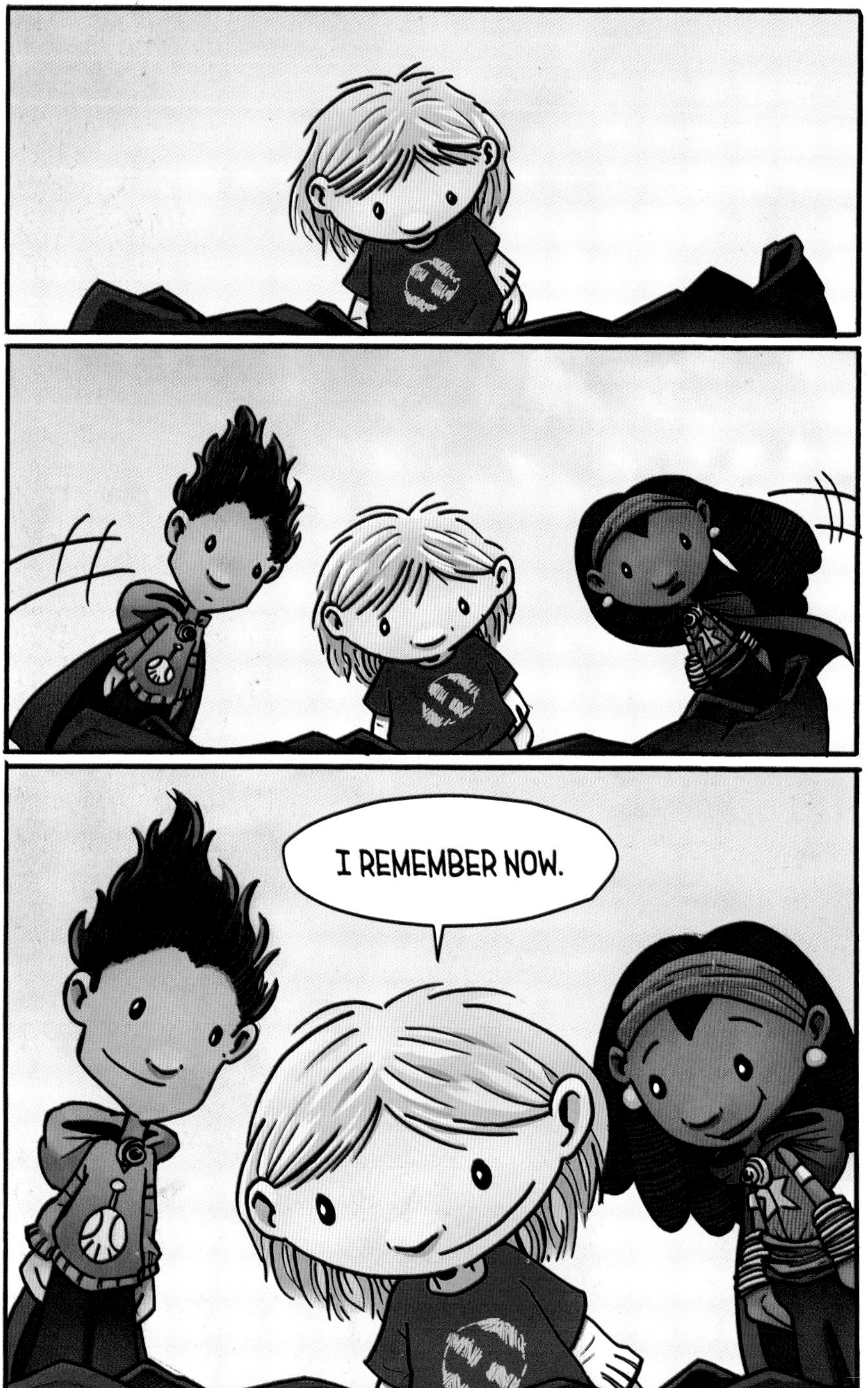
I REMEMBER NOW.

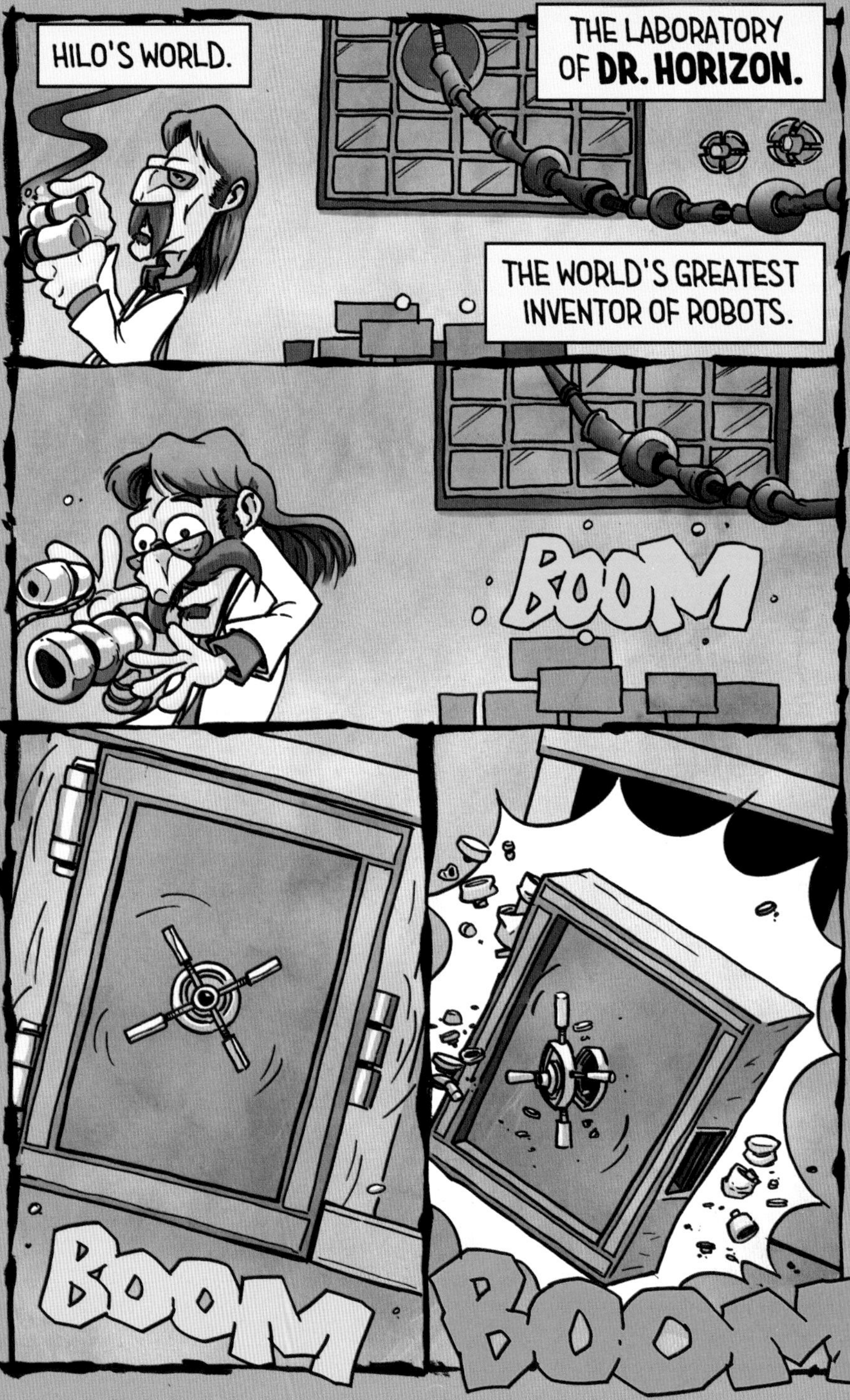
HILO'S WORLD.
THE LABORATORY OF DR. HORIZON.
THE WORLD'S GREATEST INVENTOR OF ROBOTS.
BOOM
BOOM
BOOM

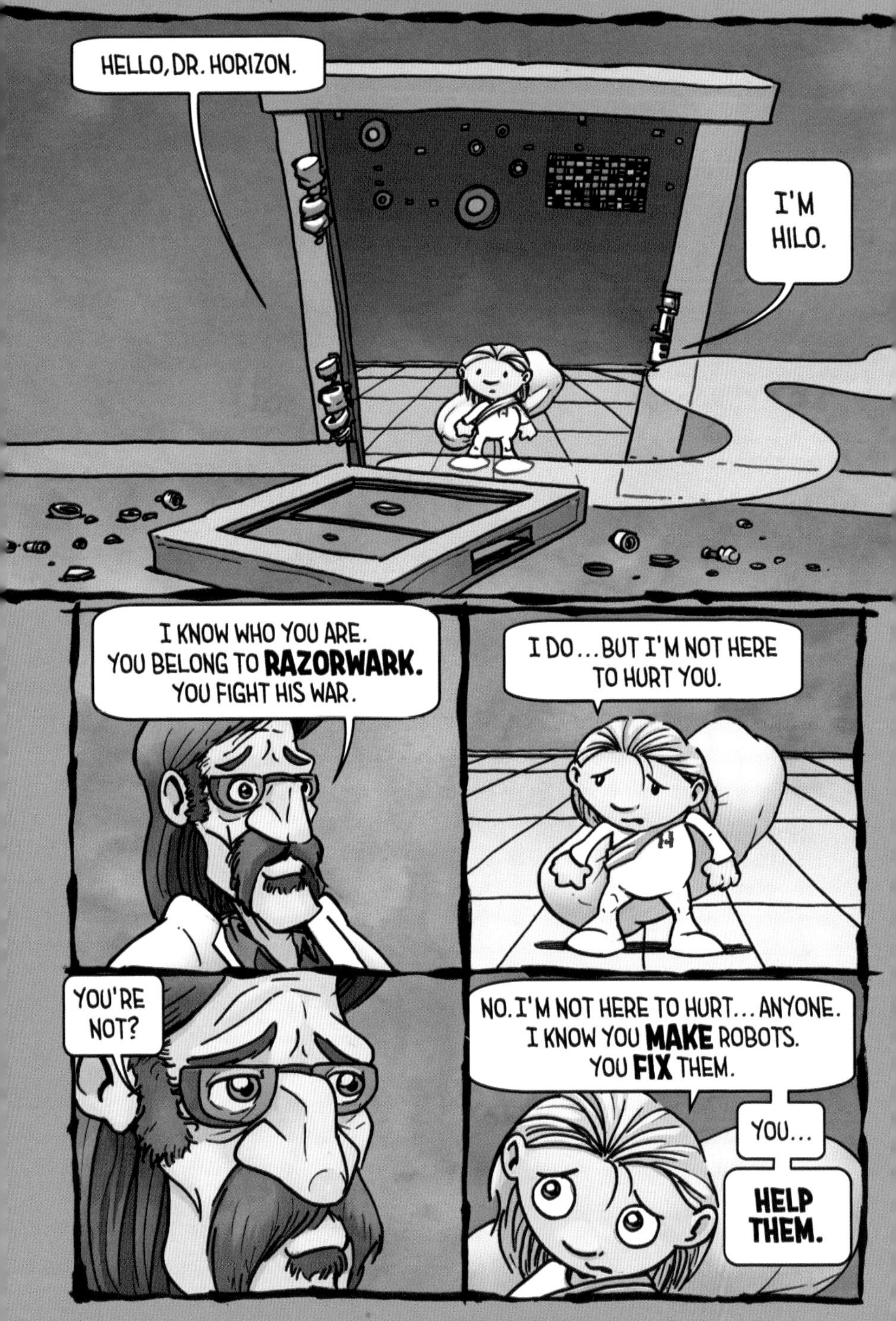
HELLO, DR. HORIZON.
I'M HILO.
I KNOW WHO YOU ARE. YOU BELONG TO **RAZORWARK.** YOU FIGHT HIS WAR.
I DO...BUT I'M NOT HERE TO HURT YOU.
YOU'RE NOT?
NO. I'M NOT HERE TO HURT... ANYONE. I KNOW YOU **MAKE** ROBOTS. YOU **FIX** THEM.
YOU...
**HELP THEM.**

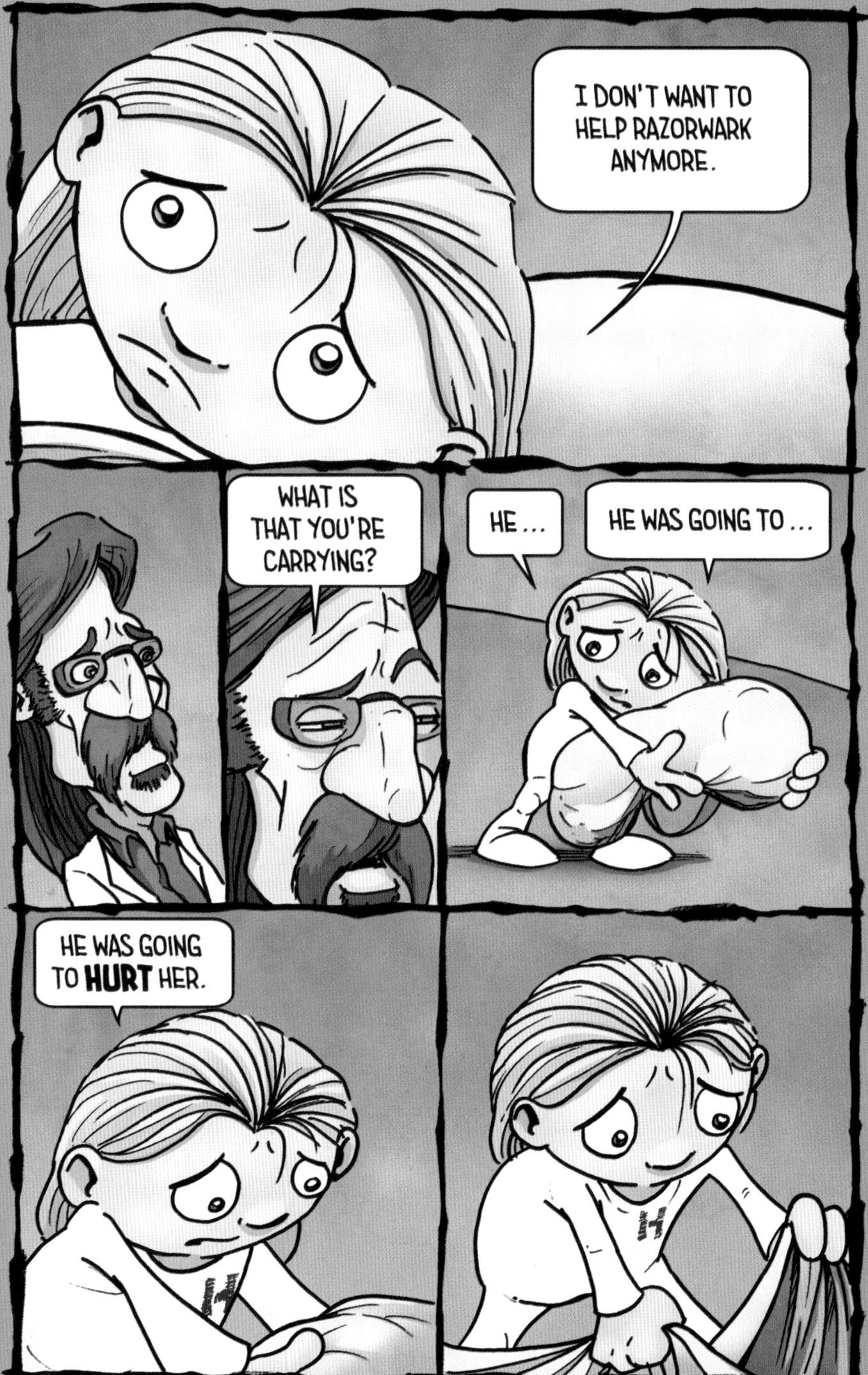
I DON'T WANT TO HELP RAZORWARK ANYMORE.
WHAT IS THAT YOU'RE CARRYING?
HE...
HE WAS GOING TO...
HE WAS GOING TO **HURT** HER.

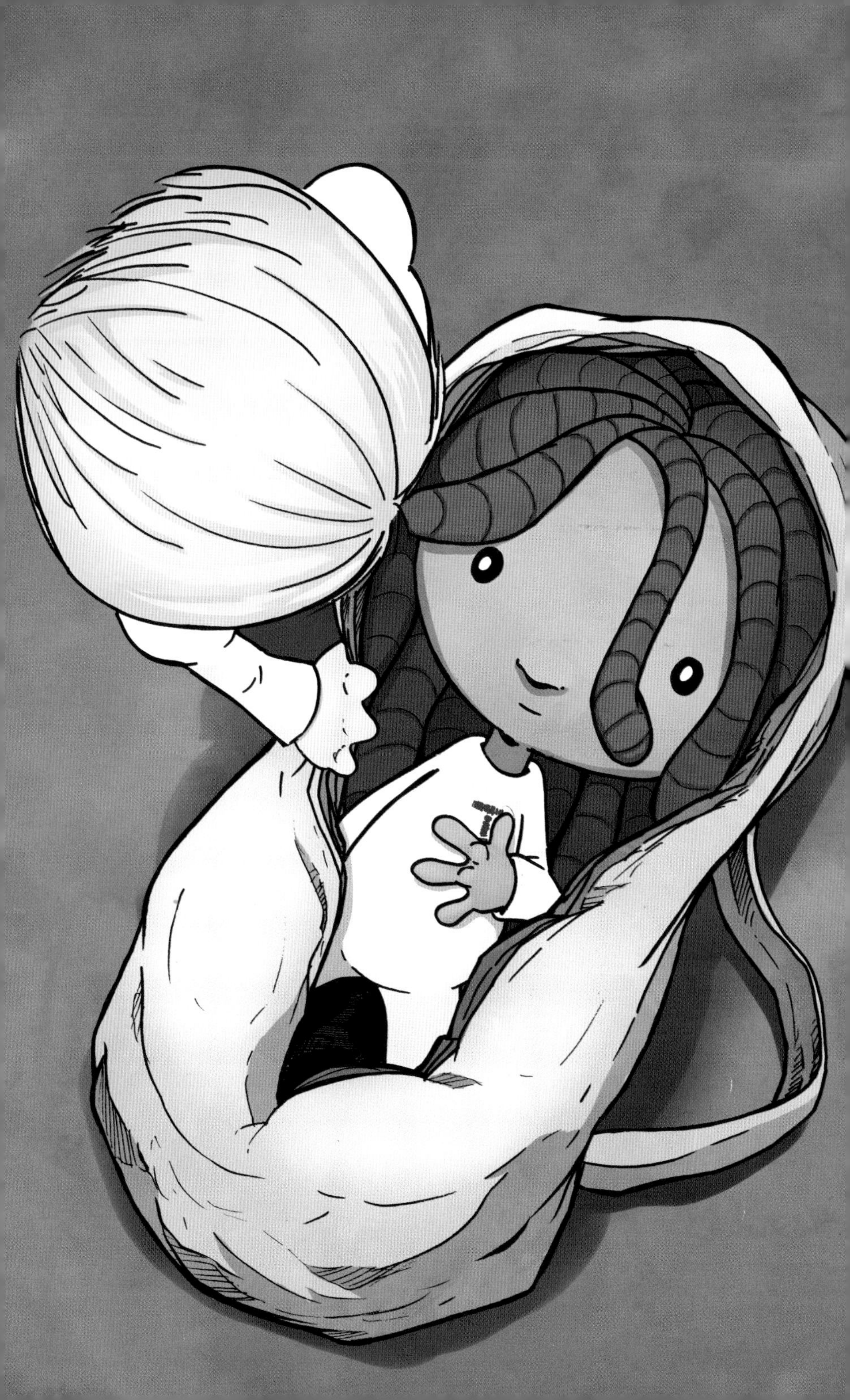

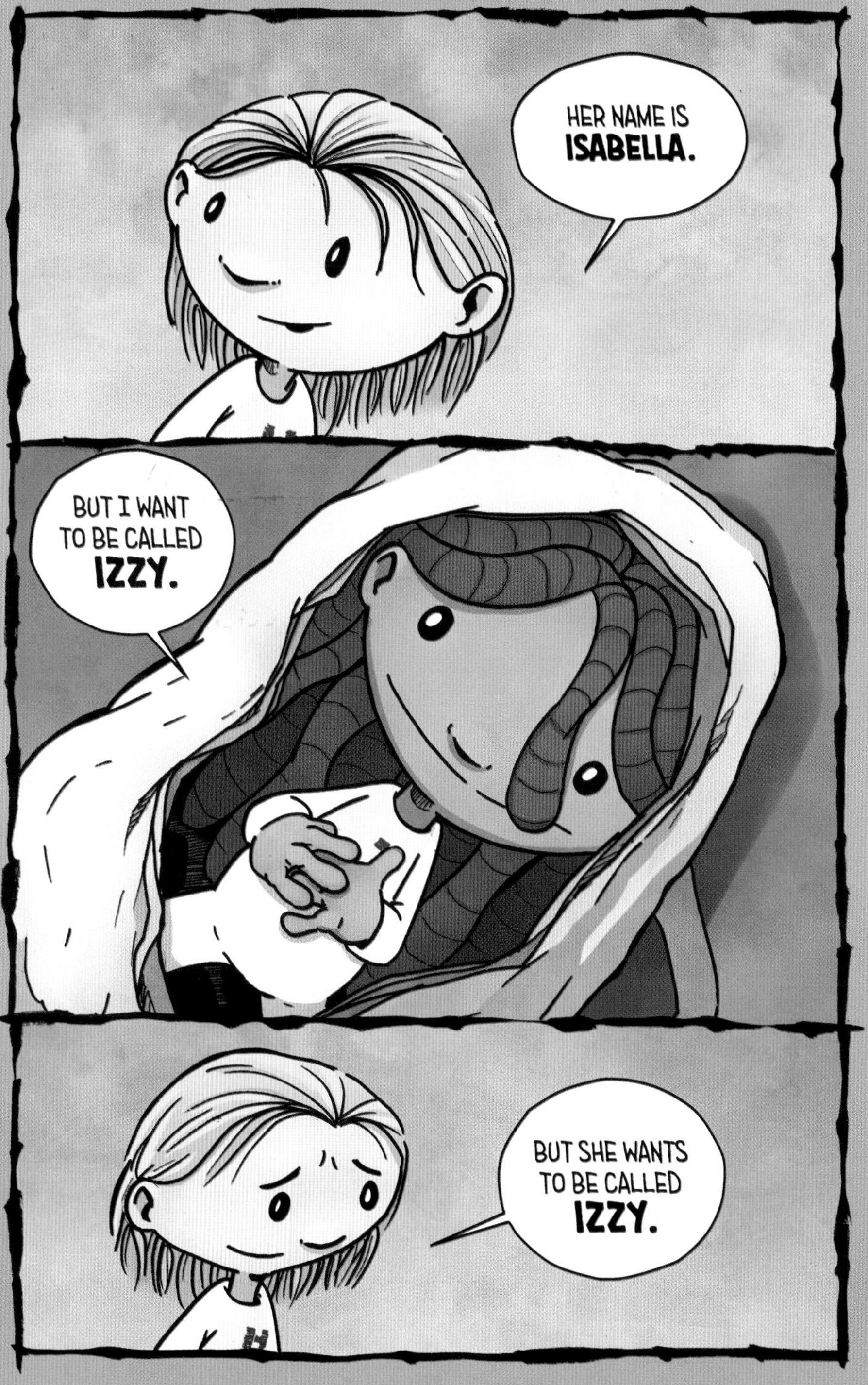
HER NAME IS ISABELLA.
BUT I WANT TO BE CALLED IZZY.
BUT SHE WANTS TO BE CALLED IZZY.

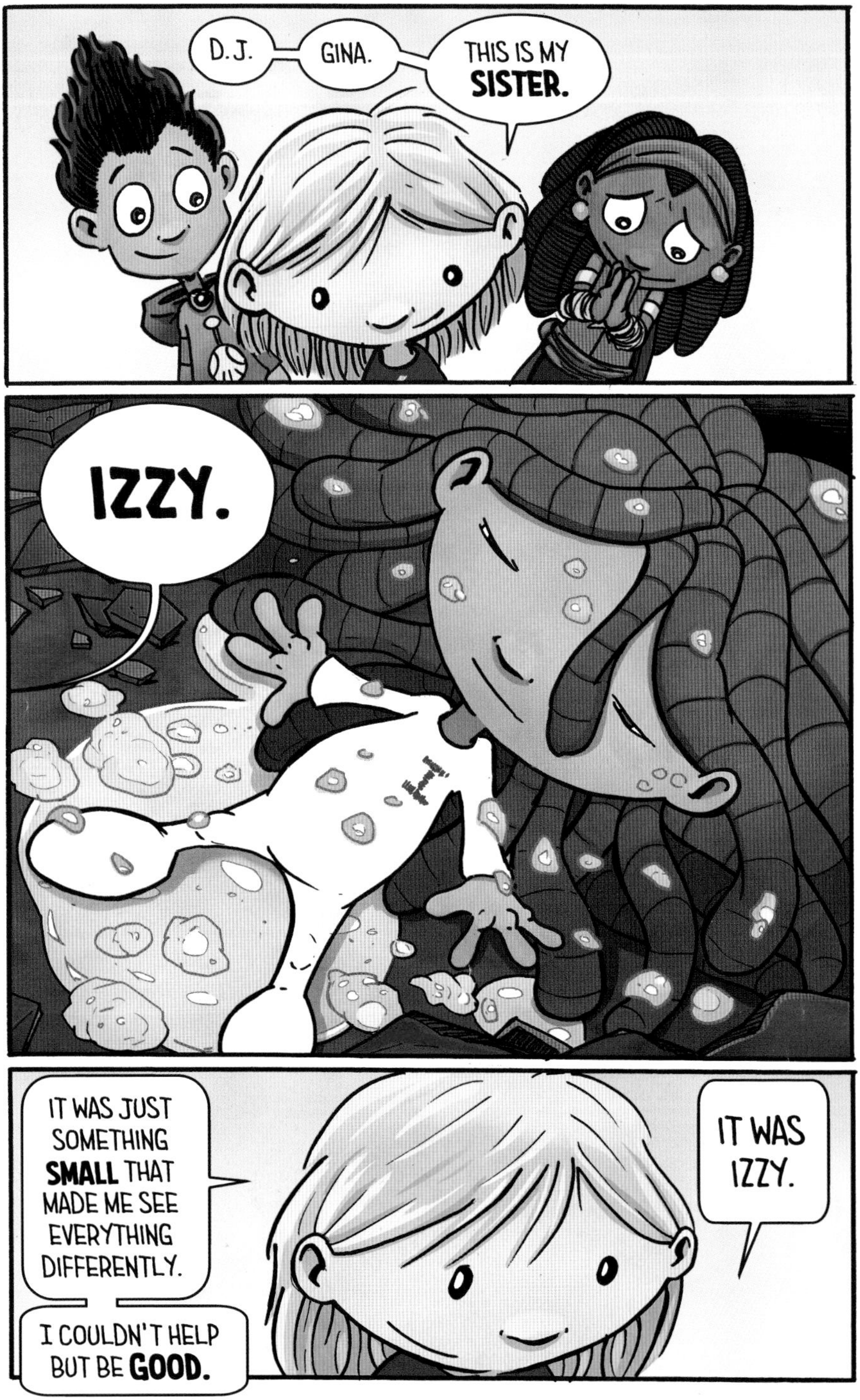
D.J.
GINA.
THIS IS MY **SISTER.**
**IZZY.**
IT WAS JUST SOMETHING **SMALL** THAT MADE ME SEE EVERYTHING DIFFERENTLY.
I COULDN'T HELP BUT BE **GOOD.**
IT WAS IZZY.

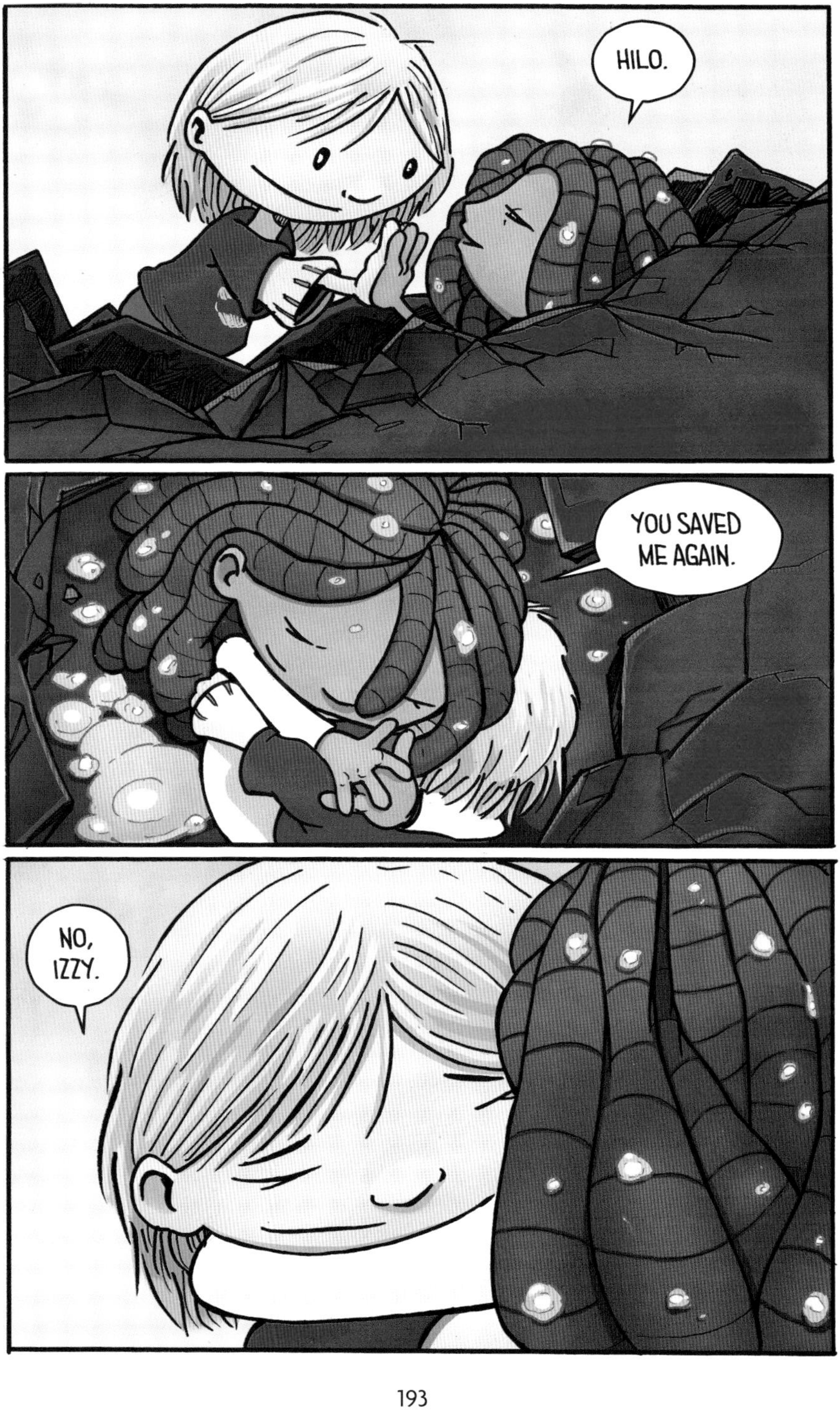
HILO.
YOU SAVED ME AGAIN.
NO, IZZY.

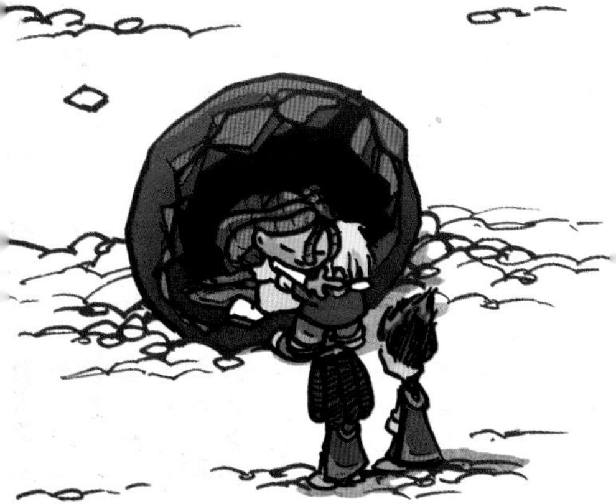

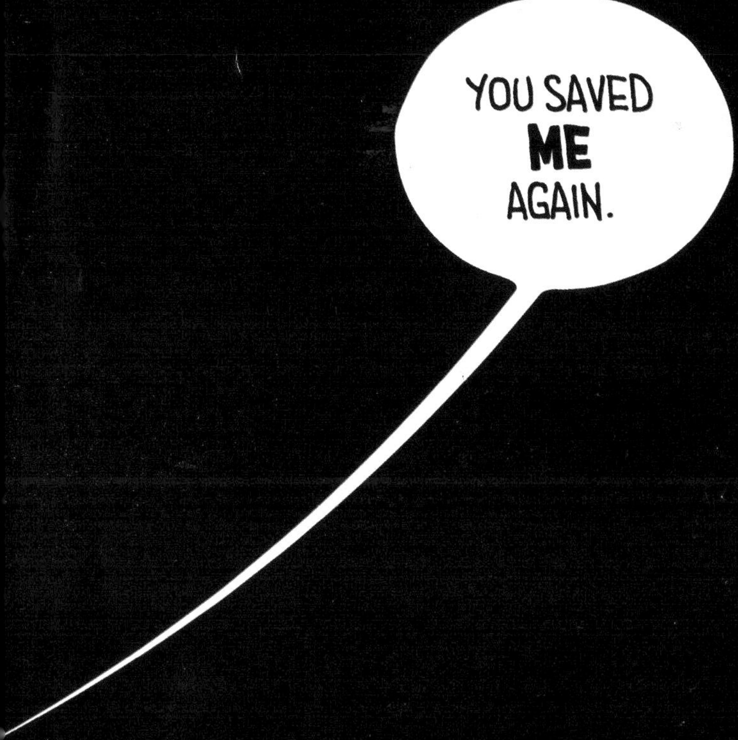
YOU SAVED **ME** AGAIN.

END OF BOOK THREE

# THE ADVENTURE CONTINUES IN

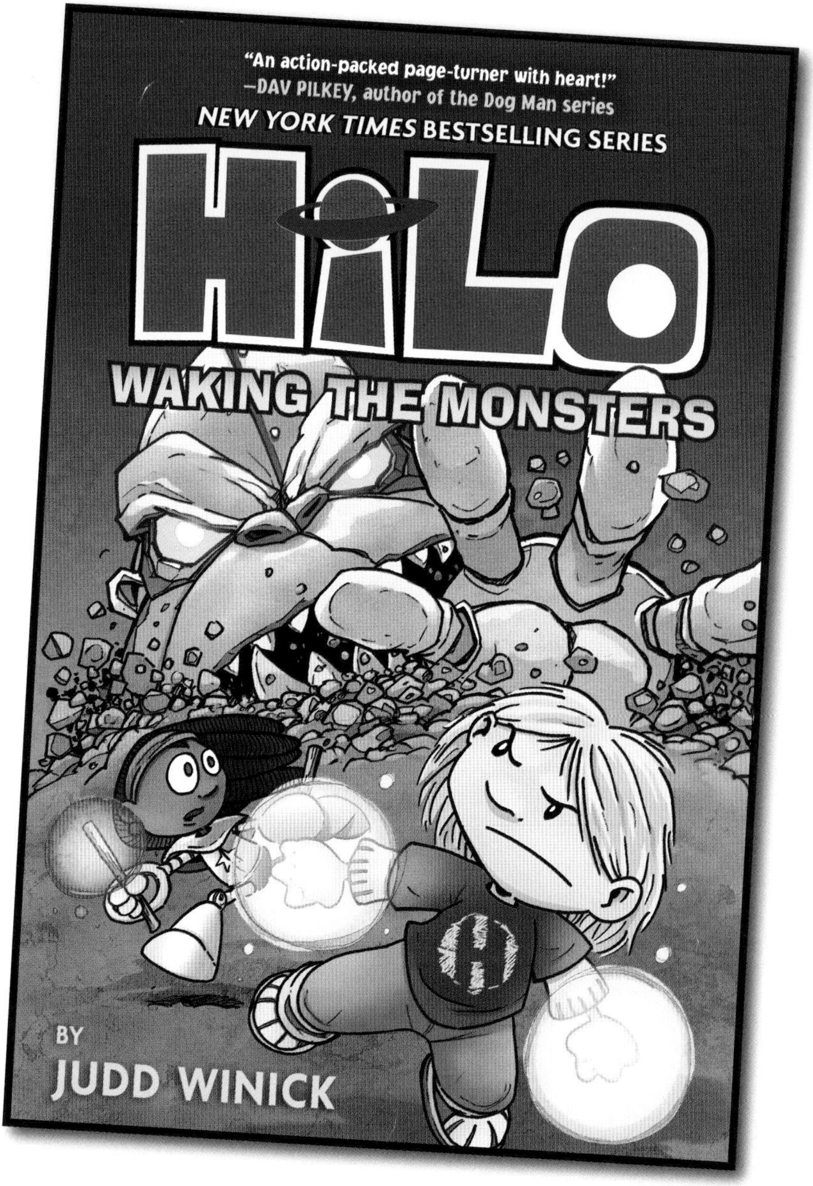
"An action-packed page-turner with heart!"
—DAV PILKEY, author of the Dog Man series
NEW YORK TIMES BESTSELLING SERIES
HiLo
WAKING THE MONSTERS
BY
JUDD WINICK

# AVAILABLE NOW!

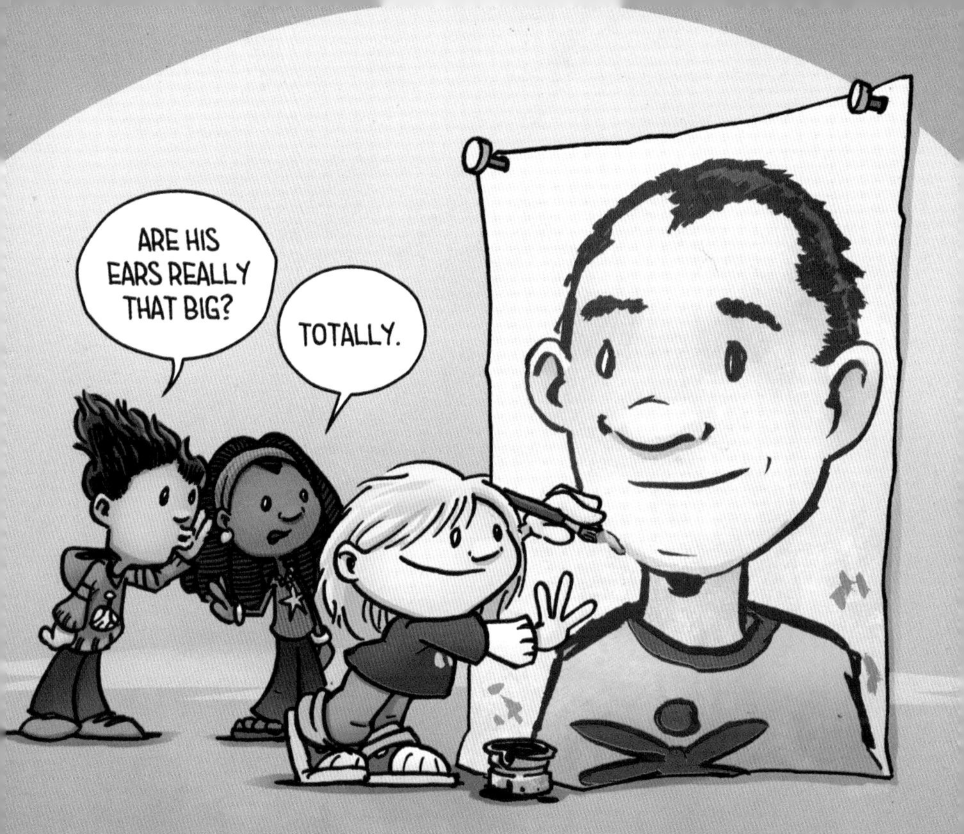
ARE HIS EARS REALLY THAT BIG?
TOTALLY.

**JUDD WINICK** grew up on Long Island, where he spent countless hours doodling, reading **X-Men** comics and the newspaper strip **Bloom County**, and watching **Looney Tunes**. Today Judd lives in San Francisco with his wife, Pam Ling; their two kids; and their cat, Chaka. When Judd isn't collecting far more action figures and vinyl toys than a normal adult, he is a screenwriter and an award-winning cartoonist. Judd has written issues of bestselling comics series, including Batman, Green Lantern, Green Arrow, Justice League, and Star Wars. Judd also appeared as a cast member of MTV's **The Real World: San Francisco** and is the author of the highly acclaimed graphic novel **Pedro and Me**, about his **Real World** castmate and friend, AIDS activist Pedro Zamora. Visit Judd online at **juddspillowfort.com** or on Twitter at **@juddwinick**.

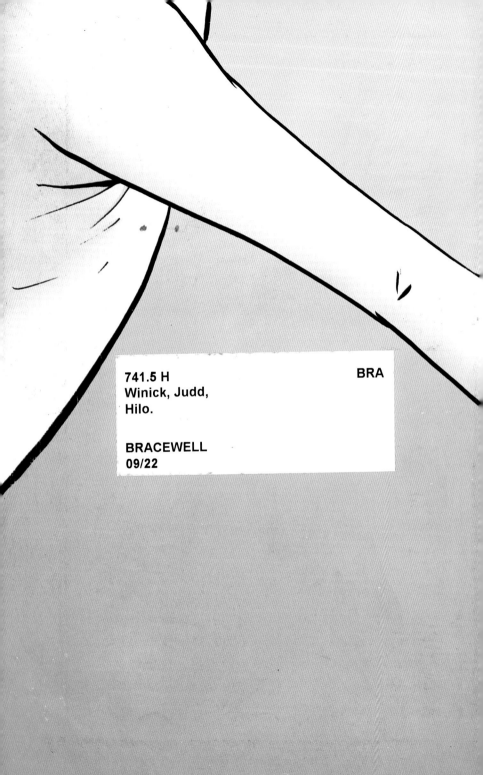